George Harley, Ethel Ale

Life of a London Physician

George Harley, F.R.S.

George Harley, Ethel Alec-Tweedie

Life of a London Physician
George Harley, F.R.S.

ISBN/EAN: 9783337849580

Printed in Europe, USA, Canada, Australia, Japan

Cover: Foto ©Raphael Reischuk / pixelio.de

More available books at **www.hansebooks.com**

Very truly yours
George Harley.

GEORGE HARLEY, F.R.S.

The Life of a London Physician.

EDITED BY HIS DAUGHTER,

MRS. ALEC TWEEDIE,

AUTHOR OF

'THROUGH FINLAND IN CARTS,' 'A GIRL'S RIDE IN ICELAND,' 'A WINTER
JAUNT TO NORWAY,' ETC.

London:

THE SCIENTIFIC PRESS, LIMITED,

29 & 30 SOUTHAMPTON STREET, STRAND.

1899.

INTRODUCTION.

WHEN George Harley was asked why he did not write his life, he replied :

'I will scribble my reminiscences when I retire from practice, for I have much to tell about strange folk and foreign lands, to say nothing of how I have watched the development of medical science.'

'But why not now?' was the question repeated again and again.

'Simply because I have not time. At seventy I mean to retire from practice, and I shall then amuse myself by sorting out and arranging the chaos lying dormant in my brain; now if I began to take down the dusty volumes from their shelves, I might never stop,' he would laughingly say.

He never lived to seventy, for he died at sixty-seven, and he never retired from practice, for he died while still in harness.

Thus cut off before accomplishing his purpose, I, his daughter, thought I would undertake the task. Full of this design, a few days before Christmas, 1897, I called upon Dr. and Mrs. Samuel Smiles. The dear old lady, with white hair and dark bushy eyebrows, looked sad.

'Sam is very ailing,' she said. 'He will be eighty-five

to-morrow, and his health has always been splendid until now.'

For some time I sat and chatted with the kindly lady, who was expecting her son to come up from Yorkshire, because of the Doctor's sudden access of weakness, and then I rose to go.

'Wait one moment,' she said ; 'if my husband is awake, you must peep at him for a moment. He would never forgive me for letting you leave the house without one word.'

She crossed the passage of their London home, opened the study door opposite, and beckoned me to follow.

The old gentleman, in his black velvet coat, was sitting before the fire thinking. The moment he saw me he rose (feebly, 'tis true), and greeted me with :

'Ah, Ethel, my dear girl, how good of you, how sweet of you, to come and see an old man.'

He seemed much changed bodily; the mark upon his forehead was more prominent, the figure more bent, and altogether the author of 'Self-Help' and a score of other well-known volumes appeared more the octogenarian than he had ever done before.

We talked for a few minutes about Eastbourne, where he had spent the autumn, and then with all the interest of youth he asked :

'What are you writing?'

'I want to write my father's Life, but I am not a biographer, and I hardly know how to begin.'

Instantly a change came over him, his eyes glistened, he sat up erect, and enthusiastically exclaimed :

'Capital, capital ! Why, your father and I both came

from Haddington, dear old Haddington. Though I was a man before he was a boy, I followed his progress with interest, and looked upon him as a great friend till the grave took him from us. I envied his career as a physician, a profession I myself forsook. Yes, write his Life, dear, —if I were younger I would help you; but I am getting old now, and often wonder whether I shall ever finish even that book;' and as he spoke he laid his hand upon a manuscript on the writing-table.

We chatted on; he was keenly interested, his mind growing every minute brighter and clearer, as he told me how to begin the Life. His enthusiasm soon became too much for his strength, for at that time and for many weeks afterwards he was very ill. He wanted to plan the volume and start at it right away, but I saw he was tired, and left with these words ringing in my ears:

'If only I were well enough, I would help you myself.'

Encouraged by this cheery push—from a veteran of the craft—along the slippery road of authorship, I determined to try and write my father's memoirs.

Many months afterwards I sent the first half of the book to Dr. Smiles—then happily entirely recovered from his illness—to look over. 'Very cleverly done,' was his comment. Thanks to his interest and sympathy, as I told the dear old man, for without them I should never have dared begin.

Thus it was, with the help of friends, I took courage, and have endeavoured to string my father's life-beads on a suitable cord; but as relations proverbially write badly of their own, and rarely succeed in presenting a faithful picture, whenever and wherever possible, the words of others have been inserted, because they are impartial, and, like the sun that shows up the seams of an old coat, outsiders see faults more clearly, and appreciate, perhaps, more justly.

George Harley was a physician, yet before everything he was a man of science; but ill-health having overtaken him when still quite young, and deprived him of the physical energy natural to that time of life, he developed many hobbies. Hobbies were his solace and his joy, and no one can deny he was a man of many sides.

Certain fragments of his reminiscences exist, totally unconnected, written at different times of his life when sickness overtook him. Under such unhappy circumstances many men would have given up in despair, but his wonderful courage kept him cheerful, and he occupied his mind by writing accounts of his life, anecdotes and stories of natural history to amuse his children, living again, during sickness, those scenes and events from which ill-health tore him away.

The life of George Harley of Harley Street was one long struggle, mental strength battling with physical weakness, and on this account it has its interest even to a casual observer. As the outside world is better able to judge a man than his own family, so the specialist is more completely able to analyze his work, therefore I quote a few words from the many columns of obituary notice which appeared in the *British Medical Journal*, November, 1896, on the subject of this memoir, as a reason why it has been compiled :

The announcement of the sudden death of Dr. George Harley on October 27, 1896, will be read with much regret by many beyond the immediate circle of his friends, to whom he was endeared by his buoyant temperament, his ever-fresh enthusiasm, and the many lovable traits in his character. . . . It would be impossible here even to enumerate all his contributions to medical science. . . .

Dr. George Harley was endowed with great abilities, and possessed by an enthusiastic devotion to science. That he had also a high courage is shown by the eminent position which he won for himself under circumstances of ill-health which might well have excused retirement from the field.

Personally, he was a man of great openness of mind. Genial to his friends, courteous to his opponents, he was ever ready to recognise sound scientific work and to applaud its spirit. Of an original turn of mind, of great industry, and holding strongly the views to which his scientific researches and clinical observations had led him, he stated his conclusions frankly, and defended them with spirit. A physician of no ordinary skill in the practice of his profession, and one whose opinion was highly valued, his published writings show that, though he did not disdain the teachings of empiricism, yet they never satisfied his intellectual needs. He was always striving to find the scientific basis for empirical practices, and the influence of his writings has extended, and will extend beyond their actual teachings. He was a ready speaker, and often took an effective part in discussions at the medical societies.

Of his social qualities, it is sufficient to say that he was a charming companion, always cheery, a mine of curious information on many subjects, and an excellent raconteur.

His most important publications had to do with the diseases of the liver, a subject to which he was naturally led by his early study of the physiology of that organ, and of the processes of digestion. In 1863 he published his work entitled ' Jaundice : its Pathology and Treatment,' a book marked by much originality of thought and method, and destined to have an important influence on the progress of medical knowledge and opinion on the subject with which it dealt. It was eventually succeeded and replaced by his large and important treatise on the ' Diseases of the Liver,' published in 1883, a work in which the writer focussed all the experience and research of many years. This book was reprinted in Canada and in America, and was translated into German.

The *Lancet* likewise filled several pages with a notice, beginning by deploring the death of ' an eminent physician from London life,' and, after paying tribute to his scientific and medical attributes, ended by saying, ' He was a man of many interests and very decided opinions.'

The *Times* gave a long notice of the scientific work of George Harley, and the ' Royal Society Proceedings ' began by stating that 'death has removed, in the midst of active labour, a distinguished physician, a true lover of science. It would take pages to give an enumeration of all George Harley's writings, scientific and medical. He was never at rest, and when he died he must have felt conscious that he had done his duty and completed his work.'

Thus spoke those best fitted to judge of his scientific accomplishments, but his life apart from work was by no means an ordinary one, and it is the story of that life I have tried to tell.

CONTENTS.

CHAPTER | PAGE
INTRODUCTION - - - v

I. EARLY DAYS - - - - - - 1

II. HADDINGTON - - - - - - 9

III. EDINBURGH—STUDENT LIFE - - - 27

IV. PARIS—A BATTLE FOR LIFE - - - 34

V. PARIS - - - - - - 56

VI. MARRIAGE OF NAPOLEON III.—WAS NAPOLEON III.
A COWARD? - - - - 72

VII. STUDENT LIFE IN GERMANY—CONDEMNED TO BE
SHOT - - - - - - 84

VIII. SLEDGING ACROSS THE ALPS - - - 99

IX. LONDON AND UNIVERSITY COLLEGE - - - 109

X. THE YOUNG PHYSICIAN - - - - 121

XI. HARLEY STREET—THE DOCTORS' ELYSIUM - - 131

XII. AN UNCONVENTIONAL WEDDING-TOUR - - 148

XIII. THE CONSULTANT - - - - - 159

XIV. BLIND - - - - - - 172

XV. TOTAL DARKNESS - - - - - 183

XVI. BACK IN HARNESS—QUEER PATIENTS - - 191

XVII. MORE QUEER PATIENTS - - - - 205

VIII. CANNIBAL BREAKFASTS - - - - 217

CHAPTER   PAGE

XIX. INTERESTING FRIENDS - - - - 228

XX. RECOLLECTIONS - - - - - 241

XXI. SQUIRE WATERTON - - - - - 260

XXII. PEEPS ABROAD - - - - - 282

XXIII. SCIENTIFIC HOBBIES - - - 294

XXIV. SPELLING REFORM AND CHAMPAGNE - - 306

XXV. A PEEP AT THE DEVELOPMENT OF MEDICAL

SCIENCE - - - - - - 316

XXVI. LAST YEARS - - - - - - 325

XXVII. DEATH, AND STRANGE WISHES - - - 337

APPENDIX

DR. GEORGE HARLEY AS I KNEW HIM (BY MRS. J. H. RIDDELL) - - - - - - 347

INDEX (COMPILED BY MISS BEATRICE JACKSON) - - 356

GEORGE HARLEY;

OR,

THE LIFE OF A LONDON PHYSICIAN.

CHAPTER I.

EARLY DAYS.

In that royal burgh, the old, old town of Haddington, my father, Dr. George Harley, was born, on February 12, 1829.

There are those who call ancient Haddington a 'quiet, drowsy place,' but such a description is not strictly accurate. Rather, its tranquil aspect suggests the well-earned repose of some famous soldier, who towards the close of life's long day, seeks far from war's alarms that peace his youth and prime never knew.

On banks sloping to the Scottish Tyne, Haddington lies basking in the summer sunshine, its magnificent Franciscan abbey and cathedral church partly in ruins, keeping faithful ward and watch over the graves of its children—ay, over the last earthly resting-place of some who in a frenzy of fanaticism tried to serve God by desecrating and well-nigh destroying one of His most beautiful temples!

Go where we will in Scotland, the same mournful story is repeated—Elgin, Melrose, Dryburgh, *Dulce Cœur*, and many another abbey, chapel, and cathedral, tell with mute

1

eloquence of that Calvinistic storm which swept through
the country and left magnificent buildings, reared by men
'who dreamt not of a perishable home,' roofless, doorless,
windowless, open to furious wind, driving rain, and in-
sidious softly-falling snow for long centuries; alas! and
alas! as those who destroyed firmly believed for the love
and glory of God.

Nature, however, has been kinder than man to the
glorious piles erected at a time ere faith, then strong, had
lapsed into the feeble dotage of superstition, and when
'shoddy' building was unknown.

Over 400 years have come and gone since those 'holy
places' were wrecked as completely as the hand of man
could compass; nevertheless, even in decay the famous
Haddington cathedral, *Lucerna Laudoniæ* ('The Lamp of
Lothian'), at all events, still lights the page of ancient
history, and repeats to understanding ears the tale of former
greatness, when it contained no less than fifteen altars,
served by sixty-one ministering priests, which number it
retained up to the time of the Scottish Protestant Reformation.

Both priests and altars have been for centuries dust, but
we know by the story handed down from generation to
generation it was one of Haddington's own sons who
wrought this ruin; her own, not by adoption, but by birth,
for John Knox was born (1505) within a stone's-throw of the
noble abbey.

As a boy he had wandered through her even then ancient
burying-ground, heard the stirring sermons, and listened to
the glorious chants which seemed knocking at the very
gates of heaven. Delicate tracery, flying buttress, arch,
groin, stately pillar, noble window, and curiously carved
doorway, must have been familiar to him as the furniture
in his father's house.

The famous Scottish Reformer was actually educated by
Friar-Warden Harley, the last Roman Catholic Primate of
this Franciscan monastery. Yet it was Knox who uttered

the edict which marred and defaced so many of Scotland's
grandest and loveliest structures, erected by men who
wrought such miracles of architecture less as those who
labour at the bidding of an earthly master than as artificers
for God. Who could replace those beautiful temples now?

We have learnt many things since Knox kindled that
fierce fire of Calvinism which destroyed so much we would
fain possess and cherish in this—it is to be hoped—more
Christian age, but we have forgotten how to build!

Grass is growing where sin-laden men and women once
knelt in prayer, birds come and go where in the olden time
anthems rose on high, desolation keeps its lonely vigil
where formerly the beauty of holiness reigned supreme, and
all is silence where the weary and worn told their griefs to
One that heareth, and laid their bitter burden on Him
who said, ' Come unto Me, and I will give you rest.'

The very house in which George Harley first saw the
light was built on land that once formed part of those wide
abbey grounds. It must have been an ideal home, with
its spacious garden filled with old-fashioned shrubs and
flowers, where birds nested in peace; its smooth bowling-
green, its lovely look-out over the Tyne and fair pasture-
land beyond to the Lammermuir Hills that stretched away
in the distance.

Both politically and ecclesiastically, the Harleys played
no unimportant part in the earlier and more stirring
times of Scottish history. Friar John Harley, who died in
1377, was Warden or Abbot of the great Haddington
Franciscan monastery. At the period of the Scottish
Reformation members of this family held high positions in
the Romish Church, and through the instrumentality of
their friend John Knox were converted to Protestantism,
afterwards rising, under his auspices, to places of dignity in
the Reformed Church.

In 1553 the Rev. Dr. John Harley, a Fellow of Magdalen
College, Oxford, and Chaplain to King James VI., was
appointed the first Protestant Bishop of Hereford; while in

1560 a cousin of his, the Rev. William Harley, became the first legally inducted Protestant clergyman in Scotland, being appointed to the charge of St. Cuthbert's, Edinburgh, in that year.

In political matters their prominence was fraught with not altogether pleasant consequences to themselves. During the second half of the sixteenth century, James Harley, a Writer to the King's Signet, stood his trial for high treason, he having assisted with a Captain Calder, in 1571, in the assassination of the Earl of Lennox, Lord Regent of Scotland, in a species of political free-fight. Previously to this, another of Dr. Harley's progenitors was condemned to death on the charge of having arrested and imprisoned Mary, Queen of Scotland. William Harley was tried at Edinburgh on April 1, 1566, along with Deputy-Sheriff Scott, for having on the night after the murder of Rizzio gone with forty armed followers to Holyrood Palace, over-powered the guard, and made Queen Mary prisoner on account of her being suspected of having connived at the murder of her lover and private secretary, in consequence of her fearing his betrayal of her intrigues with the French Court. A full account of the trial is given in No. 34, 3, 11, folio 55, of the State Papers preserved in the Advocates' Library, Edinburgh, in which it is stated that they confined the Queen in durance vile for forty-eight hours in her private chamber in Holyrood House, for which crime John Scott, who appears to have been the chief aggressor, was con-demned to be 'hanged, drawn, and quartered,' while William Harley was acquitted. William Harley fled to the Court of Queen Elizabeth, who not only gave him a grant of land, but shortly afterwards knighted him for his kind attention to her cousin.

Little surprise can be felt at the imperfect way national history is written when it is stated that in a private correspondence my father had with the late Mr. Froude, author of ' The History of Queen Mary,' it appears that not only was Mr. Froude totally ignorant of this episode in her life, but he had never, before my father called his attention to the documents, so much as seen them, or even heard of the existence of any State Papers in the Advocates' Library, and consequently was, at the time he wrote her history, unacquainted of several important facts which give an entirely different complexion to some of the statements he made regarding her conduct at the time above referred to.

It would be easy to quote other instances that would go far to show George Harley came of a fighting race, one which never lacked the courage of its opinions nor hesitated to stand by them to the bitter end.

As before mentioned, it was on February 12, 1829, that my father was born in Haddington. He may be said to have been the offspring of aged parents, his mother being forty, and his father, George Barclay Harley, sixty-three at the time of the birth of their only son. Thus young George was the last of his race who was closely associated with the little old-world town in East Lothian.

His was a charming home—one he never forgot—loving after long years to recall how a certain bedchamber originally intended for a dining-room was wainscoted throughout, while on the centre panel over the chimney-piece was painted a stirring picture of a fox-hunt: Reynard making at full speed for a hole in the cliff, hotly pursued by hounds, horses, and men. Think of how such an apartment must have impressed an imaginative child, and at every turn the same thing was repeated, with a difference ; indeed, there is before me now a statement in his own writing of how the many old and beautiful objects which surrounded him during infancy and boyhood stamped themselves on his memory.

' Since arriving at manhood's estate,' he says, ' I have ever and anon looked back and reflected concerning the powerful influence which was exerted upon my boyish mind by the speechless lessons taught me through the instrumentality of the secret and silent contemplation of innumerable

old family relics which in every corner of the house met
my eyes—relics such as pictures, miniatures, old silver,
and china bric-à-bracs; pieces of old carved oaken
furniture, in the shape of a bridal "naporie-chest," an
escritoire with secret drawers, a four-post bedstead with
carved canopy, all of which had at one time or another
been the special property of members of past generations
of the family. *Moi, qui vous parle* may here venture to
tell you how in my boyhood, when but little more than
out of the nursery, I have yearned after a knowledge of
my ancestors, and to peer into the long, far-off, distant,
hazy past. Often have I stood in rapt meditation before
the full-length miniature portrait of fair-haired, intelligent-
featured Mary Cockburn, who married Thomas Harla in
1470; and while I gazed on her calm face, as it looked
down from its picture-frame, the long since dead woman
reappeared to me, as it were, in a living vision of delight. I
believe that picture influenced my life. Merely looking at
it has again and again made me feel as if I were inspired
with all the possible ennobling influences of her nature.

' To this day I can remember, as if it had happened but
yesterday, how the mere handling of an old Spanish
rapier, whose home was the garret, filled my budding mind
with all kinds of heroic aspirations, and engendered for the
time being an unconquerable desire to enter the army and
carve my way to fame by the destruction of human life.
A mere accident alone prevented my entering upon this
career at the age of seventeen.

' That old Toledo blade was said not only to have been
the one Sir William Harley wore when Queen Elizabeth
knighted him in 1585, but the actual sword with which she
performed the ceremony. Along the blade, close to the
hilt, were engraved the words, " No me Saguas sin razon ;
no me envaines sino honor "—an ennobling chivalric senti-
ment which means in plain English, " Never draw me
without good cause ; never sheath me without honour."

' " When I am big I will go to Toledo," I used to say to

myself again and again, and years afterwards I did, when on my wedding tour.

'I know, moreover, how my taste for *l'objet de vertu*, for *meubles d'artistiques*, though only fully developed and cultivated in later years, had its origin in my familiarity with the pretty ornaments my mother's taste distributed throughout our sitting-rooms and bedchambers. Her home was full of charming little odds and ends, and no wonder these had accumulated, seeing that the Harleys lived in the locality for some centuries, and clung to the old place, never really leaving Haddington, indeed, until the last representative of the house, myself, forsook it in 1845, after all the other members of the family, with the exception of one solitary sister, had died.

'The worst episode in the breaking up of Harley House was that all the articles not wanted were sent to Elm House and put up in the garret—among them the old Toledo sword, a duck-gun, an Elizabethan clock, and the box of family manuscript papers. No more heed was paid to them till Elm House was some years afterwards let, and then it was discovered that everything had disappeared, supposed to have been taken by the men who cleared the chimney-stacks of the immense quantity of sticks the jackdaws had piled in the chimney.

'A curious coincidence occurred about this. On receiving a bill of £15 for clearing a chimney, I inquired into the matter, and found it had taken three men several days to take away the débris of the said dining-room chimney, for the jackdaws had dropped stick after stick down the aperture, so as to form a safe foundation on which they might build their nest, until the birds had literally filled it up with cartloads of stuff. When it was all unearthed, a beautiful piece of old lace, once belonging to my mother, but mysteriously lost for many years, came to light. It hardly seemed possible that birds could cause such fearful havoc, but those jackdaws pursued their work with unceasing energy for generations.

' The contemplation of the deeds of one's ancestors, be they either good or bad, but more especially if they be good, refines the thoughts while purifying the passions. The good excite to imitation—the bad prompt to repudiation. Honour is a treasure wealth cannot purchase, a gem whose brightness poverty cannot tarnish. The family escutcheon I received untarnished, and in the same condition I hope to bequeath it to my children.

' It has often appeared to me strange that none of our popular writers have ever devoted a chapter to the ennobling moral influences exerted on the minds of youth through being surrounded by old family heirlooms, because I believe the small, still voice from the mouldering relics of noble-minded ancestors is a most potent factor in creating a desire to keep alight the pure flame of manly virtues which burned in the bosoms of their progenitors.

' Nay, more : I believe that it is often from the mere impressions derived from the silent contemplation of trifling memorials of ancestors long since dead and gone—so long, indeed, removed from the stage of life that even the very dust from their withered bones has vanished from their tombs—that the instincts and talents of the sires are regenerated in the heads and hearts of the scions.'

CHAPTER II.

AMONGST George Harley's dearest memories, Haddington's 'auld kirk' on the banks of the river Tyne, and mentioned in the first chapter, plays a prominent part.

'The old church of which I am about to relate a boyish anecdote,' he says, 'was built in the eleventh century, and belonged to the Franciscan Monastery, of which Friar Adam Harley was Warden from 1522 till 1566, when it was swept away by the Reformation.

'The church, which was dedicated to St. Mary, is a Gothic fabric of a chaste style of architecture, but possesses no excess of floral embellishment, so common in old Gothic churches.

'The nave is 210 feet long by 60 feet broad, and the transept across from north to south measures 110 feet, while the square tower in the centre rises to the height of 90 feet, and it is regarding my escapade in this tower that the gist of my tale lies. In 1878 appeared from my pen, in the *Haddingtonshire Courier*, a series of articles under the *nom de plume* of " G. Virtute et Fide," on " The Ecclesiastical Buildings of Haddington," more especially on its fine abbey church—the Lucerna Laudoniæ — with which certain ecclesiastical members of my family had been intimately connected.

'Only the west portion of the building is now in repair, and this is still used as the parish church.

' In the days of Friar Adam Harley the auld kirk was in its full glory. With his and his fraternity's banishment, however, not only ended the greatness of the church, but also the ecclesiastical renown of Haddington, which is said to have commenced about 630.

' In 1560 Haddington possessed, in addition to this fine church and the Franciscan monastery, a Dominican monastery and church of its own, a nunnery, and an abbey of importance.

' The old monks knew well what they were about when they selected Haddington for their home, for not only did its river—the Tyne—furnish some of the finest trout in the world for their *maigre* days, but the fertile valley of the river an inexhaustible supply of corn and kine.

' In 1811 the west end of the church was put into a complete state of repair, and adapted to hold 1,233 sitters, but it was not until 1844 that civilization had sufficiently advanced to make people so sensitive to cold they found they could not worship in the church unless it were artificially heated in winter. Therefore it was in that year stoves and hot-air pipes found their way into the Auld Kirk o' Haddington.

' During the time this innovation was in progress I chanced to be a scholar at the Haddington Burgh Schools, and heard that a great many human skeletons had been found in opening up a passage within the church, necessary to lay down the hot-air pipes. This news proved sweet nuts for the boys, and after school hours more than a dozen of us repaired in a body to view the dead men's bones.

' The churchyard gates being open, we readily obtained access to the sanctuary, going straight up the broad walk. Separating this walk from the burying-ground there was a stone wall, but so many, many, many people had been buried there that, although the wall was about 4 feet high, the hallowed ground had risen to a level with

the top of the wall on the one side. Just think for a
moment what a mass of human beings must have been
huddled there, for their dust to be 4 feet deep all
over the extensive graveyard! At a place on the top
of the wall just opposite the side-door of the church
were ranged in a row nineteen grinning human skulls.
Some of them were beautifully clean, and in an excellent
state of preservation, with regular rows of fine, pearly
teeth. The incisors in one of the skulls proved to
me irresistible, so I pulled two of the prettiest out, and
popped them into my waistcoat pocket to treasure up as a
souvenir of Old Mortality.

' Having finished our examination of the skulls, and made
our boyish comments thereon, we proceeded to explore the
interior of the church ; but finding nothing there to suit
our tastes, and ascertaining that the way to the roof was
open—the men were putting up a chimney to convey
away the smoke—we instantly hurried to the slates.
Here we discovered a nice broad lead-way, all round the
roof of the church, and the lead being as smooth as ice, we
scampered along it, from one end of the building to the
other, towards the central tower. Here we stopped, and
looked over the parapet down into the ruined chancel
beyond. Our investigations, however, did not terminate
here. A peep up into the ruined tower revealed to our
eager eyes a broken stone stair, the fragments of the steps
of which gradually got smaller and smaller until they were
nothing more than little fist-sized knobs, projecting from
the old and time-worn wall. One boy after another
ascended the dangerous flight of steps, as far as his inclination or his courage dictated ; but all of them soon returned,
except two other boys and myself. We three continued our
path upward after the steps had ceased to be, and only
fragments of stone projecting from the wall remained. I
led the way ; they followed for a time, and cheered me on.
At length the projecting fragments of the old stone steps
got so small, and the climbing became so difficult, I was

about to retrace my steps, when, looking up, I found I was already within a few feet of a window in the tower, and that discovery proved an incentive which led me on, until the window-sill was reached. It was nice and broad, so I sat on it comfortably, and looked out, down into the chancel, on the far-off scene below. The sight was charming. There stood a group of my companions, who looked like little picaninnies, and when I called to them, a cheering shout fell upon my ear.

'After a few minutes thus spent in mirth, I turned round to address my two companions who had followed me up the dangerous part of the tower. They were gone! Looking down, all I could see was a deep, dark hole. The shades of an autumn evening were already closing in. The small-windowed, narrow-sided, gray-walled and old ruined tower looked sombre enough in every respect, and, as I said, when I gazed down into it I saw nothing but a deep dark hole. A thrill of awe ran through my heart. I turned for relief to look at my merry companions in the chancel down below. Alas! they were gone also. I tried to hear where they were, but I heard them not; and as I listened, all at once the sound of the workmen ceased, and I knew their day's labour was done. Like lightning the thought, " They will lock up the church and go away, and I shall be left alone in it all night!" flashed through my brain. Not a pleasant thought for a boy not then fourteen!

'I quickly decided to go down with all speed. But, oh horrors! though it had been easy, comparatively speaking, to get up, on looking at the small knobs projecting from the wall, the great depth of the tower, the dark abyss beneath, a feeling of fear laid hold of me, and instead of making any attempt to descend I shouted loudly for help. No response came; nothing but dead silence met my ear. In despair I turned round. I lay flat down on the window-sill, and then gradually lowered myself with my hands, groping about with the points of my toes for the knobs, but I could find none. All at once it struck me that this dreadful dilemma was a Divine punishment for having committed sacrilege by stealing the teeth from a dead man's skull. Having arrived at this conclusion, I again pulled myself up on to the window-sill, put my hand into my waistcoat-pocket, took out the two teeth and pitched them down into the chancel of the old church. Then, kneeling with my knees on the window-sill, I offered up a contrite and sincere prayer for forgiveness for the sin I had committed, and deliverance from the peril in which I was placed. And as was usual on such occasions, prayer fulfilled my mother's assurance that God would befriend me in my time of need. Once more I made the attempt to descend, and, fortified by faith in the guidance of an Almighty hand, clinging with my fingers to the wall, I let my feet down slowly, and by degrees, until they rested on a knob. Then bit by bit, and by dint of careful clinging with my very nails set in the decaying wall, I descended from one point of safety to another until I reached the ruined steps, when all became at once plain sailing. No sooner did I arrive at the level of the church roof than I rushed from the tower and ran along the top of the leaden way until I reached the trap-door, where I was suddenly met by two of the workmen, who had come up to seek for me on being told by my companions that I was still in the tower.

'In after-years my climb in Haddington old church has oftentimes afforded me a theme for theological and philosophical reflection.'

After all, however, when everything is said that can be said about the ancient glories of Haddington's Franciscan monastery and the rare relics of a picturesque and interesting past scattered about his home, it was the boy's mother who moulded his character, and made my father so straightforward, unselfish, and affectionate a man.

Somehow, it usually appears to be the mothers who make or mar their sons' lives. This seems hard on the fathers; but in this case there was no father, because he died just three years after the birth of his youngest child and only son, George.

Indeed, my father's only remembrance of his male parent was one of horror, for, most unwisely, the little lad was allowed to see his father as he lay dead in his coffin, and he never forgot the fearful chill he felt strike through his heart when he touched the clay-cold cheek on the day of burial. His restless brain, busy even at the age of three, could not be quieted, he needs must inquire into everything. At last, when he saw his father's remains being removed, he rushed out into the path, exclaiming: 'You naughty men, to take my poor papa away!' Whereupon one of the gentlemen took him by the hand and led him to his mother, who was bitterly weeping in the house.

'Why do you cry, mamma?'

'Because they are taking poor papa away.'

'Why do you let them take papa away?'

'Because, my dear, it is God who has taken him to live with Him in heaven for ever.'

'Oh, I want no gods here if they make you cry!' said the poor child passionately.

Thus it was the mother—beautiful, wise, and tender—who alone guided the young boy's feet along the straight path which leads to peace. As a woman and her granddaughter, I am proud to put that fact on record.

'Poor lady,' says her son, 'she bestowed great pains on my bringing up. She cultivated my taste for antiquarian lore, for the beautiful in Nature and in Art. She taught me to love every creature that liveth. She did all in her power to develop my intellect and to refine my tastes. How far she succeeded, it is not for me to say; but one thing is certain: she implanted in my bosom an undying affection for her.'

A statement strong as touching, yet literally true. Through all the years that followed he never changed, he never forgot ; her memory was dear to him when the evening shadows were drawing on, as her beautiful self had been in the brightness of youth's early morning. It may have been that few sons were so loved, but I am sure not many sons so remember.

His mother fostered his love of animals immensely, and the garden at Harley House was full of pigeons, rabbits, dogs, and two tame seagulls, and he used often in manhood to tell of his delightful boyhood's companion, Jacky, who was with him for years. This jackdaw was given to him by a school friend, and soon became a great favourite. When it was time to rise in the morning, Jacky used to come to his little friend's window, and peck at the glass till it was opened ; then he would sit and talk away, putting his head first on one side, then on the other, till he saw his little master's toilet was complete, when he would fly round to the dining-room window and greet him with a ' Caw-caw !' when he appeared. Then he would take a little turn, but when he saw his young master was ready for school would give another friendly caw and fly alongside of him, hopping from hedge to hedge for a certain distance, and then go back home. But when the time arrived for the return from school off he would fly again, and meet his young master at the same spot he had left him in the morning. My father often pondered on this in after-years, and never could satisfy himself how Master Jacky calculated time.

But Jacky had one failing. Continually things were missed, and the climax came—one day my grandmother's old gold watch mysteriously disappeared. It was searched for high and low, and at last was seen hanging from the window-sill of the bedroom. Evidently our wary friend had been attracted by its glistening on the dressing-table, and pulled it thus far with the intention of taking it to his hiding-place, but found it too heavy for removal !

This jackdaw was my father's companion for years, and ultimately went to Edinburgh with him and his venerable grandmother, where it soon learnt to meet him on his return from college, as it had done in the old Haddington school-days.

This love of birds and animals was probably an inherited trait in my father, for his grandfather, Patrick Harley, had nearly a hundred years before written a poem, entitled

PEDIGREE OF THE SOLAN-GOOSE OF THE BASS ROCK.*

By PATRICK HARLEY

(Born at Haddington, ten miles from the Bass, in 1717; died in 1766).

IN days of old,
As I am told,
The Barnacle or Solan-goose,
From the fruit of a tree
Was born unnaturally,
Which tree was cut down
By a gard'ner-clown,
And burnt most ignorantly,
Not knowing that its apples were changed into geese,
Which to eat are not bad, when they are not too obese.
So soon as they found themselves 'reft of their tree,
The disconsolate geese flew off to the sea;
For though they had searched o'er all Scotia's ground,
No tree like their tree had they anywhere found.
After flying about, it soon came to pass'
They got tired on the wing, and took to the Bass.
There they sullenly sat, consulting together,
Till one testily said, 'A fig for this bother!
Our plight's not so bad; for do you not see
There are birds here in plenty, and yet not a tree?
If they lay their own eggs—four, six, or e'en ten—
Why can't we lay one, and hatch it like them?'
All listened, all pondered, and at length all agreed
To try if this bold plan of his would succeed.
So the Rock they explored—then settled down there,
Resolved to lay but one egg 'tween each single pair.

A success it has proved, as all well do know
Who visit the Bass when the mild zephyrs blow ;
For there sit the geese, quite fearless of man,
Each hatching her egg as fast as she can.
Some sit ; some stand on the egg with one foot,
For all know, full well, that none dare them shoot ;
This mine own eyes beheld, when I visited there,
And marvel did I, at a sight so rare,
For while we were shooting other birds on the rock,
The geese flew round us, as if us to mock.

It must have been a hard trial for any widowed mother to place no check on her only son's passion for field sports, yet George Harley was the happy possessor of a fowling-piece while still so young that part of the stock had to be sawn off, so that he might carry the weapon with greater comfort and safety. The same course was pursued in other directions. During his summer holidays she took him with her to Ireland, the Highlands, etc.; in fact, this capable lady seems to have adopted 'Love and Common-sense' for her motto, and striven to make her boy manly, truthful, kind.

He is said to have been a funny little chap, and various stories are told concerning his precociousness, fondness for animals, and love of adventure. He had certainly one curious experience when as a lad of between ten and eleven he paid a visit to Edinburgh Castle in company with his mother and a schoolfellow, Robert Dickson, which it will be better to tell in his own words :

'Being of an inquiring turn of mind, while my mother was leaning over the parapet in rapt contemplation of the magnificent view which the landscape and Firth of Forth presented on that bright, balmy summer's day, I quietly proceeded to crawl into the mouth of that very celebrated old cannon Mons Meg—Mons being the place where it was founded, and Meg the Scottish abbreviation of Margaret.

'Without the slightest difficulty I crawled along the interior of the cannon till I reached the touch-hole, and then shouted through it in the best way I could to my

2

companion. Receiving after some short interval a jocular
reply, I bethought me that it was about time to withdraw,
and find my way out again. But oh, horror of horrors,
although it had been easy to get in, it was utterly impossible for me to get out! I was a tight fit, and as human
bones are not flexible, my thigh-joints being unbendable,
the legs were totally unable to perform any retrogressive
movement.

'There I stuck hard and fast. What was to be done?
Struggling and wriggling in the cannon were in vain; I
failed ignominiously to make a backward movement. I
could not straighten my legs. At last my companion,
becoming conscious of my dilemma, called my mother to
his aid. She came, she questioned, she looked, and in
a moment, comprehending the gravity of my situation,
besought the sentinel's help.

'He kindly tried to poke me out with the muzzle of his
musket, but his well-meant endeavours proving absolutely
unavailing, there was nothing left for it but to send for the
sergeant of the guard. My schoolfellow ran off to fetch him
in hot haste. He came, he looked, and was in dismay, for
the more the matter was considered, the more the difficulties in the way of my extraction presented themselves.
He shouted to me, he commanded me to come out, he
swore at me; but all in vain—there I remained a fixture.
He could not reach me with his arm; he could devise no
scheme for my release. There was no alternative but to
consult the Captain of the day. On having the dilemma
explained to him, he at once ordered a squad of soldiers to
follow him to the cannon's mouth. They promptly did
so, but when there they could do nothing. At length my
mother's wit was brought into action. She proposed that
a rope should be procured, and passed in to me with the aid
of a long stick; that I should grasp the end, and so be
dragged out. The idea was approved of by the Captain; a
rope and stick were brought forthwith, I hooked myself on
to one end of it, and was slowly dragged from the cannon,

humbled with shame, and covered with cobwebs, rust, and dust, but morally improved.

'The danger of Mons Meg to human liberty was speedily reported to the Commandant of the castle, and she was encompassed with a chevaux-de-frise in order to prevent the recurrence of a similar accident, within a month after my temporary incarceration in her iron womb.'

Like most spirited boys, my father appears to have frequently got within the lines of danger, occasionally from mere accident, but oftener, I fear, from indiscretion. In a sort of diary he says :

'My dear mother was constantly cautioning me to be prudent, and keep out of the way of danger, for, as she used to say, when I left her hale and hearty in the morning, she never felt quite certain that I should not be brought back to her a poor lifeless corpse in the evening. I fear, like most other boys, I often caused my darling mother's heart to ache.

'When she lectured me on being prudent, my pert reply invariably was, "There's no pleasure without excitement ; and there's no excitement without danger." I had not then learned that there are plenty of pleasures without excitement, and abundance of excitements without danger.

'When about thirteen years of age, I had one great ambition, viz., to be a good swimmer. I studied books on the subject, but they taught me little compared with what practice did. In fact, they taught me some things which I afterwards found to be false, especially one startling assertion—that a man can swim as well with his clothes on as off, if he only gets used to it. Which is just about as good philosophy as that you will catch a sparrow if you put a pinch of salt upon his tail. I was only fifteen when I unlearned, to my surprise, that it is a most difficult thing to swim with one's clothes on, and with the addition of heavy boots, beyond a very short distance, utterly impossible.

' My first narrow escape from drowning occurred in the following wise: When I was thirteen, I had learned to swim from the bathing ledge of rocks under the west wing of old Dunbar Castle to a rock about 24 feet distant, in an oblique line seaward from the cliff, so that when I had once reached and rested myself on the rock, if the tide was on the flow, I found no difficulty in getting back again, as the tide helped me onward to the landing-place. I was in the habit of daily bathing there with my friend, William Aitken, and two others of his fellow-students. They were men and expert swimmers—I a boy and but a learner. So one stormy day, when large waves were rolling in, they told me that I must not wait to bathe with them when the tide was full, but go at once, and bathe by myself before the flowing tide had made the uncovered portion of the rock more distant from the part on which we stood. This I flatly declined to do, but on being taunted that it was cowardice alone prevented me from going in by myself, and that it was the sight of the big waves which frightened me, I stripped, and in I went. With rather more difficulty than usual, in consequence of the increased force of the waves and tide, I reached my accustomed resting-place on the little island rock. Proud of my feat, I waved my hand, and raised a cheer of self-congratulation. Then one of them called out, " Hah ! my good fellow, don't boast ; you've still to get back again." Not dreaming that any danger could lie in the return journey, as the tide would be with me, I replied to him simply by a contemptuous laugh—a laugh which, as the sequel showed, might have been my last ; for a great danger lurked, hidden from mortal eye, in my return journey. That danger lay in the strength of the waves, not to overwhelm me in their surf, but to dash me with violence against the rocks.

' Once rested, I was soon again in the water, and beautifully and easily did I glide along, and then with a smiling face did I extend my hands to lay hold of the accustomed rock. But, alas! a huge *roller* overtook me, and ere I had time to place my fingers upon the ledge, it had hurled me breast-on with all its force against the hard and jagged rock. Knocked breathless, and completely stunned by the violence of the blow, I was pulled back again by the receding surf, and carried along, helpless, with the tide. The next wave again hurled me against the rocks, when John Gray, one of the gentlemen who afterwards went out in the first expedition in search of Sir John Franklin, had the presence of mind to catch one of his companions by the hand, lean over the rock, and snatch hold of me by the hair of the head as I floated senseless past.

'Drawn out of the water, I soon recovered myself, and the first thing that I saw on opening my eyes was my chest covered with blood. This was nothing serious, although it looked formidable from the blood mingling with the drops of water hanging on the skin, and thereby assuming the appearance of a much larger quantity than it really was. The hæmorrhage was caused by the scratching of the skin when I was dashed by the waves against the hard young limpet-covered rock. The scratches soon healed, and I was none the worse for my first drowning experiences.'

As a youth, one of his principal companions was Dr. William Aitken, of the Madras Army, many years older than himself; yet they remained true and faithful friends for over forty years. He was the son of an Indian judge, who retired on a pension and took up his abode in Dunbar, much appreciating the quiet and peace of that funny old town, where at one time the only excitement was the daily arrival of the coach running from London to Edinburgh. When the horn was heard, all the people rushed out to see this wonder of the age—this marvel that joined the sleepy old town to the rest of the world.

My father used often to tell of one of his early visits to Dunbar, the first time he ever journeyed alone. He was quite a little chap, about ten years old (1839), and the happy possessor of a new carpet bag—a real carpet bag, with wonderful roses and yet more wonderful leaves woven in the pattern. Armed with this treasure and a new pea-jacket, of which he was immensely proud, he was conducted by the old servant to the gates of Harley House in Haddington, there to await the arrival of the coach. Presently the horn was heard approaching, and the boy's heart began to beat quickly with excitement. At last up drew the coach, and he climbed into the interior, for the outside seats were occupied, in spite of its being a frosty December morning. His bag was reluctantly handed to the guard, for he wanted to hold his treasure tight; and off drove the coach, rumbling through the Haddington High Street, drawing up at the Old George Inn, where my father was charmed to converse with some of his school companions from his elevated position at the coach-window.

Again the horn sounded, the guard mounted, and off they rattled in great excitement; at last they neared Dunbar; then my father again looked out of the window, and as they clattered up the High Street—the horn blowing, the whip cracking, and the boy's heart thumping —there he saw his dear old friends Mr. and Mrs. Aitken waiting for him at the inn door. Out he jumped, and at once proclaiming the fact of the new carpet bag, waited breathlessly for the door of the boot to be opened to claim his treasure, when, instead of the bag, out jumped a big goose, which took to its heels and rushed cackling down the High Street, the guard and half the town running after it! Never did goose run like that one, for it was indeed flying for dear life, being on its way to grace a Christmas dinner in London. At last the goose was captured and returned to the boot, but this time its legs were more tightly tied.

Often did my father tell this story, and always enjoyed a good laugh at the dismay of all beholders when the goose took to flight down the High Street of Dunbar.

Many happy days the boy spent there until death stepped

in and took his dear old friends hence, for during the time
their own son William was in India he was truly a son
to them. On one occasion, when he arrived for his usual
holiday, the old servant Elsie shook her head and said :

' Ay, Master George, but the mistress has been more busy
than ever getting ready for you, and she has had a regular
revolution amongst the boots and shoes !'

Yes ; those were good and happy days, but they could not
last. All too quickly the years sped by and brought George
Harley face to face with his first great trouble. What her
disease may have been, how long the devoted mother
lingered by the way, or whether she lingered at all, no
record is left. In one line her son tells all we need to know :

' God took her from me on March 15, 1845.'

When he was just turned sixteen. Think of it ! Think
of his youth—how he had loved, what he had lost !

' Her death,' he adds, ' nearly cost me my life, for on her
funeral-day I was seized with a sudden paroxysm of
palpitation of the heart, which was supposed by the
leading physician in Edinburgh, Professor Alison, to be
due to some organic disease, and for years afterwards I
was but a shadow of my former self. Time, the only
healer of the wounds death inflicts, at last healed mine,
but left visions of the departed almost as fresh on my recollection as the very day they were written with sorrow's
iron pen. My mother died a confiding Christian, and
blessings for ever rest on her sainted memory.'

She was buried at the back of the old church of Haddington, where innumerable Harleys had been buried before.
There also rest the remains of Jane Welsh Carlyle and the
ancestors of Dr. Samuel Smiles.

It is a calm, tranquil spot, and the setting sun illumines
with a flood of golden glory the ancient Harley tombstone,
dating from 1500, beneath which a mother most faithfully mourned has slept peacefully for over fifty years.

CHAPTER III.

EDINBURGH—STUDENT LIFE.

Up to the time of his mother's death, I can find no mention among my father's papers either of his success or failure at the Haddington Burgh Schools, where many previous Harleys had been educated, from which silence it may fairly be surmised he did not begin to show any great evidence of exceptional natural ability till after 1845, when Harley House, with its spacious old-fashioned rooms, fair lawns, and shady gardens, was let, and the orphan boy, in company with his maternal grandmother, removed to Edinburgh.

At that period Haddington Burgh Schools, under the skilful management of Rev. N. Gunn—subsequently Dr. Gunn, Master of the High School, Edinburgh—were again in the zenith of their glory, so, in spite of the omission above stated, there can be no doubt he was well instructed during his early days, learning many things in the ancient town, which stood him in good stead when he grew to be a man.

His grandmother was eighty-three years of age and he only sixteen when they went together to Edinburgh, where for a year George Harley entered the Hill Street Institution, a school of some repute for boys in their teens.

What a change that uprooting must have seemed to both the elderly lady and the young lad—that transplanting of the aged tree and the tender sapling, even though their home was in the house of a granddaughter and the boy's married sister !

Probably the boy was too sad, the octogenarian too feeble, to leave any detailed account of how poorly the glories of an ancient and most beautiful city—then as much a centre of learning and thought as London is now—compensated for the peace of Haddington, and the thousand tender memories which must continually have seemed to be pulling them back to the town of Adda, the King, the grand Lammermuir Hills, and the clear sparkling river.

But the lad at least was in no danger of forgetting those old stories which had since childhood formed a large part of his mental nourishment.

Aged and broken though Mrs. Macbeath was, bereft of all her children and with the long gap of much more than half a century intervening between herself and grandson, her stories and reminiscences must have been a source of never-ending delight to young George.

'The old lady,' writes her grandson, 'was born at a small place called Logie, near Stirling, in 1772. She was the only child of a Mr. Lieshman, who held his land by feudal tenure. The very name indicates the form of tenure. He was a Lieshman—that is to say, a slipper of hounds ; and so long as there was a male heir in the house to perform the office of Lieshman when called upon—or, rather, if called upon—the property remained unalienable from the family. If, however, a male lineal descendant failed, the property reverted to the Crown, all except sufficient land on which to build a house and form a kail-yard,* which went by right to the daughter. When my great (maternal) grandfather died, he left no male issue, consequently my grandmother could lay claim to nothing except the small piece of land for a house and kail-yard. Woman-like, she thought she was grievously wronged, and in triumphant disdain told the legal authorities that, as they had taken her father's patrimony, they might take the land for the house and kail-yard too.

* Kitchen-garden.

For years the piece of land was carefully fenced off and remained unoccupied; but after a lapse of time, no claim being made, the fences were taken down and it was absorbed into the other property.

'My old grandmother, aged eighty-three, used to tell me many a tale of her younger days. When her father was a boy, the troops of Bonnie Prince Charlie besieged Stirling Castle (1745), and a number of them were quartered in their house. The standard was stuck into a hole on the louping-on stane,* which stood at one side of the front-door. This stone I saw as a boy when visiting the place in 1840 with my mother; the old house was then being pulled down, but the fine old orchard, although a high-road had been cut through the middle of it, still remained. The stone, from having a hole in the upper surface, and from its somewhat circular form, leads me to believe that it was originally used as the under block of a quern, or hand-mill, for grinding corn.

'Her father, she used to say, as a boy laid himself flat on his back in the valley between his home and Stirling Castle, and watched the cannon-balls as they played over his head. Before the troops arrived, all the valuables possessed by the Lieshmans, napery† included, were put into wooden chests and buried in various places about the grounds. Her mother was dreadfully indignant at the troops being quartered on her, for she was no Jacobin, and at the easy way they conducted themselves in her beautiful home. On one occasion the kitchenmaid rushed to her mistress and bitterly complained that two of the soldiers were waiting in the kitchen to steal the contents of the "dinner-pot" as soon as it was ready.

'The good lady's temper could not stand this, so she flew into the kitchen and began to scold the men, when one of them drew his claymore, and would have run her through

---

* The Scotch word for joust, or mounting-stone of English counties.

† Scotch for house-linen.

the back had her husband not in the very nick of time entered and seized the arm of the soldier ere he was able to accomplish his purpose.

'Many of the tales my grandmother used to tell with great glee referred to her own wonderful feats of horsemanship. She must indeed have been a graceful and wonderful rider; and the contrast suggested between the fragile narrator, and the handsome high-spirited girl who thought it such splendid fun to ride over "brake, bush, and scaur" in the days that could never return, struck me as most pathetic.

'There is one feat of horsemanship which I ought not to omit to mention, as it shows a little bit of the custom of the country in those days before carriages came into common use.* When eighteen years of age my grandmother was one of the bridesmaids at the wedding of the son of a wealthy laird. In those days there were no such things as wedding-tours for young married couples. The good folks were married not unfrequently in the open air, the church in which the service was performed being a green field, its roof the cloud canopy of heaven, its altar the mossy turf.

'On the occasion about to be alluded to, the company proceeded in procession to the home of the bride's father, where they partook of a substantial dinner. After the meal was over the newly-married couple were conducted in grand procession, with music and flags, to their future home.

'On this occasion the bridegroom's house was about four or five miles distant from the girl's father's, and the guests, being well-to-do people, were all mounted, the young folks on separate horses, the old married couples riding pillion.†

'As they were mounted and assembled round the door

---

* About 1780.

† In riding pillion, the man sat astride the horse in front on a saddle, the woman sideways behind on a pad. I only once in my life saw this arrangement (1839), and the couple were an old farmer and his wife.

before starting on their journey, the newly-married man stood forward on the doorstep, signalled to the bagpipes to stop playing, then held up a ring between his finger and thumb, saying: " To the girl who first reaches my house, and is there ready to welcome me and my wife on our arrival, I will give this ring. Now, off you go."

' There were six young maidens besides my grandmother, and all immediately started off at a smart canter. She stayed behind, and the other girls, looking back, laughed at her for her apparent folly. She, however, laughed in her turn, and called out to them : " I'll be there before you."

' As she was always well mounted, this caused no surprise, but little did any of them anticipate the trick she was going to play. There was a short-cut across the fields, but not used for horses, as there was an ugly ditch to cross, over which was merely a plank for foot-passengers. No sooner did the other girls get fairly out of sight than she cantered quietly down the road and turned her horse on to the footpath. Being a bold as well as a good rider, and knowing her animal's capabilities, as soon as she neared the dreaded ditch she put her horse to his full speed, kept him well at it, and over he sprang and landed her in safety on the opposite bank. Now the race, she well knew, was her own, as she had cut off a good mile or more, so on she galloped and reached the back of the house long before any of the others were in sight of the front of it. Quickly dismounting from her now panting steed, she threw the reins to one of the men in readiness to take the horses from the guests on their arrival, and observing from the front-door that her competitors were still a good way off, she ran upstairs, took off her hat, smoothed her hair, hastily arranged her dress, and ran down again. This done, she took up her position at the front-door, as if she had been there all day. She had not to wait long. The astonishment of the bride, when she rode up and saw my grandmother, whom she had fancied lagged far behind, was unbounded. The others, when they arrived, were no less amazed until the stratagem was explained. She had fairly won the ring, which, although of no great value, richly did she prize. That ring I have worn on my finger or my scarf more days than I care to own, for I prize its history.

'I began studying medicine,' continues George Harley, ' at the University of Edinburgh, but made it a practice to be home in time to take tea with my dear old grandmother at least three days a week, on which occasion she invariably asked me to " feel her pulse." She had got the idea into her head that the large veins in her emaciated arms were full of air ; therefore when I, with a great affectation of knowledge, felt her pulse in one arm, she immediately extended the other, and said, in a touchingly appealing tone : " Now, George, try this, and see if they correspond !" '

One of this old lady's hobbies was that it was right for all ' gentlefolk ' to prepare their shroud ; therefore many years, perhaps half a century, before her death she learned to weave, so that she might weave her last garment, which was made of the finest white lawn, trimmed with lace. Periodically the death-dress was carefully aired and put back in the drawer to wait till wanted. My father always remembered these periodical airings, and could describe the long white robe, the lace-bedecked cap, the white stockings and gloves, so carefully treasured by the old body. All too soon for the lonely lad the good soul was taken from him, and George Harley left in the wide world alone.

The last of the Lieshmans, who for centuries held Hirrown at Logie, Stirlingshire, did not long survive her daughter, dying in 1846, when her husband's family name also became extinct. *Sic transit gloria mundi.*

'Whatever the cause,' continues the student, 'I must confess to having passed an idle first year at the Edinburgh University. At the end of that time, however, a great change came over the spirit of my dream. Science grew to have attractions for me, which mere book knowledge never had, and I began to work at chemistry, anatomy, and physiology *con amore*.

'I never studied after twelve o'clock at night. The moment the clock struck that hour, I closed my book; no matter whether I were in the middle of a sentence or not, the book was shut; five minutes, exactly, were given to a pipe or a cigar, and then off I went to bed. On Saturdays and Sundays I never studied. In 1849 I went in for my first important examination, and came out with flying colours, notwithstanding that out of the sixty-three candidates thirty-two were rejected, and among them one of my old schoolfellows, who at school used to be my superior in everything except arithmetic and algebra. Upon him I turned the tables. I had now got into a groove of learning suited to my tastes.

'My first step on the ladder of fame was made in the April of the following year (1850). When house-surgeon at the Royal Maternity Hospital, I, single-handed and without any preparation, successfully extracted by Cæsarean section, immediately after the death of the mother from heart disease, a living child, and thus saved the life of a seven and a half months babe.*

'The child was a boy. His grandfather named him after me. When he was ten years of age I brought him up to London, and he afterwards became my page; but after being with me seven years he became so domineering with the other servants, as he laboured under the delusion that, do what he would, I should never send him away, that I had to get rid of him. From me he went as footman into another place, but he did not keep it long, and I lost sight of him until I accidentally heard that he had been an in-patient, at the age of twenty-five, in Guy's Hospital.'

Amongst the traditions of the day, in Edinburgh, were the stories of Knox, the anatomist. But a few years before he had been the brilliantly clever lecturer whose name,

* *Edinburgh Medical Journal*, July, 1850.

unfortunately for himself, was so closely connected with the famous Burke and Hare mysteries. At that time there was no Anatomical Act, neither was Warburton the statesman in power, therefore there was no supervision whatever as to how or where bodies were procured for dissection. Good sums were paid for 'subjects,' and thus it was that 'body-snatching' became a regular profession. It was no easy matter to get hold of a corpse, and even in the silence of the night great strategy was necessary to transfer one to the dissecting-rooms.

Two of the men employed by Dr. Knox were named respectively Burke and Hare, and no matter how many bodies were required, this couple always succeeded in procuring the right number. There was a mystery about it all; but even the mystery at last became more mysterious. An inquiry was set on foot, with the result that it was discovered when these two men had not a sufficient supply to quench the demand they resorted to a little strategy.

The Cowgate, Canongate, and Grassmarket, with their strange 'closes' and 'wynds,' were in Knox's day (1828) the scene of much iniquity and vice. The 'Burking' business came about in this wise. Hare had a lodger who died owing him £4; so, to reimburse himself, Hare sold the body to Knox for £7 10s. This was a tempting price to get for a body. No other lodger conveniently died, however; so late one night, meeting a very drunk old woman, Hare inveigled her to his home, where suffocation killed the poor old woman, as it did many more—fifteen in all—during the next few months.

The men were taken up, and on their trial it was proved their usual mode of procedure was to put a plaster over the mouths of their victims—even sit on them, if necessary, so as to sell their dead bodies for the anatomical rooms. This practice became known as 'Burking.'

The trial was a very ghastly one, and revealed many tales of horror; finally Hare turned King's evidence, and got off free, while Burke was executed.

The whole thing, I believe, at the time created an enormous sensation. My father often told the story, and I very well remember, when walking with him as a child in Portland Place, his pointing out a funny old man who was blind and led about by a terrier dog with a tin can in his mouth, who, he told me, was Hare, the famous body-snatcher. For years I saw that old man; he was often in Oxford Street, Regent Street, and the neighbourhood, and kindly people dropped their pennies in the bent tin can, little realizing that the 'poor old blind man' was one of the famous body-snatchers of Burke and Hare fame. His blindness, be it remarked, was the result of the fury of the mob at his turning King's evidence — they cruelly threw lime in his face.

The Edinburgh students at the time wrote some doggerel verses on the subject of the trial, such as :

> 'Midst a fiendish yell, Burke danced to hell ;
> 'Gainst him the door old Satan locks.
> Says he, This place you shan't disgrace ;
> Go back to earth and dwell with Knox !'

But Dr. Knox was entirely exonerated from any blame, and as a man did much for anatomy, then almost unknown in Britain.

My father always had a dread of a practical joke, and was most severe on us as children if we ever attempted anything of the kind. The origin of his dread was the following :

When a medical student he had a friend who vowed he had no fear of ghosts or spirits of any kind. He was not a popular man for some reason, and being fond of bragging of his valour, several of his comrades determined to play a practical joke upon him, and asked my father to join. He did not like practical jokes even in those early days, and declined.

One night several of the students determined to enter the brave young man's room with an apparent ghost, and see if he were really as fearless as he made out. Accordingly they arranged a sheet over a broom. They had a very jovial evening, and the young companions waited till they thought the dauntless one was asleep; then silently one of them glided into his room beneath the sheet, and, rattling the linen to attract his attention, quietly glided out again. They heard him strike a light, when, fearing to be caught, they stole quietly away.

The next day he confided to one of his friends that he had seen a ghost, but he would do for that ghost if it ever came again, as he had no fear of such nonsense. This was exactly what they wanted, so a night or two afterwards the students made the same preparations, and arranged their broom and sheet as before.

Two or three of these young fellows stayed outside the door while their chosen companion impersonated the ghost. He glided in. Through the darkness the long gaunt figure was visible to the drowsy sleeper, who sat bolt upright in bed. He glared upon the ghost, put his hand under his pillow, found the pistol he had bought for the purpose, took aim, and fired. The ghost stood his ground. Slowly and silently the bullet rolled back to the affrighted man across the counterpane. He fired the second chamber; the second bullet quietly rolled back again as before.

Having heard he had procured a revolver, one of the students crept up to his room last thing, and extracted the two bullets, which he gave to the ghost to roll back across the counterpane, feeling perfectly safe, as the box containing further charges had been removed.

But they little guessed what the sequel would prove. Almost before the second bullet had rolled the length of the bed, without a sound the poor young man fell back upon his pillow—dead.

And thus a silly practical joke ended in a tragedy!

Students, and especially medical students, are proverbially fond of what they call ' fun,' and it is scarcely reasonable to expect that my father should have been an exception

3

to the rule. Yet so-called practical joking was a thing he never indulged in.

'To my way of thinking,' he said, 'it is tomfoolery without wit, and as such beneath the dignity of any man with the slightest pretension to brains or a spark of gentlemanly feeling. My contempt for, and my refusal to take part in, practical joking with my fellow house physicians and surgeons in the Edinburgh Royal Infirmary once caused a serious quarrel between me and my colleagues, which ended in my literally cutting down one of them—a fellow six feet two—by means of a bedroom poker. The scalp wound I inflicted on his head was of sufficient gravity to bring to an end the system of childish practical joking which had been indulged in over a period of several months.'

But to relate a funny little story. Hats were being constantly taken by mistake by the Edinburgh students, and to avoid this George Harley christened his head-covering Golgotha. 'I cut out a piece of drawing-paper,' he says, 'to the exact size of the inside of the crown of my hat. Upon that paper I carefully drew a human skull, as large as the bottom of an ordinary tumbler, taking care to make the skull appear as fierce-looking as possible by endowing it with dark staring eyeholes and two rows of prominently-marked white teeth. Under the skull was neatly but boldly written the single word "Golgotha." When the drawing was gummed into the crown of the hat it was readily recognisable, and by this characteristic trade mark "Harley's hat" was soon well known, and regarded with some degree of interest by most of the medical students then in attendance at the University.

'*Tempus fugit* during student life more rapidly in appearance than at any other period of a man's existence, and in its flight bears on its wings many novelties. Trifles, too, carry with them an air of importance, sufficient to leave an indelible impression on the memory, and such probably is the cause why the following occurrence in my hat's history appears to me, at the present moment, worth recording.

'In the days I speak of (1847), Professor Syme gave his clinical lectures in the operating theatre of the Royal Infirmary, and it was customary on these occasions for as many of the students as possible to put their hats on the side-tables of the arena in which the Professor sat. On one occasion it happened that my hat was placed on the front edge of one of the tables, and as the students who subsequently entered the class-room put their hats on the same table, they naturally enough observed Golgotha.

'Professor Syme began his lecture, and at length, having to speak of the case of a man with an injured cranium, he requested a human skull to be brought to him, in order that he might point out the exact seat of the injury. The skull was brought, and the demonstration was nearly at an end, when the footsteps of the house-surgeon and the patient, whom he was leading in, were heard in the corridor of the theatre. Startled by their rather premature approach, and fearful lest the patient should catch a glimpse of a skull, the Professor sprang up and looked for a place to hide it. He bethought himself of popping it into a hat for concealment, and, approaching the table with this object in view, the hat which came first to hand happened, by a strange coincidence, to be mine, and just as he was on the point of dropping the skull from his hand, his eye caught sight of the drawing. He gave an involuntary start, the students understood in a moment, and one more impulsive than the rest drawled out, in a sort of suppressed murmur, through his teeth the word "Golgotha," which caused a roar of laughter, in which even Professor Syme himself was forced to join. Raising his eyes to the students for a moment, he smiled, and then carefully placed the skull in its proper place—Golgotha—thereby provoking a second burst of merriment.

'After the lecture, Professor Syme inquired who was the owner of the hat, which from that moment became famous !

'During fifteen months I successively filled the offices of house-surgeon and of resident physician in the Royal Infirmary of Edinburgh.

'In August, 1850, I graduated as a Doctor of Medicine at the University of Edinburgh ; after which I went straight off to London, and passed my examination as a Member of the Royal College of Surgeons. During the examination, Mr.—afterwards Sir William—Lawrence asked me where I had studied surgery. On being told with Syme at Edinburgh, he invited me to call on him the next day. I did so, when he asked me a great deal about Syme's treatment of gangrene. He afterwards took me to St. Bartholomew's Hospital, and went round with me, pointing out the most interesting of his cases, an honour which I duly appreciated.'

My father little thought then what a friend the great Sir William Lawrence would prove in the future. The surgeon was so much struck by George Harley's ability that he never lost sight of him, and when the young medico came to reside permanently in London, Sir William was almost the first to give him a helping hand. But in the meantime, the Napoleonic *coup d'état* taking place in the end of 1851, the newly fledged doctor went off to Paris to study gunshot wounds.

CHAPTER IV.

My father was very fond of telling children, and sometimes grown-up folk, too, what he was pleased to call, ' My Ghost Story,' which, although space does not permit of its insertion here, is a very good story, and especially interesting as regards the author, because it demonstrates so clearly that ' The child is father of the man.'

When only fourteen years old, young George Harley, as has previously been shown, accomplished a most perilous descent from the tower of Haddington old church ; and so it came to pass, quite in the natural order of things, that before attaining the age of twenty he wrestled, far from human dwelling, at midnight, in pouring rain, on a bleak seashore, inhabited only by demons, with a newly-made grave, a horrid ghost, and such inexplicable jabberings as though all the doomed spirits were making at once their terrible plaint to earth and heaven, only to find next morning grave, ghost and shrieks were ordinary phenomena!

The event occurred in 1848, but it was not till thirty years later that, yielding to the request of Mrs. J. H. Riddell, the well-known author of ' George Geith,' he wrote out his night experience on the Arran coast, and let her publish the weird tale in a magazine she was then editing.

The author did not return to Arran for about a like period; perhaps it was the publication of the story which induced him to do so in company with my mother and sister Olga, one lovely autumn when the dear old land was looking its very best and sweetest.

After that long gap, however, the people *knew him*. How wonderful that must have seemed! And yet he was not a man easily to be forgotten. 'The body changes, but the actual person within the body does not,' as possibly he himself would have said; and so it is more than probable time had left the kindly voice untouched, the genial manner unchanged, the frank face with a virtue of youth still in its features. Ah me! what a wonderful personality it was ill-health tried so perseveringly to wreck—in vain!

'My Ghost Story' was written down *thirty years after its actual occurrence* without a note of any kind.

The author was indeed blessed with a truly remarkable memory, and to the very end could give quotations, dates, facts and figures without reference, even when writing for the press.

In connection with this matter, I may mention one of my most juvenile recollections is every morning seeing my father sitting up in bed, an early cup of tea beside him, a small board in his hand covered by blotting-paper and manuscript, scribbling letters, stories, lectures or scientific books.

He never wrote at a table, but either sitting up in bed, or in an armchair, beside the fire in winter, or an open window in summer; he always looked most uncomfortable holding his board up in his left hand, but declared he liked it.

Poor mother! what she suffered over those early morning exercises! The ink flew in every direction; the more interested he became, the more oblivious to sheets, counterpanes, blankets, which received a black christening weekly.

It was lucky for him he could write anywhere, otherwise, during the many years of illness he was forced to endure, he would have lacked his greatest solace.

Two years after that lonely encounter on the lovely Arran shore, my father, having meanwhile graduated at

the Edinburgh University, bethought him it might be well
to spend four or five years at Continental seats of learning.

Paris with its warlike prospects was his first goal—one
which began an entirely new page in his life's history.

He had done well in Edinburgh, where he received
honours and medals for his work ; and being young,
energetic, and endowed with the means needful for comfortable existence, he was practically free to choose his own
career.

He chose Science, and for a time wooed that goddess
with an undivided heart.

In Paris, at the suggestion of an old college friend, Dr.
William Marcet, he entered as a private pupil the laboratory then under the superintendence of Wurtz, Verdeil and
Charles Dollfus. The terms were 100 francs a month for
instruction, while the cost of materials for work amounted
to 50 francs more, making up a total cost of £72 in the
twelve months.

'A large sum,' he says, 'but one I never grudged. It
was well laid out, for the amount of physiological chemistry
I learned was beyond all proportion to the money expended.
While working in this laboratory I made my first scientific
discovery—oh, the joy of that first success!—namely, that
the metal iron is a normal ingredient of healthy renal
secretion. This discovery was soon followed by another—
the mode of extracting in a pure state the colouring matter
of the renal secretion.'*

I have said that Paris began an entirely new page in the
young man's life story, and that statement is strictly true;
for there he gained not merely a wide and profound
knowledge of science, but made his first acquaintance with
adversity.

Although very well off, my father was by no means
personally extravagant ; still, he went much into society,

* ' Researches on the Colouring Matter of the Urine, and the
Existence of Iron in that Liquid,' *Journ. Pharm. Soc.*, 1852.

hired riding-horses when the fancy took him, lived in expensive rooms, dined at good cafés, bought tea at 40 francs a pound—the price in Paris in those days—and otherwise enjoyed himself, as was natural at his age and with his temperament.

Such a mode of life runs away with money, but he had enough and to spare; and it was not because of any wild or foolish expenditure he learnt in the gay city how speedily gold can take unto itself wings.

Unfortunately, he had among his many friends one of a speculative turn of mind—a man who looked at life through rose-coloured glasses—who, never content to leave well alone, invariably ended by making matters worse than he found them, and who advised my father so effectually how to make a huge fortune that ere long he found himself minus a very comfortable one. This loss no doubt considerably altered his ideas with regard to science as a hobby, and also turned his mind to medicine as a means to an end. He had bought his experience at so heavy a price that, although sufficient money remained to leave him without anxiety concerning his own wants, he knew if ever he meant to marry, and enjoy the expensive luxury of a home, he must direct his attention to some profession likely to prove more lucrative than pure science.

He soon made up his mind as to the course he should pursue, and 'went in' determinedly for medicine, while in Paris working with Claude Bernard at the Collège de France, and publishing in French some original researches on the saccharine function of the liver.

It was at this time my father conceived an idea that he might possibly directly stimulate the nerves of the liver so as to cause it to manufacture such an excess of sugar as would produce diabetes. Failing, however, to meet with any encouragement from Claude Bernard, and therefore feeling somewhat shy about conducting such researches at the laboratory, he decided to continue to experiment on the subject at his own lodgings in Paris. He fitted up a

small laboratory—naturally of a very primitive nature—
and having procured the dogs necessary for the experiments, enlisted the sympathies of one or two of his fellow-
students, notably Dr. John Baumann. The results were
successful; they soon had the satisfaction of demonstrating
that by the injection of stimulating liquids, such as alcohol,
aqua ammonia, sulphuric ether, and chloroform, into the
portal circulation, a true diabetes could be established.

But my father's love of knowledge and scientific research
did not stop here; he had tasted the sweetness of success,
and determined to try a series of experiments upon himself
which most undoubtedly undermined his constitution. He
found that he could render himself diabetic by living
for three days entirely on asparagus, rendered stimulating
with pepper and vinegar.

This love of scientific research was the mainspring of
his life, and certainly up to the time he married, and unfortunately, indeed, sometimes after, his experiments were
made upon himself, for, as he often laughingly remarked :
'If a man may not do what he likes with his own body,
who can ?'

Which may be all right in theory, but, unfortunately, his
experiments went so far that on several occasions they
nearly cost him his life.

It was while studying hard at the Collège de France,
however, that an incident occurred which is worth
mentioning as showing the danger those who start in the
pursuit of knowledge may have to encounter. Fortunately
I am able to tell of his battle for life in his own words :

' I was busily occupied in prosecuting a series of original
researches on the formation of sugar in the animal body,
and to enable me to carry them out it was necessary to
experiment on animals. Being prohibited alike by the
laws of God and man from sacrificing human beings on
the altar of science, I did the next best thing : I made use
of his companions.

'Having arranged with a member of the Secret Police— Monsieur Henri*—I received a certain number of dogs weekly, and paid a fixed sum per head. As Henri did not wish that Monsieur le Directeur should know of his doings with the "jeune Médecin Écossais," his visits to my domicile were usually paid early in the morning or late at night. One morning, about six o'clock, as I lay comfortably asleep in bed, a sharp rat-tat-tat awoke me.

' "Entrez," I cried, and in popped Monsieur Henri's head; after a sly glance round the room, a habit of the rogue's to see that the coast was clear, the body followed the head, and a fine full-grown brown and white English setter followed close after Henri.

' "Voilà, monsieur, un prix pour vous," said my friend with an air of triumph.

'With eyelids only half open, I looked, saw, and was satisfied, and, unwilling to have my dreams disturbed, with a "C'est très bien " I dismissed him.

'An hour and a half later the maid came with my early cup of coffee, after which I got up and began to dress. Not seeing the dog about the room, I called for him, thinking that he had gone into the next apartment, the door of which was open. Receiving no response to my call, I looked into the room, but to my surprise the dog was not there. I then knelt down and peeped under my bed, to find he was lying crouched up in a corner. I tried coaxing, but that failed to bring him out. A bit of roll was next offered him, with the same negative result. As setters, I knew, are often subjected to the lash, and in general timid, I put my hand under the bed and drew him out. Now I noticed that he had a string securely tied round and round his muzzle. It was fixed on very tightly, and in an unusual manner, being regularly bound round and round the nose many times, and with as much regularity and care as one would use in splicing a fishing-rod. " No wonder," thought

---

* Among other offices, this man's duty was to catch and kill all the stray dogs in Paris.

I to myself, " that the animal is frightened, for he must be in pain." I at once unmuzzled him, and with kindly words and fondling caresses sought to gain his confidence. He yielded, however, to neither ; and as soon as I let him go, with a sort of glassy stare in his eyes, he slunk back to his corner under the bed again.

'During my toilet I whistled to him, I spoke to him, I even sang to him, but no responsive sign gave he. Dressing finished, I prepared to take him down into the garden, where I kept my other dogs ; but as no coaxing could induce him to leave his corner, after patting his head, I for the second time pulled him out. I then tried to get him to follow me, but in vain, so sought a collar and chain, intending to lead him. On turning to put on the collar, however, I found that he had disappeared under the bed once more. Now, this rather surprised me, for he was a splendidly made animal, and possessed such a lovely coat I felt sure his late master must have been fond of him. His appearance had already won my heart. A third time I knelt on the carpet, and pulled him out, the while I began to feel astonished that all my fondling, coaxing, and caressing seemed thrown away. Such a stoic of a dog I had never before met with. Having buckled the collar, I proceeded to lead him downstairs, but we had not descended more than half a dozen steps ere I was startled by a peculiar sound and sudden tug. On looking over my shoulder, I beheld the animal gnashing and champing at the chain. His eyes, glassy as before, had now a wild glare about them, with which, in spite of all my experience of dogs, I was unfamiliar. I paused, spoke kindly to the creature, took the chain from his mouth, and again began to descend, when the noise was repeated. This time, however, the dog had one of the iron bars of the railing in his mouth, and was biting at it savagely.

'At last I saw something was wrong; but what it was I did not know, my idea, however, being that the dog was not exactly of sane mind. I pulled him hurriedly.

downstairs, dragged him out at the back-door on to the garden terrace, which was on a level with the step, and quickly fastened the chain to the terrace railings. I then retreated a few steps out of reach of his teeth and examined him at my leisure.

'"Is the dog really mad?" I asked myself. But I could not answer, for at that time I had no experience to guide me. "Is he mad, or is he not mad?" that was the first question; and how to solve it the next. The last put was the first answered. Hydrophobia meant a dread of water. "Go and get some water," said I to myself, "and try him with that." I ran upstairs and returned with a tumbler of water in my hand. When I presented it to the dog he shrank back. Again the tumbler was placed near to his mouth, again he speedily decamped to the other side, as far as his chain would allow him to go. A third time the water was placed within his reach, and a third time he walked away from it as far as he could. No doubt remained now in my mind that the dog was rabid. No coaxing would induce him to approach the water; no endearing words could persuade him to remain beside the tumbler.

'Both questions having now been settled, a third one presented itself: "What is to be done with the dog?" "Kill it," was the reply. "How is it to be killed?" I had nothing to shoot it with. Besides, shooting would make a noise, attract attention, and stop my experiments. There was, then, but one course open, viz., to fetch Henri and ask him to take the dog away.

'I looked to see that the chain was safely fastened. I locked the door leading from the garden into the house. I put the key in my pocket, got my hat, and started off at a round trot for Monsieur Henri. He lived in a street near the Panthéon, which I soon reached, and learning from the concierge that he whom I sought was at home, I rushed up the stairs and knocked at his door. No answer. I knocked again, and louder.

' "Qui est là?" was the reply.

' "Monsieur Harley," said I.

' "Que voulez-vous?" asked Monsieur Henri.

' "You, to come and fetch away the dog," I returned.

' "Est-il mort?"

' "No."

' "Tuez lui, donc, et je viendrai tout de suite," answered my kind friend.

' "No," I said, "you shall come and kill him yourself."

' "Est-il muselé?" demanded Monsieur Henri.

'Most foolishly I told the truth and answered "No," when at once the vagabond changed his tactics and defeated me by a lie.

' "Allez chez vous," said he, " et je suivrai immédiatement."

'Trusting in the word of a scamp, I went home and waited, but he did not come. Minutes slipped away, and yet Henri did not appear. Time was precious, for the other lodgers would be coming into the garden, and what if the dog should bite any of them? The thought was dreadful, for I had once seen a child in the convulsions of hydrophobia, and I shuddered to think of anyone being subjected even to the risk of having such a malady.

'Again I returned to Henri, actually running through the streets, regardless alike of what people might think or say. Almost breathless, I still managed to fly up the stairs three steps at a time. A violent knock at the door announced my presence. But no answer came. All was as still as death. Another more violent knock. Again no reply. I shook the door. I shouted aloud, "Monsieur Henri!" But not a sound from within was to be heard. Thinking that he might have gone out, but still suspicious of deception, I went on to the landing, leant over the balusters, and called out to the concierge: "Monsieur Henri est-il chez lui?"

' "Oui, monsieur," was the reply.

'Back I went to the door. Again I knocked; again I shook it. At last I got desperate, and said: "Henri, if you don't open the door I will break it open."

'Not a word was vouchsafed. I took one step backwards, raised my foot, and with all my force banged it against the panel. The door rattled in its frame, and a shrill frightened voice screamed from within: "Arretez! arretez! j'ouvre la porte."

' "Quick, then," cried I, " or down goes the door!"

'The key turned in the lock, the door opened, and I stood face to face with my adversary. Henri was a man nearly, but not quite, my own height; broader in build, and at least possessed of twice my strength. But there I was, with my blood up, the energy of despair in my frame, ready to strangle him on the spot. Had he shown fight, regardless of consequences I should instantly have closed upon him. But the cowardly villain shrank from my approach, while with white lips and a cowed air he stuttered out an apology, and declared he was preparing to come, but had only just got out of bed and dressed himself. A lie from beginning to end. There lay on the floor five or six small dogs, newly killed. On a block of wood, which served him for a seat, was a bundle, tied up in a coarse brown towel, which seemed to me to move. Following my eye, his attention was directed to the spot; he took up the bundle, undid the knots, and out rolled a recently-murdered fine young long-haired Skye terrier, worth £5 at least. The brute of a man had smothered the poor animal by tying it up in the towel and then sitting on it. I afterwards ascertained this was his usual method of despatching the dogs, and that he received 6 sous (threepence) for each dead dog he took to the conciergerie.

'Here, then, was the proof that his excuse was a lie. He had been out early, captured his prey, returned home and despatched them while pretending to have been in bed and getting ready to come to me. How could I compete with such a blackguard? Fight him with his own weapons? That was impossible.

'"Henri," said I, "you shall come along with me and take away that dog."

'"If you will only kill it," said he, "I promise to do anything you please."

'Seeing that I stared at him and made no remark, he quickly added: "If you even muzzle him, I will take him away at once."

'"Coquin!" retorted I; "you shall muzzle him yourself. So follow me."

'I began to descend the staircase, but he still hesitated.

'"Are you coming?" I called out.

'"Oui, monsieur, tout de suite; allez, je vous suis."

'Every minute being to me precious, for, as I said before, I dreaded leaving the dog in the garden, lest anyone should be bitten by him, I hurried home, now and then turning round to see if Henri was behind me. Not he; nor, as it afterwards proved, had he ever the slightest intention of coming for the dog.

'Arrived once more in the garden, I found things just as I had left them. I paced up and down, I fumed, I waited. Henri never came. It would soon be ten o'clock, déjeuner would be ready half an hour later, people would be coming into the garden to promenade for a few minutes before sitting down to table. What on earth was to be done? To wait longer for Henri was out of the question. To pith the dog seemed the easiest way of killing him, and that I determined to try.

'A word on "pithing." There is one little point in an animal (vertebrated) the mere puncturing of which with a darning-needle means instantaneous death. The French savant Flourens, its discoverer, gave to it the name *point vitale* (vital point). This remarkable spot is situated close to the top of the spinal marrow, and near the base of the brain. And while a quarter of an inch below or a quarter of an inch above it the spinal marrow may be pricked with comparative impunity, when that special point is touched by the needle, life is at an end—no restorative means can ever again bring back the vital spark. It is a knowledge of this spot that enables the matador to kill the bull by thrusting the point of his sharp sword into his neck immediately behind the head as the animal rushes upon him at full tilt. By skilled hands the proper spot is easily struck when the animal's head is still. But if the head be moved about from side to side, the operator is more likely to miss his mark than he is to hit it.

' Knowing all this, it required a little moral courage on my part to determine upon making the venture with an unmuzzled dog with rabies. I must admit that now I should think twice before attempting such a task. But young blood is more regardless of consequences than mature age, so I ran upstairs to my bedroom in search of an instrument likely to answer my purpose. I could find nothing, however, except a tooth-punch, which lay in a case of dental instruments. This I seized, together with the ewer of water, and rapidly retraced my steps to the garden. Now for a bit of strategy. How was I to get hold of the dog, and keep his head steady while I pithed him? He had a mind of his own; and with dogs, as with men, self-preservation is the first law of Nature. He had jaws, and he had teeth, strong teeth, in them. Moreover, he was foaming at the mouth, and his eyes were glaring. Was he likely to remain quiet while I deprived him of his life? "Not quite," thought I; "but I will do my best." Holding the tooth-punch between my teeth, I took the ewer in my left hand, and began ladling out the water at him.

' As I did so he shrank back from me till he could go no further. Then, dragging on the chain with his face turned towards me, his tail was at the extreme diameter of a circle, whose centre is to be regarded as the point at which the chain was fastened to the railings. Now was the moment for attack. Down went the ewer on the ground, and with

a sudden bound, in the twinkling of an eye, I had firm hold
of his tail.   Pulling him tight towards me, while the collar
kept him stretched out to his utmost length, he could not
turn to attack me.   Grasping his tail firmly with my
right hand, I bent over and seized him by the under part
of the neck with my left.   Compressing his neck as tightly
as I could, I released the tail in order to leave my right
hand free to use the punch.

'Then came the tug-of-war.   Little did I imagine that the
brute had such strength.   Instead of being able to take the
instrument in my right hand, the services of both were
instantly required to enable me to cope with the animal.
We struggled ; I lost my footing, and down I fell on the top
of him.   For a minute he almost slipped from my grasp.
He nearly freed his neck from my clutch.   He almost
mastered me.   In the struggle my face got within an inch
of his jaws, and I felt if my hand slipped from his throat it
would be all up with me.   It was indeed a battle for life.
How long it lasted I cannot tell.   When danger is great,
moments are minutes—ay, even minutes seem hours.   I
dared not cry for help.   The question therefore was, Whose
strength would hold out the longest, or whose tactics would
eventually triumph ?   I advisedly use the word "tactics";
for the dog displayed as much tact in availing himself of
my weak points as I did in counteracting his movements.
At length I got the whole weight of my body upon him—I
literally lay upon the huge creature ; and pinioned to the
ground he ceased to struggle for a minute.   My right hand
thus freed, I seized the instrument from between my teeth,
and quick as thought plunged it in his neck.   One powerful
convulsion was rapidly succeeded by another, and then all
was still.

'The dog which had seemed so formidable in my eyes a
minute before was now as nothing.   With the vital spark,
all power for ill had departed.   I lay panting for a minute
beside the poor brute, afterwards slowly rose, took out my
handkerchief and wiped the perspiration from my forehead.

4

'The battle finished, I could quietly review the scene. A moment more, and terror seized me. *There was blood on my hand!* The skin had been rubbed off my left forefinger by the chain or collar during the fray. My hand was covered with deadly saliva from the dog's mouth. Here was a nice affair. I had escaped being bitten ; but a raw surface and saliva upon it was quite as dangerous as a bite. The handkerchief was instantly employed to wipe away the secretion, and my lips as rapidly applied to the wounded surface. That done, I undid the chain, picked up the dog, and carried him with much difficulty, he was such a size, to an outhouse at the bottom of the garden. Returning to the house, I washed my hand, made myself tidy, and at half-past ten sat down with the others to breakfast as if nothing unusual had happened. Whatever my thoughts on that occasion may have been—and needless to say the wound made me a little anxious—my outward appearance bore no trace of them, and never did an inmate of that dwelling hear one syllable of the story here related.

'P.S.—Like a lady's letter, my tale would not be complete without a postscript, so here it is :

'Henri never appeared till the afternoon, when, being too angry to see him, I sent a message ordering him to take away the dog, which he did. Much as I disliked the man, I could not do without his services, so I went on employing him for many months afterwards—indeed, until I left Paris. Although I related the story to no one in the house, it was well known among my companions, and at the laboratory in the Collège de France. Everything must have an end. You have heard the dog's finish ; now let me tell you that of Monsieur Henri. After leaving Paris, I passed two years and a half at German Universities, and when returning home to England visited Paris on my way. The day after my arrival I went to the Collège de France to call on my old teacher, Professor Claude Bernard. I had scarcely entered the quadrangle, when the laboratory porter came running up to me, his face radiant with smiles, and ere he had fully completed his little congratulatory speech on my return, he burst out into a chuckle of delight, exclaiming :

' " Votre ami Monsieur Henri est au galères."

' " Thanks for the news," said I ; " and long may he stay there."

' The cause of that gentleman's visit to the galleys I do not remember, but it is unlikely his punishment was altogether undeserved.'

In reply to a friend's question concerning the definition of a mad dog, my father wrote :

' That a mad dog is not mad at all is a paradox which I shall explain. The word *mad* comes from Old Gothic *mod*, signifying rage. A " madman," in English of the present day, is synonymous with a maniac, a lunatic, a person of unsound mind. Now, a madman in this sense is a person who thinks, and acts differently in the ordinary affairs of life from the ordinary run of mankind. There exist other conditions of body in which men act differently from the ordinary run of mankind, without rendering them liable to be regarded as madmen or lunatics. Thus, for example, the thoughts and acts of a drunken man differ from those of the same individual when sober. Again, a person labouring under the delirium of disease—such as the delirium which is associated with, and the direct result of, typhus, scarlet and other fevers—is not, properly speaking, insane, although the actions of the individual labouring under this delirium are, while it lasts, as much at variance with those of sane men as those of a maniac.

' The aberrations of the mind in delirium come with the bodily fever, and depart with the cessation of the fever. The aberrations of the mind in insanity—madness—on the other hand, are not necessarily associated with any feverish condition of the body, but spring entirely from an abnormal condition of the brain, which may give rise to no tangible disturbance in any other organ of the body. Man is liable both to delirium and to insanity. The dog, too, is liable both to insanity and to delirium. The madness of hydro-

phobia, either in the dog or in the man, is the madness of
delirium of bodily disease, not of insanity.

' I once possessed an insane dog. He had not a single
symptom of hydrophobia (now called rabies), or of any
other febrile disease. He was in my possession several
days before I knew there was anything abnormal the matter
with him. The way in which I discovered that he was
insane was the same as that by which I should discover it
in a human being (barring speech), viz., by his acts. The
first insane act I noticed in this dog was his suddenly
jumping up from my feet, where he had been quietly lying
asleep, rushing to, and violently barking at, the door, as if
there were someone outside it, though, on rising and going
to the door, I found no one. The dog, as soon as the door
was opened, ceased barking, and again lay down at my feet.
This circumstance, taken by itself, indicated nothing. The
dog may have heard a noise outside the door, which was
quite inaudible to me, and his judgment might have been
perfectly correct in guiding him to bark : for which reasons
I thought nothing more of the matter, till, on the following
day, without any premonitory sign, he rushed from the fireplace where he was sitting (in my laboratory at University
College, London), and snarled and barked at the corner of
the room, as if he saw some opposing and offensive object.
Now the thought dawned upon me that the dog was labouring under some hallucination, and I began to pay particular
attention to his manners and mode of life, giving my servant
strict orders to be on the watch, and to tell me of anything
in the dog's actions which might appear to him peculiar.

' Once made alive to the dog's condition, I soon had ample
opportunity of studying his mental state and diagnosing
his form of insanity. He was a true monomaniac, and
suffered from mental delusions and hallucinations. At one
time he was troubled with imaginary noises, at another
time he saw visions, and would stand staring into vacant
space ; or else he made rushes at nothing, as if he saw real
and tangible objects before him. Occasionally he would

bark at me or my man, as if we were perfect strangers ; then, a minute afterwards, as if on discovering his mistake, would approach us fawningly, to be fondled.

'He had no dread of water ; he would drink it ; he would swim in it. He had no hydrophobia, and I had no fear of him. He constantly shared my room at the college, and was to me a most interesting, as well as a most instructive, companion. Somehow or other, it got mooted about among the students that Dr. Harley had a mad dog, and at the suggestion of the secretary my poor harmless lunatic was destroyed. I grieved over his loss, for his eccentricities and oddities had become a source of amusement and also of instruction to me. During the six weeks he was in my possession he yielded a rich harvest of medical information. He taught me the vast gulf which lies between insanity and hydrophobia. He showed me that, although there is danger in associating with a case of the latter, there is perfect safety in coming in contact with one of the former. He had his lucid intervals, just as madmen have, and when lucid behaved as rationally, in proportion to his lights, as any human being would do.

'There is a marked difference in the appearance of an insane dog and a dog suffering from rabies. The former is brisk and lively, the latter downcast and morose. The eyes of the former are clear and bright ; those of the latter are glassy and heavy. No saliva dribbles from the jowl of the former ; a frothy secretion hangs round the mouth of the latter. Coaxing and fondling are appreciated by the former, while the latter receives one and both with indifference, if not even with dislike. The appetite of the former is natural and good, of the latter capricious and bad. The former drinks freely ; the latter shuns water in every form.

'In one word, the dog labouring under hydrophobia carries with him the appearance, and possesses the symptoms, of febrile disorder, while the insane or mad animal shows none of the signs of bodily disease.

' The bite of an insane dog would, I believe, be no more dangerous than that of a healthy one, and that means not dangerous at all. If the bites of healthy dogs were liable to produce hydrophobia, I should have been in my grave long ago ; for not once, but many times, have I been bitten by them, both in fun and in earnest.

'Even the hydrophobic dog can only communicate rabies during the time he has the disease in him, just as a man can only convey small-pox to his fellow-man while the poison yet exists in his system.'

This is a divergence ; but hydrophobia is of such universal interest that a little elucidation on the subject may prove of interest, especially as we know the Pasteur treatment is now an almost safe preventive of rabies, if the patient only undergoes the treatment in time.

For Pasteur and his work my father always had the profoundest admiration ; indeed, he sent my brother Vaughan, who has followed in his footsteps, to work at the Institut Pasteur after he had finished his Edinburgh University curriculum. In the long ago, when Pasteur was practically unknown in this country, my father always maintained he was a most original thinker and brilliant worker, and considered it quite distressing how little he was known and appreciated in this country. He was ever most keen about there being a Pasteur Institute in London, and thought it disgraceful that a rich country like England should send sufferers from hydrophobia to Paris for treatment. As far as his means could allow, coupled with unlimited interest and sympathy, he was one of the most energetic men in founding the British Institute of Preventive Medicine.

'Scientific medicine,' my father was wont to say, ' is based on physiological and pathological investigation, and such results could not have been reached without recourse when requisite to experimental research, which is the quickest and surest way to discover the secrets of life, that enable us to solve the dark problems of disease.'

The man who had studied the subject deeply, and was a scientist at heart, shuddered at the cruelty practised daily in our midst by mischievous children and uneducated people. He longed for some form of steam-carriage to ease the sufferings of bus and dray horses, he turned in repulsion from the old maid's overfed pug dying from fatty degeneration, while the promiscuous administration of arsenical poison was his horror.

He was most gentle, and spared animals pain from purely moral and ethical reasons. He was loved by dogs and horses, always had a number of the former about him, and spent much time with his horses, who sought for the carrots he hid in his pockets, and with whom he played like a child.

All the time we were in the Isle of Man a jackdaw was his constant companion, either perched on his shoulder or actually sitting on his head as he wrote, excepting when Jacky in a wicked mood descended to the inkpot and, filling his beak, spluttered the contents over everything. A story he wrote of a white rat he called 'My Bosom Friend,' for the rat rushed and hid herself inside his waistcoat for protection whenever a stranger entered the room; indeed the man who was fearless of death, who experimented on his own body, who was a vivisectionist when the necessities of science demanded, was the gentlest of created beings and the champion of all animal life.

CHAPTER V.

GEORGE HARLEY was elected President of the Parisian Medical Society, and some of those who were present at its anniversary dinner—among them Sir William Priestley and Dr. Burdon Sanderson—may still remember the sad and curious coincidence which happened after that event, when the distinguished Orfila was present. Mathieu Orfila was Dean of the Faculty of Medicine under Louis Philippe. He was the most celebrated toxicologist of his age, and having investigated every department of medical jurisprudence with brilliant success, gained a world-wide reputation. At this dinner, in proposing Dr. George Harley's health, he stated 'although he had never before taken part in any of the society's dinners, the pleasing experience of that night would in future not allow him to miss an opportunity of being present at its annual reunions.'

After leaving the house, Orfila, linking his arm in my father's, walked a short distance in the rain to his carriage. Unfortunately, through having on thin boots, he was during the night seized with fatal inflammation of the lungs, and on that very day fortnight the whole of the fifty gentlemen who had dined in his company attended the great public funeral bestowed upon him by the State.

In a note-book on Orfila, written in 1868, I find :

'What a flood of fast-fading memories that name lets

loose! Back, back rushes thought upon thought to days of youthful ardour, healthy ambition, buoyant hope.

'Once more I see myself sitting among the dirty-handed, ready-witted students of republican France, listening to the brilliant eloquence of the learned Orfila, as he poured forth his seemingly inexhaustible stock of medical and legal lore, little dreaming that in after-years I should myself occupy a similar professorship on this side the Channel. "Liberté, Égalité et Fraternité," words which adorned the walls of the École de Médecine, as well as every public building and every drinking-fountain of Paris, have been buried beneath the glitter of Imperialism; but the memory of that man and the influence of his teaching will go down to posterity. Even now, although eighteen years have rolled away, I, the mere accidental student, can see his snow-white hair, his beaming smile and sparkling eye, as with cheery voice he playfully, as it were, performed the most delicate toxicological experiments, leading one almost to fancy that Nature's elements were his toys, and scientific exposition but his pastime.'

During his student days my father, who spoke French fluently, went much into Parisian society, and so devoted did he become to the gay capital that at one time he thought seriously of settling there altogether. He constantly met Louis Blanc, and sometimes his brother, whose likeness to the reformer, or Socialist, was so remarkable that it was supposed the idea of the Corsican Brothers originated from these two fat little men. Louis Blague was the nickname Paris gave to Louis Blanc. Italian and Spanish by birth, but French by education and sympathy, he spoke excellent English, which he always attributed to the lessons given him by Fanny Kemble. Meeting him, as my father did, in society, he seemed the most amiable, quiet man, for it was not often that he warmed up to discuss matters which lay very near his heart; but when he did, fire shot from his eyes, and he moved an educated audience as mesmerically as the bourgeoisie of France, though not so lastingly. Some years after this he was to be seen everywhere in London society, where he was a great favourite. Perhaps people were sorry for him in his exile. Be that as it may, he was a welcome and constant guest at many houses.

My father loved Paris, and often spoke of the two years spent in that gay city as among the happiest of his life.

One evening, when sitting in a café on a Paris boulevard, a French officer produced a knife—quite a plain dagger knife about six or seven inches long, with a horn handle, something like those Scandinavian knives which are to be seen hanging from the belt of every Norwegian and Finn. He was showing it with great glee to a brother officer, who remarked :

' I don't think it very beautiful, wherever you got it.'

' But it is very wonderful, for all that.'

' In what way ? Hein !'

' It will pierce a five-franc piece without turning the edge. Parbleu !'

' Nonsense !' exclaimed the other, handling the ordinary-looking blade.

Hearing this conversation, my father pricked up his ears, and ultimately asked to be allowed to look at the knife.

'It seems impossible that this could do anything so extraordinary,' he said.

Somewhat nettled at his remark, the officer exclaimed :

' As you both seem to doubt my word, I will show you.' Whereupon, laying a five-franc piece on the table, and raising the knife in his hand, with one stroke the blade pierced the coin, which the officer presented, hanging to the steel, to his two sceptical companions.

My father was amazed, and asked where he had bought such a knife.

' In the Rue —— near the Pont Neuf, in a little shop, but I don't know the man's name, although it was next the corner of the Rue Vert.'

'Do you think he has another like it?' inquired my father.

'I don't know, but I should think not. It is a very little shop, and I don't fancy he has much of anything.'

On his way home to the Rue Vaugirard, where he was then living, Dr. Harley passed down the street, and eagerly looked for the shop indicated, but failed to find it.

Pondering that night on the subject of the knife, he determined to again try to discover the seller, and accordingly started off next day, when his search was rewarded by finding a sort of room half below the pavement, hardly a shop at all, which seemed to contain rusty iron and rubbish generally. Peering into the darkness, he saw a funny old man working at a piece of metal, and accosted him in a friendly manner. After some conversation he asked him if he had ever seen a knife that would pierce a five-franc piece.

'Oh yes, I have. I think I have one.'

'I should much like to see it.'

'Wait a bit, then, and I'll show it to you, young man.'

The 'young man' waited while the queer old character finished his piece of work, when he began rummaging about, but his search proved futile.

'I made them myself,' he muttered—'two of them—and I only remember selling one, and that was to an officer.' At last he said: 'I can't find it; it seems to have gone.'

But George Harley was not to be put off so easily, and told the old man he should call back in a day or two, by which time he perhaps might have found it.

Impatience prompted him to return next day, but he let two or three days go by ere again presenting himself at the shop. The old man's face beamed with triumph as he said, 'I've got it,' and the young man's beamed equally with delight at the prospect of securing such a treasure.

A very dingy little parcel was produced, rolled in an oiled rag, which, when unfolded, disclosed a similar knife to that in the officer's possession, only that the latest 'find' looked very dirty.

'What a shabby old thing!' exclaimed the Englishman ; ' that could never pierce a five-franc piece.'

' Ah, wouldn't it, though ! If you like, I'll show you to the contrary.'

My father, though sceptical, placed a five-franc piece on the counter and said :

' All right ; let me see you do it.'

The old man turned up his coat-sleeve deliberately, and with a flourish stabbed the coin even more effectually than the officer had done, the blade penetrating deep into the wooden counter.

' Mon Dieu, that is wonderful ! What is the price of the knife ?'

' Thirty francs,' was the answer.

' Ridiculous ! a shabby old thing like that ; it is not worth it.'

' Very well,' said the man, deliberately rolling the knife up again in its greasy wrappings and putting it on a shelf.

George Harley, though greatly disappointed, felt rather proud at having refrained from buying such an ugly thing at so extravagant a price, and consoled himself by thinking he could get a better-looking one somewhere else at a cheaper rate which would do the trick equally well.

Time went on, he unsuccessfully tried to get a knife of the kind, and finally left Paris, feeling sure he would procure one in Germany.

He often thought of that knife, but whenever he asked for one that would pierce a coin, people laughed at him.

Two years later he returned to Paris, his real object in passing through that city on his way to London being to pay another visit to the strange old shopkeeper.

Accordingly, early one morning after his arrival, he started for the Rue ——. The shop was there as he had left it, but the old man was gone. His wife now looked after the queer old store, and tearfully told him a long, rambling tale of her husband's last illness and death and her present loneliness. He listened to all she had to say, and then asked her if she had still got the knife capable of piercing a five-franc piece.

'I don't think my husband sold it, because he only made two, and one was bought by an officer, and the other he was so proud of he never meant to sell it at all; but I don't know where it is.'

'It is on that shelf'—pointing high up.

'How do you know?'

'And it is rolled in a greasy rag,' continued the Englishman.

'Seigneur! How can you tell that?'

'Because I saw him put it there.'

'Allons donc! You? How wonderful!'

'Will you let me see it?'

'Oh,' said the old body, 'I can't reach up there.'

'Then let me.'

'Oh no, I could not; it's not for a gentleman like you to poke about such dirty places. But my son-in-law will be here this afternoon, and he shall look for it if you like.'

Next day, by appointment, he returned to find the old lady armed with the greasy parcel.

'I've got it—I've got it, sir!' she said. 'It was just where you pointed, and here it is.'

'What is the price?'

'It is marked thirty francs.'

'Here are thirty francs,' he said. 'I will take the knife.'

'Let me clean it for you first, monsieur.'

'No, no!' he exclaimed, not caring again to be parted from his coveted treasure even for an hour; and away in triumph he bore the ugly little dagger.

As soon as he arrived at his hotel he tried his skill, and, as on many subsequent occasions, the coin was satisfactorily pierced.

Long years afterwards, when staying at Whitley Hall, near Sheffield, he mentioned the incident in the smoking-room one night after dinner. One of the party, who was a great friend of Rogers, the cutler, then in the zenith of his glory, said laughingly:

'If you have a knife able to do that made by a French-man, I'll back Rogers to have twenty made by English-men.'

'All right; ask him.'

Next day they all went to look over Rogers' factory, when the gentleman repeated my father's story, and asked to be shown knives of the same kind.

'We haven't got any,' was the reply.

'Could you make one?'

'No; and, what is more, I hardly believe such a thing possible.'

Hearing this, my father stepped forward and said he possessed the knife, which he happened to have brought to Sheffield to try and match.

He produced it, and the Rogers people standing round smiled dubiously.

'Would you like to see it pierce a five-shilling piece?' he asked.

'Yes, very much. But if it can really do what you say, I should like the heads of the different departments to come and witness the performance.'

'All right; send for them.'

They came. My father was preparing to strike, when a man rushed forward with a cloth and said:

'We always test with our hands wrapped up; it is not safe otherwise. Let me arrange the cloth for you.'

'Nonsense! I want no cloth.' And in a second the knife was deep into the five-shilling piece, for he had not the strength to strike it right through so thick a coin.

'Wonderful!' they all exclaimed; but they refused to believe the edge was not turned till he handed the knife round.

Then they said they would try and make one like it, and he made a bet of £5 with the gentlemen that they could not. *They never did!*

In connection with my father's stay in Paris, I find several papers—one 'An Episode in Parisian Life just after the *Coup d'État* in 1851,' another relating to the marriage proclamation of Napoleon, a third asking 'Was Napoleon III. a Coward?'

'No sooner had I read of the *coup d'état* in the newspapers,' writes my father, 'than I at once made arrangements to start for Paris. I had a great longing to see what civil war and its concomitants were like, and discovered a good excuse for going, in the fact that I wished to study gunshot wounds.

'On arriving in Paris I found the fighting was all over, and that the grand city had resumed its usual appearance. Nevertheless, it was proclaimed to be in a state of siege and under military law, the consequence of which was everyone had to be in the house wherein he meant to sleep by 11 p.m. The first thing which opened my eyes to the fact that Paris was not in her ordinary frame of mind was seeing 40,000 soldiers, fully equipped for war, with artillery trains and all the appliances for attack or defence, marching through what otherwise appeared perfectly peaceable streets. The army round Paris at that time was reported to number 160,000 men, of which a fourth part was daily taken through a different quarter of the town, in order to overawe the inhabitants.

'It was a grand but a fatiguing sight to stand and watch such a formidable amount of military proceeding through the streets.

'Just after the proclamation of the Napoleonic Empire, I saw 80,000 soldiers reviewed in the Champs de Mars, a spectacle which, however, did not impress me nearly so much as the march past of the 40,000 men.

'At the door of the house in which I lived (46, Rue

Vaugirard), the mansion of the Dowager Duchess of Montalembert, a sentry stood from morning to night, keeping guard over the quarters of a Colonel who lived in apartments at the back of the court-yard. I thought this was a mere formality, or guard of honour, till my eyes were opened about ten weeks after the *coup d'état*, when I ventured to say while passing the soldier : " Is your gun loaded ? "

' He smiled and gave me a side-glance, but neither spoke nor moved, except by lightly placing his fingers on the stock of his gun ; and while he thus steadied the weapon with his right hand, he slowly raised the cock with the left, and thus, to my great astonishment, showed that it was ready capped and fit for instant use. It was evident, therefore, that the sentry at our house door was not intended solely for ornament.

' This fact of itself speaks volumes concerning the state of insecurity in which Louis Napoleon lived during the eventful period of the transition stage between Republic and Empire.

' These preliminary observations will render the episode I am about to relate a little more intelligible.

' It happened that a day or two after my arrival in Paris, my old Edinburgh University friend, William Marcet, now a distinguished F.R.S., invited me to spend the evening at his rooms, in company with a mutual friend, Wason, who afterwards died while on Lord Raglan's staff in the Crimea. The evening passed pleasantly away, midnight arrived ; we utterly forgot Paris was in a state of siege, and that all good citizens were required to be at their own homes by eleven o'clock at night. Instead, it was an hour past midnight when we left Marcet's hospitable board. He lived on the Quai Voltaire, exactly opposite the Palais de Louvre, and it was not until the great door of the *porte-cochère* had slammed its farewell, and we stood in the empty street, that we began to realize the nature of our situation.

'Not a soul was anywhere visible, although it was a lovely moonlight night in winter. Not a sound was to be heard. All Paris might have been dead and buried, for any sign of life about us. We looked for a fiacre, but no cab was to be seen. We both wanted cabs, and while we gazed upon the moonlit river we discussed what had better be done. A sound of wheels coming from afar fell on our ears. We stopped the driver and asked him to convey us to our respective destinations—*i.e.*, first take the one home, then the other. At first he bluntly refused to do either, but on hearing that Wason wanted to go up the Champs Élysées he volunteered to take him, as that thoroughfare lay in the direction of his own home.

'Wason was reluctant to part company, but on being assured that I should not experience any real difficulty in finding my own abode, as *all* I had to do was to get into the Rue de Seine, follow it straight up to its termination at the Palais du Luxembourg, and then turn to the right, when I should find my quarters exactly opposite the Luxembourg Gardens, he left me alone with my reflections in the deserted street.

' Having been warned against the then danger of walking close to the houses at night, many persons having been suddenly pounced upon from a door or a *porte-cochère*— only the week before a gentleman had been stabbed and robbed in this way close to the entrance to the Hôtel du Mont Blanc—instead of proceeding along the inhabited side of the street, I crossed to the parapet beyond which ran the river.

'I kept on for a considerable distance—much further, indeed, than I considered the Rue de Seine ought to run. Where on earth had the street gone? It could not have been spirited away. Neither ghosts nor hobgoblins run off with whole streets. What, then, had become of it? Here indeed was a puzzle — here a true mystery. The solemn cathedral clock had more than once chimed the hours since I left Marcet's hospitable abode. The lesser

5

fry had all followed suit. Time was rapidly slipping away, the winter's early morning air felt crisp and chill, and, although warmly clad, my hands and face rebelled against the low temperature. What was I to do?

'I had stopped dead short opposite the Morgue, and while thinking out some plan leaned over the parapet, and looked down upon the rippling, gurgling stream below; gazing upon its dark surface, dimly lighted by the moonbeams, now growing pale and sad, I thought of the many poor wretches who had voluntarily drowned their cares and their trials in its cold depths. From the spot where I stood my eye fell on the arches of the Pont Neuf, and as I glanced at that dark-shaded parapet my thoughts recurred to the multitudes of poor creatures who one day had stood on its edge, moving, feeling, thinking, living human beings, and a few minutes after they had taken the fatal leap, floated cold, motionless, in the river's dirty waters, to be in a day or two subsequently dragged from thence, swollen, discoloured corpses, loathsome alike to the touch and sight of their fellow-men.

'As I thus mused over the dark waters of the murmuring Seine, and fancied that if they had but voice they would repeat harrowing tales of suicide and murder, of misery unutterable, of love unspeakable, the sound of distant footsteps fell upon my ear. It was a measured tread, one which, though distant, echoed distinctly through the silent air. More audible still the sound is heard; nearer and nearer it approaches; eagerly I peer in the direction from whence it comes, and although I can discover nothing, a gleam of hope lights up my heart. Hark! again I distinctly hear a footfall; but, alas! it grows fainter and fainter, and soon is heard no more.

'Disappointment takes the place of expectation, and again I turn to the parapet and relapse into thought.

'My ears have, however, been sharpened by the welcome sound, and are on the alert for its repetition. Soon they are gladdened by its return. Again the measured tread becomes more and more distinct; it approaches nearer and nearer to where I stand; but from whence it came I could not decide. Just as hope again grew buoyant, hope was doomed to die. The footfall got less and less audible until it ceased to be recognisable to the ear.

' " 'Tis the tread of a sentry," I mentally exclaimed; " where *can* he be?"

' Entering a street, and keeping well in the dark shadow of the houses, I crept cautiously on. In a few minutes I received my reward, for there on the opposite side of the street gleamed in the moonbeams a bayonet. A soldier, too, was visible; slowly and firmly he approached. " Now," I thought to myself, " there is no danger," and, stepping boldly from the friendly shadow, I politely, and in the best French which I could at that time command, for I had not long been in Paris then, asked my way to the Rue de Seine.

' In an instant, to my intense surprise, the attitude of the soldier changed, a sharp " Qui vive?" issued from his lips, his gun was shifted from his shoulder, and the bayonet pointed at me.

' " Pardon, monsieur, je suis étranger,' I began, when quickly rang in my ears the words, " À l'écart!" the meaning of which was then unknown to me, but which I am now aware signifies, " Get out of the way."

' The expression of the man's face showed that he was not friendly, wherefore I began again, more politely than before, begging *mille pardons*, and gesticulating with my hands; but to no avail, for blacker and blacker his fierce countenance grew, and again " À l'écart!" resounded in my ears.

' Not knowing what to do, and not wishing to lose my chance of finding the Rue de Seine, I made a step forward to try what closer proximity would do, when, lo! I distinctly heard a sharp click, click, and saw the gun again raised to the soldier's shoulder, and its muzzle pointed direct at me. At the same moment its possessor shouted out " À mort!" Instantly I sprang back into the

5—2

dark shadow of the wall. Rapidly I placed myself out of reach of the muzzle, for it and the soldier were quite distinct to me—though I was at that time invisible to him—and quietly retreated, while the soldier continued to stand stock-still with his gun at his shoulder, ready to fire at a second's notice. When I at last emerged into the moonlight, he lowered his gun from his shoulder, but kept his eyes fixed upon me until I had removed to a safe distance. He evidently was as suspicious of my movements as I was of his.

' I ought to have mentioned ere this there were no gas-lamps lighted in the streets through which I slowly and sadly retraced my steps towards the Quai Voltaire. All at once I again heard the sound of footsteps, this time proceeding from an opposite direction. I paused and listened, and then beheld two figures appear from the end of one of the streets, slowly walking away from the spot where I stood.

' It was evident that the figures had not noticed me, so I slipped across to the house-side on which they were, and noiselessly glided after them. As they walked slowly, while I followed on tiptoe as rapidly as I could, I soon neared the men, who, to my joy, wore cocked hats and swords. They were, in fact, a couple of sergents-de-ville.

' I was within about ten paces of them when I abandoned my noiseless mode of progression, which had become irksome ; but no sooner did my footfall betray my proximity than with the rapidity of shooting-stars round they wheeled, their swords flew from their scabbards, and with the words " Qui vive ?" from both their mouths they threw themselves into an attitude of defence. I, like them, being in the full glare of the moon, they soon recognised my non-dangerous character, and after a few questions as to how I came to be abroad at a time in the morning when all good citizens were supposed to be in their beds, they told me the whereabouts of the Rue de Seine. Once put into the right way, I speedily found my way home, and quickly forgot my troubles in the arms of Morpheus.

'Having arrived in Paris with some good introductions, I dined at Madame Damot's on the following day—I should rather say same day, since before I got to bed it was nearly four o'clock in the morning—and chanced to relate my midnight adventure. An officer who sat opposite me, not understanding English, was so curious to know what had interested the other guests that, after I finished, he asked the lady who was sitting beside him to translate the tale for his benefit. I did not then comprehend conversational French sufficiently well to understand the evidently pithy comments he made upon my story; but when communicated to me subsequently I *did* open my eyes, for, instead of expressing sympathy with a foreigner placed in such a position, he censured the sentry in no measured terms for not shooting me on the spot!

'It seemed after the *coup d'état*, several of the sentries having been assassinated at their posts, orders were issued that any "man who approached a sentry after eleven o'clock at night was to be shot."

'That this order was no dead letter most unfortunately happened to be amply proved within a week after my adventure. At the first evening reception Louis Napoleon gave after the *coup d'état*, all the guests left before eleven o'clock, in compliance with the order before-mentioned. One of the company, a nobleman from Normandy, dressed in spotless white waistcoat and cravat, with diamond studs glittering in his shirt-front, was quietly walking home up the Rue de Richelieu, near the Bibliothèque Martinale, when he was challenged by a sentry, and commanded to cross to the other side of the street. He hesitated for a moment to do so; the command was repeated, and, not being instantly obeyed, "ping" the bullet rang through the air and the gentleman's heart! Though mortally wounded, he had still strength enough to stagger to a café opposite, the door of which was just being closed by a waiter, against whom

he fell heavily and then dropped lifeless upon the floor.
Thus for him ended the princely entertainment.

'Ere Paris was fully awake next day, the naked body of
the man who had so cheerily gone forth on pleasure the
night before lay stretched on a black stone slab in the
Morgue. A stream of cold water trickled over his unheeding
body to arrest the progress of its decay, and keep the
atmosphere untainted by removing from the surface of the
corpse all the effete particles which become detached during
the progress of retrograde metamorphosis. Living or dead,
our frames are ever in a state of perpetual change, the
only difference being that, while during life that which is
constantly being pulled down is as constantly being replaced
by new material, after death the material that is pulled
down is never replaced.

'Directly over the gentleman's head hung the garments
he had worn the night before. The white waistcoat and
the dress shirt, with its bright diamond studs, seemed as
if they were placed there in silent mockery of the evanes-
cent nature of human enjoyment. The true object of their
presence above the inanimate mass of humanity was, however, to facilitate its identification. Ere long friends came
in search of the missing noble, and removed his body,
which a few hours later was carried to the grave, where
kind Mother Earth concealed from view all physical
evidence that a military murder had been committed.

'No notice of this awful crime found its way into the
newspapers, though all Paris joined in a chorus of indignant condemnation.

'From this little episode I learned that I owed my life to
the forbearance of the young soldier. Young he was—that
I saw by his face—perhaps, indeed, little more than a con-
script recently drafted from some quiet village, and as yet
not heart-hardened by the rough ways of military service.
Nevertheless, the development in his brain of one harsh
thought, the pressure of one of his fingers on the trigger,
would have sent me into eternity. My time was, however,

not yet come, my work in this world not yet accomplished, my innings in the game of life not yet perfected. Since then I have sojourned a quarter of a century through this pleasant world ; but now I begin to feel as if I should soon have to lay down the bat. The damaged pitcher is often spared to make many a journey to the well, but eventually it comes to grief.'

CHAPTER VI.

'IN a man's journey through life it not unfrequently happens,' writes George Harley, 'that the quiet observation of some comparatively trivial circumstance suddenly lets in upon his brain an immense flood of light.

'I am now about to relate a circumstance that happened no less than between four and five and twenty years ago* in connection with a placard, the influence of which placard upon the feelings of men seemed to me so astonishing that it left a most vivid impression on my mind.

'One day in the spring of 1852 I was crossing the Pont Neuf in Paris, during the workmen's dinner-hour, when I beheld a bill-sticker busily engaged in pasting up on the wall a large *affiche*, headed "Proclamation."

'A short time previously I had heard it rumoured the Emperor intended to get married, associated with which rumour was another, to the effect that if he dared to take to himself a wife his last hour was at hand.

'People crowded round the bill-poster in such numbers I found it impossible to get near enough to read the *affiche*. Therefore I abandoned the attempt, placed my back against the wall on which the announcement was posted, and gazed at its readers standing in front of me. I had not gazed long before I was struck with the changing expressions on their faces. That which they were reading was evidently working on their minds to no small extent, and the conviction of

* The above was written on July 30, 1876.

this fact made me scrutinize with more care the face of each individual as he approached. Amongst the men was one who particularly attracted my attention. He was an *ouvrier* of about fifty years of age, thin, but well built; he had black, grizzled hair and moustache, bright, black, active eyes, and was clad in a dark-blue blouse and cloth cap with leather peak. I can even now conjure up the man in my mind's eye, and although I only saw him once, nearly a quarter of a century ago, I feel sure I could swear to him among a hundred others. As he approached the place where the *affiche* was posted, he muttered through his teeth (quite audibly), "Proclamation! Sacridie, qu'est ce que c'est maintenant"; then, turning round to his companion, he began gesticulating angrily, and uttering in a loud tone of voice something evidently not complimentary to the Emperor, for, interlarded in his discourse, I could detect the words *coquin, scélérat, sale fripon.* The more he spoke, the more excited and angry he became, till, his eye catching the words "Proclamation de mon mariage," his face grew actually livid with rage. He looked more like a fiend than a man. Gradually, however, his facial muscles relaxed. The dark ferocity of his expression faded; his countenance assumed a milder appearance. For some reason, slowly but surely, a change came over "the spirit of his dream." The demon in his heart began to be exorcised by human sympathies. The emotions of his mind were written in his face, and there I plainly read that anger having given place to indifference, indifference was followed by sympathy, sympathy succeeded by satisfaction, and satisfaction at length transformed into approval, so that I witnessed the human being who had approached with the rage of a tiger depart with the quiet, inoffensive expression of the lamb.

' The very nature of the individual appeared changed. The opprobrious terms of *coquin, scélérat,* and *fripon* were heard no more; but in their stead the approving words of "C'est bien," "C'est juste," and "Bravo!" fell upon my astonished ear.

The hand that at the beginning was raised in rage, and significantly drawn across the throat,* was now slapped into his pocket with an approving " Bravo ! très bien."

' Here was food for thought. What was there in the poster that worked this marvellous transformation ? What power existed therein, to convert, in a few minutes, an enemy into a friend ? Verily, thought I, man is a queer machine—paper and ink a powerful engine. The silent writing on the wall did more in five minutes than it would have been possible for a stump orator to accomplish within an hour. Language is alike potent for good or for evil ; but to be effectual, be it written or be it oral, it must come direct from the heart in order to touch the heart. Such being my conviction, every second of time seemed a minute, until I should be able to scan the placard.

' The workman's dinner-hour lasts no longer than other hours, so the stream of *ouvriers* soon passed away, and I found it possible to read the *affiche*. How I wish I had its contents now before me, to aid my memory, and enable me to put in regular order the ideas that it conveyed ! but, alas ! I have not got a copy, so I must jot them down simply in the order in which they now recur to my mind.

' The proclamation was, as before said, a notification of the intended marriage of the Emperor. It began, I think, by saying that he was one of the people, and that he intended acting as one of the people. Such being the case, as he had now attained to his position in life, he would do as other people did when they attained to their positions in life. He would marry—and where was he to seek for a wife ? Like other men in his rank, was he to go and bow at the footstool of some crowned head, and ask as a favour the hand of one of his daughters ?† Oh no ! He had

---

* ' About this time I noticed that nearly all the new five-franc pieces bearing the effigy of Napoleon upon them had an unmistakably significant line scratched across the throat.

† ' He had already knelt at a footstool and asked the hand of a petty German Sovereign's daughter in marriage, but been refused. His people, however, did not all know that.

been called a parvenu; but how could the chosen elect of so many millions of glorious French people be called a parvenu ? It was a misnomer, and he who was the chosen head of so great a nation would never condescend to humble it by begging the hand of a crowned head's daughter. No; he would do as his people did—select one from among themselves. Who did his people select? The one they loved. He therefore would do likewise—select the one he loved. Of what religion should he choose her? Of his own religion, of the religion of his people, that he and she might kneel at the same altar, offer up their united prayers for the welfare of *la belle France.*

'In this splendid proclamation, no excess of adjectives was to be found, no impassioned oratory employed. The language was simple and to the point; but every line, every word, administered to the vanity of the people to whom it was addressed, and a better, a more exact measure of a nation's character was surely never before taken.

'I have drawn the picture of one member of the nation. I have shown how he approached with the scowl of a demon, and how he departed with a complaisant smile; and although he could not be regarded as an exact counterpart of all Frenchmen, he was yet not a bad type of his fellows.

'A more phlegmatically constituted man would, of course, have been less rapidly and less decidedly acted upon by the proclamation; but he was a true Celt, and the Gallic nation is, as is well known, thoroughly Celtic, so that the influence which tho *affiche* exerted over one specimen is not likely to have been very dissimilar from the influence it exercised on the majority of Frenchmen. This, indeed, was proved by the result. So fearful was Napoleon of the consequences of his marriage that the whole thing was kept secret until within eight days of its actual accomplishment, yet those eight days sufficed to change the whole views of the nation.

'The effect which I saw produced on one man by the

proclamation was of great value to me mentally. It opened my eyes, first, to the marvellous power of human language ; second, to the value of paper and ink, as a means of mental communication between man and man ; third, it showed me the unstable nature of human emotions, feelings, and actions—how easily they can be excited, formed, and ruled by language ; and, fourth, what a powerful engine for good or for evil God had put into my hands in the shape of print.

'La Rochefoucauld said that words were given to man in order that he might be able to conceal his thoughts ; but I say that written and oral language is given to us in order that we may sway other men's minds.

'Up to the time of reading the proclamation, I held the prevalent opinion—which had been instilled into me by my French associates—that Louis Napoleon was little better than a mental muff. Report said he was the cat's-paw of the clerical party. All his proclamations were stated to be written for him by an Abbé. The Abbé was, in fact, believed to fill the place of his brains, which were thought to be either absent from his calvarium or in a state of inextricable confusion. No sooner did I read the proclamation, however, than (young though I was) I arrived at a different conclusion. "Let whomsoever may write his other proclamations," thought I, "none but the person most interested ever wrote that one." It was the language of the man-personal himself, and none other. No Abbé, no second party, could ever have coined that proclamation. Its whole wording, its reference to parvenus, its allusion to love and religion, told me, as plainly as if I had myself seen Napoleon writing it, that it proceeded from his brain alone.'

'Was Napoleon III. a Coward?

' 'Tis well known that the direction which a straw takes is a sure indication of the way the wind blows, and in like manner one act of a man's life may not infrequently afford a true index to his whole career, for which reason I now venture to relate a scene in the life of Napoleon III. which some may think stamped him as a physical coward—that is to say, a man fearful of receiving bodily hurt.

'The first time Louis Napoleon met his troops after the *coup d'état*, 1851, was on a Sunday forenoon behind the Tuileries, and within the iron railings that separated it from the courtyard of the Louvre. There the soldiers assembled to receive the decorations earned by their brilliant deeds on the days succeeding the night of the *coup d'état*.

'I had a friend who, by some means or other, contrived to obtain pretty correct information concerning all events about to take place in Paris. On the evening before the distribution of orders and medals above alluded to, he called and startled me by asking if I should like to be present at the assassination of Louis Napoleon.

'On my inquiring where and when the event was to take place, the only reply he gave me was, "Never you mind; if you want to see it, I'll take you."

' " All right," said I, whereupon he answered :

' " Then I will call for you at eleven o'clock to-morrow forenoon."

'Punctually at the hour named he appeared, and we sallied forth. To tell the truth, I did not place much confidence in what he said, for I could not believe that people bent upon assassination would communicate their plans to strangers. Where my friend got his information he would never deign to inform me, but subsequent events proved it to be well grounded. He took me direct to the Tuileries, to the gate leading from the Rue de Rivoli into the courtyard behind the palace, and there he stationed me, placing himself at my side, and saying : "Wait patiently, and watch till the review is over."

'I looked all around for the assassins, but saw no one I could even suspect. There were a number of people passing along the street, especially on the opposite side,

messieurs and *ouvriers*, but none that looked to me likely
to harbour in his bosom the dire design of murder. I got
rather tired of waiting, and felt inclined to leave the scene,
as I was less assured than ever of the accuracy of my
friend's information. However, he induced me to remain,
and in due time the military ceremony came to an end.

' No sooner was it over than the clatter of horses' feet fell
upon our ears, and, looking in the direction from whence
the sound proceeded, our eyes beheld a group of gaily
dressed and handsomely mounted officers entering the
archway under the palace, at the other end of which we
stood. Foremost among them rode Napoleon, upon whom
my eyes became instantly riveted. Calmly he rode looking
straight before him, until within a yard of the outer entrance
to the gateway by which I stood, when, in an instant, the
colour forsook his lips, his face grew deadly pale, he reined
in his horse, and there was a momentary pause. At that
instant someone shouted in a commanding voice, "Au galop!
au galop!" and off started the cavalcade, Napoleon being
hid in the midst. Whether his being instantly surrounded
by his staff was owing to a preconcerted plan, or whether it
arose simply from the fact of his reining in his horse, while
the others pushed theirs on, I know not; but certainly it
proved a most effectual way of concealing the intended
victim from his would-be assassin or assassins. At full
speed the cavalcade rushed along the street, and was soon
out of sight. I ought to have mentioned that it was preceded and accompanied on either side by a row of mounted
dragoons with pistols, loaded, capped, and ready cocked, in
their hands, who galloped with the cavalcade, but away
from it close to the pavement, their eyes fixed on the
passers-by, with the double object of overawing them and
of detecting a would-be assassin.

' My eyes had been so fixed on the face of Napoleon that
I did not see the cause of his turning so deadly pale, but I
soon learned it. The would-be assassins were ready on the
other side of the street, in the direct line of the gate, and

a number of secret police dressed in plain clothing were
stationed (apparently as ordinary sightseers) at the same
spot, ready to arrest anyone making an attempt on
Napoleon's life. At the moment when the intended victim
manifested fear, a movement had taken place in the crowd
opposite, when a number of arrests were instantly made.

'No doubt, since the plot was known to the police, it was
known also to Napoleon, as well as to some, if not to all,
the members of his staff. The one who shouted out, "Au
galop! au galop!" so promptly must at least have been
acquainted with it, or his presence of mind can only be
considered remarkable. Be the knowledge of the intended
plot as it may, I shall certainly never forget the paralyzed
and frightened look of Napoleon, together with the sudden
check he gave to the onward progress of his steed. I may
add he was so closely surrounded by his staff that, had a
bullet been fired at him, it would just as likely have lodged
itself in the head of one of his companions as in his own.
Yet, if they all knew of the plot, as far as I could see on
the spur of the moment, no one of them except Napoleon
seemed to me for an instant to lose his presence of
mind.

'Occasionally, when I have related the foregoing little
episode to my friends, I have been told that it would be an
error to regard Napoleon as a coward, because his behaviour
on the occasion of his marriage militates against the
idea that he was wanting in courage. It was commonly
rumoured that an attempt to assassinate him would be
made on the way from Notre Dame to the Tuileries. Yet
he not only drove quietly along the quay, but sat a little
in advance of Eugénie during the whole route. That is
perfectly true. I saw he did myself. He not only sat a
little in front of his wife, but he looked dreadfully pale also.
That, however, need not surprise one, for the mere act of
matrimony, with its unknown future, is quite enough of
itself to make a man, even a courageous one, turn white, so
I willingly let that pass. Still, I must add Louis Napoleon

had no great cause for fear on his wedding-day, even
although a hundred men had been ready and anxious to
take his life. He was much too well guarded—not only by
the troopers who rode alongside of his carriage, but by the
soldiers who lined his route. A better precaution against
danger I never saw. It was necessary, of course, that as
many of the soldiers as possible should see the wedding
cortège of their future Emperor; it was but a natural return
for their kind services to him, and was admirably accomplished. From the door of the church to that of the palace,
four rows deep of armed men stood on each side of the road
in front of the spectators. Four times the ordinary number
of military could therefore be eye-witnesses of the bridal
cortège. But that was not all. In order that each should
have the best possible view of the happy pair, the soldiers
were not allowed to stand in a line, as on parade, one
behind the other. Oh no ; they were zigzagged in such a
way as to be able to see between each other's heads. With
the crowd of people at their backs, it did not require much
acumen for me to discover that, while it looked a beautiful
mode to enable the soldiers to get a good view of what was
passing, it proved also a most effectual barrier against any
intended assassination. Where I stood, and I stood immediately behind the back line of soldiers, no man could even
have pointed a stick at the cortège, far less have taken aim
with a gun or a pistol. If he had held either up, pointed
it straight, and drawn the trigger, his ball must have
inevitably lodged itself in the head of some sight-seeing
soldier.

'Honour to the genius who invented this human safety
wall! A happy combination of novelty, simplicity, and
security. A more powerful argument than the preceding
has been launched against the idea that Louis Napoleon
was a coward. He was elected Emperor November 25,
1852, a year after the *coup d'état.* On the day in which
he entered Paris, after the Proclamation of the Empire, it
was generally believed that an infernal machine would be

fired at him as he passed along the boulevards. Yet, in spite of this knowledge, he boldly rode two or three yards in advance of his staff, so that, if fired at, he himself might be killed without any danger being incurred by those in attendance. So far, so good; but I am in a position to state that neither he nor any member of his staff ran a shadow of danger from any infernal machine on the day in question. My knowledge of this fact was obtained in the following wise:

'A friend, who lived in the Rue Richelieu, three houses from the end abutting on to the boulevard, invited me to witness the procession from his windows, which were *au troisième*. By putting our heads out at the window, we could see the boulevard for the whole length of the Rue de Richelieu. I went early, and while we were sitting there smoking and chatting, the door was suddenly opened and a man popped in his head. He, after a rapid but searching scrutiny of the apartment, immediately withdrew.

' " Who is that ?" asked I.

' " I do not know," was the reply; " but a similar thing occurred about an hour ago."

' " Well," said I, " that man is either a thief or a person looking for somebody."

'An hour passed away, and just about ten or fifteen minutes before the procession appeared in sight, another head was popped in, and speedily withdrawn. Then it dawned upon us that the mysterious visitors were police in plain clothes, looking out for the infernal or any other machine likely to be employed against the life of His Imperial Majesty. Subsequent inquiry showed me that not only every room with a window opening on the boulevard had been similarly inspected, but that every room in the side-streets, from the window of which it was possible to aim a projectile at the cortège, as it passed along the boulevard, had received the honour of three domiciliary visits, so that it seemed next to impossible the Emperor could have been in the slightest danger during his trium-

6

phant entry into his capital. Discretion is certainly the better part of valour.

' I was not surprised then, and I am not surprised now, that the Emperor rode so bravely all alone before the procession. At the same time, I attach no blame to the forethought which secured his safety.

' Another reason has been adduced to me in favour of Napoleon's courage—namely, the fact that he exposed himself to danger on the field of battle. That, to my mind, is a very insufficient argument, because the danger of death which the leader of an army has to face on the field of battle is about equivalent to the risk run by a first-class passenger in an express train.

' Napoleon was on many battle-fields; but it was only on the last—Sedan—that he really faced any danger at all, and it must be remembered that two causes probably combined to induce such courage. First, repeated immunity from accident invariably induces callousness to danger. A man may be perfectly careless of a danger he has constantly to encounter, and yet tremble like an aspen leaf in view of a lesser peril to which he is unaccustomed. At heart, man is anything but courageous; but habit makes him indifferent to particular forms of danger. Soldiers, when first under fire, are often in a dreadful state of fright; while after a time they think little or nothing about the matter, and before the Battle of Sedan occurred, Napoleon had ample opportunity of getting hardened to the dangers.

' The second reason is, that he well knew that his grand game was about played out. Moreover, he was in bodily pain, and that of itself makes one welcome, rather than shun, death, as I have good cause to know. It could not much matter to him, personally, whether he were slain on the field or had to surrender into the hands of the Prussians—the only two courses open to him, since to return to Paris again was impossible, and to cut and run dishonourable. His conduct at Sedan, therefore, is to my mind a most inconclusive argument in his favour.

'An old proverb says, "There is no smoke without fire." And unless there actually existed some foundation for the rumour that Napoleon III. was not a brave man, how in the name of wonder did such a rumour originate?

'Somewhere I have read, or heard, that he showed the white feather before his escape from Ham. If I remember rightly, he did so in this wise. He was disguised, and all was ready for his escape. He had said adieu to faithful Dr. Conneau, and descended into the courtyard, which he had only to cross, but when halfway over, seeing the sentry coming in his direction, his courage forsook him, and at once wheeling round, he turned, and walked straight back to his chamber, which poor Dr. Conneau vainly hoped he had left for the last time. It was not till some days afterwards that he summoned up sufficient courage to repeat the attempt at escape, which the second time proved so successful.'

CHAPTER VII.

STUDENT LIFE IN GERMANY—CONDEMNED TO BE SHOT.

THOUGH my father never kept a diary, he was through life
in the habit of jotting down reminiscences of any events
that particularly interested him, and a little bundle of note-
paper, yellow with age, and tied round with a piece of *old
boot-lace*, disclosed a few student recollections, headed:
"Burial of a Student who had been killed in a Duel,"
"Taken up as a Spy," "The Last Public Decapitation in
Bavaria," etc.

These are only scraps, but they are written in the same
handwriting by the student of twenty-five as is that of the
man who penned the last article he ever published,
"Champagne," when he was sixty-six years of age. If
handwriting be characteristic, then verily the student was
already a man, for the caligraphy is identical.

The following, states one faded sheet, occurred in Giessen,
July, 1854:

'BURIAL OF A STUDENT KILLED IN A DUEL.

'As the high-church bell tolled eight, and the shades
of evening were slowly drawing themselves in thicker
and darker layers over the quiet town of Giessen, the
streets leading in the direction of the bridge which spans
the river Lahn were thronged with people of all classes
and all ages, while here and there could be observed the
dashing caps of the corps students, numbers of whom
were in full dress—that is, wore their enormous Hessian

boots, knee-breeches (white), corps coat and hat, sword
dangling at the side, and sash hanging over the right
shoulder. The sash was, however, not the bright, gaudy
festival ornament, but one of black-and-white cloth, and
no bands appeared on the students' breasts—all were
dressed in sombre style, although none looked particularly
mournful.

'When I arrived at the bridge, it was already crowded
with students, who were standing in clusters round three
or four fires that sent up volumes of smoke, smelling
strongly of tar, not brimstone. In a few minutes the
voices of the commanders of the respective corps were
heard calling their comrades to prepare themselves, and
soon torch after torch was lighted, till the whole place was
illuminated. They now formed into order of procession.
First came three policemen; then two torches carried by
members of the corps who had lost their associate, which
fact was made known by their white caps; then came a
band of music, with torches on either side; then the
colours of the corps; then two lines of torches, carried
by 300 students; in the middle of the lines marched the
officers, with drawn swords. The procession, in this
order, entered the town, and proceeded to the house of
the deceased, where the hearse stood. This was drawn
by six horses, all deeply draped in black. On the yellow
coffin were placed numerous wreaths of fresh-culled flowers.
On the top of the hearse was a beautiful, large, glittering
golden crown. Six of the students placed themselves at
the head of the horses, and the procession once more
moved on, preceded by the band, playing a slow tune.

'While they marched through the town, I took the road
to the cemetery, and found hundreds like myself treading
in the same direction. When the procession came in view,
a truly beautiful and thought-inspiring spectacle presented
itself. A long double row of torches appeared every now
and then in sight, then as often disappeared behind the
trees with which the promenade was thickly studded; and

what rendered the scene more deeply affecting was the
sound of music which ever and anon came borne by the
gentle breeze in our direction, and as the wind died away
was lost again to our ears, just as the flickering lights were
to our eyes.

' Evening was coming on apace, but the darkness only
emphasized the glitter from the hundreds of torches, the
very smoke of which lent wild mystery to the scene. On
arriving at the cemetery, the coffin was lifted by the
students from the hearse to the grave, and the torch-
bearers formed a large circle to keep back the crowd.
The minister, a Protestant, then gave a sermon or address,
the principal part of which was devoted to tracing the
career of the departed, only nineteen years of age, and
picturing the grief of his parents, while the coffin was
being lowered. Then, after prayers, the students approached, and threw a little earth on the grave, after
which the officers of the respective corps advanced with
drawn swords, which they extended over the grave in the
form of a wheel, the united points forming a centre, the
blades glistening in the torchlight, and sung a students'
song, in which the other students joined. After they had
thus bade farewell to their comrade who had died, as they
felt, " defending his honour," they marched to the square
in front of the University, where they threw their torches
into a heap, and so made a large crackling bonfire, round
which they stood singing till all was burned and consumed,
and naught remained but ashes—fit emblem of their
departed friend.'

Although the subject of this memoir disapproved utterly
of duelling, he constantly attended such meetings, being
intensely interested from a medical point of view in the
cuts and wounds. I have heard him tell how he has seen
an ear sliced from a student's head, and that he and others
have tried to patch it on again, and have also heard him
relate stories concerning the suffering occasioned by the

inexperienced sewing up of wounds, at which, as he was rather expert, he was constantly called upon to assist.

These duels were held in a sort of shed, and five or six would take place in an evening. The combatants wore shades over their eyes, had their right arms bandaged up to twice the natural size, so as to protect them from cuts, and wore various shields on their bodies. Raising their right arms and standing in position betokened all was ready; their swords were handed to them with due pomp by their seconds, and at the given word they would begin to slash. A cut here and a cut there, and the blood would slowly trickle down their faces, and drop on to their shirts. If they were experienced, they would perhaps hit out a dozen times, the steel of the swords flashing in the light, before they succeeded in touching their combatant, and sometimes the duels continued for thirty minutes, unless a bad wound were inflicted. The combatants, often strangers to each other, soon worked themselves up into fury; they slashed and dashed at one another, the blood poured, the flesh even flew, and when a halt was called, it was but for a moment to regain their breath, and to permit the doctor to step forward and sponge their faces with cold water.

The spectators enjoyed the fun, cheered on their comrades, munched sausage or drank beer, wishing heartily they were the envied duellists instead of merely spectators, for to their mind it was a very grand thing to wound a fellow-creature. It was a hideous sight: the men's faces grew red, bloated, and swollen; their eyes got a wild look, as perspiration dripped from their foreheads; their hair was wet with blood; and so they went on and on, things got worse and worse, until one was so badly hurt and became so weak he could no longer stand up to face his foe. Then, and not till then, that duel was announced at an end, and the two combatants retired to be attended to by the doctors, while another couple came on the scene to continue the fray.

The proudest recommendation that could be given to a student was, 'He has fought in twenty or thirty duels,' and the finest badge he could wear was a cut from his ear to his nose, or a slice out of his chin!

When my father was studying in Heidelberg, pistol-shooting was a favourite pastime among the students, and he became much fascinated with it, though he never raised his arm against human life. As the men became more expert they used to practise shooting at a hard-boiled egg, and whoever shot it the most times without destroying it was the victor. Often my father shot five or six slices off an egg before it was spoilt; so in course of time, when he was elected president of the Anglo-American Students' Club, pistol-shooting was a great institution.

One day it was suggested that the English students should have a match against the Americans, and great formalities and preparations were made. When the day for final competition between the two best shots was appointed, the English were much annoyed because the date chosen by the Americans was July 4. My father was champion for England, and Mr. Vanderhost for America.

The excitement on both sides was intense, and both the champions practised diligently, but for a couple of days before the event my father said he should not shoot again, as he thought a rest was the wisest course. His backers tried to persuade him to practise; but he would not, and as the day approached he luckily became calmer. Amidst great excitement the contest began, and some wonderful scores were made on both sides, but my father came off victorious. He was hailed the hero. On the strength of it a subscription was got up amongst the English students, and a handsome china toilet-set was presented to him, with his coat-of-arms beautifully painted on it. The words accompanying were: 'Presented to George Harley, President of the Anglo-American Students' Club, Heidelberg, for having beaten the first American pistol-shot at the University (Vanderhost),

July 4 (anniversary of the declaration of American Independence), 1855.'

These treasures always accompanied him wherever he went, and he used often to tell the tale of how they came into his possession.

The next note I find is entitled, 'The Last Public Decapitation in Bavaria.' 'Decapitation with a broadsword, the criminal being seated in a wooden kitchen armchair. April 6, 1854.'

'Kuhles and Gerard came for me a little before eight o'clock. It was in Würzburg. We lighted our cigars and set out. In the street near the Council Chamber a great crowd had assembled, men, women, and children, but few of the better class. By elbowing through the throng we at last got near the Council Chamber, around which a troop of infantry was stationed, in the midst of which we saw a low common two-horse cart which had received a superficial coating of black paint, or "black-mailing"; on this stood two priests, uncovered. The culprit, a man of thirty-three years of age, was standing before them, dressed in a gray linen dressing-gown reaching to the lower part of the neck, which was quite bare; the head was also uncovered. In his hands, which were fastened before him by a cord, he held a white pocket-handkerchief and a crucifix 6 inches long. Before and behind him (breast and back) hung two black boards on which were printed in white letters the cause of his execution. Close behind his back stood a man holding a cord attached to the prisoner's arms to prevent escape. Immediately after the arrival of the cart, the magistrate approached a window on the first-floor, over the ledge of which hung a piece of red cloth, and read aloud the accusation and condemnation of the criminal. He then took a piece of black stick 18 inches long, broke it in two, and flung it from the window at the feet of the criminal, saying: "As thou hast broken the laws of God and man, thus shalt thy life be broken."

' This was the last and final ceremony in Bavaria before
an execution, and the wretched man before me had been
condemned to death for having poisoned two wives.

' The cart now moved off, and I set out over the Palace
Square in order to arrive as soon as possible on the hill
where the decapitation was to take place. On my arrival
I found the scaffold to be a round building of stone 30 feet
in diameter, 10 feet high, and filled with earth, on the
surface of which the grass was growing luxuriantly, while
in the middle was placed an armchair painted black.

' Walking quietly among the spectators, I observed an
elegantly-dressed, most gentleman-like and intelligent-
looking person in a smart white waistcoat. On inquiring
who he was, imagine my astonishment when told he was
the executioner! I find that the office of this individual is
much sought after, as it requires a clever man to perform
the duty. To cut off a head elegantly demands more skill
than letting go a rope. The German headsman receives
600 florins yearly, and 50 florins for each execution. He
lives in Munich, and is the State executioner—that is, of
all Bavaria. Already the official I saw had whipped the
head off the shoulders of fifteen persons.

' When the cart came in sight, the smart gentleman with
the white vest mounted on the scaffold, unsheathed the
sword, which was lying on the ground, and calmly laid it
down again. The sword was double-handled, and at least
$2\frac{1}{2}$ inches broad by 2 feet long, exclusive of the handle. A
troop of military now formed a circle round to keep the
spectators from approaching too near. The black cart with
its sad burden drove up, crossed in front of the scaffold,
and then passed behind. The culprit sat with his back
to the horses, his face to the priests, and I observed that
he was repeating aloud his prayers. He glanced for an
instant around, but did not look up at the scaffold. He
descended from the cart by means of steps placed for
the purpose, quietly stood for his eyes to be bound, and
was then led by the priests to the place of execution. As

soon as he had taken his seat in the chair—his face to the east—the assistant-executioner seized him by the hair and planted his fingers tightly in his locks, and the crucifix was taken quickly from his hand.

'The executioner, who had taken off his outer coat, looked for a moment; then, taking true aim, in a second —ay, less than the twinkling of an eye—the sword swept like lightning through the neck, and the head was loose in the hand of the assistant, who held it up by the hair. He unbound the eyes, which were wide open, and carried the head round the scaffold; the mouth was open, but after some seconds it closed slowly. It was a gruesome spectacle!

'The body still for a moment sat upright, as if the head were still on it, then sank back in the chair; nothing moved except the legs, which heaved upwards a little. The blood rose with a hissing sound in deep red streams with every pulsation of the heart for about a minute. The first jets must at least have risen three feet, and then they became smaller and smaller till invisible. Decapitation is not really a painful death, as sensation disappears instantly, but it is ghastly to behold.

'The priests then addressed a warning to the multitude while the body was being put into the coffin—a yellow one—and driven rapidly to the anatomical rooms to be experimented upon. I took the dead man's rosary as a memento of the event.'

When the Crimea excitement was at its height in 1854, my father was studying in Vienna. Much talked of were the adventures of Omar Pasha, the great Turkish general, who, siding with England and France against the Russians, was fighting bravely for the liberty of his country. Amongst the students the one great subject of conversation was the fearful suffering of the troops from dearth of surgeons, and the spirit of adventure prompted George Harley to start forthwith to join the army as a volunteer medico.

He applied at the British Embassy for a permit to do so, but after some days' delay was told such a thing could not be granted. At that time it was very uncertain which side Austria would take in the war, for the Government had decided not to interfere one way or the other; and therefore his own Embassy would not grant the permit.

Being very keen on the matter, he went to the Embassy every day to see if some hope could not be given; and at last one of the secretaries said :

' You seem very much in earnest, and I feel sorry for your disappointment. I think I can give you a hint. If you apply for a permit to go direct to Kalifat from here, you will never get it; but it might be granted for Trieste. You start from here by train, then by diligence. Near the river —the Pruth—you will find Omar Pasha's soldiers. Tell no one you are going; have your papers viséd for Trieste, which will enable you to get safely to Leibach; get away as well as you can from the Trieste road without attracting attention, and make your journey across the mountains on foot to Kalifat. You must be most discreet; you will require all the tact you possess.'

Thanking the secretary, my father left the Embassy, packed a few things in a knapsack, leaving all his heavy luggage behind, and dressed in stout travelling-clothes and heavy walking-boots, with £40 in French gold, started by train across the Semmering Pass, thence in the diligence towards Trieste. Taking care to secure the outside seat near the conductor—a German—he soon made friends with that individual, and very diplomatically approached the subject of his journey.

The man in charge was at first very taciturn, and did not seem at all fired with the medical student's enthusiasm; but at one of the places where they stopped, my father treated him to a good bottle of wine and an excellent cigar, the result of which was that, on returning to the diligence, they became more confidential than they had hitherto been. At last the conductor said :

'I suppose youth always likes adventures, and I'm not surprised at your enthusiasm when it is in such a good cause ; for surgeons are badly wanted. I will help you. Shortly after leaving Leibach we must cross a road which I will show you. Take careful mental note of that road, for you must ultimately traverse it on foot. Bearing to the right, it will lead you to the Pruth. When we arrive at the next village, we change horses. By that time it will be dusk.

'You can get down from the diligence as if you were going into the hotel; slip aside, and hide somewhere until we have started off again. Then you can come out of your hiding-place, go into the hotel, and appear in despair at the stupidity of our having left you behind. Show your ticket to Trieste, and say nothing of your knapsack, which in the meantime you must leave somewhere out of sight.

'Ultimately, say you will walk on to the next village, hoping there to make arrangements to drive on and catch up the diligence. I wish you all luck, and advise you to have a good meal before starting, as it may be long before you get another.'

They parted excellent friends, and the conductor was overjoyed with a generous tip.

Arriving at the next stage about 8 p.m., the little village inn presented a lively appearance from the number of bullock-carts laden with soldiers' necessaries. My father learnt from some of the drivers, to his great dismay, that 40,000 Austrians were *en route* from Northern Italy to the Pruth, where they were intended to form an army of observation.

There was nothing for it, however, but to do and dare everything ; therefore, following the friendly conductor's advice, after waiting till the lumbering coach had departed, my father entered the inn, loudly lamenting his ill-luck in having been left behind. The people, who understood a little German, sympathized with him, and, to his joy, regretted they had no spare bedroom to offer. This was lucky, as he wanted to get away ; so, after having partaken

of some coffee and rolls, finding the Fates thus far pro-
pitious, he boldly remarked that he should walk on to the
next village, and chance picking up the diligence.

So well did he play the rôle assigned him, that in about
an hour's time, well fed and happy, he started off at
furious pace to pursue the diligence on its way to Trieste.

No sooner was he out of sight of the village, however,
than he veered round, picked up his knapsack, hidden
behind a wall, and made for the road the conductor had
told him he must pursue in order to find the famous army.

It was midnight; he walked for a couple of hours; darkness continued, so he rested in a wood, tired out after his
long drive in the diligence and his trudge through a strange
region. But when morning dawned, he again started, and
walked the whole of that day, getting some simple fare at a
farmhouse he passed. By this time he found himself in a
land where he was tongue-tied. He had left the German-
speaking folk behind, and he knew no Hungarian.

In the course of that day he came across some Austrian
soldiers—poor fellows who, having become footsore, had
been left behind to follow as they could. He attended to
their wounds, and learnt corroboration of the terrible
sufferings endured by their comrades, and also of the
Turkish soldiers, from want of medical aid. Two of them
were so much relieved by the simple washings and
bandaging he had accomplished with a pocket-handkerchief
and a clean stream, that they were able to walk some way,
and gave him much useful information. They picked up
several stragglers by the road who had fallen out of rank,
and all slept in a copse that night. So passed his second
day, the soldiers sharing some of their rations with him.

It was towards evening on the third day. He was very
tired after his long journey, lack of food, and indifferent
lodging in the open. Nevertheless, he felt greatly pleased
with himself as he neared his goal, having left his footsore
friends in the rear, and looked forward to doing much useful
work among the sick and wounded.

Suddenly before him lay an army which he, in his ignorance, rejoiced to think was Omar Pasha's. When he reached the outposts, however, an officer asked in German for his passport, which he at once produced.

The officer stared hard at him, and said, ' This is viséd for Trieste; why are you here ?' Naturally, my father's answer was somewhat evasive, and without further ceremony he was immediately arrested *as a spy*.

No explanations proved of any avail now, and he was marched off between two soldiers. On they trudged; the men would not listen to him, only declared everything he said made the case against him worse; therefore, a prisoner between two armed men, he had *nolens volens* to march to the next village. Here he was at once locked up in a room with a soldier patrolling outside the door, the noise of whose booted feet loudly proclaimed his excessive zeal.

My poor father's plight was not enviable. His ambitious project had failed, and he was a prisoner. Hour after hour went by.

' *All spies are shot,*' he had been frankly told.

He was given no food, no one came to see him, and, as it was growing dark, he could not even see. He thought and thought; the position was becoming unbearable, and he resolved to try and escape. But how?

The window of his room looked on to a courtyard some twelve feet below, in which were several soldiers, while outside his door he continually heard the tramp, tramp, of the sentinel, sometimes loud as he came right up to the door, then getting fainter and fainter as he reached the other end of the long corridor.

Tired out with devising impossible schemes for escape, and sick at heart, he lay down on the floor in the small hours of the morning, assured his doom was sealed, when suddenly he heard a rustling noise at the door.

Instantly on the alert, he sprang up, and seeing something moving, he went to the door to find a small dirty piece of paper, on which was scrawled in German : ' Get out of the window, turn left, then right, and fly, or you will lose your life; they have arranged to shoot you as a spy at six to-morrow morning. I tell you this in return for your goodness to me, a poor soldier, to-day.'

In the dim light he read and re-read the words, which seemed sent miraculously. He jumped up to the small window-sill, which from below had seemed far too small for any man ever to squeeze through the opening, and he felt baffled. How was his big body ever to get through that little hole? In spite of exhaustion and hunger, he managed with the utmost difficulty to raise the window sufficiently to attempt to squeeze his body through. His head and one shoulder went all right, but the second shoulder would not, and then he suddenly realized that, even if he did succeed in getting through, he would drop down all that height on his head. He was in despair, but it was his only chance of life.

The courtyard was deserted and paved several feet below, therefore it became a problem how was he to slip down quietly. At last he thought of lowering his knapsack by means of his handkerchief and the two straps joined together; with a desperate resolve he pushed his legs out first, and somehow wriggled his body through that tiny aperture; jumping on his Rücksack, he broke his fall, and deadened the noise which would otherwise have attracted attention.

Once on the ground, he groped his way round the house, saw a soldier patrolling within a few feet of him. The man had his back to the fugitive, and was just retracing his steps by the long wall of the farm. My father waited a moment till the sentinel was at a safe distance; then, glancing round, he found no one else was in sight, so he flew with his life in his hands. Never had he ran so fast before, imagining every moment that he heard pursuers on his track, and picturing the death that they had appointed for him at six that morning.

'*Condemned to be shot*' rang in his ears and struck terror to his heart.

It was barely dawn, and all that day and night till noon the next day, he never paused to rest. For thirty hours, on the top of his previous three days' walk, he sped without stop, feeling at any moment he might be caught and shot as he stood.

By this time his ardour for Omar Pasha had cooled, and his one idea was to save his own life.

After eight days and nights' walking, with only such food as he could obtain from hurried visits to peasants' homes, and only the heavens for his bed-covering, he arrived at a little *wirthshaus* in Styria, on his way to Trieste. Looking travel-stained and wretched, he asked for a bedroom, but it was refused. Naturally his appearance was against him. He showed the woman money, and thus enticed, she led him to a room in her little inn near Adelsberg.

' When will dinner be ready ?' he asked.

' In an hour, mein Herr.'

' Very well; bring me some hot water, and I will dine then.'

Meantime he took off his coat, which he threw over a chair, and while waiting for the hot water flung himself on the bed.

When he awoke, he wondered where he was; he felt cold and shivery, and, looking around the room, saw his coat had been brushed and folded; but there was no hot water, so he rang the bell, which summons was answered by the frightened *hausfrau*.

' Why haven't you brought the hot water ?' he inquired.

With scared face and trembling voice she exclaimed :

' You aren't dead, then ?'

' Dead ?' he said ; ' no.'

' It's all right, mein Herr,' she answered ; ' no one knows you are here but Fritz and me.'

' What *do* you mean ?' he asked.

' Not dead ? not dead ?' she kept repeating. ' Ach Gott !'

' Why do you say that ? Of course I'm not dead. I want my dinner. How soon will it be ready ?'

7

'Yesterday's dinner is done,' she replied mysteriously, 'and so is supper, and so is to-day's breakfast, and to-day's dinner is now on the table.'

'God bless me! how long have I been asleep, then?' he cried.

'Twenty-six hours—and so, after all, you're not dead; but it's all right: nobody knows but Fritz and me.'

'What does it matter who knows?'

Creeping close up beside him with a sympathetic look, she whispered:

'You are a prisoner from gaol, aren't you

'Me?'

'Yes. What have you done? *I* won't tell!'

He laughed heartily, told the real story, showed his passport, and thus happily ended what might have cost him his life.

CHAPTER VIII.

SLEDGING ACROSS THE ALPS.

' IN these modern days of easy travel,' says my father in one of the little sketches he has left, ' all the world and his wife traverse the continent of Europe with very little more trouble than they stray through the more or less tortuous walks of their flower-gardens, while Switzerland and the Alps are nearly as well known to Mr., Mrs., and Miss John Bull as Hyde Park and Bond Street.

' But, common as Continental travel is to the great family of John Bull in general, I have never yet met with a single member who had gone through the pleasing ordeal of passing across the greatest mountain range of Europe seated in a sledge.

' Sledges and snow are usually associated together in the mind; but the presence of snow is not a necessary concomitant to the use of a sledge. On the contrary, I am inclined to imagine that the sledge was invented and employed by primitive races of mankind, long ere any of its members were driven to seek home and subsistence in the inhospitable regions of snow.

' Central Asia was the cradle of the human race, and man was long resident on its warm, genial soil ere he had to seek his fortunes in colder regions.

' Very soon after man knew how to domesticate animals for his own use, he must have learned not only to employ them as beasts of burden, but also as beasts of draught;

and for the latter purpose a very primitive form of carriage
was ready to his hand, in the shape of the branch of a
tree, which again, in its turn, would suggest to his mind
the manufacture of a sledge.

'When a student at the University of Giessen, in the
summer of 1854, it was my regular habit to go from
Saturday afternoon till Monday morning to the Baths of
Nauheim, which were only one hour's distance by rail, and
which in consequence of their Spieltische—gambling-tables
—were a lively resort.

'One Sunday when there, I met, coming into the village,
a number of boys and girls, leading a young heifer, who
dragged behind her the spreading branches of a full-
leaved tree, upon whose arms a girl sat, singing in joyous
glee with her companions. Here was a most primitive
kind of sledge; and more simple was the harness, which
was nothing!

'"How, then," you will ask, "could the heifer drag the
tree?"

'"Beautifully," I reply, "and by very simple means.
Her horns acted as a harness-collar, the tree itself being
the traces. In effect, one of the heifer's horns was simply
pushed through the cleft uniting the largest branch to the
main stem of the tree, which made harness and sledge alike
complete. Here, then, I think we have the counterpart of
the first invented vehicle, and the same idea which suggested itself to the children of the German village would
probably suggest itself also to the more imperfectly developed minds of prehistoric men.

'Sledges requiring little mental development for their
invention I have seen employed by mature men in the
middle of the nineteenth century. At Würzburg, for
example, in 1853, when the newly-erected, uncompleted
railway workshop was burned down, the fire-brigade
brought water to the scene of action in huge copper pans,
on sleighs roughly manufactured out of four beams of wood.
Two fastened lengthways, and two as cross-bars screwed

together, afforded another example of a primitive form of sledge.

'Wheels have now entirely taken the place of runners, except in lands of snow. There sledges still, and ever must, hold their own ; for snow beyond the depth of eight inches completely impedes the progress of wheels. In the winter of 1853-54, while I was studying at the University of Würzburg, I saw the mail diligence drawn by eight horses drive through the streets on runners, instead of on wheels, every day for about six weeks.

'Progress has gone on, and just as runners have given place to wheels, and oxen to horses, so horses have, in their turn, in a great measure given place to coals and water. And possibly the time is not far distant when land and water steamboats, and steam-carriages,* will give place to aerial navigation. We have imitated the progress of fish in the sea, we have excelled the progression of animals on the land, and I am quite at a loss to discover why the intellect of man fails to imitate the flight of a goose in the air ; for I am sure the bird is both heavy and clumsy enough, to admit of its movements being copied by a combination of the feeble brain and imperfect hands of man.

'Time conquers all things, and time will, I have no doubt, conquer aerial navigation.

'At the time I am writing of (1854), I had already spent nearly four years at French and German Universities, and thinking I might with advantage pass a winter at an Italian one, I betook myself to Padua, my object in going there being to acquire a deeper insight into the higher branches of scientific medicine. Immediately after my arrival in the old city I made inquiries regarding the capabilities of the schools for advancing my knowledge of physiological chemistry. But, alas! to my chagrin, I found that the University of Padua, once so famous, had, like our British schools of medicine, not yet wakened out

* This was written twenty years before the advent of the motor-car.

of the slumber into which it had fallen in the dark midnight of science. Indeed, I soon discovered that in Padua there was nothing for me to learn, but much for me to teach from the store of scientific knowledge I had already acquired elsewhere.

'My plans were easily arranged, seeing that I had no one to consult except myself, and off I started for Munich, viâ Como. Passing along its beautiful lake, I soon arrived at Chiavenna, a little village at the foot of the Alps, on the Italian side. Here my journeying was brought to an abrupt stop. It was now the month of October. The Alpine winter had already set in. Fresh snow had fallen and covered the roads some inches deep. The last diligence had left Chiavenna the day before my arrival, and no more would run till spring again appeared.

'Here was a nice fix. I was lodged at the Hôtel de la Poste—the only good hostelry in the place—and from its *garçon* I learned that before I could move on I must patiently wait till a sufficient number of travellers arrived to fill a certain number of sleighs, so as to make it worth their while to face the snow-clad roads.

'"Patience is a virtue" of which I have not a superabundance; but "necessity knows no law," therefore I just waited.

'On the second day after my arrival in the almost desolate hotel, I sat toasting my toes before the coffee-room stove, puffing a cigar, not one whit less melancholy than myself. Well might I say we were both melancholy; for what can be more depressing than to sit all day in the deserted coffee-room of an Italian village hotel, after having perused all its dirty old newspapers and thrice gone through the visitors' book. While looking through this book, my eye caught the names of "Baronin von Liebig and Miss Emma Muspratt," which seemed familiar to me—why, I could not think, till I remembered that my friend Herman von Liebig, with whom I shared rooms in Giessen the previous spring, had often talked about his sister and her English friend. Moreover, when his father, Baron Justus von Liebig, whose acquaintance I was so pleased to make, came to visit him, he had told us much about these two young girls, who were together enjoying the delights of Munich society. Little did I dream, as I sat looking at the visitors' book, that this then unknown girl, Emma Muspratt, would eventually become my wife.

'Even the cigars seemed to taste bad and stale. To go out of the hotel was impossible—the nature of the weather prohibited that—so I simply stared into the *kamin* and mused.

'At length the afternoon came. The door opened, and in walked a human being other than that wearisome *garçon*. He bowed, I bowed, and we began to talk. French we talked, German we talked, and at length, finding that I was an Englishman, English we talked, for he was proficient in that language also. We soon became good friends. He introduced himself as Baron von Stein; I told him my name; we smoked together, we ate together, and time no longer hung heavy on my hands. I thought my companion a very intelligent man; he knew a great deal, too, about England; he had been to London; he was acquainted with our statesmen, and understood a vast amount more about English politics than I did; I wondered at his knowledge and admired the man's manner. He had a companion with him, who spoke but little, and the little he did say was neither instructive nor amusing. The companion treated the Baron, I thought, with an exceptional degree of deference.

'A couple of days passed by, and sufficient *voyageurs* having then arrived to enable the landlord to rig out a sledge-party, we were informed that we must all rise early next morning, in order to start on our journey by daybreak, as it was necessary to accomplish the sledging part of our tour across the Alps ere the sun-setting, or we should probably never open our eyes to another day's dawn. Accordingly the Hôtel de la Poste was brilliantly illuminated at an early hour next morning. We breakfasted by candlelight, and as I emerged from the warm inn door into the sharp crisp morning air, I spied, drawn up in a row, nine small single horse-sledges. They looked, in the dim morning light, exactly like a line of gigs, from which the wheels had been removed. The ostlers, with lanterns in their hands, flitted about like so many Will-o'-the-wisps. The courier (mail-guard) was in great feather, rushing about everywhere, marshalling his passengers into their proper places. All being safely seated in the sledges, and ready for the fray, the horn was sounded, crack went the drivers' whips, and away went the cortège in grand style. Most of the sledges contained two passengers, but I was alone with a driver, and we had not started long ere I perceived the first two vehicles contained no drivers and no passengers. The first sledge, indeed, was utterly empty, while the second contained only luggage. Not until the third did I notice a driver, beside whom sat the guard, puffing away like a steam-engine at a cigar as thick as his finger and as long as his foot.

' On inquiry, I learned from the coachman of my sleigh that the cause of the two first horses being sent on in front, without any conductor or passengers with them, was in consequence of the dangerous nature of the road. The snow having completely obliterated all traces of a path, there was nothing but the tops of long poles (which had been driven in the outer edge of the road) to indicate where the track lay. Within the poles was perfect safety, without them utter and immediate destruction. The staves being close to the edge of a precipice, by which the road was bounded, there was scarcely footing for a cat outside of the poles, so that a horse and sleigh would, on attempting to round them on the outside, be at once hurled into the abyss below, there to remain till the summer sun melted the snow from the valley.

' Most curiously did I watch how the leading horse

would behave at the turns of the road round the mountains, where the dangers of the journey were most
imminent. No footprints were there to guide him on his
dangerous course. His own intelligence was his only
safety, and on that and the agility of his own limbs could
he alone depend for safety. A momentary error in his
judgment, or a single stumble of his foot, would at once
send him headlong into eternity. No wonder, then, that
I watched with anxious eye his movements. It was
beautiful to see his courage and his sagacity. Where
safety lay he boldly and rapidly trotted on, nearly touching
his nose with his well-bent knees at every step, as he
whisked before him the light untrodden snow. Where
danger lurked—close to each pole—he cautiously and more
slowly tried his way ; but when once the stake was passed
he knew full well there was naught to fear, and therefore
sped in a straight line to the next post, where again he
slackened speed. No sooner, however, was it passed than
off he went, like a hero in the chase, and never abated his
rapid trot till danger again presented itself. The sledges
following had no difficulty in escaping unharmed, so long
as their horses followed in the footsteps of their leader,
and most thoroughly did they appear to understand this,
for not an inch either right or left did they swerve.

‘ ’Twas gloriously exciting, but fearfully cold, as we
passed the summit of the Splügen Pass, and glad was I to
cover my whole head in one of the ends of my warm
woollen Scotch plaid, leaving absolutely nothing visible
except my eyes, which were kept in constant activity
during the whole expedition.

‘ We halted in our journey, baited the horses, refreshed
ourselves, and then went off again. During the short
time that we waited at the little mountain *auberge*, I think
we changed horses ; but it is so long ago that I should not
like to say positively whether this were so or not.

‘ All I further distinctly remember is, that the snow-clad
mountain-tops, the snow-lined valleys and ravines, were

enough to inspire the most callous human heart to admire
and adore the transcendent works of God, and raise his
thoughts from the beauteous mortal earth below to the
eternal heaven above.

'Between three and four o'clock in the afternoon our
sledging feat was accomplished; and precious glad was I
to get out of the sleigh and once more be able to stretch
out my legs on Mother Earth. Sitting still in one position
so long, coupled with the cold, had cramped me dreadfully.

'The sledges drew up in a row—one behind the other—
and all their occupants quickly disembarked, except one
gentleman, who remained sitting stock-still. He was asked
to get out, but made no response, either by word or sign.
His interlocutor was, on nearer approach, startled by the
strange appearance he presented, and immediately shouted
out "Der Mann ist Todt!" (The man is dead).

'We all ran to the side of the sledge, and there sat the
occupant, bolt upright, a lifeless statue. He looked most
gruesome. Seeing at once that he was frozen, yet apparently not quite dead, I had him lifted out of the
sleigh. When he was placed upon the ground, his legs
were so stiff they still retained the bent attitude of his
sitting posture. I instantly set two of the men to catch
hold of his clothes and rub them briskly against the skin,
their exertions being most ably assisted by Baron von Stein.
In twenty or thirty minutes the sufferer was sufficiently
recovered, although he could not speak even then, to admit
of his being carried into the inn, where I soon had him
rolled up in warm blankets, with hot water-bottles, and
placed on the floor in front of a blazing wood-fire, where
he slowly recovered.

'The diligence being ready to start ere the poor gentleman
was able to proceed, we left him in the safe keeping of the
kind *padrona* of the hotel, who, I have little doubt, could
give a good account of her patient, whom I never saw nor
heard of more. Before leaving him, however, I was able

to satisfy myself that his having been frozen was entirely
due to his having no rugs, a single top-coat being totally
inadequate to keep out such cold.

'After travelling with Baron von Stein for about a week,
our routes diverged at a little village on the road. On
parting, he bequeathed me—one of many friendly acts—
his courier, whose wages he had paid up to the end of the
week, and whose services during the intervening three days
I was to have for nothing, excepting any small gratuity I
might voluntarily bestow upon him.

'My suspicions having been raised that the Baron was
not exactly the person he represented himself to be, on the
day after his departure I asked the guide if he knew who
he really was.

' "Yes," was the reply; "but he told me not to tell
you."

'This remark, of course, deeply excited my curiosity; but
I asked no more. When we parted company he vouchsafed
the following information :

' "I was engaged at Lucerne to go on a fortnight's tour
with the gentleman, and he travelled under the name of
Baron von Stein. When we got to Lake Como he went to
Villa Charlotta, and on our arrival there I was astonished
to find all the servants of the house, drawn up in two rows,
commence bowing and scraping at us, as if we were very
grand folks. 'Now,' thought I to myself, 'this man's
somebody;' so as soon as I sat down to my supper among
the other servants, I managed to find out that my gentleman was not Baron von Stein at all, but the husband of
Princess Charlotte of Prussia, in whose villa we then were,
while he himself was the Duke of Saxe-Meiningen. There,
now you know as much about him as I do, and I dare say
you are much more likely to meet him again than I
am."

'At this revelation I could not help laughing, for, on
shaking hands with the Baron at parting, I had cordially
expressed the hope—which he, in words at least, recipro-

cated—that I might some day or other meet him again, if not in Germany, at least in England, whither I was then returning, little dreaming that my good-natured *compagnon de voyage* was such a " great gun."

' George, Duke of Saxe-Meiningen, was born in 1826; his wife, Princess Charlotte of Prussia, died in 1865.'

CHAPTER IX.

In 1853 my father, his happy student days over, returned
to England, with the determination of settling down and
making a home for himself. He was full of all the newest
scientific ideas gleaned from various Continental Universities; he had hardly a relation in the world, and had
lived too long abroad to have many friends in England.
Nevertheless, full of hope, enthusiasm, and ability, he
believed the time had come to give up wandering, and
turn his knowledge to practical account. He says himself:

'After my connection with the Royal Maternity Hospital,
and the success of the Cæsarean section, I thought of
turning my attention specially to midwifery, and starting
as an accoucheur. In France I had applied myself
diligently to this subject, and, although I had no actual
understanding with Professor Simpson (afterwards Sir
James), from various little things he said I certainly looked
forward to commencing my midwifery career as one of his
assistants, and therefore travelled to Edinburgh in order to
see him about the matter.

'He, of course, inquired minutely concerning all I had
seen, read, and done, and at his request I left him my
published papers on " Urohæmatin "* and " The Saccharine
Function of the Liver," also the volume of Robin and
Verdeil's " Chimie Anatomique," in which some of my

* *Pharmaceutical Journal*, 1852.

work in the laboratories of those gentlemen is referred to. As a result, he asked me to breakfast with him on the following morning. After breakfast we went into his study, and as soon as we entered he closed the door, with the intention, I naturally imagined, of suggesting I should become his own assistant, for I had now determined to try and earn some money in medicine instead of spending it on science. My blank astonishment—horror, rather—may be more easily imagined than described, when, without the slightest word of preface, he said :

' "You won't do for a howdie;" then, seeing my look of disappointed surprise, he immediately added : "You have educated yourself too well for a howdie. Start for Birmingham this afternoon ; they want a professor there. I can give you letters that will get you the appointment."

' I was so bewildered, as well I might be, at this extraordinary address, that I sat perfectly mute while he looked up Bradshaw for the train he wished me to catch. He found what he wanted, mentioned the time it left Edinburgh, told me to " call in on your way to the station, and get two letters to take with you."

' Not a word more was spoken, for he had stricken me dumb, and we parted.

' I left the house, the words " educated yourself too well for a howdie " ringing in my ears with anything but a pleasant sound. Of what use, then, was education, if it could not give me my heart's desire? All my plans in life seemed blasted, for my idea was that Professor Simpson, not desiring my services, was only using polite words in order civilly to get rid of me.

' After partaking of an early dinner, to which I brought no appetite, I started on my journey, Birmingham, as the Professor had planned, being reached about twelve o'clock that same night, in a damp, depressing drizzle. I told the coachman to drive me to the best hotel, ate some supper, and went to bed, not in a very good humour.

' In the train I had already settled my plans for the

future. If Simpson thought I was too good for a howdie, I thought myself too good for Birmingham, and consequently made up my mind, unless Birmingham proved much better than I expected, to stay there no longer than was necessary to see what its attractions might be.

' My bedroom window being at the back of the hotel, on pulling up the blind in the morning a murky atmosphere and dingy brick walls tended to confirm the disagreeable impression produced on my mind the previous night in the rain.

' After breakfast I walked straight to the college, and there gathered from the porter all the information he could give, which, beyond that the students were eighty in number, was not much. I then proceeded to the hospital, and was shown over it, ascertained the hour at which Mr. Sands Cox made his visit, left my card for him, and departed.

' Afterwards I strolled round the town until the time came for Mr. Cox to be at the hospital, when I purposely called at his house, left Simpson's letter and my card. Very glad to have got over that piece of business without encountering Mr. Cox, I returned to the hotel, had luncheon, paid my bill, drove to the station, and took the next train back to Edinburgh.

' I had seen quite enough of manufacturing Birmingham to know it would not suit my perhaps too ambitious views.

' Having tasted the alluring sweets of scientific discovery, and having the wherewithal to gratify my tastes, I resolved to return to the Continent for another couple of years, and at German Universities train myself still further by the prosecution of biological research for the duties of a scientific physician, feeling convinced that pure science is the true road to all successful healing art.

'Next day, so soon as breakfast was over, I called on Professor Simpson, who, the moment I entered his room, greeted me with :

' " I thought we settled you were to go to Birmingham ?"

' " I have been there and come back again," was my reply.

' " How is that ?" he asked.

' Summoning up all my courage, I bravely answered :

' " You told me that I had overeducated myself for a howdie, and advised me to become a consulting physician. I have made up my mind to follow your counsel, and intend to go abroad for two years in order to obtain more information. At the end of that time I think I may probably know enough to enable me to start in London."

' Looking me hard in the face, he inquired :

' " Did you tell Cox that ?"

' " No, for I never saw Cox," I replied. " I called at the hospital and called at his house, but each time missed him."

' " And where is the letter I gave you for him ?"

' " I left it at his house with my card."

' " Without any explanation ?"

' " Yes."

' " Confound it !" burst out Simpson. " He'll take us for two fools. You ought not to have left the letter."

' Instantly realizing the mistake I had made, and knowing the nature of the man I had to deal with, I murmured some apology, backed out of the room as soon as possible, and never entered it again until two days later, when I went to bid my friend good-bye, ere starting for Germany.

' Professor Simpson I had known since I was a boy of fifteen. As a student he had experimented upon me with chloroform. I believe I was the third or fourth person who was ever rendered insensible by the drug. He had given it to me in soda-water, but the result had not been very satisfactory. Of course I was delighted to be experimented upon, but I gave him an awful fright ; suddenly the respiration ceased. I turned livid and the pupils became widely dilated. Simpson told me afterwards he had feared it was all up with me ; but he pulled me round, and many are the experiments I have since made with chloroform myself.

'When at the Maternity Hospital I had assisted Simpson on many occasions. He had read my paper on the case of Cæsarean section for me at the Medical Chirurgical Society.* I had plenty of opportunities, therefore, of knowing the Professor's temper, and so thought it only prudent to keep out of his way till my escapade was forgiven.'

Germany was at that time in its zenith (1850-60) as an educational centre, and my father studied histology under Kölliker and pathology under Virchow.

'Leaving Edinburgh,' he writes, 'I journeyed direct to Bavaria, in order to study the microscope with Professor Kölliker and chemistry under Professor Scherer. I was particularly desirous of going to the latter, as he had in a review of my paper on the subject questioned the correctness of my statement concerning the existence of iron in the normal renal secretion, and I desired to prove to him I was right, which I soon did, for he afterwards complimented me publicly at the Academy for my discovery, and I was shortly elected a member of that august body.

'During the eight months I passed at Würtzburg I worked in Kölliker's private room. He was then bringing out his large book on histology, and I worked *pari passu* with him on the same subject. From Kölliker I learned much, also from Virchow, and thus laid the foundation of the knowledge which afterwards stood me in such good stead. In Scherer's laboratory I continued my researches on urohæmatin, and before leaving Würtzburg published papers on "Urohæmatin und seine Verbindungen mit Animalischem Harze," etc., for which I had the honour of being made a corresponding member of the Physicalis.

* Published in the *Edinburgh Journal of Medical Science*, July, 1850.

8

'Life in Würtzburg in those days was indeed primitive. Maidens fetched water from the well as in the Middle Ages; the streets were lighted with oil-lamps hanging in the middle from a string suspended from window to window. At 8 p.m. the gates of the town were closed, and no one was allowed to go out or enter the town after that hour.

'How different it all is now, when the old gates are done away with, the old ramparts are disappearing, the streets are gaily lighted with gas, and water is laid on to all the houses!

'From Würtzburg I returned to Giessen to learn more of inorganic analysis, and after remaining there for one session visited during the three next months the hospitals of Berlin and Vienna, coming back by Heidelberg in order to study gas analysis under Professor Bunsen. After spending nine profitable months there, I returned to England with the view of turning the scientific knowledge I had acquired to practical account.'

The time spent abroad (five years in all) seems to have been admirably employed, for it enabled my father subsequently to make a most elaborate series of researches on the chemistry of respiration, and to obtain grants from the Royal Society to further his investigations, and he had the honour of being elected a Fellow of that learned body at the age of thirty-six.

Speaking of his successful youth, he writes :

'The day after my second return to Edinburgh (1855), Professor Bennett offered me £150 per annum to assist him in conducting a class of practical physiology which he was about to establish in the University. On communicating this offer to Professor Simpson, he advised me to have nothing to do with it. He had evidently forgiven my former escapade, and, after hearing all about my work since we parted, pointed out an advertisement in the *Lancet* for a teacher of Practical Physiology and Histology in University College, London, and told me at once to start off and make inquiries about it, as the following Saturday was the last day for receiving applications for the newly formed post.

' He favoured me with no letter of introduction this time, having apparently not forgotten my treatment of the Birmingham one, but he kindly gave me leave to use his name, and write to him if I wanted anything. To London, therefore, I proceeded without delay, arriving at Euston about eight o'clock on the Monday morning.

' After breakfast and a good bath, I repaired to University College and inquired for the secretary. On being shown into his room I saw a little, white-haired old gentleman sitting primly behind his writing-desk, whom I soon informed that I had called with the view of obtaining information regarding the lectureship of practical physiology and histology. Then the following dialogue ensued:

' " What do you want ?" he asked.

' " To secure the lectureship," I answered.

' " Oh ! who are you ?"

' " George Harley."

' " And what testimonials have you got ?"

' " None."

' " Then where have you come from ?"

' " Abroad."

' " I don't know anything about you, and I know less of those foreign Universities, so I don't think you'll do. You look a mere boy."

' " Are you the person to give the appointment ?"

' " No—not exactly."

' " Well, who is ?" I asked.

' " The Council."

' " I suppose I can't see the Council ; but I should like to see someone else, please."

' But that he did not think possible till I let him know that I could easily get introductions from the Edinburgh professors, when his stern tone somewhat relaxed ; and, still refusing the slightest particle of information, he told me to go and see the Dean.

'Ascertaining Professor Ellis was the Dean, and that I should probably find him at the opposite end of the building, I proceeded to his room, where my reception, though more polite, was little less formal than it had been in the secretary's office, our brief interview ending in my being handed over to Professor Sharpey.

'"You had better see Dr. Sharpey," said the Dean.

'"I know his name quite well as a great physiologist. Where can I see him?"

'"I will send you to him."'

'And accordingly I was conducted by a small boy through various corridors to a private room.

'There sat the genial, world-renowned Sharpey, whose enormous head and wonderful gray hair made a vivid impression on me.

'Sharpey, as soon as he heard my name, said:

'"Ah yes, I know all about you; you have been working with Kölliker, from whom I lately received a letter telling of a young Englishman for whom he predicted a brilliant future."

'We chatted pleasantly about foreign places and scientific men, and then suddenly Sharpey said:

'"Oh, I forgot you came about this post; you can leave your testimonials with me."

'"I haven't got any."

'"What! you haven't got any? Why, the appointment is to be made in five days, so what are you going to do?"

'"I don't know."

'"Can you get any testimonials?"

'"I suppose I can if I ask."

'"Well, young man, you had better go away and ask at once, and let me have them the day after to-morrow."

'I did go away, wrote to my various old teachers in Edinburgh and abroad, and in due time a batch of testimonials arrived from Edinburgh, but none from the Continent.

'I thought I would take copies of my published papers in my pocket : two in English, one in French, and two in German. So, armed with these precious documents, I retraced my steps to University College, where I found Professor Sharpey in the professors' common-room. I gave him my papers, when he told me to write to Simpson for an introduction, and come back and see him on Saturday forenoon.

'Pleased with the interview, I passed the rest of the day in looking for lodgings, and ended by taking up my quarters in Mortimer Street, Cavendish Square. I wrote to Professor Simpson, told him what I had done, and asked him for a formal letter of introduction to Sharpey. The remainder of the week I spent my time in visiting the different hospitals and calling on Dr. Bence Jones with a message from his old college friend, Professor Scherer. On my telling Dr. Bence Jones that I wished to get the lectureship at University College, and giving him a comic description of my interview with the secretary, he laughingly said :

' " You will be a clever fellow if you get in there."

' Not a very cheering remark, certainly, but one uttered, I am sure, from what I afterwards knew of the man, in the most perfect good faith.

' Saturday morning brought a laconic note from Sir James Simpson. With this note was a fat letter for Dr. Sharpey.

' At eleven o'clock I proceeded to keep my appointment with my new friend, and found him alone. He received me most courteously ; said that he had read over the papers I left with him, and was glad to see that I took such a broad view of biological research as to think that, besides physiological and histological knowledge, it was necessary also to have a thorough chemical training. I thanked him for his compliment, and we soon got into the

full swing of a biological conversation. After remaining
with him for more than an hour, I rose to take my
departure, but just as I was going out of the door I
suddenly remembered that Professor Simpson's letter was
still in my pocket. I instantly stepped back into the
room, and presented the letter with an apology for having
until then forgotten it. Sharpey took it, and asked me
again to be seated. He was on one side of the fire, I on
the other, and most carefully did I watch his face in the
hope of gathering the tenor of the letter from the expression of his countenance. But his face remained
immovable until he had got nearly through the epistle,
which was a long one, consisting, as I saw, of two sheets
of notepaper. Then he raised his eyes, looked straight in
my face, and asked :

' "Do you know what is in this letter?"

' "No," I answered, rather surprised.

' "Did the letter come to you open?" was his next
question.

' "Yes," I replied ; " it came in exactly the same state
as it was in when I gave it to you."

' "Did it come with another letter?" he then asked.

' "Yes," I answered; and pulling Simpson's note to me
out of my pocket, I presented it to him.

' He at once read and returned it, without making any
remark, and then resumed the perusal of his own letter.
No sooner had he finished reading it than he said :

' "This is the last day for sending in applications, and
as the Council meet very shortly, you had better sit down
at that table and write your application now."

' I took a sheet of notepaper from the case, dipped a
pen into the ink, but then had to stop. I had not an
idea what to say. After reflecting for a few moments, I
turned to Sharpey, who was busy re-perusing Simpson's
epistle, and exclaimed hopelessly :

' "I don't know how to write a letter of application. I
never wrote one in my life. Besides which, I have been

so long out of England, and so little in the habit of either speaking or writing English, that I find great difficulty in expressing myself properly."

' "Very well," said Sharpey, "I will dictate the letter, and you shall write it."

' After having worded the formal part of the application for me, he went on :

' " Now give a short account of your medical education ; mention the places where you have studied abroad, and state the titles of the papers you have written."

' That finished, he told me how to sign myself, and then asked me for the letter. After reading it over, he handed it back, remarking that it would do nicely, and telling me to put it in an envelope and address it to the President of University College. When I had done so, he said :

' " Give me the letter, and I will see that it is laid before the Council this afternoon," adding : " The office of Curator to the Anatomical Museum is vacant—it is worth 50 guineas a year—would you take that in the meantime, till we settle about the lectureship ?"

' Seeing I hesitated ere replying, he proceeded to explain the advantages which would accrue from accepting the position, even if only for a short period, viz., having a room assigned to me to work in, and a man who would assist, etc. When the thing was placed before me in this light, I of course said I should be glad to accept. We then parted.

' At nine o'clock on the same night I received by post a polite official letter from the secretary, who had snubbed me five days previously, offering me the post of curator to the museum ; informing me the Council had postponed the day for receiving applications for the lectureship on Practical Physiology and Histology till that day three months, but that if I chose to accept the office of curator I might begin my duties on the following Monday (Saturday was the day on which the letter was written and received), when the honorarium would begin.

'I accepted the offer, and forthwith commenced my duties as curator, or, as it was then styled, Assistant-Director of the Anatomical Museum, on the Monday morning indicated.

'Thus in 1855, a stranger in London, and without so much as even an acquaintance at University College, then the best teaching school in London, I acquired a paid appointment within five days of my arrival in the Metropolis.'

My father was then only twenty-six years of age, yet he received an intimation that the college would keep open for three months the lectureship on Practical Physiology and Histology then vacant, to enable him to obtain some more testimonials and send in another formal application.

CHAPTER X.

'FROM fortune to failure there is but a step; but from failure to fortune the road is both long and weary,' confided George Harley in his diary in later days. 'I was surprised then, but I am not surprised now I have gained experience of public institutions and their ways, that Dr. Bence Jones should have thrown up his hands in amazement when, a few days later, I called to inform him of my appointment as curator.

'Thus happily began my Metropolitan career. My next move was to take a dining-room with a study behind and a bedroom above, and put my plate on the door of 22, Nottingham Place, W.

'When quietly settled down I again wrote to all those professors with whom I had worked abroad for the required testimonials. Answers speedily came, and in due time I received the appointment of first Professor of Practical Physiology in England, my most formidable opponent being Dr. Augustus Waller, already an F.R.S. I held this professorship until 1869, when the chair was taken by Professor Michael Foster, who had most kindly delivered my lectures for me when I was away through ill-health. Strangely enough, on Foster's going to Cambridge, my old Edinburgh college chum, Professor Burdon Sanderson, succeeded to my chair at University College.'

The young scientist in after-life often referred to his keen

excitement and pride on being appointed to a professorship
in London. He had seen such splendid work done abroad
that the poor condition of medical science in England
horrified him ; and he frequently told of the opposition he
experienced when trying to introduce new methods, such
endeavours invariably being met with a querulous reference
to his ridiculous 'new-fangled notions.' But my father
would warmly declare, ' A truth cannot be got rid of by a
simple denial; and in an argument each thinks he knows
best.'

George Harley was not easily daunted, and, if he considered a thing to be right, would plod diligently until he
beat the subject or it beat him. His natural ardour and
enthusiasm, however, met with such constant rebuffs that
he was often tempted to give up the fight. What was the
use of fighting against a stone wall of old customs and
habits ? But, although at the time often laughed at for
such ' absurd scientific ideas,' he did struggle bravely on at
his pioneer work against the odds of prejudice, walking
himself often, alas! arm in arm with the odds of ill-health.

It made him miserable to see how far England was behind
France and Germany in science. His great ambition was
to help raise the standard of the old country to the foremost rank.   England in the fifties was lagging sadly
behind, and only now, nearly half a century later, is she
taking a proper position, one which bids fair to be snatched
from her ere the century dies by America, who is to-day
rapidly marching to the front in scientific work.

' In May, 1856,' the doctor writes, ' I began my lectures,
and for thirteen years continued them to gradually increasing classes.

' In that summer occurred the celebrated trial of Palmer
for poisoning Cooke, with strychnine, and as next to nothing
was then known concerning the physiological action of
strychnine, I gave three lectures *to the students* on the
subject.

'As the so-called lectures were not only experimental, but entirely original, I was advised to publish them, and for that purpose took my manuscript to the office of the *Medical Times and Gazette.* The editor, not having any idea of the value of what I had left, let some time pass without publishing my paper; so in high dudgeon I returned to the office and demanded it back. On my way home I met Dr. Marshall Hall, and related the circumstance to him.

'"Let me read your manuscript," he said.

'Very willingly I handed him the despised parcel, which he put in his pocket. Next morning, just as I had finished breakfast, who should appear but Marshall Hall, who, without any waste of words, exclaimed :

'"Your paper is first-rate ! Come with me to the *Lancet* office, and I'll get them to publish it at once."

'I went, he introduced me to old Wakley, and in the next journal my paper appeared.'

In the obituary notice of George Harley in the *Lancet* we read :

Immediately after the great trial of Palmer for poisoning his friend Cooke with strychnia in 1856, and at a time when little was known regarding the toxic effects of that substance beyond that it induced tetanic convulsions, Dr. Harley published a series of papers which threw considerable light on the physiological action of strychnia on the animal body. These papers are referred to in the appended bibliography. In these articles he showed that the poison acts in precisely the same way, though with different degrees of rapidity, however introduced, and that, notwithstanding that it is called a nerve poison, it has no direct action on the nervous system whatever, but only affects it through the intermediary of the circulation. He found experimentally that the tetanizing action of strychnia on the nerves is entirely due to the chemical changes it produces in the constituents of the blood. Moreover, he showed that strychnia operates most quickly when introduced into a vein near to the heart. He was the first also to demonstrate that strychnia and wourali (arrow poison) have the property of reciprocally neutralizing the toxic effects of one another, so that an animal poisoned by one may be cured by the administration of a hypodermic dose of the other when too large a quantity has not been taken.

'Little did I think,' says my father, 'that paper on poisoning would get me into trouble; but it did. No sooner had Professor Sharpey read it than he came to me in a great fume, and asked what I meant by publishing the notes of physiological lectures delivered in the college, without first consulting the authorities! This was a turn of matters I never anticipated. However, I at once answered I did not know I had done anything wrong in publishing notes of my own lectures; surely my work was my own, and the only reason I had not told him of my intention was simply because I had not seen him between making up my mind to publish them and their actual appearance in print.

'He accepted the apology, but gathering from that experience the good doctor liked to know what I was about, I shortly afterwards showed him a paper on Respiration.

'After he had read it, he advised me to let him present it to the Royal Society. I did so somewhat bashfully, and was most agreeably surprised when a letter arrived from the society, saying they had awarded me a grant of £50, and would be much pleased if I would continue my researches and furnish the society with the results. Thus the goddess of Science again smiled graciously.'

Yes, he had bought his door-plate, had taken it home with pride, fixed it to the outer door, and positively walked up and down the street to see what his name looked like in such a distinguished position!

Of course practice would come. Like every other young medico, he imagined that a door-plate had only to be seen for patients and their guineas to come rolling in; but, alas! his hopes and ambition were doomed to be disappointed.

' The door-plate,' he states, ' on No. 22, Nottingham Place, proved no success. It did not bring practice. At the end of my first year I had only pocketed five guineas, out of which two came from a lady in the drawing-room of the same house !

' Having to pay extra for the satisfaction of seeing my name on the door, and finding that it brought no patients (a consulting practice I was determined to have, and nothing short of that would I condescend to take), I with a sigh took off the plate I had bought with such pride, locked it up in my portmanteau, rented a drawing-room floor in Somerset Street, Portman Square, and there determined to wait quietly until my professional services were called for.

' This turned out an excellent move, though undertaken contrary to the advice of all my friends, one of whom, Dr. Marshall Hall, jeeringly told me if I took off my door-plate I should "never become anything but a scientist."

' Having ceased to be anxious about practice, however, I felt I might devote my energies—meantime, at least—to scientific research and literature, and I added to my experience by penning articles for the *British and Foreign Quarterly Review* in the evenings, while I worked hard at science all day long at University College.

' During my second year in London, old Dr. Wakley, the editor of the *Lancet*, asked me to join the staff of that journal, and write leading articles for him ; but when I consulted Professor Sharpey on the subject, he advised me most emphatically to decline, as I could afford to wait to earn an income, notwithstanding the terms offered would have greatly conduced to my interests in a monetary point of view.

' A great change about this time came over the spirit of many a medical-journal-editor's dream, and instead of finding a difficulty about placing my papers, as in the case of that on strychnine, I received even from our best-known

dailies numerous applications for articles, and sometimes
wrote scientific leaders.

' The weekly medical journals do not pay for original
articles, but I eventually found that for a good paper they
would sometimes bear the expense of woodcuts—a point of
no little importance to a beginner.'

A medical obituary says :

Consulting practice came to him sooner than he expected, and from
a quarter little anticipated.   The first medical man who called him to
a case was the late Sir Thomas (then Dr.) Watson.   In December, 1856,
Dr. Harley had shown at the Pathological Society, of which Dr. Watson
was then president, a large encysted hepatic intestinal calculus
(weighing 450 grains), and had explained how he thought it got into
the duodenum by ulceration direct from the gall-bladder.   The theory
given being not only perfectly new to Dr. Watson, but appearing both
reasonable and ingenious, led him, as he afterwards said, to put his
"mark upon the young man," and from that time until he gave up
practice he repeatedly consulted with Dr. Harley, not only in liver but
also in renal cases.   This may be said to have led to Dr. Harley's
subsequent success as a consulting physician.   In 1858, immediately
after he had been elected a Fellow of the Chemical Society, his career
was nearly brought to an untimely close by his taking, by way of
experiment, between 3 and 4 drops of pure nitro-glycerine.   Its effect
was first to send up the pulse to 130, and then to reduce it to less
than 40 per minute ; at the same time it gradually paralyzed him
from the feet upwards, without, however, in the slightest degree
affecting his consciousness.   After the administration of ammonia and
brandy the alarming effects passed off in about an hour and a half.
This accident happened a couple of days after a paper on the effects of
nitro-glycerine had appeared from his pen in the *Medical Times and
Gazette* in April, 1858.   In the *Lancet* during the same year he published articles on the Histology of the Suprarenal Capsules, organs
which at that time were attracting a great deal of attention.   At the
meeting of the British Association for the Advancement of Science,
held at Leeds in that year, Dr. Harley communicated a paper entitled
' Notes of Experiments on Digestion,' written to show that pure
pancreatine unites in itself the digestive functions of the salivary,
gastric, and biliary secretions.   This discovery of these compound
effects of pure pancreatine had much to do with the subsequent
employment of pancreatic emulsion as an artificial digestive agent,
though it was many years before the suggestion of employing pure
pancreatine as an artificial digestive agent was carried into effect.

In 1859 Dr. Harley was appointed to a second chair, Professor of Medical Jurisprudence in University College, London. In the year following, in the *British and Foreign Medico-Chirurgical Review*, appeared an original article on the Chemistry of Digestion, in which he showed, by the result of experiment, that the reason why the living stomach is not itself digested is because it is protected from the solvent action of its own gastric juice by a layer of alkaline mucus, which is as rapidly replaced as it is removed during the digestive process. About the same time he communicated to the Royal Society a paper on the Saccharine Function of the Liver.

I have inserted this little bit to show how continuous was my father's work, and how his experiments sometimes nearly cost him his life. Columns and columns of this obituary notice in the *Lancet* did not contain half of his contributions to scientific and medical literature. He was a most prolific writer.

George Harley became editor, in 1859, of a new year-book on medicine and surgery. This was brought out for the New Sydenham Society, and was a novel idea of keeping an epitome of science applied to practical medicine. He was helped by such able men as Handfield Jones, Hulke, Grailey Hewitt and Odling; but it caused the general editor much worry, and he worked for its success unceasingly for some years.

He laboured steadily at science and literature for four years, occasionally, though very occasionally, being called into consultation by some appreciative medical friend; at the beginning of the fifth year, however, he discovered that his knowledge of scientific medicine began to be in request; general practitioners often sent for him, and were most flattering; and about the same time, having the good fortune to be elected Professor of Medical Jurisprudence, in the place of Dr. Carpenter (a second chair at University College), seeing a practice coming by leaps and bounds, he ventured, again under the advice of Dr. Sharpey, to take a house—No. 77, Harley Street (now 25)—this time feeling he might really dub himself ' Consulting Physician.'

When my father first settled in London, he soon became

a guest in many delightful houses, where he met numbers of interesting people. Up to the time of his death he frequently talked of the social evenings spent at Mrs. Loudon's, where the artists and literary folk of that day assembled weekly. She was a most charming woman, who possessed the happy power of attracting old and young. Her husband was a great botanist, and after his death she edited one or more of his books. She loved travelling, and, although by no means rich, journeyed all over Europe. Everywhere she made friends, so that when her numerous foreign acquaintances came to England she was able to introduce them to some of the most interesting people in London.

When, consequent on her death, that charming home was broken up, people said it caused almost as great a blank in the social world as the closing of Gore House, where for so many years Lady Blessington reigned supreme.

Many pleasant evenings were spent with Robert Bell, to whose house eminent literary men of the day constantly resorted. Bell was himself an author of some repute, and edited ' The British Poets,' which was, perhaps, his best-known contribution to English literature. Thackeray, Dickens, Mark Lemon, Samuel Lover, John Leech, S. C. Hall, Louis Blanc, were frequent guests.

When my father was a young man, spiritualism became very much the fashion; indeed, in the early sixties it was the rage of London, and at many of the houses where he visited séances were in vogue.

The doctor used often to relate how much he was impressed with a saying of Orfila's in Paris at one of the lectures of the Collège de France. Spiritualism was then in its infancy, and Orfila, after explaining that it was the offspring of alchemy and mystery, finished: ' Les hommes qui y croient sont des fous, et les hommes qui le pratiquent sont des charlatans.'

My father knew Home well; but, somehow, whenever he was present at one of his séances nothing ever happened. Many and many an argument he had with friends on the subject, as one by one they became converts to spiritualism ; and the more he knew of Home, the more he admired him as a ' superb impostor.'

Mrs. Milner-Gibson was at first infatuated about this spiritualist, but eventually she swerved from her allegiance, and at last never referred without amusement to the time of her ' delusion.'

At one of Mrs. Milner-Gibson's parties my father was much struck with Catherine Hayes' singing. Music had for him no charm, but on this particular occasion he happened to be near the piano, and could not move before the song began. Miss Hayes' voice was weak, but so tender and sympathetic that her melodies always proved attractive. On the occasion mentioned she sang the simple song ' He will return; I know he will' with such pathos that the young doctor was spell-bound, more especially as he noticed towards the end that tears were pouring down her cheeks. When she rose from the piano, she advanced to him, and, taking his hand, said: ' Thank you for your sympathy, but please take me away; I must get home.' He gave her his arm, and, seeing how much she was affected, remained silent for a time, then begged her to go and have some refreshment before he saw her to a cab. She did so, and after a cup of tea, which seemed to refresh her, he got her cloak and put her into a cab. She was a very delicate woman, whose lover had died suddenly, and this grief had quite broken down her health. Within ten days from the time the poor sensitive creature sang her song she caught cold and died. Often afterwards my father said it remained in his memory as the most thrilling thing he had ever heard.

Shrewd as he was as regards spiritualism, my father did not always come forth scatheless from an interview with the plausible impostor, as the following anecdote will prove :

One evening a gentleman called, and, after telling him a sad tale of woe about one of his children being dead in Edinburgh, and explaining he was an intimate friend of

Dr. Sharpey's, whom he had gone to see with the intention of asking him for the loan of £5 to get back to Edinburgh by that night's train, he went on to state that, finding that Dr. Sharpey was from home, he ventured to call on Dr. Harley, and beg his assistance in so sudden and great an emergency. As related it seemed such a pitiful story that the £5 was at once handed over.

A few days after, when my father saw Sharpey, he said to him :

'What a sad case that is of your friend Mr. B—— !'

'*My* friend!' exclaimed Sharpey. 'I never saw him in my life till he came to borrow £5 to take him to Edinburgh, where his child lay dead. He told me he was an old friend of yours, but you were out of town ; would I therefore help him ? And I did.'

Tableau of the two dupes !

CHAPTER XI.

THERE follows a sudden break in my father's early London experiences which might seem well-nigh inexplicable did we fail to remember a precisely similar pause ensued upon the death of his mother.

Of what he suffered at leaving Haddington, the beloved familiar house, the never-to-be-forgotten gardens, the old Franciscan burying-ground where so many belonging to him 'slept well,' how he faced the unaccustomed life in Edinburgh, how he bore the uprooting of all old ties, we are told nothing—absolutely nothing.

That he won his battle we know; but of the incidents that preceded his victory, of aught which befell him by the way, he scarcely speaks.

If we ask whether he found the short road smooth or rough, stony underfoot, or easy to travel, we are met by silence—a silence so strange, and at first sight so foreign to the simple frankness of his whole character, we are driven to the conclusion that when stricken by grief or elated by happiness, when toiling for success or proud the laurels Fortune so soon showered upon him, he retired to some inner sanctuary and became as one dumb.

Concerning matters which lay close to his heart, whether sorrowful or joyful, he refrains from speech, and only on one occasion, as we shall see later on, breaks those fetters of reticence wherewith Nature, and probably education, had bound him.

9—2

Under such circumstances, it may be well, before proceeding further, to sum up the facts he has left on record :

He came to London knowing no single individual in its
length or breadth, yet he made friends immediately.
Armed merely with his own unsupported statement of work
done abroad, no one deemed him an impostor. Simply
backed by Sir James Simpson's letter, which, arriving as
it did at the eleventh hour, might well have been an
impudent forgery, he obtained an appointment within a
week of coming South, from which time success followed
success.

Considering the months and years some men have to
wait for the faintest smile from Fortune, such astonishing
favour on the part of that fickle goddess might well have
turned a much older brain ; but it produced no evil effect
on him—he continued to labour steadily at the college, at
his profession and his literary work.

How did he gain such an immediate footing ? it may be
asked. My answer must be : 'I do not know, except it
were through the force of his own personality.'

He was the soul of truth. A statement from him might
be believed with more absolute conviction than aught sworn
on oath from many another. He was not vainglorious ; to
the last he seemed to regard himself but as ' one gathering
shells beside the vast ocean of knowledge'; he was *thorough*,
and, although he had learned much, ever showed himself
anxious to learn more. 'The strongest minds,' he would
say, ' are always the most open to conviction ; 'tis the fool
that never changes his opinions.'

Throughout life he had but small tolerance for arrogant
imbecility, but felt that some fact worth knowing might
be gleaned from the talk of the most simple creature.
' Wisdom is progression,' he would avow. It was these
traits among others that perhaps gained him such stanch
friends amid scientific men, friends who never changed,
but held true to the end.

At first he did not fully furnish the house in Harley

Street, but everything he bought was of the best, and slowly, but surely, success followed success in practice. It seems strange to relate that in 1860, when my father put up his brass plate in Harley Street, there were very few doctors' plates in that thoroughfare, or, indeed, neighbourhood. Now they abound on all sides. He chose the street because of family associations; Robert Harley, the statesman, having been made the first Earl of Oxford, all the streets round that neighbourhood are connected with the Oxford family, or named after the women they married. Then, again, it was only a quarter of an hour's walk from University College, and, excepting Portland Place, the first really good street going west. Thus, Harley Street became the home of the young London physician, as it did to many others in a few years' time, until it has verily become 'the doctors' Elysium.'

My father's house was that in which the Baroness Burdett-Coutts spent all her girlhood; and his near neighbours for many years were Sir William Jenner, Sir John Williams, Sir Alfred Garrod, and Sir Richard Quain.

Science to George Harley was a watchword. He declared it the shortest, as well as the cheapest, road to truth, and the longer he lived the more impressed he became of its magic power. He often said that science and medicine would in the future march hand-in-hand, and the more progress was made, the more would science become indispensable to the successful results of medicine.

When he first started practice in London, science was at a very low ebb; indeed, few of the medical men of that day knew anything about it in the true sense of the word. Still, there were some few exceptions, and amongst them such men as Sir Thomas Watson, Sir James Clark, Sir William Ferguson, and Dr. Bence Jones, who, although not fully acquainted with its mysteries, nevertheless appreciated its marvellous possibilities, and acknowledged the great factor it must become in the future. My father was one of the first doctors in England who combined scientific work with practice, and it was principally owing to this that his success as a young man proved so great. On one occasion his opinion was asked in a very complicated case which baffled all the experts. After a careful examination of the patient and bringing all his knowledge to bear, working with the microscope aided by chemical analysis, he decided it was cancer. The other doctors were all against him, but he still stuck to his diagnosis ; and when asked by some of his older colleagues why he would not yield to their larger experience, he replied : 'I cannot. I admit *my* judgment might be wrong, for I am not infallible; but science never errs, her laws are fixed and never change, therefore I still hold my opinion.'

When further pressed, he said : ' I will give you a homely example of what I mean. If you walk into a field believing that rabbits have been in that field, and you find none, you come to the opinion there are none, and would state that as your opinion ; if just as you are leaving that field, how-ever, you should chance to spy a very little rabbit, you change your mind, and come to believe there are rabbits in that field. In like manner, after microscopical examination, I can only arrive at the opinion this case is one of cancer, and time will show whether I am right or wrong.'

He saw no more of the patient for some months, when he was suddenly sent for, to find that cancer was unfor-tunately an established fact. Later on, at the post-mortem, it was proved that his diagnosis had been correct in every particular. It was a very uncommon and interesting case, and one which attracted much attention at the time.

And socially ? Well, young, possessed of genial manners and many talents, a rapidly rising man of ancient family, it is not wonderful that ere long he was eagerly welcomed in circles where he met the best minds of that day—which was a famous day—brilliant talkers, caustic wits, deep thinkers, learned theologians, and last, but by no means least, clever women—charming women. Often have I heard my father speak of those delightful parties he so much enjoyed, when such women as Charlotte Cushman, Miss Hosmer, Mrs. S. C. Hall, Catherine Hayes, Helen Faucet, George Eliot, Mrs. Charles Kean, Mrs. Kemble, Mrs. Dallas Glyn, Mrs. Stirling, added grace and charm to the evening's pleasure, while Mazzini, Kossuth and Louis Blanc threw a certain halo of political romance over society.

Faraday, Graham, Tyndall, William Ferguson, Sir Henry Holland, Sir James Clarke, Dr. Bence Jones, Dr. Sharpey, Sir David Brewster, Frank Buckland, then shone in the learned Societies; while in the literary world George Harley was brought in constant contact with Thackeray, Dickens, Matthew Arnold, Theodore Hook, Mark Lemon, Samuel Lover, Robert Bell, etc.

The artistic circle in which he moved was that of Sir Edwin Landseer, Charles Landseer, Cruikshank, Sir Charles Eastlake, John Leech. Those who are old enough to recollect those then familiar faces—which, alas! I am not—will remember the charm of their society, when each and all seemed to try and outvie the other in pleasant and instructive talk. Those were days my father always looked back upon with pleasure. He had endless tales to tell about them, but, unfortunately, committed few to writing.

I now come to a very important event in the London physician's life, which occurred thus:

Returning one day from Haddington, whither he had journeyed to receive his rents and sell some land, he chanced to meet at Manchester an old fellow-student, Meidinger of Heidelberg, who, stating he was going to see another fellow-student, resident near Liverpool, persuaded my father to travel with him to that town. When in due time the friend appeared at their hotel, he proved to be E. K. Muspratt, who most cordially invited George Harley to accompany Meidinger on a visit to Seaforth Hall, where his father lived. The young doctor was much surprised to find in the person of his host's daughter the girl whose name, recorded in the visitors' book at the Hôtel de la

Poste at Chiavenna, he had puzzled over—Emma Muspratt
—destined to alter his whole after-existence.

The romance of this unexpected meeting was, however,
somewhat spoiled by the fact of my father suddenly
remembering late at night that he had left the money
brought from Haddington in a satchel hanging behind his
bedroom door at the Liverpool hotel. This untoward act
of forgetfulness compelled him to leave Seaforth very early
next morning, for which reason he did not again see the
young lady till several months had passed, when they met
for the second time at the house of a well-known artist in
London.

Concerning the lost money, some reader may be interested
to know that, after driving along country lanes and a tract
of beautifully silver sandy shore at the mouth of the Mersey,
where now stand part of the Liverpool docks, my father
at a most unearthly hour sprang out of the gig which had
brought him from Seaforth and rushed up to his bedroom
in the hotel, where he found the satchel he had so carelessly
left with its contents intact! He used often to wonder in
after-life how he could have done such a stupid thing, and how
it happened the satchel had not been stolen by someone.

The incident afforded food for much badinage when the
young couple met again, and the acquaintanceship so
strangely begun soon ripened into friendship. George
Harley, the young London physician, often ran down to
Lancashire for a few days to enjoy the almost regal
hospitality vouchsafed by old James Muspratt, 'the father
of the chemical industry,' whose eldest son, Dr. Sheridan
Muspratt, was author of the well-known volumes, Muspratt's ' Dictionary of Chemistry.'

On the subject of my grandfather I quote the following,
from the *Chemical Trade Journal*, as his life was remarkable, apart from his being the founder of English chemical
industry :

Romance, adventure, and enterprise, are comprised in the career of
James Muspratt, who was the father of the alkali trade in this country.

He was born in Dublin on August 12, 1793; his father was an Englishman, whose brother was a director of the East India Com·pany; his mother, who was a remarkable woman of fine character and culture, was a Miss Mainwaring, one of the Cheshire family of that name. They resided in Dublin, and to a commercial school in that city sent their son. We picture the boy amongst his play·mates, a strong, broad-shouldered lad, one with whom one would not lightly choose to provoke a quarrel or encounter in a scuffle. His features were even more noticeable than his form; he had a high, broad brow, eyes well set and full of fire, large aquiline nose, and massive chin; it was a head indicating dogged determination, strong will, and quick, powerful intellect. In the classes he made his mark, excelling his companions in their studies, and winning prizes in many subjects. In these days scholarships and exhibitions would have fallen to his lot, and probably a distinguished University career; but in those days the boy of promise was early sent to engage in the battle of life, and at fourteen years of age he was taken from school and apprenticed to a Mr. Mitcheltree, a wholesale chemist and druggist, in Dublin, with whom he remained between three and four years. A chemist's laboratory would have many attractions for such a lad. Chemistry at that period retained much that still appealed to the imagination; it was not wholly divested of the mysterious and magical. The spirit of the old alchemist continued to move amongst its retorts and stills, its furnaces and phials. Experiments were made with the crudest apparatus, and there were no text-books that enabled it to be studied as an exact science. The youth rejoiced to devote what time he could spare to the study of such books as the ' Dictionary of Chemistry,' by Nicholson, and a translation of the works of Guyton de Morveau, and also to the making of experiments.

In the year 1810 he had the calamity to lose his father, and in the succeeding year his mother died. She had excited in him devoted love and veneration, and to his latest day her memory was sacred to him. Just before his father's death the young apprentice had for some cause quarrelled with his master, and was at home unoccupied when he lost his mother. An orphan, his heart heavy with grief, and his prospects darkened, the slight inheritance left him by his parents wasting away in Chancery proceedings, he was attracted by the excitement of a warrior's life, and determined to seek a career in the army. All Europe was at this time watching the exploits of Wellington and Napoleon in the Peninsula, and to this strife of heroes James Mus·pratt, full of strength and valour, went.

The cavalry of England had won much glory in these campaigns, and he was determined in it to obtain a cornetcy. But commissions in mounted regiments were retained for those favoured in high quarters, and Muspratt was only able to obtain the offer of a commission in the infantry. This he scorned to accept, but, still attracted by military and camp life, he followed in the wake of the troops.

Two or three days after July 22, 1812, he visited the bloody but glorious field of Salamanca, and during the next month or two was with his countrymen in Madrid. Wellington received the acclaims of the Madrilenos on August 12, on his triumphant entry into the capital. General Hill, to whose keeping he handed over the city, was compelled to retreat ten weeks later, and during that time the fever, which had hovered around the pathway of the armies and their halting-grounds, seized on young Muspratt. He received scarcely any care or attention of any sort, and had he not had a splendid constitution he must have succumbed to the disease.

Before he had risen from his sick-bed the city was full of tumult at the rapid approach of the French forces in overwhelming numbers, and a hurried retreat had to be made down the valley of the Tagus westward. Weak as he was, he determined not to fall a prisoner into the enemy's hands, and set out to follow the English, who had abandoned the city. It was then he accomplished the remarkable feat of walking 100 miles in two days, and made his way to Lisbon. His diary contains graphic accounts of the great hardships which he underwent; the history of that campaign relates how wretched was the state of the country, and how great were the sufferings of the troops and the inhabitants from hunger and sickness. Muspratt would gladly have got back again to his own country, and he hoped that at Lisbon he would find a vessel that would convey him home; but in this he was disappointed. Although his warlike longings had failed to be satisfied in the army, he succeeded in securing an appointment as midshipman in the navy, and in his ship, the *Impetueux*, he took part in the blockade of Brest, and was engaged in the chase of the United States frigate, the *Constitution*, the ship that vanquished the *Guerrière* in one of those celebrated naval duels.

He was promoted to rank of second officer in a smaller craft than the *Impetueux*, but the stern discipline and irksomeness of his post, accompanied, as was too often the case, with insult and humiliation, was intolerable to him, and he determined to desert. A comrade joined him in this resolve, which they carried out one dark night when the vessel lay in the Mumbles roadstead, off Swansea. The boatman who rowed them ashore only performed his perilous task under the terror of threats that if he did not do it they would throw him overboard. In this escapade these young fellows ran great risk of disgrace and death, for such would have been their fate had they failed. Not until the morning was their escape detected, and then pursuit was fruitless. The hard experiences through which he had passed had quenched the spirit for military adventure ; his ideas, derived from songs and romances, had proved illusions that faded amidst the stern realities of life. As soon as he could he made his way back from Wales to Ireland. His affairs were still in Chancery, and for the termination of the suit he was compelled to wait ; but little of the property that had been left him would come into his possession—the greater portion had been wasted in its passage through the court.

His literary and artistic tastes drew him during this period of leisure into the society of authors and actors. A young man, about twenty-one, of a romantic and adventurous turn such as he had shown himself to be, would be filled with enthusiastic admiration for a star of unusual brilliancy which at that time attracted great attention in the dramatic world.

As the name of this star was Miss O'Neill, the famous actress, the most beautiful woman of her day according to my grandfather, the following may be of interest :

In the year 1791, at Drogheda, was born Eliza O'Neill. Her father was an indigent stage-manager and actor. The pretty little child might often be seen running about the streets of the dirty town, barefooted. She was compelled, before she reached her teens, to appear upon the stage with her father, and when she was but twelve years of age she drew large houses, attracted by the charms of her acting. She was only a girl when she played the part of Juliet, in Dublin, which excited the greatest enthusiasm, and by the time she was one-and-twenty she inspired the line of a prologue :

' Then fair O'Neill ranks first on Britain's stage.'

Lord William Lennox wrote : ' She was loveliness personified ; her voice was the perfection of melody ; her manner graceful, impassioned, irresistible. In Lady Macbeth the Siddons was unrivalled ; while O'Neill, in her matchless representation of feminine tenderness as Juliet and Mrs. Haller, was faultless.' Her character was one of singular modesty and gentleness ; she ' wore the white flower of a blameless life.' She married, in 1819, William Wrixen-Beecher, M.P. for Mallow, who succeeded to a baronetcy, and the poor little maid of Drogheda became Lady Wrixen-Beecher. James Muspratt came under the spell of her beauty and genius, and, although only a young man, was honoured in being able to assist in bringing her before the fashionable Dublin circle. Probably it was at this time that he made the acquaintance of the youth who afterwards became his intimate friend—the humorous, pathetic, romantic, artistic, poetical Samuel Lover.

The man to whom he felt most drawn was James Sheridan Knowles, the celebrated dramatist, actor and scholar, whose gift of authorship dawned on him when a mere child, and who when he was but fourteen years old wrote the extremely popular ballad, ' The Welsh Harper.' The intimacy of this friendship is seen in the fact that James Muspratt named two of his sons, James Sheridan and Edmund Knowles, after him. These early friendships revealed traits of character and tastes which were strikingly developed in after-years. James Muspratt loved literature, especially romance, poetry, and the drama ; he highly appreciated the gifts of literary and scientific men, who found in him a worthy and congenial friend.

As soon as his small inheritance came into his hands he determined to use the knowledge he had acquired during the years he spent with the Dublin apothecary. He began by manufacturing a few simple chemicals, one of which was hydrochloric acid, but in the course of a short time he was joined by a Mr. Abbott, who put more money into the business, and then they made prussiate of potash, for which there was a good demand. He was the first to carry out the Leblanc process on a large scale. He would now be a young man of about five-and-twenty.

John Tennant, the father of Sir Charles Tennant, and my grandfather were at one time partners in some sulphur-mines in Sicily. After they had spent large sums of money in developing the mines, the King of Sicily put a duty of £4 per ton on all sulphur exported, except what was exported by a French company. This led to the stoppage of the English mines, and owing to a rush of water into the works, it was found unremunerative to start them again. The English Government (Palmerston being Foreign Minister) complained that the different treatment of the French company's exports was an infraction of the favoured nation clause in the treaties with England, and sent the English fleet to Naples to bring the King to his senses. The duty was then levied on all sulphur exported, but in the meantime Tennant and Muspratt began to use pyrites in the place of sulphur, owing to the high price of the latter ; and as the reopening of the mines required more capital, they parted with them, having found a substitute.

Half a century afterwards we find the sons of these two men president and vice-president of the great Alkali Union ! '

The cause of education found in James Muspratt an ardent promoter ; himself such a lover of books and reading, knowing the priceless value of knowledge, he did great service to the cause of popular instruction by the work which he and his friends, James Mulleneux and George Holt, accomplished in connection with the Mechanics' Institute in Liverpool. The work of mechanics' institutes became somewhat obsolete, and this institution was transformed into an ordinary public school—the Liverpool Institute—which to-day ranks among the first schools of the class in the land.

In politics he was no less enthusiastic. He was a thoroughgoing Liberal, one of the earliest supporters of the Anti-Corn Law movement. His Free Trade principles were so strong that even when his own manufacture of prussiate of potash was threatened by German competition, and those in the same trade in this country were agitating for Protection, he protested with scorn against such action ; if they could not hold their own they deserved to be beaten, and the consumer had the right to buy in the cheapest market.

He was fond of Continental travel, and at times took up his residence in Giessen and Munich, to enjoy the companionship of Baron Liebig and of the scientific circle in which he moved. He also travelled with his own carriage through Greece and Italy. He was gifted with an extraordinary memory, which was enriched with an extensive and accurate knowledge of the best English poetry ; even in his eightieth year he could repeat the whole of Goldsmith's ' Traveller ' and ' The Deserted Village.' Those who were the companions of his travels remember how he would repeat whole cantos of ' Childe Harold ' and Rogers' ' Italy.'

James Muspratt probably inherited his love of travel and adventure from his great-uncle, Captain Denham, who went the first voyage round the world with the famous Captain Cook. My great-great-great-uncle's coat and sword are, I believe, reposing in a glass case at the Greenwich Hospital.

The article continues :

His extensive reading, romantic adventures, and social tastes made him a delightful companion. He gathered round him in his home at Seaforth a circle of literary and artistic friends, as well as comrades with whom he had fought hard battles for the social and political progress of the people. Many a young artist found in James Muspratt a true and generous patron. He was an intense admirer of the sculptor's as well as the painter's art. It was his design to have made a collection which would have illustrated the progress of English art during the first fifty years of the century; but this he was prevented from achieving. How he would have rejoiced to have seen how splendidly his idea was carried out in the Manchester Jubilee Exhibition of 1887!

He had in his own collection some very valuable pictures; he greatly admired Linton's landscapes, and he possessed Sir George Harvey's ' Battle of Drumclog.'

He died when he was ninety-three years of age, at his home, Seaforth Hall, near Liverpool, on Tuesday, May 4, 1886, and was buried in the parish churchyard of Walton. In him there passed away from the stage of life a remarkable man, who had acted many parts. Physically and mentally he was robust. We have seen how his strong constitution bore him through the dangers and hardships of his youth, and enabled him to battle bravely through his stormy business career. Strength was his great trait—*ein kräftiger Mann;* he signalized himself by strength of body, by strength of intellect, by strength of purpose, and not unfrequently by strength of expression. He was a man of strong emotions as well as deep convictions. He was a character long to be remembered, bold, daring, impetuous, self-willed, and restless; a man to cherish as a friend, to dread as a foe. He believed in progress, realized that ' knowledge was power '; was ever ready to utilize talent and invention; literature was his delight, and men of letters his boon associates and companions. The mark he left upon the trade, which he did so much to found and to build up, was not that of an inventor; he will not be remembered as an eminent chemist or engineer, but as a man of unusual energy, of keen perception, of indomitable perseverance, and of far-seeing enterprise, and such men have been large contributors to the greatness of their country as well as to the fortunes of their families.

As will be seen from the foregoing, old James Muspratt's house was a centre of light and learning, and therefore when the two celebrated American actresses, Charlotte and Susan Cushman, came over to England, it seemed quite natural for them to bring introductions to the hospitable home at Seaforth Hall, so near their landing-place. At this time Charlotte Cushman was well known as the greatest tragedienne of her day. She had created an enormous sensation as Lady Macbeth, as Queen Catherine, and such-like parts. In the ' Life of Charlotte Cushman,' by Miss Stebbins, we find the following :

By the packet of the 10th I wrote you a few lines and sent a lot of newspapers, which could tell you in so much better language than I could of my brilliant and triumphant success in London (1845). I can say no more to you than this : that it is far, far beyond my most sanguine expectations. In my most ambitious moments I never dreamed of the success which has awaited me and crowned every effort I have made. To you I should not hesitate to tell *all* my grief and all my failure if it had been such, for no one could have felt more with me and for me. Why, then, should I hesitate (unless through a fear that I might seem egotistical) to tell you all my triumphs, all my suc- cesses ? Suffice it, *all my successes put together since I have been upon the stage* would not come near my success in London ; and I only wanted some one of you here to enjoy it with me to make it complete.

In the next letter, dated March 28, we see she is reaping the full measure of her success, not only publicly, but socially.

I have been so crowded with company (she says) since I have acted, that upon my word and honour I am almost sick of it. Invitations pour in for every night that I do not act, and all the day I have a steady stream of callers ; so that it has become a joke among my more particular friends that I am never with less than six people in the room ; and I am so tired when it comes time for me to go to the theatre that Sallie [her famous black servant] has to hold my cup of tea for me to drink it.

It seems almost exaggerated, this account ; but indeed you would laugh if you could see the way in which I am besieged, and if you could see the heaps of complimentary letters and notes you would be amused. All this, as you may imagine, reconciles me more to England, and now I think I might be willing to stay longer. If my family were only with me I think I could be content. Sergeant Tal- fourd has promised to write a play for me by next year. I have played Bianca four times, Emilia twice, Lady Macbeth six times, Mrs. Haller five, and Rosalind five, in five weeks. I am sitting to five artists. So you may see I am very busy. I hesitate to write even to you the agreeable and complimentary things that are said and done to me here, for it looks monstrously like boasting. I like you to know it, but I hate to tell it to you myself.

That was in 1845. So successful were these performances that Miss Cushman opened her second engagement
in London at the Haymarket Theatre on December 30 of
the same year, and then it was that she and her beautiful
sister Susan made their first appearance together in
Shakespeare's tragedy of ' Romeo and Juliet.' They acted
the play according to the original version of Shakespeare,
and so wonderful was the performance of these two women
—the Juliet a most beautiful girl—that they gave upwards
of eighty representations in London alone, in those days a
most remarkable feat.

Charlotte Cushman, although such a marvellous actress,
was a very plain woman; but her sister was, I have heard
my father say, one of the most beautiful visions ever seen.
Her graceful charm as Juliet aroused the enthusiasm of all
London. Then it was that my uncle, Sheridan Muspratt
(author of Muspratt's ' Dictionary of Chemistry '), fell in
love with this fascinating creature, and in March, 1848, he
married the celebrated Susan Cushman, who then retired
from the stage.

The theatrical world is often so misunderstood that I
venture here to quote a letter from the great Charlotte to
my aunt, Mrs. Sheridan Muspratt, on the death of her
youngest child, Ida, for it shows the love of these two
women and the trust in a higher Power of the woman who
was dazzling the theatrical world with her brilliant performance :

I grieve from my heart, dear Sue, for all your sadness and depression; but can you not think that God's will is best—that perhaps you
needed something to draw you nearer to heaven, and so this best and
purest and dearest was taken to remind you that only such can enter
into the kingdom of heaven in all its purity, and that your whole aim
must be to fit yourself to be able to join her there ? That the taking
away of this lovely child was for some good and wise purpose, though
through our earthly eyes we cannot recognise it, we are bound in
humble confidence to trust and believe; and in striving more to do
God's will, in aiming for a more truly Christian life, we shall show
that we feel His wisdom and power, and are willing to bow unto it,

eager only to be fitted to rejoin her at the last. How hard it would be to die, if we had all the joys and happiness that we could desire here! The dews of autumn penetrate into the leaves and prepare them for their fall. But for the dews of sorrow upon the heart, we should never be prepared for the sickle of the destroyer. And so does God wean us from this world by taking what we love most to His world; and the purer He takes them, the nearer are they to His glorious presence, the more blessed and blessing angels, who ever see His face. Could you wish her back from this? Could you be willing that she should ever know again the chances of such suffering as you witnessed in her little agonized frame? No, I am sure not; and if one of God's angels should give you the choice, you would say with uplifted hands: ' Keep her, O God, from the suffering and sorrow she knew even in her little life; keep her ever near Thee!' And you must try not to grieve too deeply, for sorrow in such a case is almost rebellion. Feel, as you kneel to God morning and night, that it is her spirit which takes you there, and ever mediates between you and Him. That you will and must miss her is most certain, and this will be wherever you may be situated. Even I, who saw so little of her, never think of any of you without missing her smile and pretty ways. How much more, then, must you! But if you suffer it to be a means of bringing you nearer to God and to heaven, you will find in time that it will prove a tender rather than a harrowing sorrow, and you will be indeed saying: ' Thy will be done.' I know it seems almost folly in me to attempt to write you upon such a subject, but I have felt so much—do feel so much for you in it—that I must say what little I can to induce you not to despond, and to trust to a higher Power than we can understand, but who ordains everything for our good, and who chastens in love and merciful kindness.

The beautiful Susan did not live very long; she died in May, 1859. But by that time she had endeared herself to all the family.

Charlotte Cushman remained ever welcome in London society. Although a big plain woman in reality, she had a certain fascination, especially when she began to talk, for her conversation was always interesting. She, too, had a marvellous power when she sang, and, no matter how animated the conversation might be, when she began to sing silence reigned, and in spite of her want of voice—she herself called it ' declaiming the music '—every heart was

10

stirred when she repeated Kingsley's well-known song
' Call the Cattle Home.'   It was most thrilling.

In those days one of the most welcome guests everywhere,
and another constant visitor at Seaforth Hall, was jovial,
round-faced Samuel Lover, a typical Irishman in appearance and manners, kind-hearted and genial, and apparently
without a care or trouble in the world, although he had
many, one being the death in early womanhood of a clever
and dearly-beloved daughter.   Even my father's non-
musical soul was stirred to enthusiasm when Lover went
to the piano and sang ' The Angel's Whisper,' ' The Four-
leaved Shamrock,' ' Molly Bawn,' or ' The Low-backed Car,'
the gems of his creation.   In the most crowded drawing-
room as soon as he began to sing silence reigned, and
people were moved to tears or to laughter; this was all
the more marvellous because he really had no voice, yet
for years he riveted the attention of the public, for he
gave entertainments by himself in Great Britain and
America from his own writings which were most successful.
Some people preferred his entertainments to those of
Charles Mathews (the elder), who was the first to provide
any amusement of the kind, which has since been so successfully followed by John Parry, Corney Grain, and George
Grossmith.

Samuel Lover was a wonderful miniature painter; he did
one of Paganini, quite a work of art, which is in the possession
of my uncle, E. K. Muspratt, at the old house at Seaforth,
who has several other beautiful miniatures by this gifted
Irishman, besides busts of Sheridan Knowles, Charlotte
Cushman, Charles Dickens, etc., which were executed for my
grandfather and greatly valued by him.

Thomas Moore, the poet, was another of this little
coterie, while James Sheridan Knowles, as mentioned in a
former page, was a great friend of my grandfather's; indeed,
several of his plays were partly written at Seaforth Hall,
among them ' The Hunchback.'

James Sheridan Knowles, the lexicographer, was a short,

thick-set man with a remarkably handsome face and penetrating eyes ; he possessed the most marvellous spirits ;
indeed, when in a frolicsome mood he was like a schoolboy out for a holiday, and proved most excellent company, full of anecdotes, which he related with the keenest
pleasure.   In his youth, when he studied medicine, he was
befriended by Hazlitt the elder, who introduced him to
Coleridge and Lamb ; then he took to the stage, played
Hamlet and Macbeth, ' badly, badly,' as my poor old grandfather used to say, and at Macready's suggestion wrote the
drama ' William Tell,' the success of which soon made him
famous as a dramatist.

Unfortunately, he outlived his youthful spirit, and when
my grandfather used to relate many amusing tales of him,
my father could hardly believe he was speaking of the
same man he met frequently in London society, where his
marvellous personal appearance attracted universal attention.   Instead, however, of being the jovial, happy boy
described by Mr. Muspratt, he had changed into a melancholy, morbid man, with a very theological mind.   Sheridan
Knowles was one of the original committee formed to
purchase Shakespeare's birthplace at Stratford-on-Avon, of
which he was ultimately offered the custodianship.

It was into this interesting circle the young Harley
Street physician entered when he went to claim his bride
at Seaforth Hall.

CHAPTER XII.

AN UNCONVENTIONAL WEDDING-TOUR.

GEORGE HARLEY'S was a happy life, one so full that there lacked but the magic of domesticity to complete its bliss.

Small wonder therefore he writes, shortly after taking 77, Harley Street, with that brevity which distinguishes so many of his important utterances :

' Like most men who have arrived so far as to possess a house of his own, I began to wish to transform it into a home, and for this purpose on April 4, 1861, married Emma Jessie, youngest daughter of James Muspratt, of Seaforth Hall, near Liverpool. The wedding took place in Sefton Church, where the ceremony was performed by the Rev. Thomas Williams, then Incumbent of Flint. We went for our honeymoon first to Paris, then to Lyons, then to Marseilles, skirted along all the towns of the South of France, from Toulon to Perpignan, then over the Pyrenees to Figueras, "and so," as Pepys would have said, to Gerona and Barcelona.'

That must have been a delightful time of travel, when Hope and Joy journeyed with them, when amongst their luggage not a hidden anxiety concerning the future crossed any frontier, when ' all the world was still so young ' it seemed as though neither sorrow nor death could ever enter their Eden. The manuscript goes on to say :

' Next to Valencia by steamer ; then by rail to Madrid viâ
Almanza and Albaceta ; visited Toledo, the Escurial ; then
across the Quadarrama Mountains to Valladolid, Burgos,
Vitoria, Tolosa, and out of Spain ; back again over the
Pyrenees to St. Sebastian ; from there to Bayonne, Bordeaux,
and Tours to Paris, whence we returned home just in time
for me to begin my medical jurisprudence lectures the next
morning at ten o'clock.'

How different was travelling in Spain in those days from
what it is now that railways have made it easy!

' Diligence travelling in Spain,' says my father, ' differed
a vast deal from diligence travelling in any other country
in Europe.

' When my wife and I went to Spain in 1861 for our
wedding-tour, we entered the country by diligence at the
southern end of the Pyrenees, travelled right through its
very centre, and bade adieu to the country in a diligence
at the northern part of the Pyrenees, so that I am in a
tolerably favourable position to give a correct idea of *ye
habits, manners, and customs of ye Spanish diligences.*

' A Spanish diligence differs in no marked degree from
the various members of its species met with in France,
Germany, or Switzerland, save in one particular ; but that
particular is a very curious one, consisting as it does in the
nature and number of the cattle by which it is drawn.
Mules are in Spain used instead of horses, with the result
that from thirteen to twenty animals are employed at a
time instead of four or six.

' Our first journey was from Perpignan in France to
Figueras in Spain. Nothing noteworthy occurred on the
journey across the Pyrenees, but when we reached Figueras,
much as I had read of the fortress being underground, I
felt greatly surprised at being challenged by a sentry at its
gates before I was even aware we were near a fortified city.
Figueras has stabling for 500 horses under the ground, but,
as my French guide-book to Spain informed me, the most
curious feature in this quite impregnable fortress is " that

during the time of peace it is always held by the Spanish, while during the time of war it is invariably in the hands of the French." Such a cruel cut at the Spanish nation makes one wonder that this French guide-book is ever permitted to cross the frontier.

'By diligence we journeyed to Gerona, and thence to Barcelona, and the thing that struck me as most curious on the road was that the rivers we passed which contained no water (it was the middle of a nice dry April) were invariably spanned by bridges, while those where the stream was deep enough to touch our animals' girths had no bridges whatever. This was no doubt due to a *lusus naturæ*, thoroughly Spanish.

'Another thing that struck me about Spanish diligence travelling was when we crossed the Guadarrama Mountains, on our way from Madrid to Valladolid—we had fifteen mules and two horses in the traces. The horses, being docile, were used as wheelers. Spite of all this traction power, however, we seldom exceeded a speed of six miles an hour.

'To manage this wondrous team, we had a driver sitting on the box, and a little wiry chap of a postilion, who varied his amusements by running alongside the mules, occasionally riding on one of their backs, but more frequently sitting perched like a monkey beneath the driver's footboard. His erratic movements, associated as they were with a succession of noises, emanating chiefly from his powerful lungs, but partly from the energetic cracking of his whip, proved an unceasing source of amusement to me. Seated as we (my wife, Sir Edward Baker, and myself) were in the coupé, I saw and heard almost the whole programme of our versatile friend's accomplishments. When running alongside, he was generally yelling " Ar-re ! ar-re !" at the top of his voice. " Ar-re !" is the word which all Spanish muleteers employ when urging on their teams ; hence the common name for a muleteer in Spain is an *arrieros*. The origin of this cry " Ar-re !" is very ancient, and probably

Asiatic. Sir Emerson Tennant, in his "Wild Elephant,"
says that the mahouts in Ceylon direct the movements of
elephants by modulations of the words "Ur-re, ur-re,"
while the drivers of camels in Turkey, Palestine, and
Egypt encourage them to speed by shouting "Ar-re!
ar-re!" exactly the same words that are used by the
Spanish muleteers, which probably were carried into
Spain from the East by the Moors, who, I believe, call
"Ar-rak!" to their camels and asses.

'The guttural "Ar-r-re!" of our postilion was something
never to be forgotten when heard by ears previously unaccustomed to such an unusual burst of sound. When not
entirely engrossed with the on-goings of his "chickens," as
he jocularly called his hybrids, our friend would occasionally deign to crack a joke, instead of his whip, at the head
of one of the road-repairers as we passed along; but that
was but seldom, his attention being, as a rule, devoted to
his stubborn mules. The driver did but little more than
hold the reins, and occasionally crack his long whip, which
sounded feeble when compared with the pistol-shots of our
postilion's fourteen-inch-handle battering machine. My
word! he did make the sides of some of those mules ring
out a formidable note, when the thong was thoroughly
applied to them. The echo was distinctly audible to our
ears in the coupé.

'That postilion was indeed a wonderful fellow! He
seemed to live without either sleep or food. From the
time we left Madrid till we reached Bayonne, he never
to my knowledge, had a moment's rest, except once, when
he fell asleep on the top of a sack of corn, laid across the
under-carriage immediately below the footboard of the box-
seat. That half-hour's sleep served him during the three
days and three nights we occupied on the journey.

'Spain in 1861 was a troubled country. The men
employed in repairing the roads beyond fifty miles from
Madrid were all provided with a military musket, which
we invariably saw lying in company with their coats and

dinner-cans at the side of the road; and while crossing the
Guadarrama Mountains we met patrols of police every few
miles both night and day. Notwithstanding these precau-
tions, the very diligence in which we were travelling had
been stopped and robbed by banditti just three weeks
before our never-to-be-forgotten journey.

'It was the very end of April when we crossed the
Guadarrama, and we had been indulging in green peas and
strawberries at Barcelona; yet the cold at night was so
intense we could scarcely keep ourselves from freezing,
although the coupé windows were closed, and we huddled
together like sheep under our rugs. The vapour of our
breath was frozen into hard flakes of ice on the glass, and
truly thankful did we feel, when the mountains were passed,
to find ourselves once more snug on the lowlands.

'On entering Spain, we were much struck with the
difference between French and Spanish soldiers, the former
in those days being smart, polite, and thoroughly military-
looking men, while the latter were a slouching, dirty set of
fellows, who did not seem to know what courtesy and
politeness meant.

'In many of the small towns the houses consisted of
only one room, divided by a curtain, behind which, we
presumed, the family slept. Hardly any of these dwellings
boasted any glass in the windows, which were either open
spaces or papered over, in which latter case the only light
admitted was through the doorway, which, however, was
very large.

'I am not going to trace our route from Valladolid to
Burgos, from Burgos to Vitoria, from Vitoria to Tolosa;
all I want to record is the journey by the diligence, so
that I must at once take a great leap to the Pyrenees—
not, however, back to the Pyrénées-Orientales, but forward
to the Basses Pyrénées, by which we returned from Spain
to *la belle France* again. Well may I call her *la belle,* for
from the time I left her till I saw her fair face once more I
never had a dinner! What with garlic, stinking fish, and

pigskin wine, I say advisedly I never had a dinner the whole time I was in Spain, except at Barcelona when I entered it, and at St. Sebastian when I left it—two places sufficiently near France to have acquired some knowledge of civilized cookery.

' After this little digression on feeding, let me return to the diligence and the Pyrenees. One part of the hills was so steep that, although we had by that time *nineteen* animals in the traces, seventeen mules and two horses, they could not drag the vehicle up to the top, and had all to be unyoked, except the two wheelers, and replaced by no less than eight pairs of oxen. These were driven by eight men, one to each pair, and urged on by goads, sharply-pointed long sticks. The oxen did not draw from the collar, as horses and mules do ; they pushed from the head, against a bar of wood placed across the brow of each pair, a chain to draw by being wound round the roots of the horns, and attached to the middle of the bar just mentioned. Their draught was slow, but sure, and hard they seemed to work, notwithstanding that they had little to pull save the diligence and the luggage, for all the passengers alighted and walked up the terrific hill.

' When we reached Bayonne, after having spent three days and nights in the coupé, we were all glad to anchor ourselves in " blanket bay." We were literally black and blue from the joltings, and, although our postilion assured me he was not tired, I am certain he felt thankful to lay his active head on a pillow.'

Food at the hotels in those days was, as a rule, something too dreadful, and the travellers were almost famished, since, with the exception of bread and chocolate, it was well-nigh impossible to swallow anything set before them. Bread was excellent everywhere, however, and the chocolate would have been, too, had it not been made quite thick like a paste, in which the spoon stood up straight, and it was served with a tumbler of cold water, the idea being to take a spoonful of hot chocolate, and then sip some cold water.

The meat was atrocious, and in Madrid quite putrid. This, however, was evidently considered a delicacy, for when my father complained about it to some Spaniards, they remarked : 'We treat our meat as you do game; you keep that till it is " high " before cooking.'

Fish it was simply a necessity to eat tainted, or not at all, for it had to be brought on the backs of mules over the wide plain which surrounds Madrid.

Taste is a queer sense, and almost entirely dependent on education. When George I. came to England, he ordered oysters as a great treat for dinner when he landed. They were brought to him, and he ate one, smelt the rest, then, putting them aside, said : 'Es sind nicht richte Austern, sie stinken nicht.' He was accustomed to them so 'high' that he found fresh oysters tasteless !

But to an Englishman the drop which filled his cup of misery to overflowing was that everything tasted of garlic —everything, even the eggs. This was dreadful, and my father formed a grand theory that all the fowls in Spain were fed on garlic. Years afterwards, however, at a large dinner-party given by Sir Rowland Hill, when he was expounding this theory, one of the Secretaries of the Spanish Embassy politely interposed :

'No, no, monsieur! the hens are not fed on garlic at all.'

' Then, how does it happen that the eggs taste of garlic ?'

' Oh, it is all the cook.'

' Nonsense ! the cook can't get inside an egg.'

' No, no, monsieur; but the cook takes a piece of garlic and rubs it on his hands, then he take the egg and rub it in his hand, then he pop it in the pot very quick, and the garlic go into the egg.'

Thus, to my father's great regret, his grand theory was dispelled.

Concerning Toledo, a most interesting place, which, as
we know, he purposely visited, because of a boyish resolve
to see from where the old Toledo blade in the garret in
Haddington had come, he says :

'It is a strange, queer old town ; the streets so narrow,
the shops so small, and with no windows, only a single
opening, which has to serve for window as well as door.
We went into one of these small shops, wishing to buy a
genuine Toledo knife ; but what was our amazement, when
the shopman showed us his best knives, to find on them
the name of Rogers!

'Unfortunately, it turned out a wet afternoon, so we could
not walk about much, since in the streets not only did we
have the benefit of the rain, but also that of the water-
pipes from the house-tops ; for here, as in many Spanish
towns, a water-spout projects into the middle of the road,
and from this spout, when it rains, there pours a perfect
stream of water, which it is impossible to escape, the
streets are so narrow.

'We were fortunate to see a performance of "Don
Quixote" at the principal theatre in Madrid. On each
anniversary of the birth of Cervantes this famous romance
is acted by the first actresses and actors in Spain, who
consider it a great honour to be invited to take part in the
celebration. The play was most admirably mounted, and
the acting excellent. Sancho Panza was Sancho himself,
and the Rosinante was perfection ; wherever and however
such a horse could be produced was a mystery. Although
so many years have passed since the romance was written,
yet the Spain of to-day is in many ways identical with the
Spain Cervantes describes—just as primitive, just as unique.
It is utterly different from any other country. The finale
was exceedingly pretty and characteristic. At the conclusion of the play the curtain was again drawn up, and
the author's statue stood alone on the stage, when each of
the actors came in procession and laid a laurel wreath on

the marble statue, the greatest actor and actress in Spain reading an address to Cervantes.'

The young couple had many charming introductions, and thoroughly enjoyed Madrid society for a few weeks.

'The Professor of Chemistry in the University of Madrid,' writes my father, 'was an old friend of my wife, and anxious to show us the real home life in Spain, therefore it was arranged we should visit his house one evening when they were *chez soi*, which proved a primitive but most hospitable entertainment. We were invited for " tea," so had dinner at six, and arrived at the house about eight. When we were assembled in the drawing-room, the eldest daughter, a girl of twelve, played the piano beautifully, after which her younger sister danced a minuet very prettily. At 9.30 we were summoned to the dining-room, where the cloth indeed was laid, but nothing appeared on the table except wine-glasses, and in the centre an enormous tray piled high with cakes of every description. Presently plates were handed to each person and immediately filled with cakes, then came chocolate with its usual accompaniment—cold water—afterwards various kinds of ices, which were followed by a number of delicious sweets, creams of all sorts, candied fruits, and lastly a quantity of various fresh fruits. We were perfectly over-whelmed with the abundance of good things, and our kind host and hostess seemed quite distressed because we could not eat of every dish. Even after this " tea " or supper, when some extra fine wine was produced from the cellar, and our host found we really could not touch anything more, he said :

' " Well, I will send some of these trifles to the hotel to-morrow morning, so you can take them with you *en voyage*."

' Accordingly, when we were sitting at breakfast, a large clothes-basket was brought for *Madame*, containing the remnants of the feast, which we packed into the coupé of

the diligence.   Just as we were about to drive away, however, up rushed our kind friend with a bottle of wine under
each arm and an immense spray of oranges in his hands,
which he thrust through the window, calling out, " Bon
voyage !"

'How thankful we were for his generous thoughtfulness
during the next two days no one can imagine who has
not travelled across Spain in the long ago.'

A most interesting place, and one which my father often
described, was the Escorial.   This is what he says about it :
' The Escorial is in its way quite unique.   To see that vast
pile of palace, monastery, and church surrounded by small
gardens, chiefly composed of beds of box about 2 feet high,
fantastically cut into all kinds of shapes, is most extraordinary.   It stands in the midst of a great bleak plain,
which looks a very region of desolation ; for outside the
royal domain not even a tree can be seen for miles—
nothing but rugged rocks and mountains, those in the
background being tipped with snow.

' The church is gigantic, gray, and sombre, and near to
the high altar is the room of Philip II., the room which
was his study and where he died—the man who boasted he
could govern the whole world from that small chamber at
the foot of a mountain !

' So wild is the surrounding country, that when out
walking early one morning I came across a young wolf,
which stared at me, but happily retreated on my remaining
perfectly still and staring back at him.   He could not have
been very hungry, or he would not have retired so quietly.
Later in the day we picked up the tail of a wolf just on the
outskirts of the town.

' Some horrible cases of brigandage were told in all
places, especially at Toledo, where the dreary mountains
have served from time immemorial as fastnesses for
highwaymen and criminals of the worst type.   We ac-
counted ourselves very fortunate, for we were not once
attacked.'

Thus the subject of this memoir returned to London with the fairest of prospects before him. He was strong and well, happy and contented, possessed a charming wife, and was the owner of a comfortable home and small private income. He had a keen desire to alleviate the sufferings of mankind, to improve modern science, and to simplify all roads to the diagnosis of disease and its eventual cure.

CHAPTER XIII.

THE CONSULTANT.

AFTER the pleasant house in Harley Street had been thus completely transformed into a delightful *home*, consultations fell more frequently to the young doctor's lot.

'No stray patients ever knocked at my door, notwithstanding the name-plate,' he states frankly; 'all came in consultation with doctors who knew my work, yet every month seemed to double the number seen in the preceding one.'

'I continued,' he goes on, 'to work at the college and publish the results of my scientific researches, but the mere reporting of medical cases in the journals was a practice I despised. Yet the journals far preferred medical cases to scientific truths, however startling the latter might be.

'For ten years I went on collecting the outcome of hard labour in my medical field, before I printed a single case, and no doubt this occasionally stood in my way a little, but I did not mind that.

'For example, I read at different times three scientific medical papers at the Royal Medico-Chirurgical Society, none of which appeared in their Transactions; they were too scientific, I suppose, although I considered one sufficiently important afterwards to publish in the form of a book, while another was thought so good by the Royal

College of Surgeons as to merit the award of their fifty-guinea triennial prize.

' On the other hand, after sending in the report of a case on intermittent hæmaturia, which required but a modicum of brains to work out, the Royal Medico-Chirurgical Society deemed it sufficiently meritorious to find a place in their Transactions !'

During the holidays in the autumn after their marriage, George Harley and his wife went on a visit to Baron Justus von Liebig, the great German chemist, who accorded them a warm welcome.

Curiously enough, it was during the time Emma Muspratt, when a girl, was staying at his house that he made his wonderful discovery of the soup which has since saved the lives of so many. It happened in this wise : She was attacked by typhoid fever, at that time very prevalent in Munich, and when the crisis was passed, Dr. Pfeuffer, who had much experience in such cases, said to Liebig :

' Now I can do nothing more—our dear invalid must die.'

' How so ?   If, as you say, the crisis is past, surely now she will recover !'

' By no means ; the crisis is past, but exhaustion has set in and its progress cannot be stopped, because in such cases the stomach is unable to digest food : assimilation is impossible, and thus exhaustion kills.'

Baron von Liebig was in despair, not only because he was fond of his guest, but because he felt how dreadful it was that one in early girlhood, who had been left in his charge when her parents returned to England, should die in his house. This feeling haunted him for hours. He paced up and down his laboratory in despair. His wife and daughter Nannie added to his misery by imploring him to do ' something to save the English girl's life.'

All at once it dawned upon him that if food could be artificially digested by some means before being taken into the stomach it might supply the necessary want. It was late—too late to begin the experiment that night; but he could not rest, and up and down, up and down, he paced, thinking out all the pros and cons, and considering every detail of his new experiment. At early dawn he sent out for a chicken and started his work; he himself minced it, pounded and prepared it most carefully, weighing out every gramme, then added a few drops of hydrochloric acid, which practically digested the meat in a short space of time. Then in a perfect fever of excitement, for verily the patient was sinking, he administered the product at intervals, one teaspoonful at a time.

Happily it had the desired effect (see Liebig's letters on Chemistry), and his visitor gradually recovered. Thus my mother was the person for whose benefit this wonderful discovery was made.

But at the time poor Liebig passed through a terrible ordeal. All Munich knew of the illness of the English girl, and the papers, taking the subject up, said it was a dreadful thing that even a friend staying under the scientist's roof was not safe from his experiments. Fortunately, Dr. Pfeuffer, who carried out the treatment, saw the marvellous results it produced. Thus the idea of digested food for such serious cases first originated, as Liebig himself wrote to my mother years afterwards :

'Your illness, which at the time was the cause of such grief and sorrow to us, has indeed been turned into a blessing, for not only have many lives been since saved by your soup, but just lately our dear Agnes, who, as you know, has had a very bad and long illness, has lived on your soup alone for twelve months. It has saved her life, as it did yours.'

This soup led to the further discovery of the world-wide renowned 'Liebig's Extractum Carnis,' which has now so many imitators.

During that visit my father realized what his wife had so often described to him—the charm of Liebig's society.

11

To him it was particularly fascinating, for he felt that he was ever learning something. The delightful chats when the Professor was propounding some difficult problem which was then baffling him were most interesting, and as the doctor sat riveted in attention he felt the fascination of Liebig's deep penetrating eyes.

The house seemed to be ever thronged with more or less interesting people, for in those days no one of any standing went to Munich without going to Liebig's hospitable home; and all her old friends in Munich hastened to call on the 'Frau Professerin,' as they called my mother.

Next door lived the Thierschs; the old gentleman was then very feeble, but still interested in seeing old friends, and gave my father a kindly greeting; his son Carl had married Liebig's second daughter, Johanna (Nannie), and they were on a visit to the old people. Thus my mother was again with her dear friend Nannie Liebig, and the girlhood love remained as tender in the newly-married wives.

Herr Geheimrath Professor Carl Thiersch ultimately became one of the most distinguished surgeons in Germany, and was at one time Rector of the University of Leipzig. Many years after this, when I was about sixteen, I went to stay with the Thierschs in Leipzig for six months, and thus the friendship descended to the third generation. And as I write visits have even been interchanged by the fourth generation between these friends!

Ludwig Thiersch, another member of this distinguished family, who had just finished some frescoes in the Pinakothek, greeted the young couple most warmly.

Geibel, the poet, with his young wife, gave them a most cordial welcome, as also Kobell, the mineralogist and poet in Bavarian dialect, who wrote the following lines in English without any correction to my mother:

TO MISS EMMA.

I never in my life forget
    A girl like a star—
So splendid looking and so fine,
    And now like him so far.

I praise the waves of Liverpool,
    Which see her every day;
I praise the air which bright and fresh
    Can find to her the way.

And going on the chamois-chase,
    I often think with pain
That all the rocks are not so high
    Of her a view to gain.

It was a most enjoyable time, and Liebig and his wife
were filled with delight at this pleasant reunion. Time
fled all too quickly, and promises were made that the visit
should soon be repeated; but, alas! it never was, and
years afterwards, in 1890, when my father and mother
again saw Munich, all those dear friends had passed away;
even the very house that Liebig lived in was pulled down.

In the early sixties the great chemist took life easily, for
his greatest work was done; indeed, from the time he left
Giessen he rested on his oars and enjoyed his days, but
during the time he was in that town he worked incessantly.
It is said that at one time when doing some great research
he was so interested he never left his laboratory for many
days. His food was taken to him there, and he lay on
the sofa at intervals to have a few hours' sleep, but after
he went to Munich he never worked so hard. His mornings were spent in the laboratory, but as a rule he gave
up the afternoons to recreation. There was nothing he
enjoyed more than the society of young people; he would
enter into all their pursuits and pleasures with the greatest
zest, and his one great recreation was a game of whist in
the evening. He was an excellent whist-player, his splendid
memory standing him in good stead, and, although he never

11—2

lost his temper if defeated, he was most triumphant when he won, and went off to bed quite happy !

My father was very busy on his return from Munich. Again quoting from the obituary notice in the *Lancet*, we read :

At the request of his friend the late Frank Buckland, Dr. George Harley published in the *Field* a paper entitled 'A Dead Heart Pulsating,' in which he showed how the physiologist has the power of producing the wonderful sight of a dead heart in a living body by means of antiar (the arrow poison of the Bornese), as well as a living heart in a dead body by means of wourali poison (the arrow poison of the Guianese).

During the year 1862 Dr. Harley communicated to the Royal Medical and Chirurgical Society an elaborate paper on 'The Pathology and Treatment of Jaundice,' which showed that jaundice was not, as it had hitherto been supposed to be, a disease, but only a mere symptom, like pain, of many widely differing pathological conditions. The advanced views Dr. Harley then enunciated have been adopted by every subsequent writer on diseases of the liver. It was in this year also that he had awarded to him by the Royal College of Surgeons of England its triennial prize of 50 guineas for his dissertation on 'The Anatomy and Physiology of the Suprarenal Bodies.' He was likewise an active member of the committee appointed by the Royal Medical and Chirurgical Society to study the subject of suspended animation by drowning, hanging, etc., the experiments for which were made in his laboratory at University College. At the meeting of the British Association at Cambridge, in 1862, he read the results of an elaborate investigation into the post-mortem appearances met with in animals slowly poisoned by daily minute doses of arsenic; also a paper on 'Ozone and Antozone,' exhibiting a rare form of fluorspar (given to him by Professor Baron von Liebig), possessing the extraordinary property of emitting a strong odour of hypochlorite of lime when pounded in a mortar, and yielding to distilled water an oxidizing agent, which, by its reactions with different chemicals, he showed was, as Schönbein had asserted, antozone. Heating the mineral causes it not only to lose the property of giving off any odour, but also of transforming HO into HO_2.

Ether was more or less known, and had been used as an anæsthetic for some little time before Dr. (afterwards Sir James) Simpson really brought chloroform and its use to perfection. Ether had been discovered by an American chemist, further perfected by Baron Liebig (whose name often occurs in these pages), Sir Humphrey Davy, etc., when chloric ether was made by mixing ether with chloroform.

When Simpson was appointed physician to Queen Victoria, he wrote to his brother Sandy : ' Flattery from the Queen is perhaps *not* common flattery, but I am far less interested in it than in having delivered a woman this week without any pain while inhaling sulphuric ether. I can think of nothing else.'

Professor Simpson was a remarkably religious man, and he said : ' I most conscientiously believe that the proud mission of the physician is distinctly twofold, namely, to alleviate human suffering as well as to preserve human life.'

In spite of all his strict religious belief, he warmly declared that no medical man would be justified in withholding this relief to a woman's sufferings, and thus Simpson became the chief agent for the use of chloroform, in spite of all the abuse he at first met with. He experimented on himself with the anæsthetic, and he experimented, as mentioned elsewhere, on my father, when a student, and to this fact George Harley often attributed his love of research and insatiable desire for knowledge to alleviate human suffering.

My father was a few years later one of those appointed to investigate into the better methods of giving anæsthetics. The results of his experiments led him to suggest the mixture of chloroform with alcohol and ether as a safe anæsthetic. This was afterwards known and much used for years as the ' A. C. E. mixture,' and owed its existence to his work. Science, however, is always advancing, and his discovery was again superseded by a better ; but each discovery helps to plant a new rung on the ladder of success.

Chloroform was a very dangerous drug in its infancy ; now its use is so perfected that death from its effects is only one in four or five thousand, which practically means the danger is nil. Women probably reap the greatest benefit from its discovery.

If such saving of pain and life can be gained, as we know, by the use of anæsthetics alone—to say nothing of disinfectants—surely this one success should be sufficient to silence the cry of the anti-vivisectionists—who are themselves the real cruelists. It is only through the use of anæsthetics that surgery has made such vast bounds during the last half-century.

Mrs. Garrett Anderson, then Miss Elizabeth Garrett, was the brilliant pioneer of medicine for women, as everyone knows. When she was studying, all doors of learning were shut to her in London, and she used to go to my father and get him to repeat his lecture to her privately, as she was not allowed to be a listener at his class.

In 1865 she obtained a license to practise, but even that did not open the doors to women, who had a stern fight, now ably won.

In June, 1863, Dr. Harley communicated to the Royal Medical and Chirurgical Society a paper on ' The Ordeal Bean of Old Calabar,' in which he drew an interesting comparison between its action and that of belladonna, woorali, and conia. In August, again, he furnished the British Medical Association with an account of the botanical characters and therapeutical properties of the ordeal bean, which was translated into French and published by Professor Robin in the *Journal d'Anatomie et de Physiologie* of Paris. In 1863, also, was issued Dr. Harley's work on ' Jaundice : its Pathology and Treatment,' the appearance of which marked a distinct advance in the study of diseases of the liver and pancreas. We may also refer, as a clinical curiosity, to ' An Extraordinary Case of Spasmodic Cough in a Girl aged Fourteen Years.' The number of times the girl coughed was carefully counted at intervals by students specially appointed for the task, and ascertained to be at the rate of 70 per minute—that is to say, 4,200 times per hour ; and reckoning that the girl coughed only twelve out of the twenty-four hours, she coughed the enormous number of 50,400 times daily. Under antispasmodic treatment she completely recovered.

In 1864 Dr. Harley took an active share in the foundation of the Edinburgh University Club. He belonged to its first council, and it was on his proposition that Sir David Brewster was chosen its first president. (Extract from the *Lancet*.)

My father until the day of his death was a very active member of the Edinburgh University Club; he sometimes took the chair at the dinners, and often spoke, being always reliable as a good after-dinner speaker.

I remember rather a funny story in connection with Dean Stanley at one of these dinners. The great divine sat down beside my father, took up the menu, read it carefully through, and with a sigh put it down again.

' Very sad, Harley,' he said, ' very sad, my friend; but I have got such an awful attack of indigestion I dare hardly eat anything, and haggis is my favourite dish.'

The doctor condoled, and they chatted pleasantly for a while, but at last, though much engrossed by the conversation of his neighbour on the other side, my father was surprised to hear the Dean's squeaky voice saying :

' Waiter, waiter ! don't you hear me ?' as he prodded the offending attendant in the back with his fork ; ' bring me some more of that haggis before it is all gone—and be quick.'

This was the man with indigestion !

In 1864 George Harley was an active member of the committee appointed by the Royal Medical and Chirurgical Society to report on the physiological and toxic effects of chloroform, the experiments on which, like those on drowning, were performed in his laboratory at University College. At the Bath meeting of the British Association in 1864, Dr. Harley for the first time appeared in the ranks of the anthropologists, and read a paper on ' The Poisoned Arrows of Savage Man,' illustrated by the exhibition of poisoned arrows from every quarter of the globe. Dr. Harley aimed to demonstrate that both North and South America were originally peopled from different parts of Asia, more especially from Borneo and China. He proved his theory as regarded South America by showing to the meeting the blow-tubes and poisoned spikes of the Malays and the inhabitants of Guiana respectively. There is, however, a most remarkable difference in the physiological nature of the poisons employed, for while in Borneo it is the antiar, heart-paralyzing poison of the upas-tree, in Guiana it is the limb-paralyzing poison woorali of the *Strychnos toxiferos* tree. In

1865 Dr. Harley published in the Transactions of the Royal Medical and Chirurgical Society notes of two cases of intermittent hæmaturia, bringing before the profession for the first time the important fact that in certain forms of malarial disease all the constituents of the blood may be eliminated by the urine, making the liquid either chocolate-coloured or quite red, and yet that scarcely a single whole blood corpuscle may be detected in it by the microscope.

' The next favours I received from Fortune,' states my father, ' were domestic ones—a boy and a girl. The name of Ethel was given the little maid to please her mother, that of Brilliana to please me. Brilliana I called her out of respect for the only woman of the name of Harley who added by her writings to the celebrity of the race. " The Letters of the Lady Brilliana Harley," 1625-43, wife of Sir Robert Harley, of Brampton Bryan, Knight of the Bath, were reprinted by the Camden Society, with introductions and notes by Thomas Taylor Lewis, M.A., Vicar of Bridstow, Herefordshire.

' Of men authors we have had an abundance ; of women only this one. No wonder, then, that I wished our daughter to perpetuate her name.'

' Ethel had the honour of having Baron Justus von Liebig for godfather. This is his letter on the occasion of her birth :

' DEAR EMMA,   .

' I always thought my wife had written to you and told you how much we were pleased with your good child-birth, and to congratulate you for your little girl. Only to-day I hear that she always meant to do it, but never found time. I can imagine quite well how happy you are in possession of your child, especially as you always loved children more than anything else. . . .

' I shall be most happy to be the godfather of that dear girl, and I hope to live long enough to see her grow and prosper. It is impossible for me to travel, dear child, otherwise there would be nothing to prevent my coming to

London this summer ; but the danger is too great with my lameness; I am too much occupied with my book ["The Natural Laws of Chemistry"], and I fear that I have to spend all my holidays in doing this book.

'What is the matter with Mrs. Jane's and Richard's journey to Munich ? Edmund told me of their intention to come and see us.

'Last Saturday the mathematical physic part of our Académie elected, after my proposal, Dr. Harley as correspondent for the Académie. Now, there is only the whole Académie who has still to vote, and the King has to give his consent. It will last till October, but I don't doubt for a moment that he will be chosen.

'Give Mr. Luna my love. Marie will be very happy to get the gift he will send her.

'Be very cautious, dear Emma, about your health, and think always of your child, which gives to you new duties to fulfil. As I already take the part of a godfather, I have some right on this child, and am allowed to care for her future. May I not?

'Good-bye ; my sincere greetings to Dr. Harley, and
'Believe me your ever-loving friend,
'J. VON LIEBIG.'

Yes, those were years of success and happiness. Fortune smiled, the joy of the domestic hearth was complete, and my father, though still a young man, had gained many honours and was surrounded by charming friends.

At the very first dinner-party given after his marriage he was pleased to be able to recall among his guests some interesting people : Sir Rowland (one of his most valued friends) and Lady Hill; Dr. Sharpey, the secretary to the Royal Society, and his 'patron saint,' so to speak ; Humphreys, coroner for the county of Middlesex ; Professor Graham, Master of the Mint ; Michael Faraday, of Royal Institution fame ; Charles Landseer, secretary to the Royal Academy ; Delepière, secretary to the Belgian Minister, etc.

On one occasion when he had a gentlemen's dinner, Sir Edwin Landseer, his brother Charles, and George Cruikshank were of the company. After the meal was over, as it was a lovely summer evening, they adjourned for a smoke to the leads at the back of the house—those dreary leads Londoners know too well—where grew—indeed, still grow—two fine plane-trees, much taller than the tall London house, the last remnants of several that formerly flourished in Harley Street.

As Cruikshank did not smoke, he amused himself with wandering about, and suddenly embraced the trunk of one of the trees, when Charles Landseer exclaimed :

'What *are* you doing, George?'

'I am taking the girth of this tree; it is such a size to have grown in this little space.'

'Nothing wonderful in that; it is easy to see London air soots (suits) it,' exclaimed Charles, for Cruikshank's immaculate white waistcoat, of which he was always very proud, had a broad black line across it.

Charles Landseer was famous for his repartees, which some people said he prepared beforehand; but Dr. Harley always quoted the above anecdote to prove that one of his smart sayings, at all events, was impromptu.

Had not Fortune been gracious to the orphaned lad who went to Edinburgh in 1845 to seek her favour? What was there the heart of man could desire she had not given him? Fame, friends, position, home, happiness, a wife who was his very right hand, tender as prudent, wise as unselfish, sensible as sympathetic, a helpmeet indeed.

During the year 1864 he was elected a Fellow of the Royal College of Physicians of London, having been a Fellow of the Royal College of Physicians of Edinburgh since 1858.

In 1865 the Royal Society thought fit to dub him a F.R.S., and then the climax of his professional honours was reached. The Microscopical Society of Giessen, the Medical Society of Halle, the Badish Society of Medical

Jurists, the Royal Academy of Medicine of Madrid, the Academy of Sciences of Bavaria, had all honoured him with their respective diplomas of Corresponding Member ; so with these, and the others before mentioned, no more societies were left for him to conquer.

But at that very moment, though all unconscious of the fact, dark clouds were gathering over his head. Let the summer be long as it may, it cannot last for ever ; and his, full of sunshine, was rapidly drawing to a close.

The tale of trouble which wrung from him that exceeding bitter cry previously referred to can, however, be only thoroughly understood after reading the record of pain cheerfully borne, and disappointment manfully endured.

CHAPTER XIV

As we saw in the last chapter, the London physician had his feet well on the ladder of success, the rungs of which he was climbing steadily but surely.

All the world seemed fair, he had as many private patients as he could conveniently see, he spent two afternoons a week at University College Hospital, where for sixteen years he was consulting physician. He went nearly every day to University College in order to deliver lectures to many students on medical jurisprudence. Among those still living may be mentioned the names of Sir John Williams, Dr. Frederick Roberts, Dr. Sidney Ringer, Sir Douglas Powell, and Dr. Carlton Bastian. He also delivered a postgraduate course, where his students were generally qualified men much older than himself, which gained him much renown.

I never heard my father lecture, but have often been present when others were speaking about the wonderful power he possessed of explaining even the most difficult subject, so as to make it plain to anyone. Some few years ago I met the Rev. Dr. Cobham Brewer, author of ' Child's Guide to Knowledge,' who died in 1897 at an advanced age, and who continued writing till his death. He was then a very old man, who had known my father in Paris, and praised him warmly, saying he had saved his wife's life some years before when all other skill had failed; then all at once he added : ' But his great forte was lecturing; it was simply wonderful. I am not a scientific man, but I attended your father's class for advanced students, and although my want of scientific knowledge made it difficult for me, yet it was all so interesting, and he lectured so simply I could follow perfectly.'

George Harley worked with delightful contemporaries, mostly men older than himself, for he was a very young professor. Among them at the College were Sir William Jenner, Sir Russell Reynolds, both afterwards Presidents of the Royal College of Physicians ; Sir Alfred Garrod ; Sir John Erichsen, afterwards President of the Royal College of Surgeons ; Sir Richard Quain, author of Quain's ' Dictionary of Medicine '; Mr. Walsh, the eminent surgeon, etc.: for in those days University College was in the zenith of its glory.

He loved University College, and some of the best years of his life were devoted to its service, but from a monetary point of view it was not remunerative. Scientific work seldom pays, hospital work rarely reaps pecuniary reward. How little the public appreciate all that is given to them, and how much more inclined they are to grumble than to thank !

The young physician worked very hard all day, and at night, when the household had gone to bed, he sat up and wrote books. Among other things he strove determinedly to improve the somewhat primitive microscopes then in use, and invented a new microscope which bore his name. Perhaps in those days no man in London did more microscopic work than he ; indeed, in the early sixties microscopes were a rarity in England, and many men in leading practices not only did not possess such a thing, but hardly knew how to use one. He believed firmly in the most precise inquiry into everything connected with disease. His microscope was one of his most treasured possessions, and many diagnoses he completely overturned by careful microscopic analysis.

Writing in 1873, several years after the actual event, he says :

'It was long past midnight, the family at rest, and I sitting alone in my study according to my wont, working the microscope with a small lens under a great illumination, when I suddenly saw blood on the lens. I took out the glass and cleaned it, but on putting it back I still saw that blood-spot. Again I removed the lens and rubbed it well, but still the blood remained. Was I awake or dreaming? It was blood—fresh blood; and yet the lens showed no signs of it. Deciding I must be overtired, I packed up my things and went off to bed and to sleep, for although I had worked with a microscope for fifteen years and never seen this before, I put it down to fatigue.

'The next morning I had almost forgotten the event till I stood before the mirror to shave, and then I saw the blood had not been on the lens at all : I had ruptured a bloodvessel of my left eye!

'As I was in the middle of my course at University College, and the accident caused me no immediate pain, instead of ceasing work like a rational individual, I deemed it my duty to continue the course as long as I possibly could. So on I went till, when finished, I found that the course had nearly finished me. After two months an acute attack of retinitis set in, followed by glaucoma in both eyes. Light became unbearable; the employment of an ophthalmoscope by an oculist set up an acute attack of inflammation which nearly drove me mad.* From the sofa I was driven to my bed; from a semi-dark room to one of total blackness, where I lay for three long weary months in perfect darkness, suffering excruciating torture. No horrors described by Dante in his " Inferno " could have been more hideous than the agony in my eyeballs, the mental anguish in my mind.

'Twelve hot poultices were applied to my eyes in the

* The medical side of this extraordinary case of blindness was reported in the *Lancet*, February, 1868.

course of every twenty-four hours; sleep I could not. The terror of even the edge of the pillow or the bedclothes touching an eye was indescribable. The agony of mind as well as of body that I endured little can any human being realize. A morphia draught was at my bedside within reach of my hand, yet I resisted it. Knowing it could do my disease no good, and that, although it might give me sleep, it would upset my other organs, for a long time I refused to follow the well-intentioned but mistaken advice of my friends to resort to narcotics. My bedroom being totally dark (and few persons know what that means; an ordinary darkened room would have seemed a lighted one to me in the then sensitive state of my eyes), friends could only stay in it for a few minutes at a time. Luckily, my brain found occupation in composing articles, one of which, on the abolition of double consonants from English spelling, I only submitted to paper ten years later.

'Time passed slowly away, for pain and want of sleep —especially the latter—tortured me. The desire to sleep was intense, yet still sleep would not come. I passed the almost incredible number of twenty-one days and twenty nights without ever having dozed for sixty minutes at any one time. That I knew from having heard every hour strike during the period mentioned.

'Driven at last to desperation, I got out of bed, and, finding my shirt in the dark, tied the body round my back, the sleeves round the strong wooden post of the bed, in the hope of being able to fall asleep in an upright position. How long I stood thus I know not; I was dreadfully weak, and must have fainted, as I have no recollection of having stood more than a few minutes in this queer fashion ere I found myself lying twisted over a chair, with my body hanging uncomfortably attached to the bedpost. As soon as I sufficiently recovered I untied the shirt-sleeves, crawled back into bed, put out my hands, laid hold of the bottle containing the draught of morphia, and drained it to the bottom. This was about one in the morning, and I must afterwards have slept nearly eleven hours, for it was past noon ere I awoke.

'My wife and friends had been in several times, but, finding me soundly sleeping, did not disturb my repose.

'The feeling the opiate produced was heavenly. It lifted me from purgatory into paradise, and I made to myself a vow never to be hard upon an opium-eater after having myself tasted of its bliss.

'Once having begun the sleeping-draught, I took regularly $\frac{1}{6}$ grain of morphia with $\frac{1}{2}$ grain of quinine every six hours, so that I was always more or less under the influence of the drug, sometimes being sound asleep and at other periods in a state of conscious divine beatitude. What a blessed change from the torments of the damned that I had previously suffered!

'Two months passed away in this manner, and then my confrères began to get as anxious I should discontinue the drug as they were at first desirous I should take it. I was not, however, inclined to give up my angel friend; I had too vivid a recollection of the agony previously endured, which, indeed, had been so awful that I again and again conned over the pros and cons of suicide, remembering an ancient philosopher had said that "the mere act of self-inflicted death is the strongest proof that a man can give of his sovereignty over himself." I worked the problem of its expediency and its justification well out in my mind, and arrived at the conclusion that when the troubles of life become permanently greater than its comforts, a man is philosophically, though not morally, justified in slipping his cable and setting sail for the unknown shore.

'My case, however, did not come within the range of my own philosophical reasoning; my wife's devotion held me back, besides which I had not lost hope that my troubles were only temporary, while if they proved not to be temporary, I felt my cable would soon be slipped by another hand than my own.

'I have heard of a man committing suicide on account

of a paroxysm of gout; I have even read of the case of a gentleman who took away his own life in an attack of toothache; but neither of these was a philosopher according to my doctrine, and whether they were to be more blamed or pitied it is not for me to decide.

'As the result of three months passed in bed and darkness, my body finally became reduced to little more than a skeleton. The continued use of opiates, together with utter inaction, had almost entirely destroyed my appetite, and, taking an insufficiency of food to replace the tissue waste, I got small by degrees, though not beautifully less.

'Strange to say, however, though my health and my means of life had been taken from me, I did not lose my spirits. In proof of this, I may mention a remark which I heard drop from a clerical friend, a cousin of the famous Matthew Arnold, just after he had left my room and before the door was properly closed behind him.

'In the passage he met his daughter, who said :

' "Dr. Harley must be better, for I heard you laughing."

' "Don't imagine that, my dear. He is not better ; but he'll crack jokes with the undertaker when he comes to bury him."

'A pleasant remark for any dying man to hear, but one which proved of service, for although it only afforded me a laugh at the time, it set me thinking that possibly, if I did not discontinue the opiate, I should ere long require the services of the undertaker. Having arrived at which conclusion, I instantly resolved to give up taking morphia.

'In the course of the same forenoon a medical friend called, and began preaching, as he had several times done before, about the impropriety of continuing the opiates, which I was then taking in enormous quantities. I abruptly interrupted him by saying that I did not intend to swallow another dose, hearing which he began another sermon on what he considered the easiest way to break off the habit, evidently thinking I could not do so, for dram-drinking is as difficult to give up as alcohol to the drunkard.

12

Again, however, I abruptly stopped him by saying: "Have no fear; not another drop shall pass my lips."

' A doubting laugh was his only reply, and we changed the subject.

' Next day he again called, evidently with the view of ascertaining if I had been able to keep my resolution. Twenty-four hours having elapsed since his last visit, four doses of morphia had been due. Cunningly he began by kindly inquiring how I had slept. On being told I had not slept at all, he quickly asked if I had not taken any morphia; and on my answering in the negative, he mildly advised me, if I had another sleepless night, to take one single dose.

' "No," said I, "not a particle of opiate will I take, even if I don't sleep for a dozen nights."

' "Friend," he returned, " don't boast; you are human, like all the rest of us, and you have too long indulged yourself in the habit to be able to give up the use of morphia, or some other narcotic, all at once."

' To this I made the jeering answer :

' "Man, if I made up my mind to cut off my own arm, I would do it; and with the morphia-bottle within my reach, I shall lie here until Nature gives me sleep, or until I change my mind. My resolve, however, I will *not* break."

' At that time most of my friends felt certain I was dying—so certain, indeed, that after I began to get a little better, one of them told me they had, " in case of the worst happening," prepared a suitable epitaph, one line of which especially took my fancy, viz., " He adored brains and hated humbug."

' Day after day my medical friend repeated his visit, because, as he expressed his opinion, he considered I was " a fine psychological study "; and day after day he found the morphia-bottle by my bedside untouched, while hour after hour I passed in misery, unrelieved by one wink of sleep. Eight nights passed thus. The ninth followed, and then—oh, then!—I received my reward. Calmly I fell asleep, and after ten hours' sweet repose awoke comforted and refreshed.

'From the first hour I left off morphia I never again returned to it, so my sceptical medical friend was forced to become a reluctant convert to "the power of resolve."'

Having decided not to have the bad eye removed to 'save the other,' as his oculist friends suggested, and believing entire rest from work and light might restore his health, the invalid decided to go into the country for the sake of perfect quiet and fresh air. In London he could see no patients, deliver no lectures, write no books, and was, in fact, as completely cut off from life as if he were dead; so that no good purpose could be served by remaining in town. About this time also another small addition arrived in the family, and my mother was most terribly ill. Small wonder, after all her nursing and anxiety; the only surprise was she did not die, for the plight of the young couple on whom the world had smiled so brightly was now sad indeed.

Then it was that my father went down to Ellough Rectory on a visit to his kind friend Mr. Arnold, and he actually insisted on travelling from London to Suffolk alone, blindfolded and weak—a very foolish step, as he himself allowed in after-years.

Concerning his stay at Ellough, he writes:

'Ere long I was strong enough to walk from one room to another on the same floor, and matters were speedily so arranged that I occupied one darkened apartment during the day and a different bedchamber during the night. A gleam of light I never saw. Not a glimpse entered; layer upon layer of dark calico blinds covered the windows and came far across the walls to prevent the slightest ray from entering, so acute did it make my suffering.

'Nothing further worth mentioning occurred after the morphia abstention, until I ventured, on a darkish night many weeks later, to go downstairs about ten o'clock, my eyes tightly bandaged—with the view of taking a walk. My nurse was leading me, and when we arrived at the carriage-gate opening to the road, in her anxiety to steer me safely through, she took her hand off the gate, which, immediately closing with a bang, struck me a blow on my bad eye. A dazzling light instantly followed; I became sick and faint, and must have fallen to the ground but for the support of my companion. Opposite the rectory stood the church, and close beside a small gate opening into the graveyard. Knowing there chanced to be a flat tombstone immediately within the enclosure, on which I could sit down, I told the nurse to lead me to it, and, as I heard she was crying because of the accident she had unwittingly caused, laughingly added, "I want to go to the churchyard in order to become better acquainted with the place in which I shall so soon have to lie."

' As a consequence of this remark, I was scarcely seated on the tombstone ere a succession of muffled sobs greeted my ears, and in a minute more, to my utter consternation, the woman fell into violent hysterics. This was a nice mess to be in, sitting helpless on a grave, unable to see, and yet conscious that almost within touch a woman was lying on the ground, weeping.

' At first I tried condoling with her, regretting I was incapable of rendering her assistance; but soon, finding sympathy was only making matters worse, I changed my tactics, and began blowing her up. After a time this line of conduct had the desired effect, for the screaming ended in a fit of sobbing, and by degrees she got more and more calm, till at length she regained sufficient self-control to help me to rise from the tombstone, on which I had been sitting so long that I was nearly perished with cold.

' We returned to the house. I went to bed, and there I lay for fourteen days in agony, the blow having induced a fresh outbreak, and again the excruciating pain I endured no one who has not suffered from an agonizing attack of neuralgia could conceive. It was exactly as though a violent toothache were raging in my eye.

'Bad news came from London. My wife was worse, and for weeks I was in great anxiety on her behalf. Indeed, the world seemed very sad; but things brightened gradually, and at last she recovered sufficiently to be able to join me, when I was transported to Devonshire, where nothing special occurred until I went to live at Southwood House, in Shaldon, on the opposite side of the river from Teignmouth, about four miles from Torquay. I was then strong enough to sit up all day, so I contrived a capital apartment in which to receive visitors.

'The drawing-room possessed a fine bow-window, and I had every article of furniture removed from the room except an easy-chair, a sofa, and the centre table; the fireplace was shut up, and a close iron stove put on the hearth, so that during the winter the apartment could be kept warm without my eyes being troubled. Those changes being effected for my own comfort, the next thing was so to arrange the room that my friends could talk to me at ease, which was in this wise managed: The bow-window was divided from the rest of the room by thick curtains, through which not a ray of light could penetrate. In the part thus partitioned off, two chairs were placed, also a table, writing materials, and some few books.

'When any friends called upon me, they remained in the lighted compartment, while I stayed in the obscure chamber, and chatted to them through the drapery. I had numerous visitors, who were very kind to me. Daily I held a levée, which was so managed that never more than two had audience at a time.

'When not engaged with these leveés, I took a walk round my table; but finding that it was impossible for me to resist now and again counting the times I circumnavigated it, by reckoning how often I passed a corner,

I had the square table replaced by a circular one, and, with my finger against the edge, round and round I went like a horse in a mill, timing the length of my stroll by a striking clock on the chimney-piece. My usual walk was for half an hour four times per diem, and at the rate I walked I calculated I averaged five miles a day.

'Besides these little amusements, I had more serious work on hand; I dictated a scientific book to a young lady who acted as my amanuensis, sitting on the light side of the curtains. The strain of remembering where I was, and recalling facts without notes, was very exhausting. The book was printed and published as soon as I came out of my purgatory.*

'In spite of my misfortune, I tried not to let time hang heavily on hand. The newspapers, journals, and conversation of my various friends kept me *au courant* with all that was taking place in the outer world, and by having books of travel and science read to me (at that time I did not care for novels, except those written by personal friends), I had ample mental food for digestion, though I realized fully, health is the most precious kind of worldly wealth.'

Cheerful words from a man who felt so deeply his sufferings that he rarely allowed himself to give them utterance!

Blind, blind, blind! All his hopes in life suddenly blasted. His work and success swept from before him. Every rung in the ladder of fame he had so painfully climbed broken beneath his feet. For many dreary months he could not see his patients; he could not read his lectures: he was an exile; his vocation in life was gone. The physical suffering, though acute, was nothing to the mental agony endured by the man, stricken down in his youth, who seemed only to have tasted the sweets of success in order to more fully realize the bitterness of such an unexpected and cruel failure.

---

* The book was entitled 'The Urine and its Derangements.' It was reprinted in America, and translated into French and Italian.

CHAPTER XV.

TOTAL DARKNESS.

'For nine long weary months,' continues the doctor, 'I never saw a human face, not even my own, and many were the strangers introduced to me during that time, regarding the appearance of every one of whom I formed a definite mental photograph, always, without a single exception, better looking than the original.

'We pity the blind for not seeing, and justly too; but little do seeing people dream that those devoid of physical sight live in an imaginative world of their own, far more beautiful, far more perfect, far more minute in its detail, than any which the visual eye is capable of creating for us. On one occasion I was taken to *see* a shipwreck, and as a number of persons stood gazing at it, I heard the howling wind, felt the bitter beating of the blast, and eagerly listened to every remark which fell from each individual member of the group. From the observations made around me, I built up a perfect picture of the wreck; the broken topmast; the torn and tattered sails; the idly dangling cordage; the black, battered, water-logged hulk, and the white surging foam rolling over her from bulwark to bulwark; the life-boat's crew striving to board her—these things were all clearly, and as it were visibly, before me.

'A few days later some friends came to dinner, and as I sat at table with my eyes still bandaged—for I was now able to join the family meals—I tried to interest my lady neighbour by telling her all about the shipwreck, till at last, hearing nothing but the sound of my own voice, I suddenly stopped short and inquired of my companion what was wrong.

' "Why," said she, with a laugh, "they are all listening to your vivid account of what you never *saw !*"

' A blind man, as I before said, lives in an ideal world of his own, infinitely more beautiful than the real world surrounding him ; but I must contradict the statement constantly made, that a blind person has a just appreciation of the things with which he comes in contact. That idea I can authoritatively declare is absolutely and totally false.

' For example, the lady who acted as my reader and amanuensis was minutely described to me—the colour of her hair, her complexion, figure, size, features and manners. Another girl who was a frequent guest, and an almost nightly companion in our walks, was also described to me with the same minuteness. At the end of many months, a few weeks previous to my liberation from darkness, I felt every feature of their faces with my hand, and, by repeating this operation at intervals of a few days, imagined I had formed so true a picture of them both in my mind that I should not experience the slightest difficulty in recognising the one from the other when I really saw them before me. The day for putting this matter to the test at length arrived. I had several times used my recovered sight for a few minutes at a time, so it was settled I should place myself with my back to the window in the dining-room, exactly opposite the door of entrance, that all the subdued light in the apartment might fall directly on the face of the person entering. Another couple of girls, comparative strangers to me, were also to enter, walk twice round the table, and then retire without uttering a syllable. For, of course, if they spoke I should at once recognise the voice. One after the other all four entered the room, went through the little pantomime indicated, and withdrew.

'The startling result was that I *failed to recognise* either of my fair friends! In fact, I expressed my strong conviction a trick had been played upon me, for not one of the damsels realized in the slightest degree the picture I had formed either of my amanuensis or her companion.

'When they spoke I instantly knew them; but, oh, what a disappointment! I hid my feelings, for neither of them came up in any way to my imaginings. I had been living under a delusion. The colour of their hair, the shape of their faces, even their complexions, bore no resemblance whatever to my blind ideals. And the most curious thing of all was that many weeks passed away before I could dissociate the ideal from the real person. That is to say, when they were not actually before my eyes, and I spoke of or thought of them, it was the ideal, not the real, individual that presented itself before my mind's eye.'

These words of my father's, written some years after the actual event, are very cheery; but although he never put it on paper, my mother tells of the days and hours of mental anguish and depression when he felt he should never get back into harness, never live to see the small children around him grow up, when despair settled upon him and he was as one crushed. But when friends appeared he regained his spirits and was the life and soul of the party.

One of George Harley's kindest friends at this time was Mrs. Brookes, the wife of a doctor at Shaldon, and appealing to her for any information, she tells the following little stories:

For many months Dr. Harley lived in a dark room with every small crevice that could let in any light pasted up. He was fed like a child; his days were monotonous both with regard to pain and pleasure. At night we led him out on smooth roads, with many-fold bandaged eyes, and an open umbrella over his head to keep off the light of the stars. As he still declared he saw chinks of light, Tom and he concocted some plaster to cover his eyes, which eventually, but temporarily, removed his eyelashes and eyebrows. No one ever saw his face, so it didn't really matter; but, still, it grieved him, and consequently he had to resume his walks in the middle of the night, and then only when there were no stars, for he could not bear their light even with his goggles on.

On the cliff-top one night I was leading Dr. Harley as usual, and we met Edward Stevenson leading a large Newfoundland dog. Pointing to it, Stevenson said, ' That's a good sort of animal to lead about.'

' Yes ; not an inviting looking specimen,' I replied.

Long silence. Then poor Dr. Harley, who, of course, had not seen the dog, said sadly, ' Those remarks may be true, Mrs. Brooks; but it would have been kinder to pity the sorrows of the blind.'

How we laughed over the explanation !

At the back-gate of Platway I turned, for a second, hearing voices. In the moonlight I saw the poor patient with his umbrella struggling over the ground, his hat off, apologizing profusely to someone for his stupidity ; then he called to me to 'just say something polite.' All his bows and apologies were to a cow !

After his illness, several of us rode one day to Stoke. We had ordered casually for him Moore's horse—an awful yellow lout of a creature. I see Dr. Harley's face now as he stood contemplating the steed, while putting on his immaculate white gloves—reins thick with greasy black, and saddle-stuffing all oozing out. He was an excellent horseman, and a dandy in dress, so we all enjoyed the scene.

He gave Tom some ' Harley's Analgiæ.' It removed acute pain instantly and thoroughly.

He used to say I wrote very good English, but we always quarrelled over the wording of telegrams—mine were terse, his too verbose for pocket or purpose.

Jokes were exchanged unceasingly ; he always kept his good spirits, but it was a terrible life for him.

Perhaps one of the strangest symptoms or results of my father's banishment into the land of darkness was that, instead of losing his visual power by blindness, his vision became excessively acute ; but he did lose for a considerable time the power of differentiating colours : everything appeared to him as either black or white, a very good description of which is given by Mr. Cornish in his volume, ' Animals at Work and at Play.' Gradually the invalid became able to discriminate between blue and red, yellow and green, and would have little pieces of silk of the different colours placed before him and pick them out, adding their names as he handed them to my mother. At first he was often totally wrong, and, strangely enough, the last colours that he was ever able to classify were grays and mauves. For the first month all mauves, blues, greens, and yellows appeared perfectly white, while grays, browns, and reds looked distinctly black.

More than this, my father had entirely lost the capacity for calculating distances, even the shortest, by the eye. Two facts which he maintained prove that the calculation of distances and the distinction of colour by the sight are not intuitive, but rather the offspring of education, and explain why infants continually knock over the things they try to take hold of.

George Harley continues :

'When my health was sufficiently re-established I returned to London, having been absent from the scene of my labours for exactly two years and a day.

' So little is one missed in this modern Babylon that on coming downstairs the next morning in my dear old Harley Street home two letters were put into my hands asking for consultations by persons who were unaware either of my illness or my absence : one was from Winchester, the other from Sydenham.

' This seemed most gratifying, for I had returned home broken in spirit as well as feeble in body, with the idea that I was a ruined man, my most hopeful view of the future being that I might *perhaps* make a couple or three hundred pounds during the first year—not even enough to pay house rent.

' I had to wear dark goggles for many long months, but managed to get about with comparative comfort, though for a couple of years longer I never wrote or read anything myself. After remaining at home for two days my wife urged me to call on Sir Thomas Watson, who had been most particularly kind in his inquiries during my absence.

Accordingly I went, and after receiving a warm welcome naturally enough communicated to him my dread that I stood on the brink of ruin.

' " I do not believe it," he said cheeringly. " Quite the contrary ; before six months are over you will have all your practice back again."

' These were kind and pleasant words, but too hopeful for me to accept as true, so I valued them at what I thought they were worth, the friendly expressions of a generous heart. Judge my surprise, therefore, when I found Sir Thomas Watson's prophecy was likely to be fulfilled.

' During the first month after my return I only made seven guineas, for I could not go to anyone outside my own door and could not *see* them in my study, though I could hear and feel ; but in the second month my fees increased to twenty-two, while in the third they actually rose to sixty-two guineas.

' A truly joyful change for me, a change so joyful that I hurried off, my fee-book in my pocket, with many appointments booked, to tell Sir Thomas Watson what had happened. I entered the room smiling, consequently my friend promptly rose to congratulate me, laughingly saying, " I see that you bring good news."

' " Yes," I answered, " and here is my fee-book for you to see."

' We sat down by the fire, and I soon told my story. When I had finished, he asked :

' " Now do you believe I was right when I predicted before six months had passed you would have all your practice back again ?"

' " Yes," I replied, " I believe it now, though you only said so to cheer me."

' In a moment the kind old man started from his seat, and standing before me, with his back to the fire, exclaimed in accents more indicative of sorrow than of anger :

' " Dr. Harley, you do me a great injustice. I never said so for the mere sake of ' cheering you.' I said what I did because I knew my words would come true, and I will tell you why."

'I began to stumble out an apology, for I saw I had wounded most unintentionally his *amour propre ;* but he instantly stopped me and went on :

' "When we first met, while I was President of the Pathological Society, I put my stamp upon you, I felt interested in you ; I have watched your whole career, and never known you publish a lot of trifling cases to bring your name before the public, as young men generally do. What you have written has not been popular. It has been above the heads of the majority of your profession, but it could not fail to benefit the thinking medical men. You made yourself useful to us. While you were away I felt the want of you, and I know that others, too, did the same, and we are all glad to get you back again. Had you gone in for the public, and not for the profession, the public would have forgotten you, and you would indeed have been a ruined man ; but as you went in for the profession, the profession has not forgotten."

' These words, and the deliberate manner in which they were uttered, made a most profound impression upon me.

' Seeing my discomfiture, he reseated himself, and in a persuasive voice said :

' "Look at your book, and tell me from whom your patients came."

'I began at the beginning, and went over them one by one, when, to my surprise—for I had not noticed the circumstance before—I found I had been consulted by forty-one new patients brought me by medical men whose names I mentioned to Sir Thomas.

' When I had finished, he quietly observed :

' "Now you see I was correct in saying your professional brethren had not forgotten you."

' Sir Thomas Watson's prophecy came literally true, for at the end of six months I had almost all my practice back again.'

Thus the world smiled once more. The London physician began his profession for the second time successfully. He was still weak and ill, the strain had told, and but for his wife, as he often proudly said, he could never have managed. She learnt to work the microscope for him, and soon was able to prepare all the slides and make any simple examination. When the subject became too complicated, and it was impossible for her to proceed further, she would get the slide ready, when, lifting his dark goggles with black silk rims, he would peep for one moment and solve the mystery.

How many women thus unostentatiously help their husbands along the stony paths of life, and by their incentive and encouragement make men's success! My mother has always been the most retiring of women, but most undoubtedly it was to her resource and sympathy, her encouragement and aid, that my father owed much of his triumph over cruelly hard obstacles, and what she did for her husband she has also done for her children. She was and is the mainspring of that Harley Street home.

CHAPTER XVI.

Back in London. Ah, what unspeakable happiness those three words meant! Back in the world, the world of intellect he loved so keenly; back in the home, with all its domestic ties; back in harness, the harness of his own choosing, the traces of which he had himself adjusted; back, with his shoulder to the collar, in the life of medicine and science, which to him was the goal of happiness. Like a schoolboy let loose for the holidays, his excitement was ecstatic; he could scarcely contain himself after two years of what to him had been mental penal servitude. He had so many plans for the future, so many scientific experiments in his brain, so many theories to put to the practical test, that he could hardly wait to begin his work. All the world seemed *couleur de rose* to the man taking up his life's work for the second time.

At this time my father was not yet forty years of age; but though full of ambition, absorbed by love of science, and acutely energetic mentally, he was still physically a sufferer: for the complete breakdown of a couple of years before had not only been the result of the burst bloodvessel, which brought on temporary blindness and nearly rendered him sightless for life, but the inevitable outcome of having lived at high pressure in a brain-exhausting profession. To quote his own words, written after he had thought the whole trouble out dispassionately: 'My train I drove

at express speed; by day I never let it rest, and by
night it got an insufficiency of repose. Being as fond
of the fascinations of intellectual society as of original
research, I consumed my little candle at both ends with
such wasteful extravagance that in 1865, when I had only
attained the age of thirty-six, it very nearly went out.'

More than this: during the years of his enforced absence
the house in Harley Street had been going on just the
same; the stables had continued to be an expense, for
every month my father hoped against hope to return
to his professional duties. A country establishment,
small children and nurses, to say nothing of his own
nurse, had rendered life a very expensive affair, and
he returned to harness feeling great responsibilities rested
upon his shoulders, though still strong in hope concerning
the future.

It was at this time George Harley made a gallant
attempt to resume his professional duties at University
College. The day came for which, in suffering exile, he
had wearied and prayed for two long years; he was
eagerly impatient to get back to his laboratory, in order
to work out the thousand and one experiments his busy
mind pleased itself with planning during those months
of darkness. Not content to do things like other people,
he must needs prepare a new and original lecture on
'Age and Development in Relation to State Policy,' with
which to open the course on May 1, 1868, on his return to
work. He never read his lectures, his notes being often so
meagre as only to fill the back of his visiting-card, for, as I
have before remarked, his memory was wonderful, and
could always be trusted; but on a very important occasion
he would prepare more fully, and write out whole pages, to
which, however, he seldom referred. His language was
terse and clear, for he used to say, ' If you wish to teach,
always use commonplace language; eloquence extinguishes
lucidity.'

Bounding down the stairs, with the exuberance of delight

in his step, my father went off happily one morning to resume his lectures. His parting words to my mother were that he 'felt life was worth living again, and all would now be well.' His eyes, however, were still far from strong, in spite of being most carefully guarded by those hideous black goggles which he constantly wore for years. His reception at the class was most cordial—everything went well. He spoke for an hour, only occasionally referring to his notes. The subject was an important one, however. At the end of the allotted time he had only half finished his discourse; therefore, bidding his students farewell, he told them he would complete the subject on the morrow.

Alas! when that morrow dawned he was in bed shrieking with agony.

'My eyeballs felt like molten metal,' he says. 'Although nearly a *thousand days* had gone by since the original accident to my sight, the eyes were once more burning with a consuming fire, and I was again driven to confinement in a darkened room. Three months of this banishment, fortunately, sufficed to bring me back to where I was before the relapse; but those three months witnessed a mental battle. It was a cruel wrench to have to give up the work I loved, to relinquish the goddess Science, at whose shrine I had worshipped for twenty years of my life, just when I had planned to conquer so many worlds. Seeing it was useless, however, to think of ever resuming my lectures, I resigned my professorship at University College, a hard trial, but a wise step; for, having already made a reputation, it was then much more important, for the sake of my young family, to go in for the golden fleece than only to pursue the phantasmagoria of honour, which indeed is

> ' "Like the poppy red :
> You snatch the flower, the bloom has fled." '

Yes; he sent in his resignation. The words were written

13

with his heart's blood. His hand could barely hold the pen that literally signed his own death-warrant so far as scientific work was concerned. But he was philosopher enough to know that if we cannot get the whole we had better accept the half than lose all. He could not continue his work in its entirety ; he might accomplish something by undertaking less. Sleepless nights, plodding up and down his room, loss of appetite, and depression, had been followed by a final resolve to give up his professorship, and once the mental battle was over and the die cast, he was a happier man for his decision.

' Some months later,' he tells us, ' finding that even my hospital visits became too much for me, having to go whether well or ill, I resigned my physicianship to the hospital, and thus severed myself entirely from University College, after having been connected with it close upon fifteen years.

' The only other public appointments I have since held are those of Examiner in Anatomy and Physiology to the Royal College of Physicians ; for, alas ! I had to realize, as far as public work was concerned, my train was shunted. And I was not yet forty !'

These are but simple words, but to a man of my father's energy they were cruel facts. The dream of his life was ended.

Stricken down in his prime, he had never given up hope, and though the medical profession had shaken their wise heads, and declared he would not only never see again, but never be able to resume his professional duties, he had always buoyed himself up with the belief that by complete visual rest he would not only regain his sight, but, through pluck and determination, manage to resume his professional life. That hope had buoyed him up for two long years. He was right in a great measure ; his sight had returned, and perhaps it may be well here to mention that when he died, at sixty-seven, his eyes were stronger than those of any ordinary man of the same age, since, beyond using glasses for reading, as nearly all people at that time of life do, he could see farther, bear stronger light, and make more continued use of his sight than anyone around him. The rest, indeed, seemed to have improved his vision and strengthened his eyes, though it took many years to do so.

Here he was, then, back in London, brimming over with enthusiasm, determined to conquer new fields, all his scientific experiments planned, the newest schemes calmly and quietly worked out, during those thousand long days of solitary confinement, and just as he lifted the cup to his lips it was again dashed from him!

Being a bit of a philosopher, however, as may have been gathered from the foregoing pages, he did his best to get well during many sad months of relapse, and managed, in a carefully-shaded room, to see a few patients each day. Medical men wrote to him for advice, which letters were read by my mother, who took down the replies from his dictation, and thus from a bed of suffering he managed to relieve others and collect his practice about him.

Mental strength was battling with physical weakness, and the man who had appeared physically ruined and mentally shelved, blindfolded though he was, and handicapped by the shackles of ill health, slowly but surely stepped back into practice.

It is a strange story, and one that makes me pause and think, for though I was too small a child at the time to understand these struggles, I can still picture my father sitting in black goggles, with drawn blinds or shaded lamps, and remember how I grew up without even knowing what his eyes looked like. Some of his most devoted patients never saw his eyes at all until he had perchance saved their lives and looked after their well-being for years. No one realizes the difference it makes in a face if you cover the eyes, especially to a man who wears a large military-

13—2

looking moustache, as my father always did, for the mouth
and the eyes are the two expressive features of a countenance, and therefore animation, love, sympathy, anger, and
amiability, are entirely lost to the world.

Despite all these physical obstacles, having decided to
relinquish the joys of University College and the alluring
pleasures of science, my father slowly but surely succeeded.
Every month his practice seemed to double the returns of
the month before, and, as he says himself, at the end of
six months, or at all events by the end of the year, he was
again making a large income.   He needed it, for the coffers
of the exchequer had been largely drawn upon during his
compulsory absence, and he was like a young man beginning life again, except that, unlike a young man, he was
surrounded by serious expenses and responsibilities in the
shape of home and family.

The second year proved even more successful than the
first : guineas rolled in, and my father would have been
making one of the largest incomes, probably, in the profession had he been able to accept the numberless biddings for
consultations from all parts of Britain.   But experience had
told him not to trifle with his strength, therefore it was
some years before he ever undertook long journeys, and I
think one of the biggest fees he ever received was for going
to Belgium, when he was away for thirty-six hours and
came back with a very large cheque in his pocket.   On
that occasion he was sent for as ' the first authority on
diseases of the liver in Europe '—such at least were the
words of the letter ; and the money was well expended, for
he saved the patient's life.

I will here relate an anecdote about money-making, as it
may serve to point a moral :

' After I had been in consulting practice for a few years,'
says my father, ' I one day heard Professor Todd remark
that he felt it a bore to have to pay a daily visit to Fulham,
despite the fact that he pocketed five guineas each time he

went. " Oh," thought I to myself, " if anybody would give me five guineas for going to Fulham, I should never feel it a bore. In fact, I would make as many visits a day as they liked at the same rate."

'Alas ! how little we know of our own nature until it is put to the test ! How little did I then dream that *I* should ever find it a bore to pocket a fee nearly half as large again on similar terms. Yet when the time came I actually did so. As the circumstance was peculiar, I will explain it. One morning before breakfast a note was put into my hand asking me to go immediately to Southwood, let us say. The letter was apparently from a stranger, so I told the messenger, a groom on horseback, to ride home and say I would follow as soon as the carriage could be got ready. I breakfasted, and within half an hour after the groom rode away I was driving to Southwood at the rate of eight miles an hour. I had a capital pair of horses, and we did the seven miles within the hour. When we arrived at the turning the letter had told me to take, a man was there ready to direct the coachman to the house. Arrived at the entrance gates, we found them wide open, and another man stationed there to hasten us forward. Into a beautiful park I drove, which I afterwards learned was 250 acres in extent, and soon we came to the house door, where stood the butler ready to receive and conduct me into the medical attendant's presence. After a word or two of conversation that gentleman took me to the sick-chamber, where I beheld a man paralyzed on the left side from shoulder to toe, conscious, but speechless. As I approached the bed a convulsive twitching of the right eye immediately took place, and gazing steadily at the patient for a moment, it occurred to me that the twitching of the eyelids was voluntary, and intended as a sign of recognition. On asking if the patient knew me, his regular attendant said not as far as he knew ; but no sooner was the remark made than the twitching became more violent than before, and all at once it dawned upon me that the sick man was an old patient of mine, who had been in the habit of consulting me at my own house. Instantly I addressed him, the eyes responded to my words as intelligibly as his lips could have done.

' " Well ! " I exclaimed, " that horse was just too much for you this time." '

My father had not recognised the name on the letter, because this mysterious patient, who had consulted him at intervals for years, had studiously avoided telling his name or residence. The only thing the physician knew about him was that he rode into London on a most magnificent horse, which he put up at the Langham, where he always lunched. My father had warned him the animal's temper was such that he would some day play him a nasty trick and cause a bad accident, which proved now to have taken place.

' The whole medical history of the case,' said my father, ' at once stood clear before my mind, and bad as he seemed and was, I immediately felt hope that with care he might recover.

' When the doctor and I retired to talk over the case, he surprised me by asking :

' " When did Mr. X. consult you ? "

' " The paralyzed man," was my reply, " has been a patient of mine off and on for five or six years, and I long since warned him against the danger which has now overtaken him ; but if you were not aware that he was my patient, how did you chance to send for me ? "

' " That is just it ; you have no idea the difficulty we had in finding out you were the person he desired to see. It took *twenty hours'* hard work to discover. In the first place we had to find out he wanted some book. The whole household was occupied in bringing up the books from the library shelves ; we were in despair, for none of these satisfied him, and I was at my wits' end to know what he could possibly want, when my eyes fell on the Post-Office Directory lying on the writing-table. I seized it and.

marched upstairs, when to my great relief I found this was the wished-for volume. Then matters became comparatively easy, for we turned over page after page, naming every street in succession until we arrived at Harley Street, which he soon made us aware by his twitchings was the thoroughfare he had in his mind. While we read down the names he remained perfectly quiet, though evidently very anxious, until we uttered yours, when in a moment the twitching of his eyelids became so violent as to leave not a shadow of doubt you were the person he longed to see; indeed, until the letter begging you to come was written and sent off, his excitement was intense."

'Which curious statement the doctor afterwards supplemented by remarking:

' "Now I understand the whole affair. About six years ago he suggested a consultation, but I told him one was not necessary. Therefore he must have gone off and seen you on the sly, and that accounts also for his never afterwards taking any of my medicine."

'I wisely held my tongue, but I thought much that the speaker would have scarcely liked to hear.

'To make a long story short, I may at once say that I received a daily fee of seven guineas—forty-nine guineas a week for visiting that patient whose house was exactly seven miles from my door; but before six weeks had passed by I grew sick and tired of the journey, and, despite every entreaty to the contrary, went to my patient on alternate days. Ere long I tired even of that, and went but twice a week. He gradually got better, and at last was able to be taken into another room, when I dropped my visits to once a week, and as soon as he could be carried daily downstairs to his sitting-room, I said I would only drive out once a fortnight. The road to his house had become insufferably irksome. I did not feel the slightest objection to pocketing the seven-guinea fee, but I detested the monotonous journey, which interfered materially with my other work.

' Just at that time, as ill-luck would have it, I had in the shape of a distinguished Asiatic traveller a very bad case, exactly five miles distant from my house, in a diametrically opposite direction from Mr. X.'s residence, and not being bodily strong, jogging over the stones (even in my easy Cee spring carriage) tired me horribly. Driving over the London pavements for an hour at a stretch is not a pleasant experience, especially when it extends to three or four hours a day, and truly glad was I when the ordeal ended.

' Seven guineas a day seems a large fee, yet it was but " a drop in the ocean " to my patient. The park round his house was 250 acres in extent, and his medical man told me he had been offered £1,000 per acre for building purposes. He was, in fact, a millionaire, so that he had no occasion to grudge the poor doctor's fee. Yet it is singular that the doctor got so soon tired of receiving such an amount ! Facts are, however, stranger than fiction, and this is one (as Lord Dundreary would say) " which no fellow can understand."

' One day another old gentleman was shown into my study, and after our consultation we chatted about many things, and when he left he said :

' " I think and hope your medical treatment will benefit me, for I believe you understand my case; anyhow, our pleasant conversation has done me a great deal of moral good, and I hope to continue it another day."

' He came to see me from time to time for months, and was always most genial and charming, and happily improved under treatment. On one occasion he asked :

' " Do you ever make up your accounts ?"

' " Oh yes," I said, " but fear I am not such a good business man as you are, from your own showing."

' " Were your accounts all right last week, or was anything wrong ?"

' " Well, now you mention it, I think I was a guinea short, somehow."

' " I am glad you know even that much, but I suppose you have no idea who did not pay you ?"

' " No, I can't imagine ; but, from your question, I fancy it must have been you."

' " You are quite right there, but why didn't you ask me for it before I left the room ?"

' " To tell you the truth, I didn't notice it ; but it doesn't matter, for of course you will pay it now."

' " Oh no, I won't—it will be a much better lesson for you if I don't pay at all, then you will remember it, and won't again be so silly as not to look after the guineas."

' After a chat he went away, and only paid for that consultation. After some weeks, he came very jauntily into my study one morning, saying :

' " Well, I have cheated you again."

' On my inquiring how, he said, " This time you are the loser, but not from your own fault," and, rubbing his hands triumphantly, exclaimed : " I met another poor chap who suffered as I used to do, and so I just had your prescription made up and gave him the bottle ; now he is quite well, and thinks me a first-rate doctor."

' " You old rascal !" I exclaimed ; " you not only keep guineas that you owe me, but you steal my prescriptions !"

' He chuckled and often referred to his cleverness. So years went on, and from time to time we had many a pleasant interview.

' One year, on my return from my autumn holiday, I took up the *Illustrated London News*, and, seeing a portrait in it, exclaimed : " Why, here is my old patient Mr. A. !" and on glancing at the obituary notice read, " He was a most charming and delightful companion and full of humour ; and now that he is dead, we are at liberty to say he is the man who for many years has given £1,000 each year to most of the London hospitals, and who did not wish this fact to be made known during his lifetime." '

Yet this was the man who gloried in having cheated Dr. George Harley out of a guinea !

' Another eccentric character, a patient of mine,' my father used to say, ' was an old gentleman who came periodically to see me, generally accompanied by a meek and mild young man, who never said a word unless spoken to.   After several visits, the old gentleman said :

' " If you will come and lunch with me, I will give you the best bottle of hock you ever tasted in your life—so good that I am sure you will say that even I may drink it with impunity."

' When I inquired his address, he said : " Colney Hatch will find me."   He seemed altogether so eccentric that I really thought Colney Hatch might some day be his address, and, attaching no importance to his invitation, thought no more about it.

' One day I received a summons to go into the country, and finding I could not get back in time to see my patients next morning, sat down to write to them, when I found Mr. D.'s name amongst them.   " God bless me !" I thought, " I don't know where he lives, so cannot write."   On thinking the matter over, however, and knowing what an irritable old gentleman he was, I determined to run round to Sir William Fergusson, who had sent him to me, and was, I knew, an old friend of his.   I just caught Sir William as he was going out, told him my dilemma, and asked him to help me out of it.

' " I would with pleasure, my dear fellow, if I could ; but though I have known this man well for years, I have never been able to find out where he lives."

' " Have you never dined with him ?" I said.

' " Yes, often in former years at his club : but he has given up his club now for a long time, and will never tell me where he lives—there is some mystery that I have never been able to solve."

' " Well," I exclaimed, " what am I to do ? for he will be

furious if he has a journey for nothing, for, as you know, he experiences the greatest difficulty in getting about."

' " I see nothing for it," said Sir William, " but for you to write him a letter, leaving it with your servant, and tell him it is quite his own fault you could not write to him, as he would not give you his address."

' This I did, and when I returned home the next day found Mr. D. had arrived as arranged, and was in an awful fury at having had his journey for nothing, and vowed he would never come again. Nevertheless, after some days he did turn up again, and then *I* got into a fury and told him his ridiculous stupidity had put me to no end of trouble and annoyance and loss of time, and his old friend Sir William Fergusson also.

' He was so astonished that he forgot to be angry, and exclaimed :

' " Well, I may have been a fool, but it's worth a good deal of folly, sir, to have been able to lose my identity so completely. In future, when you want to write to me, address Colney Hatch ; I shall get it all right. Meanwhile fix a day when you will lunch with me, and you shall have directions how to come."

' Time passed on, but, though often asked to Colney Hatch, I never could manage to accept my curious patient's invitation. One day, however, the quiet, melancholy young man appeared in my study to tell me the old gentleman was dead. Then I asked for an explanation of the mystery, and he said :

' " I am not at liberty to explain, but there is a mystery, and, of course, a woman is at the bottom of it. I have been his secretary for years, and he has paid me well—indeed, is even now paying me well—to keep his secret ; therefore, of course, I must not betray it. Still, there is one thing I may tell you, viz., that you are the only man I ever heard him invite to enter his house. It is a pity you never came, for it was the most lovely home you can imagine, containing the most interesting relics and precious treasures, but so hidden in a wood from the public gaze that no one could find his way there without a guide."

' And so ended that mysterious patient.'

My father for years always wore a piece of jade attached to his watch-chain, concerning which there was a history. A patient was sent to him from New Zealand very ill indeed; when he was cured, some months afterwards, he came to bid my father good-bye on leaving England, and, with tears in his eyes, said he could never repay the debt of gratitude he owed for all the skill and kind consideration he had received, then added :

' I wish to give you one of the greatest treasures I possess, and what I would not part with to anyone else; it is this piece of jade, which I beg you always to wear on your watch-chain. As you see, it is a perfect piece— that is a rarity — and I have had it mounted in gold for you. I have worn it for years as a charm round my neck, and it hung by a thong of human gut, as the natives arrange such charms. It was given to me years ago by a Maori chief far away up country, to whom I had been of some service, and was his greatest treasure in the world. It had belonged to his father and grandfather before him, and he assured me so long as I wore it I could come to no harm and no violent death—above all, never be drowned. I don't hesitate to say that I cannot divest myself entirely of the old man's implicit faith in this charm, and I hope it may be as a good talisman for you.'

My father wore the charm ever after, but never ceased to regret the human thong, with its romantic history, had been thrown away and replaced by a golden band.

CHAPTER XVII.

MORE QUEER PATIENTS.

PEOPLE should never grumble at their doctor's fees. No profession, probably, requires longer years of study or costs more money, and as few consultants start before they are thirty years of age, it must be borne in mind that they have to be recouped in after-life for those ten or twelve years spent at the Universities at home and abroad. Patients should remember also it has taken the specialist sixteen, perhaps twenty, years to acquire the knowledge of which he gives the benefit for twenty-one shillings.

Wages of all kinds have increased during the last century —everything is more expensive; but, strange to relate, although everyone receives bigger salaries and fees, the physician is still the recipient of the guinea—a coin no longer in existence—while his poor colleague, the healer of souls, fares even worse, for the clergymen's incomes have actually decreased.

A guinea is a physician's actual fee, but nowadays for a first visit, or for subsequent visits when analysis is required, two are usually expected. As men get on in age and position they often double their fees. A letter after consultation requires another fee, which some patients fail to realize, and among these was a certain gentleman who always expected his visit and a letter, perhaps two, for a single guinea! This man was a patient of my father's for years, and one day he came into the study, saying:

'I have just arranged for a lot of advertisements to appear that will cost me £60,000.'

My father dropped back in his chair amazed, for twenty-five years ago such a thing was unknown.

'How—why?' he exclaimed.

'For my pills,' replied the stingy patient. 'I am Blank's pills, and last year I spent £25,000 most successfully in advertisements; this year I am spending £60,000, and should that prove equally profitable, I will spend £100,000 next year.'

This was the man who wanted to cut down his physician's miserable guinea, and died a millionaire!

But to show how differently people are constituted, a man who was very ill consulted Dr. George Harley, frankly owning he could not afford to pay. It was a troublesome case, but my father treated the patient for months, and finally sent him away cured. When they parted, he whose health had been restored said to his doctor:

'I believe I have seen you twenty-six times : is it not so?'

My father assented, and they bade each other good-bye.

A year or two passed, and there arrived a cheque for £100, with a pretty little note from the grateful patient, saying he had come into a fortune, and therefore sent his fee with interest.

Most truly has someone said, 'It takes all sorts to make a world!'

All kinds of patients were in the habit of coming to 25, Harley Street, but one fine day a gentleman arrived who created quite an unusual sensation.

'D—— it, I must see him!' this strange person roared, to the consternation of a decorous butler, who, however, managed to repeat :

'The doctor is out, sir.'

More strong words, more unusual remarks, uttered in a strange idiom, but finally the new-comer decided to wait.

'I'll wait; do you hear, you soft-tongued devil!—wait, I say; and as soon as ever the doctor comes in tell him

I'm here! Confound it! d'you hear?' And the name fairly rang through the whole house.

He was a very celebrated person, the head of an ancient Irish family. He was a fine-looking man, over six feet in height, with a wonderful head of snow-white hair; for, naturally, as a child I was interested, and peeped over the balusters to see what this noisy personage could be like.

That was the first time he came to see my father, but by no means the last. The old gentleman lived to be nearly ninety, and for many years was one of Dr. George Harley's queer patients.

I believe he used to tell the most wonderful stories of wild adventure. He was very proud of acknowledging himself to be the last of the duellists, and frequently declared he had been the principal in over twenty such performances. His life had been a most extraordinary one; he spent part of it in South America; then for fifty years he represented an Irish Constituency. Two years after his retirement he returned to the House, because Mr. Gladstone said he missed him! The old gentleman was full of good jokes and a most entertaining companion.

He was an extraordinary patient; he either arrived before the time and swore and fumed at being kept waiting, or arrived long after his time and raved and swore 'at large' about having been detained.

A message arrived one day asking my father to go at once to attend a very important case, so obscure that diagnosis was well-nigh impossible; for the sufferer could not speak, but lay groaning in agony, unable to utter a word. The carriage was ordered, off went the physician, delighted at the opportunity of studying any disease so interesting and intricate as the one he had been called to. The patient, however, was not a man, nor a woman, nor a child, but a gorilla! Many visits did my father pay to that gorilla, who resided at the Zoo. They soon became fast friends, the poor beast seeming instinctively to realize the strange man meant him no harm and could ease his pain. The creature was suffering from a diseased liver and jaundice, surely showing one more link with ourselves. Unfortunately, his disease was too advanced for treatment, and he died.

The doctor at one time worked a great deal at the Zoo, especially in connection with snake-poisoning, for he dearly loved all animal life. One favourite horse of his went lame by fits and starts, and suddenly trotted as if in agony. My father finally had the horse killed, gave his body to the lions, and himself dissected the foot, where, to his surprise, he found the chalky symptoms of gout.

The subject of this memoir had no sympathy for the *malade imaginaire*, and as it is true that the shoemaker's wife is always the worst shod, it often happens that the physician's family are the worst attended. When we were really ill, he would have nothing whatever to do with us, but always called in another medico. When we had a cold or a bilious attack, his invariable reply was, 'Have a pill and go to bed, and you'll be better to-morrow.' And yet the man who did not sympathize with little ills concentrated all his energies on any case of real disease ; no one had greater power of diagnosis or a larger grasp of medical subjects, and no one loved more keenly to unravel the mysteries of an obscure ailment, probe its origin to the very root, and think out every possible scheme for its betterment. George Harley was one of the pioneers of scientific medicine.

None know, except those intimately connected with medical establishments, the enormous amount of good and kindness vouchsafed by medical men *gratuitously*. Certainly, in the case of my father, there was hardly a day passed that he did not see someone without charging a fee at all, or at most only half; yet, although he was kind and generous in these matters, he hated to be imposed upon, and told several little tales, with great bitterness, of the ghastly way in which well-to-do people worked upon his credulity, as, for instance : A certain lady who came to consult him told a long story of her poverty as she reluctantly placed her fee upon the table, at the same time saying she would never be able to come back again, because she could not afford to do so. It was a bad case ; my father's interest and sympathy were aroused, but, thinking her fairly well dressed, and therefore able to pay something, he told her he would include her next visit in the same fee. She thanked him very much, declaring how sadly poor she was, and how necessary it was to dress as well as possible to keep up appearances, for the sake of her husband's professional position, and departed. Her tale was so pitiable my father regretted he had not refused to take any fee, and determined to see her again and again, if necessary, free of charge.

Putting on his hat to attend a consultation in Queen Anne Street, for which he was late, the lady having detained him, judge his surprise to find, as he turned the corner of Harley Street, that this very patient, now robed in a splendid sable cape, was calmly seating herself in a magnificent victoria, drawn by a pair of spanking steeds, and ornamented with two men-servants in the smartest of livery and cockades. Their eyes met, and the triumphant smile upon her face faded. She had left her carriage round the corner to play her rôle of poverty and save a guinea or two. He determined to see her once more as he had promised, and at the end of the interview to tell her what he thought of a patient who could be guilty of such meanness.

But the lady never came again !

One day, about half-past one o'clock, another lady, arrayed in a very handsome sealskin jacket reaching to her feet, a black silk skirt, and a smart bonnet, came and inquired if Dr. George Harley were at home.

'Yes, madam,' replied the butler.

'Is he disengaged ?' she asked sweetly.

'No, but he will be in a moment;' and he was pro-

14

ceeding to show her to the drawing-room, as he was laying the luncheon-table, when she exclaimed :

' Oh, I cannot go upstairs ! If Dr. Harley will only be a few moments, I would rather wait in the hall.'

This the man naturally did not like, so, opening the dining-room door, he said :

' If you don't mind sitting here a short time, I think you will be more comfortable.'

The lady went in. He closed the door, and, expecting the doctor's bell to ring every moment, quietly stood in the hall looking out of the window. He had not been doing so more than a couple of minutes when the dining-room door opened, and out came the lady, all smiles, saying :

' Oh, will you tell Dr. Harley, as I am only in town for the day, and have a great deal to do, I will just run round to Marshall and Snelgrove's, and be back in half an hour ?'·

The butler, with due ceremony, bowed her out, and then returned to the dining-room to complete his table arrangements ; but, lo ! when he went to the plate-basket standing on the what-not he found all the silver had disappeared ! The lady had left the table untouched, probably guessing that the butler would notice the removal of the spoons and forks the moment he opened the door, but she had decamped with the entire contents of the plate-basket except a butter-knife.

She had only been in the room about two minutes, but that short time served to tell her all the spoons and forks were the finest old Scotch silver, which had been in the family for years, and was therefore valuable not merely because of its actual worth, but from association. The discarded butter-knife was only electro ! The lady with the sealskin coat, which no doubt contained ample pockets, departed with a large amount of plate, which was never seen or heard of again.

Another story was of a more simple nature. A telegram arrived from my father one evening when he was at

a meeting, ' Sending for top-coat. Give it messenger.'
Whereupon a top-coat was looked out, and, a messenger
arriving in due course, it was handed over. The telegram
had emanated from a thief, and the messenger confis-
cated that garment.

This is almost as good a story, but not so disastrous, as
that one of a famous judge, who, commenting on absence
of mind in court, avowed in a fit of forgetfulness he had
himself left his watch upon the dressing-table the same
morning, and had not noticed he had done so till a moment
before, when he put his hand in his pocket.

When he returned home in the evening, his wife exclaimed :

' What a funny thing for you to leave your watch behind,
and then send for it!'

' Send for it!' he exclaimed ; 'I never sent for it!'

Someone of gentlemanly appearance, hearing the judge's
profound observations in court, had gone to his house, and
kindly asked for his lordship's watch, not, however, to
return it to the exponent of the law, but to add it to his
own worldly goods.

Romance is sometimes interwoven with medical business.
To quote only one instance: My father for many years
attended a well-known Countess. At last the day came
when old age and disease baffled skill, and the aged lady, to
whom he had really grown very much attached, fell sick
unto death. It was necessary for a doctor to remain in
the house at night, but, despite all entreaties and tempting
offers, my father distinctly declined to do so.

Thus it was he picked out a young man of his acquaintance, thoroughly qualified, but struggling on the fringe of
practice, to undertake the post of resident physician. He
was a very charming young man, good-looking, and well
educated, and he and the daughter spent many hours
together watching by the patient's bed. A common
interest ripened into sympathy, sympathy developed into
love, and finally the pair were wed. A curious story !

14—2

The life of the London physician, however, is, as a rule, far from romantic—on the contrary, rather prosaic; for although everyone has not the strength to rise morning after morning at six o'clock, as the late Sir Andrew Clark used to do, in order to answer his entire correspondence with his own hand; still, breakfast at eight or half-past is a very ordinary hour, and then, in quick succession, the successful consultant sees patient after patient until about two o'clock. From four to six hours of this class of work proves a great mental strain: there is always the anxiety of diagnosis; there is an endless stream of new faces. He may perchance only see the patient once, and afterwards be able to treat him by letter; but in very obscure cases it is often necessary for the sufferer to be left in a home in London, so as to be under the direct superintendence of the specialist. In any case it means that the London physician is always seeing new people; his circle is ever increasing, and into each case he has to throw his whole heart and soul, take an individual interest, and when that person returns months, possibly years, afterwards, remember when and why he saw him, and how he treated him. This involves a great strain, one under which many men physically break down.

Then, after luncheon, he must attend consultations in the homes of those who are too ill to come out, besides spending certain afternoons in the hospital, added to which, in the case of my father, many hours a week were allotted for lecturing at University College.

A physician's evenings are not altogether free, either, for there are endless meetings of medical societies at which any particularly interesting new case is generally brought up for discussion, to say nothing of the medico who is also an author, and therefore has to spend his evenings, often far into the night, in compiling medical books or writing scientific papers.

It is a busy life, but a happy one, full of human interest and sympathy, and while the doctor, like the lawyer, may know the worst side of men's characters, he also has an opportunity of seeing its best, its noblest, and its most unselfish. That doctors do vouchsafe sympathy to their patients is proved to be true, because patients generally become most devoted friends and admirers of their medical attendant. Do they not prove it in hundreds of little ways ? A certain old lady, knowing my father's predilection for fresh eggs, sent him half a dozen fresh eggs in a little basket weekly for years. A rich patient in Wales always despatched the first woodcock shot on his estate every autumn to my father.

One of the doctor's greatest treasures was a white knitted bed-spread. It was composed of the most wonderful patterned little squares, and was big in size. This marvellous piece of work and patience was done for him by an old lady nearly ninety years of age, when she was almost blind, and the letter that accompanied the gift to her ' dear doctor ' declared : ' It contains many thousands of stitches, but not even they equal my undying gratitude to you ; believe me, every stitch was a stitch of love, and bears a friendly wish for your happiness.'

All these little acts—and they are numerous—are very touching, for although it is charming to receive a handsome piece of silver at the happy conclusion of a long illness, it is the ever-recurring slight remembrances that touch the heart. And, verily, if the doctor gives the best his skill, care, and knowledge can prescribe, he usually reaps reward a thousand-fold in the gratitude of his patients ; although there are cases, as every medical man can affirm, where ' out of sight out of mind ' is the order of the day, and there are people who resent paying a doctor's fee, and avoid doing so by every possible device.

There is a strange old law of the College of Physicians which may not be known to all, viz., that a Fellow of that illustrious body must never send in his bill. Thus, it has become the fashion to pay the physician in money rolled up in a piece of paper at the completion of every visit, although, for the convenience of patients who require to be seen several times, this practice sometimes stands over, with a request to the doctor that he will let them know at the end of the month how many visits have been paid.

There are many strange old laws connected with the Royal College of Physicians of London. No one is admitted a Member until he gives his consent to the following :

' You give your faith that you will observe and obey the statutes, by-laws, and regulations of this College relating to Members, and will submit to such penalties as may be lawfully imposed for any neglect or infringement of them ; and that you will to the best of your ability do all things in the practice of your profession for the honour of the College and the good of the public.'

There is a strict rule in which it says that no member of the college ' shall be engaged in trade, or dispense medicines, or make any engagement with a chemist or any other person for the supply of medicines, or practise medicine or surgery in partnership, by deed or otherwise.'

From which it will be seen the ' doctors ' who advertise quack medicines and pills are not doctors at all !

There are many more interesting and strict rules in connection with this august body, which is most particular that ' none of its Members or Fellows should ever advertise themselves, or give laudatory certificates, of medicinal and other preparations, or medical or surgical appliances, which they consider derogatory to the dignity of the profession, and contrary to the traditions and resolutions of the Royal College of Physicians.'

They are very particular in upholding their dignity, and when a man infringes their rules they have him up before the Council and his membership is taken from him. If, then, the public choose to employ medical men whose names their own College have thought necessary to expunge from their list, the public must not be surprised at the results; and thus it is that the unfortunate medical cases which appear periodically in the public press are the result of persons consulting men with little or no proper qualifications, or men who have been ostracized by the profession. Medicine properly practised is one of the most noble and elevating of the arts.

As the public sometimes fall a prey to unscrupulous so-called medical men, so doctors, unfortunately, fall easy victims to their speculative patients. Of course there are many men in the profession who double and treble their capital by wise investments, but there are also those who fall victims to the wily tongues of plausible rogues. My father was once taken in. He was always being given the most marvellous ' tips ' that would make a fortune, and, as he himself owned in after-life, he was ' once foolish enough to swallow the bait and invest a few thousands in this mine and a few thousands in that. Alas ! the mines quickly gobbled down my hard-earned guineas, and gave me no golden nuggets in return.'

One more patient story, and I have done with these queer folk. A certain man was very ill, but he would insist on drinking champagne, in spite of my father's orders to the contrary. The man got worse, and one day my father was summoned to Carlton House Terrace to see him. He again returned to the champagne charge, and declared the symptoms were being aggravated by alcohol. Denials from the patient. Finally the doctor left, feeling sure the man took alcohol, and probably champagne, in spite of all his protestations. As the consultant drove away in the carriage, he opened his fee-paper to put the coins in his pocket, when to his amazement he discovered 7s. 6d. Some mistake, of course; but imagine his surprise when the paper which had contained the money proved to be a bill,

and the bill said, ' To patent champagne corks, 7s. 6d.,'
dated the day before, with the patient's name in its head-
line !

Caught in his own trap !

Verily medical men come across all sorts and conditions
of men.

CHAPTER XVIII.

CANNIBAL BREAKFASTS.

ALL his life 'George Harley, of Harley Street,' as his friends called him, had a strong predilection for strange foods, and would warmly maintain almost everything was good to eat, and that we waste more than we use. For instance, during his travels in Russia he became accustomed to the red fungi which are dried and strung up on strings in rows in the rafters of the peasants' cottages, exactly as onions are tied to a stick in England. The common superstition in this country is that these red fungi are absolutely poisonous, but I have seen my father eat those with red tops and orange insides on many occasions, and they certainly never produced any ill effect.

On one of the many driving tours we made through England and Wales we stopped at Buxton, in order that he might take the waters. Nicholas Chevallier, the delightful artist who accompanied the Duke of Edinburgh round the world, was also staying there at the time for the same purpose. He had travelled in Russia, as well as my father, and I vividly remember, little girl though I was, our all going out together for a picnic tea, boiling the kettle on the gipsy caldron, while these two good men solemnly sat beside us munching the red and orange fungi which we small folk gathered for them.

The heading to this chapter is a strange one, but not more curious than the entertainments it describes, for every kind of queer food from the remotest corners of the earth was served at these meals.

Most of my father's friends were busy men like himself, often deeply engaged in the evenings, either at their own particular Scientific Societies or in writing books which made them famous, and therefore it was he evolved the idea of gathering a few friends around him on Sunday mornings for breakfast. These functions took place at 9.30, and the number of guests seldom exceeded twelve, from eight to twelve congenial spirits being, he considered, the essence of good company. The 'cannibal breakfasts' were not a freak taken up for the season and discarded at its wane, but were given at different times during many years of his life. His guests were only men; but among those men were some of the most interesting personalities of the time, although, unfortunately, as I have remarked elsewhere, my father has left no notes of their conversation. Whether he thought it unwise to do so, or whether he merely trusted to his memory for retailing a good story, I know not, but records there are none.

Of course, I was too young to recollect much of these assemblages, but I know that among those present were George Cruikshank; the brothers Charles and Edwin Landseer, R.A.; Charles Dickens, then in the zenith of his glory; John Leech, of *Punch*; Professor Sharpey; Sir James Simpson; John Tyndall; Sir William Gull; Sir John Erichsen; Sir William Savory; Sir Richard Quain; Robert Bell; Louis Blanc; Sir William Crookes; Sir Rowland Hill, of Penny Post fame; Frank Buckland, the naturalist; Professor William Milligan; Benoni, for many years the curator of Sir John Soane's Museum; Bond (afterwards Sir Edward), librarian at the British Museum; Sir John Evans; Sir Spencer Wells; Paul du Chaillu, who first discovered the gorilla; Catlin, the friend of North American Indians; John Rae, discoverer of the Franklin remains; Lord Playfair; S. C. Hall, etc.

Everywhere in society in those days one met Octave

Delepierre, brother-in-law of Lord Napier of Magdala, one of the most genial and charming of men. For many years he was the First Secretary of Legation to the Belgian Minister, who was then M. van der Weyer, universally respected and beloved in this country during his many years of office. Both were constant visitors at my father's.

The origin of the cannibal breakfasts, I believe, came from the fact that at one of the first of these functions my father, with much difficulty, procured a Pomeranian goose-breast, the first to be landed in this country. Greatly delighted with his purchase, he decided to have a breakfast, and accordingly invitations were issued, which evoked the following replies :

Colonel Addison, whose father tried the famous Colleen Bawn murder case, was a most original and interesting companion, full of humour and jollity, who, on receiving the invitation to this particular breakfast to partake of the goose-breast, answered immediately, for my father received the reply a few hours after having sent out the invitation. It ran somewhat thus :

> I've invited been to breakfast, at half-past nine,
> So to George Harley I'll surely go, and shall so feast
> (I shan't require to dine),
> For I should indeed be twice a dunce to shun my kindred goose.

Another answer, equally prompt, came from Dr. Hamilton, of Jamaica, which said :

> You've invited me to *anser ;** I accept with pleasure.

On another occasion donkey sausage formed the *pièce de résistance*, and some wit replied that ' Don Key accepted with pleasure, would elongate his ears for the occasion to hear all good things, and not forget to bray his own trumpet to perfection.'

Subjoined is a list of some of the Chinese delicacies that appeared on these occasions. Each breakfast was, as a rule, representative of a certain country, and as far as

* Latin for ' goose.'

possible the produce of that particular land alone was given.

Placed in small dishes on the table were:

Four plates 'relishes': one-thousand-years-old eggs, pork, fowl, and salt fish.
Four plates preserved fruits: Ginger, apricots, plums, melon.
Four plates fresh fruits: Oranges, water-chestnuts, olives, and pomeloes.
Four plates dried fruits: Peanuts, walnuts, almonds, dried melon-seeds (the latter are eaten with all the courses, like bread).

> Mandarin fish, boiled.
> Bêche-de-mer (sea-slug).
> Japanese fish.
> Spring olla (rats and mice).
> Fowl stew with lily-seeds.
> Ducks' tongues (stew).
> So-called sago, supposed to be a kind of seaweed.
> Corean fritters (fried pork fat).
> Winter mushrooms.
> Bright bones (fish maws).

It must not be supposed from these menus that nothing of a more substantial nature was provided, for my mother, with her practical mind, always insisted on having eggs and fish, to say nothing of cold ham for such folk as came to enjoy the conversation, but were unable to digest the odd repasts.

Gradually, as years rolled by, the cannibal breakfasts were given up, but the love of extraordinary viands remaining as strong as ever, my father sometimes inserted a couple of dishes into the menu of his dinner-parties. I am afraid that few of the lady guests appreciated these queer concoctions, and therefore it was that two of such specialities were found sufficient for an ordinary dinner-party. Some of these things were really very nice indeed, but, then, it was more a matter of good cooking, quantities of excellent stock and well-flavoured sauces, than the thing itself. I can remember as perfectly palatable the dish known as ' one-thousand-years-old eggs.' This choice production arrived from China, where I believe every egg cost £5, and although it is not at all likely that they had been buried for a thousand years, it is a fact that they had been rolled up in clay and kept for a very considerable number of years for the right transformation to take place. Preparing these eggs for table was a great event. The egg had to be carefully shelled ; it was never cooked at all, be it remembered ; but by process of time the clear white had become a beautiful dark transparent brown, about the same colour as dark brown vinegar, only that it was gelatinous. The yolk had turned a creamy green and was soft and pliable, and not only resembled in colour, but also in taste, ripe Stilton cheese. These precious eggs were cut in thin slices and carefully laid on buttered toast. Then, placed in an entrée dish, they were smartly decorated with bits of parsley or coloured flowers by the doctor's own hands, ready to be served.

Some of the little ' sun-dried shrimps ' he also prepared himself, arranging them neatly in little paper cases. They had quite the flavour of our English shrimps ; the little shrivelled-up, dried atoms, after being soaked, swelled out to the size of large prawns and were quite palatable.

Of course he had bird's-nest soup, which, I believe, can now be bought in England, but which my father was the first person to taste in this country. For many years he tried fruitlessly to procure a bird's nest, and then one fine day, to his joy, some were sent him from China. They looked like a brown gelatinous mass, and when soaked swelled tremendously, but tasted of absolutely nothing until good rich stock was added. The poor cook sighed at wasting her good soup on such ' a dirty mess.'

Although all ordinary wines were offered at the dinners, yet as something ' extraordinarily special ' and very delicious indeed there was served a spirit which individu- ally I should call ' liquid fire.' This and other deadly concoctions sent home with the greatest care, and prized most highly by my father, luxuriated in such thrilling names as 'Shamshow of tiger's bones,' and, served warm in proper Chinese fashion, were simply awful !

'Essence of rose leaves' and 'lily-flower water' sounded delicious, but in reality skinned the throat and burnt the tongue, even when only taken in sips from a liqueur-glass.

Great was the consternation of our dear old cook Elizabeth (who was my father's housekeeper before he married, and remained in his service for thirty years, ultimately dying as a pensioner), as to how she was to cook these extraordinary viands—' Dr. Harley's messes ' she called them, and being persuaded of the fact that they were messes, nothing would induce her to taste them, therefore when she added a little pepper or a little salt, a little spice or a little sauce, she always went up to the study, saucepan in hand, to make ' the master ' give his opinion as to their palatableness.

Many of my father's patients got to know of this strange love of queer foods, for they often heard him expounding the theory, when on the subject of diet, that everything was good to eat if we only knew how to cook it, and consequently some of the people who lived in far-distant lands, and had come back to Britain specially to consult him about their various liver complaints, sent him most extraordinary contributions when they returned to their far-away homes.

The climax, however, arrived one day in the shape of an earthenware jar from the West Indies.   It was delivered at a time when my father was away, and as the cook had been long expecting some particular delicacy from 'foreign parts,' she thought she had better open the jar and put its contents in a safe place.   Carefully she undid the string and the paper, cut the parchment sealed down round the china top, and lifted up the lid.   Something dark was inside, and not being able to see what it was, she took it to the window for further examination.   The reader can only faintly imagine her horror when she discovered that the jar contained a little nigger baby sent home for scientific investigation !

Here is a list, written by a Chinaman, of specimens sent
' to George Harley, Esq., F.R.S., by a grateful patient ':

> Bird's-nest soup.
> Shark's-fins soup.
> Almond (thick white soup flavoured with almonds).
> Duck stuffed with ' valuables ' (untranslatable).
> Pigeons' eggs, in clear soup.
> The thousand pearls (untranslatable).
> The silver ear (fungus).
> Dried Ulurex.
> Cutting seaweeds.
> Dried lily flower.
> Rose Shamshow. ⎫
> Shantung whisky.
> Newchwang whisky.
> Rice Shamshow.
> Distilled liquor. ⎬ Drinks.
> Green peas Shamshow.
> Glutinous rice Shamshow.
> Tiger's bones Shamshow.
> White shark fins. ⎭
> Black shark fins.
> Fungus.
> Salt eggs.
> Preserved eggs.
> Seaweeds.
> Shellfish.
> Black bêche-de-mer.
> White bêche-de-mer.
> Birds' nests.
> Isinglass.
> Cuttle-fish.
> Dried bean curd.
> Edible seaweeds.
> Flat fish.
> Fish maws.
> Dried oysters.
> Dried shrimps.
> Green seaweed (to be treated till quite crisp and eaten with
> curry).

The wife of a celebrated judge in the East sent home
many interesting things from Japan, among them :

Soy mer—a very nice sauce.

Tori nabi, or bird pot.

Fine white seaweed for soups.

Salt plum. The plum is packed in a *umi boshi*, sort of pirilla leaf which gives the aromatic salt flavour. The Japanese eat them the first thing in the morning with moist sugar, to clear away the 'fog' caused by a night's rest.

Sometimes the 'cannibal meals' were Russian, Italian, Australian or Canadian, instead of Chinese ; then we would have black bear, raw salmon, elk, buffalo-hump (quite delicious), beaver tail, elephant's foot, kangaroo tail; in fact, I believe there is hardly any food that has not found its way into that Harley Street dining-room. The kangaroo tails were sent home by Sir Charles Todd, Postmaster-General of South Australia—the man who laid the first cable across that continent. They were a great surprise in the seventies when they first came, and now twenty years later a consignment of 1,000 tails has arrived for disposal at Leadenhall Market !

Ideas have changed much in the matter of food during the last twenty-five years, and we who enjoy kangaroo and goose-breast, smoked salmon, and such-like delicacies to-day, little realize that a quarter of a century ago they were almost unknown in England.

Kind reader, have you ever eaten hedgehog ? If not, let me recommend it to your notice ; it is very good.

For several summers we had a farm at Meopham where we children were sent during all the hot months. My father used to come down from Saturday to Monday, and I well remember many little expeditions we had in pursuit of the hedgehog.

Hedgehogs are not so difficult to find as to catch. The large black retriever used to nose them out, and by his vigorous barks and general excitement disclose their where-abouts ; but he absolutely refused to catch Mr. Hedgehog, for even when he patted the strange creature with his toe the little spikes pricked, and the poor retriever retired on three legs with a woebegone expression of countenance. My father then came to his assistance, and having caught the hedgehog and killed him, he rolled him into a cloth brought for the purpose, and one of us children carried him home slung at the end of a stick across the shoulder. Oh, what performances we used to have under the magnificent walnut-trees skinning the hedgehog, which operation was generally performed by my father with the aid of a penknife! We assisted and capered around, and thoroughly enjoyed the ghastly entertainment. Somehow the first hedgehog was not a great success; it did not taste sufficiently like tender chicken, and my father determined to find a gipsy woman and from her learn the real art of hedgehog-cooking. He and I rode for miles round Kent in pursuit of the gipsies; we found many, but they were not the true kind, and did not understand the mystery we desired to learn. At last one fine day we discovered a little encampment of real true gipsies born and bred, not merely wandering vagrants; these folk and my father became great comrades; he learnt much of their habits and customs, which he afterwards discussed with his old friend Charles Leland, who at that time was writing much about gipsy tribes.

Well, the good woman explained that the hedgehog was to be rolled up in clay without being skinned. That a hole in the ground was to be made, a fire kindled, and the clay pudding buried therein. When sufficiently done, the clay would break and out would come the cooked hedgehog, all the prickles belonging to which would remain firmly embedded in the clay. We went home triumphant; we caught the hedgehog, and followed out the directions. The result was still not satisfactory. Nothing daunted, my father and I rode back another day to the gipsy encampment, and he made a bargain that the woman should come over and prepare a hedgehog for him her own way. She came, and cooked it in the back-orchard; her bake was perfect, and the white flesh of the hedgehog proved delicious. It was very much like frog (grenouille), such as one gets in Paris.

15

During many years my father was greatly devoted to horse exercise, and as he did not like riding up and down the Row alone, at seven years of age he put me on a horse, 15 hands 2, called Leibchen. Every morning for many years he and I were members of the 'liver brigade.' So began the early training, under a very critical master, which enabled me afterwards to ride across Iceland astride, through Morocco, etc.

We had tea and bread-and-butter; started at 7.15, returning at 8.45 for a bath and breakfast; then he went to his study, I sallied forth to school. When illness made it necessary for him to give up his daily rides, he was very sad, for it also deprived us of our happy Saturday afternoon expeditions (my school half-holiday) to Harrow, Richmond, Surbiton or Barnes, where we used to have tea at some small inn and the 'little missy' was given new-laid eggs, home-made jam, or watercress. But twenty years have changed all that. The inns are now public-houses, Kilburn is a suburb, Harrow a town, and West Kensington's fields are modern flats.

Samphire was another great dish during the year we lived in the Isle of Man, when my father was so ill that he had for a second time to retire from practice. He learned to enjoy the samphire pickle. It is a form of seaweed—a green thing which looks almost like thin, long beans. And a second dish he particularly appreciated was sloak, another form of seaweed, which the Manx people are very fond of serving as a vegetable, boiled. It is an ugly dish, being a brown, glutinous mass, but it is not bad when eaten like spinach. Perfectly delicious were the Manx cray-fish we used to enjoy for supper every Sunday night during that long and tedious waiting for health in the Isle of Man. Looking back upon it, it seems incredible that a man should twice in a short career have been obliged to give up his profession absolutely and entirely, on different occasions, for over a couple of years. Was it not enough to break the stoutest heart—to bring despair to the bravest ? And yet he bore these illnesses resignedly, amused himself by reading, writing reminiscences, and taking the widest interest in everything about and around him.

It was in the Isle of Man he wrote a series of natural history stories that had happened to himself. Each one bears a dedication on its cover for the child for whom he intended it. The following are the titles:

> My Bosom Friend—a White Rat.
> A Blackbird's Widowhood, Wooing, and Second Wedding.
> A Narrow Escape from Drowning.
> Vigo, my First Pet.
> Did a Whale swallow Jonah ?
> Half a Day with Poisonous Snakes.
> Do Snakes swallow their Young ?
> Nannie Cairncross.
> Fragments in the History of Two Robin Redbreasts.
> My feathered Pet.
> Little Jenny Wren.
> A Sail in a Tub.
> A Visiting Dog.
> Toss ; or, The Life of a Skye Terrier.
> My Ghost Story.
> Poisoned Arrows.

These papers contain a vast amount of information woven into interesting stories of animal life, suitable for children from six to twelve years, as we were at that time. He only published a few, and the rest were laid aside ' till he had time to attend to them.'

Alas ! that time never came. Death outstripped its laggard footsteps.

CHAPTER XIX.

As may be gathered from the foregoing pages, my father had a vast number of charming friends. While in society, he met everyone of note. 'Be a listener,' he would say, 'in the society of the wise, and a talker in that of fools. Never say a nasty thing; nastiness is the wit of the uneducated.' Perhaps it was these rules which made him so popular as a conversationalist.

I have, however, carefully avoided relating anecdotes of the living, rarely even mentioning names.

One living friend I must mention, however, viz., Dr. William Marcet, F.R.S., grandson of the famous Mrs. Marcet, of Botany fame, who was one of the founders, with Alfred Tennyson, Charles Kingsley, John Hullah, and Frederick Denison Maurice, of the 'first college open to women,' for the jubilee of which event I edited a booklet.* I name Dr. Marcet because, in writing about George Harley's death, he speaks of their 'true, un-alloyed friendship during forty-seven years.'

Such a friendship between two men is a record. They took their degrees at Edinburgh together (1850); they worked side by side in Paris in 1852, at the laboratory of Wurz, the distinguished chemist and Dean of the Faculty of Medicine.

Dr. Marcet and my father ran in double harness, so to speak. Each lived at a later date in Harley Street, with

* 'The First College for Women'—Queen's College, 1848-1898.

their brass plates upon their respective doors, each became Fellow of the Royal Society, and each worked at University College—one as professor, the other as experimentalist; and finally, after forty-seven years, Dr. Marcet writes : ' The matter is gone, but the soul is preserved, and we hope and believe that the imperishable part of his nature will for ever live. His old chum has indeed nothing but kind and affectionate thought to bestow on the friend of well-nigh half a century.'

One of the pleasantest friendships the London physician made in later years was that of Lady Charlotte Bacon, the original of ' Ianthe,' whom he had known by name all his life. Lord Byron was a very intimate friend of her mother, the Countess of Oxford. The Earl and Countess of Oxford were also great friends of Queen Caroline, and to be near her they removed with their family to Italy. At the same time Byron was in Italy, and it was then he wrote the prologue to 'Childe Harold.' He went to Athens, but on his return he again joined the Oxford family in Italy, and was so much struck with little Lady Charlotte Harley's beauty and cleverness that he dedicated ' Childe Harold ' to her, and wrote the final lines to her as ' Ianthe.'

She was then not quite twelve years old, and not, as stated in many editions of Byron, fifteen. A year or two after this event Byron's admiration for the little girl developed into something warmer, and consequently when she was about fifteen he wished to marry her. She would none of him, however, and later on married, at the Embassy in Paris, Colonel Bacon, a very distinguished soldier. He had gone all through the Peninsular War, and fought at Waterloo, where he was wounded in the last charge, carrying the bullet embedded in his flesh to the day of his death. He also served in India, Portugal and Spain, and died with the rank of a General Officer, having satisfactorily quelled the rebellion against Queen Donna Maria of Portugal.

Thus the life of Lady Charlotte Bacon had chanced to be a very varied one, and when my father met her first in the eighties, he found her experiences were many. The beauty and charm of the young girl had developed into a most interesting and original personality, and at the age of seventy she fascinated my father immensely. Many were the long chats he enjoyed with her in Harley Street or at her own home in Stanhope Place. She was never tired of talking about Lord Byron, many miniatures and relics of whom she possessed. She said ' he was very handsome, witty, sarcastic—venomous, even—and sullen-tempered at times, principally owing to his club foot, but also to his wife's utter inability to appreciate his undoubted talents.'

With her died the last of the Oxford family ; the title had become extinct, her brother, the late Earl of Oxford, leaving no male heir. She was a wonderful old woman, but time had wrinkled her face, and it always seemed to me utterly impossible when looking at her to believe she could ever have been the lovely girl depicted as 'Ianthe.' She was very fond of young people, and it was at her house I enjoyed my first ball, quickly followed by theatricals, in which the old lady took the keenest interest, showing each and all how to act the parts. At the last rehearsal, how-ever, she was taken ill, and shortly afterwards died.

After her death one of her daughters begged my father to go and see her mother, because ' she looked so beautiful ' —and truly she did. When he beheld her, he could hardly believe his eyes ; 'the lines graven by care and length of days on the aged woman's face were all gone, and the beautiful girl of the famous " Ianthe " portrait had come back again.'

My father knew well also another most interesting in-dividual, Trelawny, the friend of Byron. A true Bohemian, his life had been full of romance, and he was consequently a most delightful and interesting companion, whose stories were always fascinating. He was the trusted friend of both

Byron and Shelley, with whom he had spent months in the most intimate association.

Trelawny during the latter years of his life was a sad invalid, and used to remark, ' This enforced solitude makes my brains dull and my wits contract, but it amuses me to conjure up visions of Shelley, the tall, blushing, feminine boy, the lithe stripling who was excommunicated by the Church of Rome for his opinions, deprived of his civil rights by his Lord Chancellor, and disowned by every member of his family.'

' Shelley was a delightful companion,' he would say; ' he was all strength and fire in his writings, all weakness and mobility in his person.' Many years of Trelawny's life were spent with Shelley; they were much in Italy together, and when poor Shelley was finally drowned off the Italian coast (1822), Trelawny was then commanding the steamer *Bolivar*. He was commissioned to exhume the remains, and have them cremated according to Shelley's wish. Trelawny often described this scene to my father—the terrible recognition of the man he had so loved in the long-buried corpse. Then how he had had the almost unrecognisable remains of a once-brilliant being placed in an iron furnace, and there burnt and reduced to ashes on the sea-shore. These ashes he afterwards placed in a box which he had lined with black velvet, carefully fastened down the screws, and himself guarded as far as Leghorn !

The old gentleman loved to dwell on the past, and his conversations were always so interesting that my father spent many an odd hour in his company.

Trelawny had not the same profound admiration for Byron that he had for Shelley; indeed, he would say, ' Byron himself thought Shelley the most imaginative poet of the hour, and owned to me that it was at Shelley's suggestion he wrote much of " Childe Harold." ' Trelawny used to speak of Byron as ' a solemn farce with a superb memory, and,' he continued, ' he never could argue about anything, and his ways were niggardly. We often made

expeditions together, and Shelley was generally paymaster.
I repaid my debt at once, feeling it dishonourable not to
do so.   Byron always shirked repayment until absolutely
compelled to part with his money, and certainly after poor
Shelley died, and his charming and brilliant wife was left
in such straitened circumstances, Byron never did anything at all to help her—in fact, to my mind, behaved
most ungenerously.'

Although Trelawny did not have the same profound
admiration for Byron as for Shelley, the 'ladies' poet'
fascinated him, and they were much together, and, strangely
enough, it was Trelawny who packed up Byron's effects
after his death from fever at Missolonghi, where he had
died a few days before Trelawny's arrival.   Among these
effects he found a fine cambric handkerchief marked with
a lady's name, much stained with blood, a ringlet of hair,
a glove, and a ribbon.

The last time my father saw Trelawny was not long
before the old gentleman died, when he was sitting before
the fire with both his shoes and his stockings off, and his
toes roasting near the glowing coals.   His daughter, who
was very beautiful, was in the room, and rushed forward
to tell her father to put on his shoes as Dr. Harley was
coming.

'Put on my shoes?' he said, 'what nonsense !   I am not
ashamed of my feet, and if Dr. Harley has got as good a
pair as I have, he need not be ashamed of his, either; and
for all I care, he can take off his boots and socks and warm
his toes too, if he likes.'

I only quote this as an instance of the utter uncon-
ventionality of the intimate friend of two of the greatest
poets of the century.

Robert Browning was here, there, and everywhere in
those days; his commanding appearance attracted notice,
and he and his brilliant wife were always welcome guests.
My father summed them up by saying : 'Browning was
such a gentleman, and his wife such a dear.'

These two people, who made their mark in the literary world of their day, and lived an ideal family life as well as a brilliant social one, have passed away, and verily nothing remains but the empty palace on the Grand Canal at Venice, with its magnificent rooms devoid of life. No laughter rings through those halls ; the place is, as it were, dead, yet contains many treasures, and its size and position, besides its interest, beg for the old palace to be turned into a museum, in remembrance of one of the most brilliant couples of the century.

At the time my father was writing on 'Stones and Pearls' he had much correspondence with Ruskin, who was also greatly interested in the study of crystallization. Being anxious to compare notes, it was arranged that Dr. George Harley should pay Ruskin a visit, when, in his genial way, the great art critic wrote 'that the turret chamber should be all ready' on a certain day. Accordingly, my father made his appearance at the Lakes about dinner-time, when he was ushered into 'the turret chamber,' and soon after dinner, being weary with the railway journey from London, retired to rest. At daybreak he rose to draw up the blind, and when he came to a queer-shaped window in a corner of the room, stood absolutely transfixed by the beauty of the scene which the sun, rising over the mountains at the head of Lake Coniston, illumined.

A little later the servant brought him a cup of coffee, with a message from Mr. Ruskin that he hoped Dr. Harley would enjoy it, as he had just made it for him ; he would not get such every day.

This was the first little act of kindness which continued all through many delightful hours they spent together. Besides being a most charming companion, John Ruskin is surrounded by innumerable treasures of all sorts ; in fact, his house is a perfect museum of curios. Not the least interesting are the pictures by Turner in his bedroom, which, as he says, he looks at first thing every morning and last thing every night, and 'When I die, Dr. Harley,' he added, 'I hope they may be the last things my eyes will rest on in this world.'

My mother and sister Olga (then a very little girl) were left at the hotel at Coniston, as they were all going on to Scotland afterwards. My father had said nothing about them, not dreaming of taking them and a maid to Ruskin's house; but when Ruskin heard they were at Coniston, he insisted on my father at once writing a note to the hotel saying the carriage should be sent for them in an hour's time, and *they must come and stop* at Brantwood.

When the great art critic discovered my sister Olga's love of animal life, he was quite enchanted, and entered into all her enthusiasm and pleasure, just as if he were himself a child; hand-in-hand the old gentleman and the little girl walked about for hours, he explaining the beauties of Nature and the habits of animal life to her interested little ears.

Thus it was that one of my father's most delightful holidays was spent with John Ruskin. They afterwards corresponded constantly, but I, unfortunately, can only find a couple of letters, which I give:

'Brantwood, Coniston, Lancashire,
'*June* 15, 1887.

'DEAR DR. HARLEY,

'It is entirely comforting and exhilarating to me to have your letter and Olga's, and to hear of all those wonderful things in crystals, just when what I thought was clearest in *me* and hardest has become clouded and frangible. For everything I thought I *knew* of minerals (you know, I never *think* except that I thought I knew) has been made mere cloud and bewilderment by what I find in Field's address at the Geological of planes of internal motion, etc., and all my final purposes of writing elementary descriptions of them—broken like reeds. I can only now study tadpoles with Olga. If, indeed, you could leave her here awhile on that Scottish run North, there will be an entirely kind and prudent chaperon staying in charge of a girl from Girton whom Olga would love, and who is going to undertake the elementary music at the village school. But I can't write more to-day. Olga's letter is beautifully written, but chills me with the fatal idea of her going to school! I think there should be *no* schools, nor pensions, nor academies, nor universities—that all children should be always at home with papa and mamma, seldom out.

'Ever gratefully yours,

'J. RUSKIN.

'Don't send me back the topaz. Let it stay with yours, which it properly companions. I have more here than I shall ever see.'

'Brantwood, Coniston, Lancashire,
'*June* 16, 1887.

'DEAR DR. HARLEY,

'Indeed I *should* like to come, and have a little pink riband fastened by Olga to my breast-buttonhole, and be led wheresoever she chose; and, indeed, I should like not to talk, but to hear of the wonderful things you scientific people are doing, for I am quite crushed now, and am resigned in a pulverulent state of mind, to be radiated or coagulated into whatever new forms of belief or apprehension are possible to me in my old age.

'But, alas! I am not able any more but for the quiet of evening among the hills. And you know this is our loveliest time—the trees and grass at their greenest, and roses beginning to bud—it is the time we wait for all the year; and we are bound to do it reverence and be thankful.

'Please don't think me ungrateful—either Mrs. Harley or Olga or you—you have made me happy beyond my wont in thinking that you would care to have me, and I am, to all of you, a very faithful and grateful friend.

'J. RUSKIN.

'Your postscript is really tantalizing; I wait to hear what Olga says.'

My father always referred to John Ruskin as a delightful man. ' He always spoke,' he said, ' in the softest, gentlest voice, was deferential to others, never dictatorial in anything, even art, and keenly appreciative of any information.' 'I never knew a man use more beautiful language in ordinary conversation than Ruskin,' my father would say ; ' words tripped lightly from his tongue—well-chosen words, well-arranged sentences, and excellent matter.'

Sir David Brewster was one of the London physician's kindest friends. Although Vice-Chancellor of the University of Edinburgh, he constantly journeyed to London in order to attend scientific societies, and thus the old and the young man often met. Although originally a Presbyterian minister, Sir David Brewster became extremely scientific, inventing, among other things, the kaleidoscope.

Among some of my father's notes are the following on ' The Man in whose Brain originated the Idea of the World's Fair ' (the Great Exhibition of 1851, the first idea of its kind the world ever saw):

' To-day* I made the acquaintance of Francis Fuller, aged seventy-one, and from his own lips learned the history of the origin of the " World's Fair," the Great Exhibition of the Industry of all Nations in Hyde Park, London, in 1851.

' Francis Fuller was one of the executive committee, who, being an active member of the Society of Arts, accompanied Mr., afterwards Sir, Digby Wyatt; Mr., now Sir, Henry Cole; and Mr. Scott Russell, F.R.S., subsequently secretary to the Royal Commission of the Exhibition, to the eleventh National Exhibition held at Paris in 1849. It was then the idea of a great International Exhibition sprang up in the mind of Mr. Fuller, an idea which has since exercised an immense influence not only on the fine arts and industry, but upon the commercial development of all nations.

' The four gentlemen returned to England separately,

* August 20, 1877 (Boulogne-sur-Mer).

Mr. Fuller viâ Southampton, where he met by accident Mr. Thomas Cubitt on his way to London from Osborne, where he was then engaged in building for the Prince Consort.

'While the train was speeding on its way to London, in the course of conversation the seeds of the idea were sown by Mr. Fuller mentioning what he believed England to be capable of doing in the way of a gigantic international exhibition of art and manufacture, and advising him to get his royal master to head the enterprise, which if successful would raise him enormously in the world's estimation.

'Mr. Cubitt acted upon this suggestion, with the result that Mr. Fuller was introduced to the Prince Consort, who listened with great interest to his scheme : Mr. Fuller was accompanied by Mr. Scott Russell, then secretary to the Society of Arts, and Mr. Cole. The Prince, having received satisfactory replies to his many questions (he was a cautious man), there and then consented to entertain the subject, with the express understanding that no use should be made of his name until he formally gave his consent, which he was unwilling to do until he had consulted with the members of Her Majesty's Government.

'In July, 1849, Messrs. Russell, Cole, and Fuller were summoned to meet Her Majesty's Ministers at Osborne, in order to explain their views on the subject of the World's Great Exhibition.

'At that time Sir Robert Peel, who was then Prime Minister, declared that, however beneficial an exhibition of the kind might be, he would not advise the Prince to attach his name to it until they had the unmistakable assurance that the manufacturers of Great Britain were, as a body, in favour of such a scheme.

'Messrs. Russell, Fuller, and Cole then ascertained the views of every manufacturer of note in the kingdom, the whole expense of doing which was defrayed out of Mr. Fuller's private purse, and reported the result of the inquiry to the Prince at Balmoral in September, and after another meeting of the Ministers, ways and means were discussed, and a contractor was sought who would take upon his own shoulders the whole responsibility of paying all incidental expenses, and erecting the building at a cost not exceeding £150,000, "upon the understanding" he should receive two-thirds of the net profits, and the Society of Arts one-third, and at the same time undertake to bear any loss which might ensue. Mr. George Munday accepted the contract, and deposited in the hands of the Prince £20,000 as a guarantee that he would erect the works to the satisfaction of His Royal Highness and the Ministry (without which deposit the Ministry refused to entertain the scheme).

'A Royal Commission was then appointed, which, on finding Mr. Munday would in all probability make £100,000 by the contract, put an end to it by giving him a compensation of £5,000, awarded by Mr. Robert Stevenson's arbitration, over and above all his expenses. The Commission then replaced the responsibility of the contractor by a guarantee fund that in the end amounted to £257,000, subscribed by twenty-eight gentlemen, the Prince heading the list with £10,000. Upon this guarantee the Bank of England advanced £35,000, no more money being required in consequence of Mr. Fuller succeeding in collecting by public subscriptions £67,896 12s. 6d., and a clear profit being made by charging 5s. for entrance fee during the course of building the palace.

'At first the Prince was frightened at the responsibility he had incurred, and ordered every copy of the minutes of executive committee to be sent to him, saying that if they were correct he would not answer, but if wrong he would immediately write. In this he kept his word, for on one occasion, finding the minutes inaccurate, he with his own hand corrected them and returned the corrected copy to Mr. Scott Russell, who acted as honorary secretary.

'How the enterprise was subsequently opposed by the unenlightened press, and the many difficulties that were encountered in its progress, are matters of history, and had it not been for the steady adherence of the Prince to the plans first agreed upon, and his persistence in having them carried out to the letter, London would never have had the honour of holding within its precincts the first grand international exhibition of the world's industries in 1851.

' Mr. Fuller is a man of six feet, bright and merry, and as full of fun as he is of sense. Fond of repeating a joke also, as the subjoined examples show.

' The first is of his friend Theodore Hook, who while at dinner with a gentleman overheard the servant tell him the tax-gatherer was waiting to be paid, and on his host telling the servant to bid him call again, wittily said :

> ' " Mr. Winter has called for the taxes ;
> I advise you to pay whatever he axes.
> Nay, pay him at once, and without any flummery,
> For tho' his name's Winter, his actions are summary !"

' Another equally good one I heard him tell was of the conversation of a Turkish gentleman with a fair English belle. Said the lady :

> ' " I can't abide you Turkish folks,
> Who take your wives by twenty ;
> In England *one* is found no joke,
> And most men find *one* plenty."

' To which the Turk made answer :

> ' " In England true this plan may do,
> And be as well as any ;
> But all the charms they find in *you*
> We only find in many." '

In turning over a mass of papers and letters I chanced to come across a communication from Mrs. Lynn Linton, written in February, 1896, and as it is a very characteristic note showing the kind-heartedness of a woman whom the public looked upon as ' severe and acid,' and may therefore be of interest at a moment when this dear old friend has just passed away, I venture to give it :

‘ Brougham House, Malvern,
‘ *February* 2, 1896.

‘ Dear Dr. Harley,

‘ I write just a line of thanks to you for your kind reception of my friend Mrs. —— It cheered and "uplifted" her greatly. Her story is a very sad one, and in all her trials she has conducted herself with an unselfishness, a faithful regard for duty and high principle, beyond all praise. She has been driven to this step of independent work by simple starvation—the word is no exaggeration. Her husband must be the very vilest man that ever lived, and she has been truly an angel under provocations that would have almost justified—well, what? I was going to say murder! If she can make her way in the profession she has chosen, the law will *now* protect her and let her keep her children. She learnt the basis and main part of what she knows while assisting her husband to study medicine, which he never did study, and wherein he took neither a degree nor passed an exam. He simply lived on her money and vapoured; when he had eaten her poor little portion he lived on her mother, whom he vilified and accused of crimes that would have merited the Old Bailey. I cannot write half; but I do know this little creature's sterling *worth*. She seems, too, to have made herself professionally capable.

‘ My warmest and kindest remembrances to you all : the dear wife and daughters, and that delightful son, and your own good and generous-hearted self.

‘ You will be glad to hear that Malvern air suits me, and that I am well here and free from all my old trouble of bronchitis and the like.

‘ Sincerely and gratefully yours,

‘ E. Lynn Linton.’

CHAPTER XX.

For some years Gladstone lived in Harley Street, and it was his habit every morning to leave home about half-past nine or ten and walk down to his work. It was also the custom for my sister Olga, then a very little girl, to go out with her nurse about the same time to the Regent's Park for her morning walk. Some twenty or thirty houses divided my father's from Mr. Gladstone's, and therefore, as the elderly statesman and the little girl both left home about the same time, they very often met in that short span.

'Well, how is dolly this morning?' he would say, and then he would chaff the little lady on not having washed dolly's face, or tell her that the prized treasure wanted a new bonnet. In fact, he never passed the child without stopping to pat her on the head and make some little joke such as children love. She became so fond of her elderly friend that she was quite disappointed if she did not meet him as she went for her walk, and would come home crestfallen if she had not seen 'my friend Mr. Gladstone,' as she always called him.

It was when Gladstone first came to Harley Street that the mob broke his windows, and shouted and yelled at his opposition to Disraeli's policy about the Russo-Turkish War. The Jingo fever was at its height. It was a tremendous excitement, and the street ultimately had to be cleared by mounted police. To the surprise

16

of everyone, in the midst of the tumult the Gladstones' front-door opened, and out walked the old couple, arm-in-arm, right into the midst of the very people who had been breaking their windows. With the manner of a courtier, the elderly Minister took off his hat, made a profound bow to the populace, and walked down the street with his wife.

It was a plucky act, and one which so surprised the boisterous assembly that they utterly subsided, and quietly went home in peace.

For Thackeray my father always entertained a profound admiration. 'He was always such a gentleman,' he was wont to say. 'Somewhat sarcastic and intolerant, but most genial to those he liked, and ever ready to appreciate talent and lend a helping hand if needed.'

One of their great bonds of union was Thackeray's profound devotion to his mother, which almost equalled my father's veneration for his. Thackeray died a few years after the doctor settled in London, but even during those few years he was very kind to the young medico.

Dean Stanley, like my father, was a great tea-drinker. On one occasion Thackeray was standing by, when he exclaimed : ' Why, you would both be reduced to as great a state of misery without that cup as would my good old friend Twining, the City tea merchant, if we deprived him of his first T.'

Of Catlin, author of ' Wanderings among the North American Indians,' my father often spoke. The most delightful time he spent with Catlin was during one summer when they agreed to join company at Ostend, where for days they talked and compared notes. Many years after poor Catlin's death my father visited America, one of the greatest inducements to do so being to see for himself something of the country the indefatigable traveller had so graphically described. On nearing a certain part of the great plains of the West, my father asked the conductor of the luxurious train if they did not pass through some of the wild prairies described by Catlin. The man was so surprised to find how much the English traveller knew about the country that he promised to call him in the early twilight, when they would come to an old disused, but once celebrated, Indian camp. When they reached the place, my father was immensely impressed and astonished at the truthful vigour with which Catlin had described every detail.

I find in his notes the following:

'Now for the prairies! Now for the scenes of the wandering of my dear old friend George Catlin, whose tales concerning the noble Red Indian savages in their primitive state inspired me with an intense longing to visit them in their own wild homes! Poor Catlin, alas! is now no more, so I cannot fulfil my promise of telling him how I found his old and well-beloved friends, or what I thought of them.

'Catlin first dwelt among these strange folk in 1832, and I had a copy of his original map with me, showing where the different tribes of North American Indians had dwelt at that time. When I travelled over the same ground fifty years later in a train, what ravages the white man had made! Of the Chippeways I saw none, except a young woman of about twenty-three, with a baby of eighteen months old. They were on board the boat between Port Arthur and Duluth. She did not understand a syllable of English, and only smiled when I gave the child 25 cents. It was the Mandans, the Crows, and the Blackfeet, as described by Catlin, that had most interested me — the first on account of their peculiar religious customs, the second on account of their chiefs wearing long hair. One of these Crow braves' hair Catlin measured, and found it actually 10 feet 7 inches in length! The women's locks were, comparatively speaking, short. The Blackfeet, again, interested me on account of their having been a very important and intelligent tribe in Catlin's time, numbering, he said, 16,000 souls. I may here mention that it is an

16—2

absurdity to call any of the North American Indians " Red-skins," since red-skinned in any sense of the word they are not. Neither are they black, having, in fact, pale-brown complexions. Some tribes are, indeed, almost fair, being more sallow yellow than anything else.

'From those I saw, I should say they most nearly approach Mongolians, Asiatics, and the tribes of men we call gipsies ; for they have straight black hair, bright black eyes, and straight, sometimes even slightly aquiline, noses, all of which prove that they have, like the gipsies in Europe, an Asiatic origin. Owing to the men having no beards and wearing long hair, they are often by tourists mistaken for women.

' Oh, what a disappointment I met with as regards these Indians ! No more of the " noble-faced, straight-limbed, well-fed, and self-confident men " of Catlin's time were to be found amongst them. Their " nobility of nature " had disappeared, and the debasement of a " barbarous civiliza-tion " usurped its place. His lofty expression had passed from him with his lands and his freedom. Blankets and trousers had taken the place of buffalo robes and moccasins. An English bridle and a Mexican saddle were seen instead of a twisted thong and a bare back. . . .

' 'Tis well that poor Catlin is not alive to hear my sorrowful tales of the fate and appearance of a people who were so good and kind to him in the days of their pros-perity and wild magnificence.

' Not one single buffalo did we see, though we travelled a thousand miles and more across the prairies where in Catlin's time they were to be met with in millions. Skeletons and horns were all that remained to tell the tale of their past existence.

' The poor elk, too, has almost disappeared. We saw none alive, though we passed dead ones and fed upon their flesh.

' As we journey onwards, innumerable high - pointed hillocks, abruptly and boldly standing out on the prairie, are visible on all sides; but now, instead of appearing as bare earth, they are shrouded to the top with grass, indicating, as it were, an older development. No sooner did we get among them than I anxiously looked out for one high hill in particular, Catlin told me could be seen many miles distant, which had a tall pole stuck on the top of it to mark the last resting-place of the famous chief O-ma-haws (Blackbird), who, when dead, seated on his war-horse, was taken to the top of it and there entombed, the earth being gradually piled round the horse till the creature was suffocated, and then up and around his dead rider until both were completely buried in. There it was exactly as Catlin had described it to me twenty years previously.'

My father always cherished Catlin's memory as that of a true and valued friend.

Some years after this trip across Canada and home by the States, the doctor published a paper, 'Comparison between the Recuperative Bodily Power of Man in a Rude and in a Highly-civilized State : Illustrative of the Probably Recuperative Capacity of Men of the Stone Age in Europe.'

This was written after he had given a lecture at the Anthropological Institute (November, 1887), to show how, in spite of the refining influence of civilization, it deteriorates the recuperative bodily power, and that, while we are taller, live longer, and perchance look handsomer, we have not the same healthy recuperative power. He worked the subject out with his usual untiring energy, and apropos of the North American Indians above referred to I give one extract :

'Now for the case of a North American Indian. While I was passing from the rugged volcanic geyser district of Montana into the fertile plains of the Columbia River in Oregon in 1884, the conductor of our train pointed out a one-legged Indian standing at the depot, whom I mistook for a woman, from his being like the squaws, as devoid of hair on his face as they are of projecting bosoms, and not only being dressed in a similar costume, but wearing his head-hair in the same long and lank fashion as the women do. This man, the conductor said, had hacked off the lower part of his own leg with a tomahawk in order to extricate himself from a crane, and afterwards crawled more than a mile to his wigwam before he could get assistance. Yet, in spite of all this, he was able within a fortnight to hobble about minus his leg.'

That American trip my father thoroughly enjoyed. He loved travel, and the habits and customs of strange folk fascinated him. The next note, I find, is on my own marriage, which evidently revived many memories. He says :

'My daughter Ethel has just married (1887) Alec Tweedie,* who is a grandson of Dr. Alexander Tweedie, F.R.S., formerly of Brook Street, whose portrait hangs in the Royal College of Physicians, London. Old Dr. Tweedie's work on fever was very well known, and the London Fever Hospital was built under his supervision. Strangely enough, he examined me when I first came to London to take the membership of the Royal College of Physicians.

'But the connecting-link is even stronger, for Alec Tweedie is first cousin to Sir Alexander Christison, my old Edinburgh chum, who took his degree with Murchison and myself on the same day in Edinburgh. My son-in-law is, therefore, a nephew of dear old Sir Robert Christison, whose classes I attended as a student.

'On his mother's side, Alec is the grandson of General Leslie, K.H., and great-grandson of Colonel Muttlebury, C.B.K.W., a very distinguished soldier, who was in command of the 69th at Quatre Bras.

* He died in 1896, five months before the subject of this memoir.

' My son-in-law is also a nephew of General Jackson, who was in the famous charge of Balaclava, so that on his mother's side he is as much connected with the army as on his father's he is with medicine.'

Curiously enough, I have come across an old indenture between my husband's grandfather, Dr. Alexander Tweedie, and the great surgeon Sir William Lawrence, who was so good to my father when he first came to London. It is such a strange old document, dated November 1, 1839, showing how young men in those days took up medicine and surgery, there being hardly any teaching schools or organized hospital work, that I here insert it:

ARTICLES OF AGREEMENT, of three parts, indented, had, made, concluded and agreed upon this first day of November, in the third year of the reign of Queen Victoria, and in the year of our Lord one thousand eight hundred and thirty-nine; BETWEEN William Lawrence, of Whitehall Place, Westminster, a Member of the Council of the Royal College of Surgeons in London, of the first part, Alexander Tweedie, M.D., of Montague Place, Bedford Square, Middlesex, of the second part, and Alexander George Tweedie, son of the said Alexander Tweedie, of the third part, as follows, that is to say: THE said William Lawrence, *for and in consideration of five shillings of lawful money* of Great Britain, to him in hand, paid by the said Alexander Tweedie, at or before the sealing and delivery of these presents—the receipt whereof he doth hereby acknowledge—and also for and in consideration of the Services of the said Alexander George Tweedie to be done and performed for him, as hereinafter mentioned; DOTH for himself, his Executors and Administrators, covenant, promise, and agree, to and with the said Alexander Tweedie, his Executors and Administrators, by these Presents, that he, the said William Lawrence, shall and will receive, accept and take, and he doth hereby agree to receive, accept and take, the said Alexander George Tweedie to be the articled STUDENT OF THE ART AND SCIENCE OF SURGERY OF HIM, the said William Lawrence, for the full space and term of four years, to be computed from the day of the date of these Presents; if they the said William Lawrence and Alexander George Tweedie shall jointly so long live. And also shall and will, well and faithfully, according to the best of his power, teach and instruct, or cause to be taught and instructed, him the said Alexander George Tweedie in the Art and Science of Surgery.

AND the said Alexander Tweedie, for himself, his Executors and Administrators, and also for the said Alexander George Tweedie, and also the said Alexander George Tweedie for himself, DO, and each of them DOTH, covenant, promise and agree, to and with the said William Lawrence, his Executors and Administrators, by these Presents, that he the said Alexander George Tweedie shall and will, well and faithfully, serve the said William Lawrence during the whole of the said term of four years, to be computed as aforesaid, and perform, obey and observe all and every his lawful commands and directions, and shall not, at any time or times, absent himself from the service of the said William Lawrence during the said term, without his license and consent; nor shall do, nor cause to be done, any act or thing which can, shall, or may be hurtful or prejudicial to the said William Lawrence, his Executors or Administrators, or any of his Patients or Employers; and that he the said Alexander George Tweedie shall not, nor will, either directly or indirectly, during any part of the said term of four years, practise Surgery on his own account or for his own benefit.

AND, MOREOVER, it is hereby mutually declared and agreed by and between the said Parties to these Presents, that he the said *Alexander Tweedie shall and will find and provide, or cause to be found or provided, for the said Alexander George Tweedie, good and sufficient Board and Lodging during the said term of four years; also during the said term, good and sufficient Wearing Apparel of every kind suitable to his state and condition,* and all such Advice and Nursing in case of sickness as may be necessary. IN WITNESS whereof the said Parties to these Presents have hereunto severally set their hands and seals, the day and year first above written.

WILLIAM LAWRENCE.
A. TWEEDIE.
A. GEORGE TWEEDIE.

PRESENTED before me at the Court of Examiners on the day of the date hereof.

ROBERT HUNTER (or HEATH), Pres.

SEALED AND DELIVERED by the said William Lawrence in the presence of

EDM. WILFOURD, Sec. to the College.

SEALED AND DELIVERED by the said Alexander Tweedie and Alexander George Tweedie in the presence of

EDM. WILFOURD, Sec. Royal College of Surgeons.

But the young Alexander George Tweedie did not care for being 'fed and clothed' by his father, or taught the art of surgery by Sir William Lawrence, and after a short time left and went into the Madras Civil Service, where his son Alec was born.

Broadly speaking, the five persons who most fascinated my father, for the reason that they gave him the greatest number of new ideas, were Baron von Liebig, the author of the 'Letters on Chemistry'; Professor Sharpey, the Secretary of the Royal Society; Catlin, the North American traveller; John Ruskin, the great art critic; and Charles Waterton, the naturalist.

Of Liebig I have spoken in a former chapter, particularly in reference to his preparation of the famous extract which he evolved to save my mother's life.

Of Liebig's first meeting with Von Humboldt, the well-known traveller, my father used to tell an amusing story.

In the summer of 1823 the former gave an account of the analysis of fulminating silver before the Academy of Paris. When he was packing up his preparations at the conclusion of his paper, a gentleman stepped forward and asked him many questions about his studies and future plans. He catechized minutely, and then ended by asking Liebig to dinner on the following Sunday. The young scientist accepted the invitation, but when Sunday came he remembered that he had forgotten to ask his strange friend either his name or address. He felt very much ashamed of himself for his stupidity, and was, of course, unable to keep his engagement. Early next morning, in walked a friend, who greeted him by asking:

'What on earth did you mean by not coming to dinner with Von Humboldt?—he even invited a lot of chemists to meet you, including Gay-Lussac.'

'I was thunderstruck,' said Liebig, 'and rushed off as fast as I could run to Von Humboldt's lodgings, and made the best excuse I could.'

The great traveller seemed very angry at first, but was ultimately satisfied with the explanation, at the same time adding it was unfortunate for Liebig, as he had invited several members of the Academy to his house to meet him, thinking it would be greatly to the young scientist's advantage; 'however,' added the famous man, 'you must come next Sunday to dinner, and I think I can promise you a pleasant meal. Do not forget who I am again, or where I live,' he added with a merry twinkle.

This was a very happy dinner for Liebig, for there he made the acquaintance of Gay-Lussac, who was so much struck with the wonderful enthusiasm and capacity of the young German that he invited him to work with him in his own private laboratory, and together they continued the investigation of the fulminating compounds.

Baron von Liebig was intimately connected with our family history, as the tone of the following letter to my mother will show:

'*May* 29, 1867.

' MY DEAR EMMA,

' The little box with all the things arrived some days ago, and I hasten to thank you very heartily for all the proofs of love and affection. You are a good girl.

'Your Ethel is very sweet, and this kind of photo was quite new to me, and you can imagine that her baby-work was much admired. Give her a kiss for me, and tell her that she and Mother Emma must very soon come to see us. Mamma Liebig was very much pleased with her present, and never thought that Ethel was already as clever as that. I beg you, too, to thank your father for the beautiful book about Cobden, and tell him that I made Cobden's acquaintance on the occasion of the Peace Congress, and that I always esteemed and admired him. Please ask him his opinion of the " Development of Nations," which I sent him ; he is a man of very high spirit, on whose opinion I count a great deal.

' Marie and my wife thank you especially for the needles and the little work-basket which looks like a boot. I am busy with my preparations for my travel to Paris ; I am obliged to hire several rooms, as I will take George [his son] with me. He is to stay with me for a month, and afterwards Edmund or Harley could, perhaps, come to me with their wives ? How I am longing to see you, my dear child ! and if I can manage it, I have a great wish to cross the Channel. Let us see.

'How sad is the long-suffering of your husband ! but it seems in your letter that you have not yet given up all hope. Will you please thank him for the two nice little works, and tell him that I was glad to hear that my pamphlet pleased him ?

'Marie is going to Erlangen on Monday next; if I am right, I told you that Carl Thiersch [his son-in-law] has got a call to Leipzig as Director of the Surgical Hospital and Professor of Surgery. I am so glad, as I think, with his capacities and talents, it is luck to leave the small place which Erlangen is. Leipzig is a world-renowned town, and his annual income will be much higher. Thiersch has got, too, a prize from the Académie of Paris, for his work about cholera. Some weeks ago Nannie lost her youngest child, and she is still very sad. In about a fortnight Thierschs start for Leipzig, and Marie will accompany them to help with removal.

'As I heard through a letter from Mr. Froude, editor of the *Fraser's Magazine*, my article for my defence will appear in the April number. I am anxious to hear your opinion about it.

'My wife and Marie send you their best love. I love you as always before, and am your true old friend,

'LIEBIG.'

With the name of Sharpey was interwoven the whole of the young physician's earlier life. Speaking of Dr. Sharpey, my father said :

'Poor old gentleman ! his innings over, he has carried out his bat with honour, and now, while he is quietly drifting with the tide to that far-off, unknown shore whither we are all bound, his kindness to rising physiologists is gratefully remembered in almost every quarter of the globe.

'For nineteen years he was secretary to the Royal Society, and for nearly forty Professor of Physiology at University College; thus for years he held the destiny of many young men in his hand. A word of generous encouragement from his lips gave strength to the feeble stem, while one of censure would have nipped the opening bud. Be it to his honour said, that though he never held forth his hand to the undeserving, he never withheld it from those who merited recognition. In no case that I ever heard of did his judgment prove at fault. The false, though it glittered ever so brightly, he never failed to detect. The true coin, were its surface ever so dim, he never failed to recognise.'

My father's first meeting with Dr. Sharpey was mentioned in a former chapter. In connection with this great physiologist, I remember an amusing story. One day at luncheon, a meal he often took on Sunday in Harley Street, Dr. Sharpey said suddenly :

'I'm going to be married, Harley.'

'What !' exclaimed my father, looking at the old gentleman, who was almost blind, in perfect amazement; then, recovering himself, he added : 'I hope you will be very happy, and are getting a nice suitable and sensible wife, who will look well after you.'

'Nonsense ! nothing of the sort !' replied the elderly scientist indignantly. 'I'm going to marry a most beautiful girl of seventeen or eighteen.'

My father hardly knew what to reply, for Dr. Sharpey was now seventy and had been a bachelor all his life.

'Don't you approve of my idea,' asked the intending Benedict, ' that you sit there so silent ?'

'I feel rather knocked over; I'm a little surprised.'

'What ! that a girl will have me ?'

'Oh no, not at all; but that you, with your confirmed bachelor ways, should think of a girl.'

' Well, the fact is, I don't think I shall live long now ; that is why I have decided to marry.'

This information only made his determination the more remarkable, until he vouchsafed the explanation that for some fifty years he had been a subscriber to a Scottish Widows' Fund, his mother having thought it a good thing for him to begin as a youth. When, however, he got to about sixty and still found himself unmarried, he wrote to take his name off the fund. This the company refused point-blank, declaring *nolens volens* he must go on paying to the day of his death. At seventy he again appealed to be released from his yearly payments, but with the same result ; and so now, feeling his days were numbered, he laughingly declared he was ready on his death-bed to provide for some young and beautiful damsel, provided the lady were willing to marry him at so late an hour in order to secure the pension to procure which he had paid premiums for half a century.

Alas for the sake of the unknown charmer, the good man died unmarried !

One day when we children descended for luncheon, we found a strange gentleman, who puzzled us greatly, already seated at table with my father. First, he addressed the head of the establishment as 'George,' a most unusual occurrence, and spoke with a very broad Scotch accent ; secondly, he wore extraordinary white muslin cuffs outside his black cloth coat. This individual was, however, no less a personage than Professor William Milligan, of Aberdeen, at one time Moderator of the Church of Scotland, and one of the Revisers of the Bible.

The little white muslin cuffs, which much resembled those still worn by widows, were what were known in Scotland as *weepers;* but I imagine he must have been one of the last to wear this strange form of mourning, which he did for his mother, and certainly such a curious decoration was a revelation to the ordinary Londoner.

Professor Milligan was a considerably older man than the London physician, although a great deal of their youth had been spent together; but finally, when the learned Scotch divine went to live in Aberdeen, and my father took up his abode in London, their lives drifted apart, and it was only when Milligan came to London, generally as the guest of Dean Stanley, at the Deanery, Westminster, upon business connected with the revisions, that they met.

One evening I was talking to Dr. Ginsburg, one of the Revisers of the Old Testament, who told me how the work was divided into two parts : one the Old and one the New ; how the Revisers worked concurrently, although the Old Testament was much the more severe and took by far the longer time. I asked him whether he had ever met Professor Milligan.

'Of course I have,' he said, 'a most excellent scholar and learned gentleman.'

'He was my father's first cousin,' I explained.

Ginsburg was much interested, and told me how after two or three meetings the Revisers were one day assembled in the Jerusalem Chamber, when quite unexpectedly a man clad in a gray suit arrived from Scotland, looking much more like a country squire than a learned divine. The Bishops and Orientalists stared at the new-comer in amazement, till Aldis Wright, the secretary, rose and said :

'Gentlemen, let me introduce to you Professor Milligan, of Aberdeen.'

'Hardly had the new-comer been in the Chamber a quarter of an hour when some very critical discussion took place. He at once joined in, and we soon discovered, to our amazement, that he was one of the very best and ablest scholars amongst us all. Milligan's knowledge was profound. I may tell you that at the time we all had to pay our own expenses—although they were afterwards refunded—and Professor Milligan, living so far away as Aberdeen and having a very large family, always travelled to London the cheapest way possible, which meant by sea. It was on one of these journeys that he caught the cold which ultimately brought about his death, and therefore I have always looked upon Milligan's life as sacrificed to the revision of the Bible.'

It was in our Harley Street drawing-room about 1887, if memory do not deceive me, that the very first graphophone exhibited in London was shown at an evening party. My father provided the instrument, little dreaming of the amusement which would be provided by his guests!

George and Weedon Grossmith were present, and being fascinated with so new a toy, for their own pleasure, and, as it proved, infinitely for the pleasure of everyone present, began to play tricks with the graphophone. George sang many of his famous songs, such as ' See me dance the Polka,' down the instrument, when everyone laughed so heartily that it struck Weedon that it would be a good idea to bottle up a series of laughs. The company formed a circle, the machine was turned on, and the various sounds of merriment were recorded in its depths. Some gave hysterical little laughs, others deep haw-haws, while Madame Antoinette Sterling, who was present, hummed a tune which would have done credit to Maurice Farquhar's laughing-song. When thirty or forty people had contributed their best to the entertainment, the amusement had become so intense at the strangeness of the whole proceeding that the single laughs had degenerated into one huge roar; the machine was stopped, the wax plate was adjusted, and then the graphophone was turned on for the benefit of the bystanders. Nothing more ridiculous could well be imagined.

Some years have gone by since that evening ; the graphophone is no longer a novelty, and therefore it is difficult, perhaps, now for anyone to realize the wonderment with which clever scientific and literary folk listened to this marvellous invention.

Amongst those present was the late Sir Andrew Clark,

then President of the College of Physicians. He was so
immensely struck with this instrument that he called the
next morning to ask my father how and where it was to be
procured, as he would like to have it exhibited a few nights
later at the soirée of the Royal College of Physicians.

We live in such an advancing time that what is a modern
invention one day is history ten years hence, and almost
forgotten in twice that length of time.

I remember my father often saying: 'Nothing is impossible; although I am not a very old man, I have lived
long enough to see the railway-train come into universal
use, vernicular railways toiling up Swiss mountains, ladies
going in hansom cabs alone and walking about London
unmolested and unnoticed—ay, even to see young girls
climbing unchaperoned to the top of an omnibus! I have
lived to see electric light invented, the telegraph, and the
telephone, and now, at the close of my life, even carriages
without horses, and I should like to live long enough to
see transport through the air.'

When I was of an age to 'come out,' my father asked
me if I would like to have a ball.

' No,' I replied; ' I should prefer some private theatricals.'

Here was a startling piece of information, one which
literally took his breath away ; however, as I had evidently
set my heart upon it, he consented, and, poor man! as I
look back now I feel conscience-stricken to remember all
the horrors he endured.

We chose for a play W. S. Gilbert's charming little
comedy ' Sweethearts.' Sir William Magney played Harry
Spreadbrow, Mr. Dow the gardener, Mrs. Beerbohm Tree
maidservant, and I Jenny. Some funny little incidents
took place in connection with this performance in the back-
drawing-room. I was only allowed to have it on condition
I painted the scenery, a task I gladly undertook, being most
ably helped by Mr. Weedon Grossmith, a young artist
whose studio was but a few doors away from us in Harley

Street, one of his pictures being then exhibited upon the line at the Academy. Since those days he has become an actor-manager, and married an old school-fellow of mine, May Palfrey, the daughter of a doctor in Brook Street.

Never was scenery painted under greater difficulties. Large canvases had to be stretched—a bit at a time—along the small wall in the storeroom. We got into such messes with our jam-pots of paint, pails of whitewash, and packets of every conceivable kind of powder, that we found it necessary to wear the most remarkable costumes—which shall be nameless—to keep our own clothing from being spoilt.

My father took the keenest interest in it all, however, and used to make little expeditions to the storeroom to see 'how we were getting on.' General Anderson most generously painted a proscenium representing Comedy and Tragedy, and the stage was built entirely by an old coachman who had been in our family for many years.

On one occasion my father came upstairs to compliment him on his work, when, bubbling over with delight and almost expiring with the heat, he exclaimed:

'I'm only the carpenter; Miss Hethel 'ere his the harcitect.'

The girl who was to have played the maid fell ill, unfortunately, on the morning of the first performance, so I had to rush off to Queen's College to get a substitute. Thus it was that Mrs. Beerbohm Tree made her first appearance in public in the back-drawing-room of 25, Harley Street.

We gave seven representations of the piece, each time to an audience of about 120 friends. The result was so satisfactory that we became ambitious, and a few months afterwards played ' New Men and Old Acres.'

It is amusing now to look back and remember how Mrs. Beerbohm Tree played with us, her husband giving many valuable suggestions; how L. F. Austin, the writer, was one of the company; how Weedon Grossmith helped us over many difficulties; and how my father smiled

17

approvingly at everything, although the discomforts he had
to put up with were truly appalling.

L. F. Austin, who has taken the late James Payn's
place on the *Illustrated London News*, is the author of that
clever little book ' At Random '—which I may, perhaps, be
pardoned for quoting—for it gives an amusing account of
the perils of the amateur actor, penned methinks from
recollections of our theatricals :

> Well, all went fraternally till a certain lady of our acquaintance
> wrote a play. She was an arbitrary young daughter, and her father,
> a distinguished physician, resigned himself to misery while she turned
> his house upside down. She painted the scenery, designed the foot-
> lights, and hammered the stage with her own fair hands, at a ruinous
> cost in nails. The wretched physician could not walk upstairs without
> stumbling over lamps and cans of paint ; if he opened a door un-
> expectedly, fragments of wood fell on his head like a booby-trap ; at
> meals he listened to jargon about ' flies ' and ' wings,' till he asked with
> inopportune satire whether the great enterprise had something to do
> with entomology. Eventually he took refuge in his consulting-room,
> where he slept on a camp bedstead, and complained that the servants
> brought him pots of rouge when he wanted soup. I was told that his
> patients at this time were much disturbed by his distraught appearance,
> and that they usually called for the purpose of giving *him* medical
> advice. . . .
>
> Now, my friend the popular actor had been cast for the sentimental
> hero, and I was to impersonate a comic servitor who had to overhear
> the villain plotting the abduction of the heroine. But the hero some-
> what irritably suggested that this was not romantic, and that he ought
> to come upon the villain by accident, and there and then put him to
> the sword. This was the first rift between Damon and Pythias. Next
> day I received a note from the arbitrary young daughter, telling me
> that the villain was down with chicken-pox, that the substitute she
> had chosen refused with disgusting selfishness to give up a ball on the
> night of the performance, and that I must come to the next rehearsal
> with the villainy letter-perfect. A glow of triumph ran through my
> soul. Damon was in the sulks, was he ? He should see that Pythias
> could meet him on his own ground. Farewell, low comedy, the
> merry jest, the guttural chuckle, the slightly inflamed nose, the
> resounding slap of the thigh, all these subtle characteristics which
> had made my comic servitor the joy of true connoisseurs of dramatic
> art ! Come, genius of romance, envelop me here with the atmosphere
> of elegant iniquity, curve my nostrils with horrid scorn, and touch

the outer corner of the sinister eye with the gleam of diabolical purpose ! . . .

There is a popular actor whom I never see without recalling the days when we played in private theatricals together with immense gravity. Some of his friends suspect me of jealousy, for when they invite me to express admiration of his undoubted gifts, I often reply, in pensive abstraction, 'Ah, you should have seen him as an amateur !' The truth is that as soon as he sets foot upon the stage I am promptly carried back to our exits and our entrances in the back drawing-room, where it was difficult to get on or off without crumpling up landscapes and bringing whole castles about our ears.

We were the best of friends in those happy times, when our cheeks were 'partially obscured by whisker'—not sacrificed on the altar of art, but carefully veiled on occasion by layers of grease-paste. Ambition had laid an imperative summons on us both without causing any collision of temperaments ; for he was a sentimental hero, while I contributed a gaunt figure and lugubrious countenance to the service of low comedy. Perhaps you never saw my Perkin Middlewick, suitably enlarged by pillows, which had an uneasy habit of wandering round to the back. Mr. Bunter, too, was one of my great parts. You do not get such acting now, for, of course, I am speaking of the palmy days of the amateur stage !

It was about this time I had an offer to go upon the stage. Breathless with excitement, I rushed downstairs to tell my father of the plan and to receive his approval. He heard my story, looked very sad, and declared it should never be with his consent. He had worked hard for his children, he added, ' as hard as health would permit him, and of all professions for women he disliked the stage most, especially for anyone so young.'

I was not only young, but impetuous, and, needless to say, very angry, for all of which reasons I bounced out of the room, declaring that if I were not allowed to make my own living by such excellent means I would never act again.

I am sorry to think of that pettish answer now, when it can never be recalled !

CHAPTER XXI.

SQUIRE WATERTON.

PROBABLY one of the most interesting personalities of the day was Squire Waterton, the naturalist, and as my father often stayed with him at Walton Hall, and wrote down a few reminiscences of its strange owner, I am able to append the following in his own words, which appeared in *Nature Notes* :

' Squire Waterton, as he was called in his own domicile and district, I came in contact with on account of the interest we both took in the poisoned weapons of savage men, he having been the first to describe and bring to England the arrow-poison of the natives of South America, named respectively, according to the tribe employing it, Woorara, Wourali, Curar, or Curara, and I the first to discover that it is a true physiological antidote to strychnine, as well as to find out several other of its peculiarly interesting properties : for example, that a frog may be poisoned with it, and even after 100 hours, when its legs are already shrivelled and its webbed feet withered, be again resuscitated by merely putting it into, and carefully heating it in, a steam bath for half an hour or so.* Thus it was that

* 'Notes of Lectures on the Physiological Action of Strychnine,' *Lancet*, 1856. ' L'Action de la Strychnine et Curar,' *Compt. Rend. de l'Académie Française*, vol. xliii., p. 470. ' The Treatment of Tetanus by Wourali Poison,' *Lancet*, September, 1859. ' A Dead Heart Pulsating,' *Field*, 1861. 'The Poisoned Weapons of Savage Men,' Brit. Assoc. of Science Reports, 1864.

Squire Waterton and I took a personal interest in each other, and were mutually desirous of meeting, which desire on our parts was sympathetically nurtured by Mrs. Loudon, the well-known authoress of books on gardening.

' When I received his polite invitation to pay a visit at Walton Hall, it was accepted with feelings of pleasure and uncertainty—pleasure at the prospect of replenishing my exhausted stock of arrow-poison, as well as not merely making the acquaintance of a celebrated traveller, but also of an individual whom even his friends had taught me to regard as an interesting curiosity; and of uncertainty, as to how I should get on with a man who had been, as I imagined, not unjustly branded as an unblushing story-teller.

' Waterton's " Wanderings " startled the reading public with what was considered a most extraordinary animal's portrait as a frontispiece to the volume. This animal was described by Waterton as a " Nondescript," which he had met with in the backwoods of Guiana. Its appearance astonished people even more than did my old friend Du Chaillu's description of a gorilla, which all know appeared at the time incredible enough. For the sake of those who never saw the portrait of the nondescript, I may mention that it represents the head and hairy shoulders of a monkey with the visage of a man, the face that of a human being of classic Caucasian type, or, as Waterton himself speaks of it, " a Grecian cast of feature." This was not, however, thought at the time to be the only startling romance in the book; for, in addition to the nondescript, the public was asked to believe in three other almost equally incomprehensible animals, which the Rev. J. G. Wood, the most lenient of Waterton's critics, commented upon in the following sarcastic language : " One was a bird with a bill a yard long, which had the voice of a puppy-dog, and laid its eggs in the hollow trunks of trees. The other, a beast which ate its food suspended, slept suspended, walked suspended, and rested itself suspended ; in fact, spent its whole life in a perpetual state of suspense. While the third swallowed a tortoise, hard shell and all, and then consumed it at its leisure, much in the same way as the Court of Chancery does a fat estate when it gets it into its rapacious maw."* But these, indeed, were not the only wondrous things Waterton was reported to ask his readers to believe, for although there is no mention made of it in his "Wanderings," it was asserted he had said the Indians of South America used a poison so powerful that when an arrow dipped in it was shot into the bark of a tree, the tree immediately began to sicken and die; while among his own exploits he narrated how he had not only sat on, but ridden astride upon a living cayman—an alligator! All of which tales his reviewers stigmatized as falsehoods, and told the public that their author must either be a knave or a fool, or most probably a bit of both.

'However, as the pleasing portion of the invitation more than counterbalanced the disagreeable features associated with it, to Walton Hall I went.

'It was on a bright sunny morning in the spring of 1856 that I drove up to the high gate, or rather door, in the still higher stone wall surrounding the park of Walton Hall, situated three miles from Wakefield, in Yorkshire.

'Once within the park gates, a pleasing view met my eyes of a richly-verdured and well-wooded glade sloping down to a large lake, the placid waters of which were glistening with the rays of the sun. Before and around me all things wore a soft, subdued air of calm and sweet repose; the rooks in the distant rookery, whose harsh cawing was softened by distance, were an appropriate accompaniment to the scene.

'There is not, I believe, in England a more interesting place than Walton Hall, which is built on an island at one end of a lake, 25 acres in extent, and in a park of 300 acres, surrounded by a stone wall three miles in length. It contains, or did when I knew it, many curious contrivances of its

* Really the toucan, sloth, and boa constrictor.

owner for the nesting and protection of birds. Not only was there a rookery—the common accompaniment of a Yorkshire country-house—but a heronry with thirty or forty nests, an owl-haunt, a pigeon-cote, and an ivy-clad tower for starlings and other birds to build in.

'My first glimpse of the mansion itself was disappointing, for either I had not heard or had forgotten that the feudal hall of the ancient Waterton family, with its drawbridge and stately oaken doors, had long since disappeared, and a modern, plain, three-storied house without any artistic features now occupied its place. The drawbridge, too, had been replaced by a modern iron foot-bridge, which did not allow carriages to approach the dwelling.

'When I reached the Hall, the door was already open and the butler waiting to receive me, and no sooner had I crossed the threshold than all my feelings of disappointment vanished. The loveliness of the view from the window of the room into which I was shown drew me towards it, and, finding a telescope on a table close by ready for use, I had just placed my eye to the instrument, when the window opened and I found myself face to face with Charles Waterton, the famous traveller and naturalist. To me, at the time, he looked a man under the average size, but he assured me afterwards that he was within half an inch of six feet in height. He had a clean-shaven face and closely-cropped hair, reminding one, in those days when the fashion of wearing the hair short was not so common as it is now, of a person recently discharged from prison. Mr. Waterton's dress was hardly less of a surprise to me than his personal appearance, for he wore snuffy-brown trousers and a bright blue swallow-tailed coat with gold—real gold—buttons, a costume common enough in his early days among Yorkshire country gentlemen. His feet had never forgotten the freedom from restraint of his American explorations, when he usually went barefoot, for they were now encased in a pair of down-at-heel slippers.

'The reader will, perhaps, think I formed a poor im-

pression of my host. If so, let me tell him he is mistaken, for, as the Scottish bard pithily puts it :

> ‘What tho’ on hamely fare we dine,
>   Wear hodden gray, and a’ that;
> Gie fools their silks and knaves their wine,
>   A man’s a man for a’ that !

And so it was in Mr. Waterton’s case. No one could catch
a sight of his beaming smile, or receive a glance from his
speaking eye, without feeling that, no matter how *bizarre*
might be the appearance of the outer man, the inner was
lit up by a genial, highly-cultivated mind and sympathetic
heart. The cordial clasp he gave my hand, and the words
of warm welcome with which he greeted me, associated as
they were with a charming expression of truthful sincerity,
at once drew me towards him, and our subsequent acquaintance only tended to strengthen the bonds of a friendship
thus auspiciously begun.

‘ Our sojourn in the drawing-room was of short duration,
for no sooner did Mr. Waterton understand I required
neither rest nor refreshment, than he proposed to introduce me to his curios—a proposition to which I eagerly
assented.

‘ Once again in the entrance-hall, my eye detected that
the oil-paintings covering its walls were mostly German
works of art, and on my manifesting surprise that such
should be the case in the abode of a Yorkshireman, he
smilingly remarked:

‘ “ No wonder, for I bought the whole of them in
Würtzburg.”

‘ “ What,” I said ; “ is this old Barwin’s collection ?”

‘ “ Yes,” he replied ; “ but what do you know about old
Barwin ?”

‘ “ Why, I lived for eight months in Würtzburg, and
heard both of old Barwin and the collection he never for-
gave himself for having sold so cheap to an Englishman.”

‘ Waterton chuckled with delight, and remarked :

' " I am not surprised at his regretting his bargain. For I could have sold the lot as soon as it came here for four times more than I paid for it.'.'

' Trifling as this episode was, it contributed not a little, I believe, to cement our friendship.

' While ascending the staircase, I was struck with the novelty of its arrangement, for the banister, the whole way, was lined with a gradually ascending series of glass cases, filled with objects of natural history, chiefly collected in his " Wanderings " in South America—birds and butter-flies, quadrupeds and reptiles, each specimen being of rare beauty, as regards fur, feather and form. So life-like in attitude and perfect in preservation were they, that I muttered, " How splendidly they are stuffed !"—words which I thought complimentary ; but evidently my host was not of the same opinion, for he suddenly wheeled round upon me, and with flashing eyes exclaimed :

' " What do you mean ? *Stuffed*, did you say ? Allow me to inform you that there are no stuffed animals in this house." Then, thrusting his fingers into his waistcoat pocket, he drew from it a key, and unlocking the door of the case opposite to him, extracted from it a finely preserved polecat. Extending it somewhat brusquely towards me, he said, in a piqued yet commanding tone of voice : " Take hold of the head, and hold it firmly."

' I did so, when he immediately gave the specimen a sudden jerk, and left the head in my hand. Astonished and dismayed, I immediately began to stammer out an apology. But instead of paying the slightest attention to what I said, he cut my speech short by saying :

' " Look into the head—what do you see ?"

' " Nothing," was my answer.

' " Then put your finger into it, and tell me what you feel."

' " Nothing," was again my reply. No stuffing, no bones, no skull, could I either see or feel. It was simply empty. It contained *nothing*.

' " How, then, can you dare to say my animals are stuffed! Have you never heard of my method of preserving them ?"

' " No."

' " Then, sir, I will show you; you shan't leave this house until you have not only seen but learned the whole process. Give me back the head, please."

' On returning the head to him, to my still further astonishment—which he evidently thoroughly enjoyed—he gave it a half-twist, and twirled it immediately on to the neck, just as if it had merely been the lid of a box. Then after he had smoothed down the hair with his forefinger the polecat looked as perfect as if it had never been decapitated.

' The specimen having been replaced in the case, we had ascended the staircase but a step or two further, when my eye alighted on a lovely large purple-winged Oriental butterfly, standing alone on a pedestal. Not only its life-like attitude, but the exquisitely delicate bloom on its wings, surprised me. Observing that my attention was attracted to the insect, he opened the case, took it out, and placed it in my hand, saying:

' " What do you think of that ?"

' But one reply was possible.

' " It is most beautiful, and looks as if it were still alive," said I.

' " Ah! but that's nothing; no moth or weevil will ever dare to dine off its wings."

' " How so?" asked I, well knowing, by sad personal experience of fly-hooks, that feathers and such-like things are readily eaten and destroyed by moths and weevils.

' " That butterfly, like all my other butterflies, and every feathered and furred specimen in this house, has been thoroughly protected from attacks of all kinds of vermin. Corrosive sublimate is my talisman against evil-doers. Nothing that liveth will face corrosive sublimate. If it did, it would die. And according to my experience, all sorts of vermin are much too fond of life to run the risk. All I did to protect this butterfly was to dip it, for a few seconds, in an alcoholic solution of corrosive sublimate. That was done fifty years ago, and there you see it is, as you yourself said, looking as fresh and spruce as if it were still alive."

'This was a thing worth knowing, and having often since then put it in practice, I can confirm every word Waterton said regarding the marvellous protecting powers of corrosive sublimate—the bichloride of mercury, of chemists.

'While thus conversing, a clock, close at hand, struck twelve. Instantly he snatched the butterfly from my hand, popped it back into its case, and said:

'"Come along with me to my bedroom; I have lots to show you, and, as I dine at three, there is no time to be lost. You can look at these things to-morrow."

'Off we started at a brisk pace upstairs. As we passed the clock on the landing, I remarked:

'"What a fine tone the bell of that clock has!"

'"I am glad you like it," said he. "It is three hundred years old. It belonged to Sir Thomas More, who was one of my ancestors, and it still keeps capital time."

'It was an old-fashioned "waggity-waw" hanging against the wall, and noticing that it had only one hand, I said:

'"Poor thing! it has lost a hand."

'"Not a bit of it," was the retort; "it never had but one. There was no need of minute hands when it was made. People did not go rushing and pushing furiously, and fussing about to catch stage-coaches, steam-boats, or express trains, when it was born. A few minutes more or less counted for nothing three hundred years ago. Minute-hands were not thought of until high-pressure engines and high-pressure living came into existence, and I heartily wish they never had!"

'By this time we had reached Mr. Waterton's bedroom door, and no sooner was it opened than I was almost struck dumb with astonishment. For this apartment which he had so euphoniously designated, not only contained no bed whatever, but possessed neither a washstand nor a toilet-table—nay, not even so much as a carpet ; in fact, it had no appurtenance whatever in it that I could see to give it the smallest right to the title of a bedroom, especially the bedroom of a country gentleman in the position of Squire Waterton. What did it contain, then ?

'Well, the first thing that caught my eye was a big baboon swinging in the air, suspended from the ceiling by two strings. The next thing was a small deal kitchen-table, on which lay a dead rabbit in company with a black paint-pot, a broken-necked glass beer-bottle, an old brown canvas apron, and a number of tools. The room also contained a high old-fashioned chest of drawers, a cupboard, and three kitchen-chairs. On one of the chairs stood a plain white stoneware washhand basin, and a chipped-lipped companion ewer, while alongside, at the corner of the chair, was an old cracked china saucer, doing the duties of a soap-dish, the soap it contained being of the yellow odoriferous wash-house quality. To complete the toilet arrangements, on the chair-back was spread out to dry a common rough-grained brown hand towel.*

'Round the walls of the room again were hung, besides a map of Guiana, a few old engravings, and nailed against them were a couple of unpainted, unpolished common deal shelves, on which were arranged a few books. Such may be said to have constituted the sum and substance of Squire

---

* Lest some reader who knows nothing of the man I am writing about should fancy that were he alive he might be offended at seeing these details in print, allow me to inform him that exactly the reverse would be the case, for the Squire gloried in doing nothing like other people. He even carried his eccentricities so far as to occasionally pass himself off as one of his own servants, and he invariably had a hearty laugh when he related with what skill and success he performed the part. In fact, nothing pleased him better than hearing himself described as a *rara avis* or even a *lusus naturæ.*

Waterton's sleeping apartment, which evidently did the tripartite duties of a study and workroom as well.

'No sooner was the door shut behind us, than, walking round to the off-side of the baboon, he placed his hand beneath it, gave it a smart tap, when up the creature bounded into the air like a child's balloon. Then, with a smiling face, he said:

' "Do that, and tell me what you think it's filled with."

'I did as I was bid, and up again bounded the baboon, exactly like a wind-ball, spite of the fact that it looked not only substantial to the eye, but felt even so firm to the finger-touch as to convey to the mind the idea that it was a solid body.

' "Well, Mr. Waterton," I replied, "I am astonished; your air-stuffing is superb. Your imitations of Nature, without the intervention of visible means, are marvellous. Had I not seen and handled your specimens, I never could have believed it possible for any human being to fill a skin with nothing but air, and yet give it the form and contour of a living animal. And not only so, but even the similitude of life itself."

' "So, friend, that's the way you compliment me, and yet you have seen little more than one-half of my skill. Just look here."

'Pulling out one of the drawers of the cupboard, he extracted from it a bundle of clean white bones, and, with the triumphant air of a conqueror, tossed them down on the bare wooden floor at my feet—where they fell with a loud clatter—at the same time exclaiming:

' "Now, sir, behold! here you have the perfect specimen of the baboon hanging. And please to tell me what one among your London taxidermists furnishes you with a perfect preserved skin and a perfect skeleton from the same animal? When your stuffers preserve the skins they ruin the skeletons, and when they preserve the skeletons they destroy the skins. Here you see the vast superiority of my method, which enables me to preserve, at one and the same

time, skin and skeleton.   And that, too, no matter whether
it be of bird or beast."

' He soon proved this to me by turning again to his
treasure drawer and pulling forth from it a magnificently
plumaged large-sized barndoor cock, and saying " Catch !"
pitched it across the room into my hands, which I held out
ready to receive it, when plop into them came the cock, as
light as a feather; and well it might, for it, too, consisted of mere skin and feathers, filled with air like a
bladder.

' A finer specimen of a large, well-plumaged barn-door
fowl I never saw.   Its splendid tail feathers were as fresh-
looking and as gracefully curved as any live cock's could be.
Its bright red comb stood erect, as if in the excitement of
life.   And, from its not yet having been mounted upon a
stand, its very legs, feet, and claws stood out in as inde-
pendent-looking symmetry as if they had been still attached
to a living body.

' Apparently satisfied with the bewildering effect his
taxidermic talents had upon me, he replaced bird and
bones in the drawer, and handing me a chair, while he
took the only remaining empty one, we drew near the table,
and he proceeded to initiate me in the mysteries of his art,
which I soon found consists in two main peculiarities :
firstly, the rendering the skin of the animal as hard as
iron, and, secondly, the moulding it into the form of the
living creature to which it belonged.

' The first part of the procedure, being purely mechanical,
any man, woman, or child can readily accomplish.   The
second, alas ! requires other talents.

' In order to make the skin—whether it be covered with
fur or feather, scurf or scale—hard, all that is required is
to steep it in a spirituous solution of corrosive sublimate
from three to nine hours, according to its thickness.   The
strength of the solution Waterton gave was a teaspoonful
of powdered corrosive sublimate to a wine-bottle full of
spirits of wine; but I afterwards ascertained for myself

that the best proportions to employ are six grains to the ounce of spirit.

'On removing the skin from the solution and drying it for a short time in front of a good fire, it begins to stiffen, and so rapidly does it harden that it is advisable to roughly mould it into the shape of the animal to which it belonged during the drying process. Indeed, not until the general contours of the bird, fish, or quadruped are maintained by the partially dried skin is it to be left to itself. No sooner, however, is the desired shape found to be retained by the skin, and it has acquired a similitude to the animal to which it belonged, than it may be attached to a couple of pieces of string, and hung up to become thoroughly dry and hard. This it will readily do within two days.

'Then commenced the difficulties of Waterton's taxidermic process—the moulding of the hardened skin into the exact form of the living animal. This was accomplished by the combined action of the fingers and a set of tools similar in shape to those employed in the modelling of clay. Each part of the skin is operated upon separately, and the portion intended to be acted upon has first to be moistened with a sponge soaked in tepid water until it becomes thoroughly soft and pliable. While in this condition the skin can be coaxed, by means of alternate outward and inward pressure, into the required shape.

'It is absolutely necessary to possess four things before one can expect to be a successful air-stuffer. Firstly, an abundant supply of patience; secondly, plenty of time at one's disposal; thirdly, an intimate knowledge of the physiognomy and shape of the animal; and, lastly, a no inconsiderable amount of "artistic talent." Unless one have all these four elements at his disposal, he need not, I think, trouble himself attempting to rival Mr. Waterton.

'When the dinner-bell rang, I suggested going to my bedroom to wash my hands.

'"Oh no," said my host; "there is no time for that; you can wash them here."

'And from the baboon skeleton cupboard he forthwith produced a basin. I washed as I was desired, and he handed me a small nail-brush, at the same time informing me it was manufactured by cutting the shank from an old toothbrush ! He said he kept all his old toothbrushes for that purpose, as they acted admirably, and strongly advised me to adopt his plan.

'Well, even the toothbrush was not quite successful in cleaning my ebony tips, for we had been messing about dreadfully, and they were consequently very dirty. So, fertile of resource, my obliging host again dived into his cosmopolite cupboard, and returned with a small bottle of oil of turpentine with a feather stuck in it, and, assuring me it was excellent stuff for the removal of dirt, smeared the points of my fingers all over with it. I dared not say nay, yet I was in mortal terror lest my hands should smell unsavoury at the dinner-table. Most vigorously did I scrub away, and, to my joy, my fingers became beautifully clean, and, to my greater joy, a good after-lathering of soap sufficed entirely to remove the nasty smell of turpentine. So after drying with rather a queer-looking towel, I stood radiant with smiles of satisfaction, while my host in the same basin went through the same process. He was a character, this man with a property worth £150,000 and a large income to boot.

'Having now time to look about me, I examined the apartment more closely for any sign of a bed. He said it was his *bedroom*, but not a vestige of a bed could I see. At first I had supposed the bed must be in a recess into which the cupboard door opened, but I had looked into the wonderful cupboard from which he extracted so many different articles, and there was no place for a shut-up bed there. "True," thought I; "but he may, by some further conjuring trick, extract from the cosmopolite cupboard a bed and bedding too." Yet it did not seem probable ; so I gazed earnestly about me, trying to find the missing article. The Squire was endowed with sharp eyes, and behind them he had a quick brain; so he soon detected that my vagrant orbs were in search of something. While he dried his hands, he asked me what I was looking for.

' " Why," I replied, " you told me that this was your bed-room, but I can see no bed in it."

' " So it is my bedroom ;" and, giving a kick to a rolled-up bundle in a corner, which gradually unwound itself into a strip of cocoanut matting and a block of wood, he added, " These are my bedclothes, and that is my pillow."

' Here was startling news—the Squire of Walton Hall to have a block of wood for a pillow, a roll of matting for bedclothes, and the hard floor for a mattress !

' " Since my wife's death, three-and-twenty years ago," he explained, " these boards have been my only bed—that mat my only covering."

' How could I but revere the man who stood before me ? He was a Roman Catholic, and acted strictly up to the doctrines of his Church and faith. He had dearly loved his wife, and he performed self-inflicted penance for her soul ! Although I had no sympathy with his religious views, I could not fail to admire his faith and self-denial.

' Our toilets being finished, we descended to the drawing-room, and took the two Misses Edmonstone (his sisters-in-law) in to dinner. As soon as we were seated at table, he informed me he did not drink wine, but hoped I would take as much as I pleased. The meal was simple, the conver-sation delightful, and that funny little dinner-party will always be a charming recollection.

' My first evening at Walton Hall was spent in examining and discussing various specimens of woorara placed on a small table in the drawing-room. The Squire kept the poison carefully rolled up in beeswax, and it retained its power perfectly, as I afterwards ascertained, for fifty years. He most kindly gave me some of all his specimens, and after we had done with the woorara, we joined the ladies, who were ready to refresh us with tea. While we sipped the exhilarating beverage and engaged in light chat, a large

18

tabby tom-cat entered the room at the heels of the butler, and approached the little table on which we had placed the woorara. Miss Edmonstone immediately cried out that the creature would be poisoned, and, although there was not the remotest danger of that, as the poison does not act when swallowed, but only when introduced by a wound, both the Squire and I rushed to handsome Tom's rescue. No sooner was pussy in a place of safety than the Squire performed a feat which astonished me.

'He was nearly seventy-five years of age, be it remembered, yet, standing beside the little table, he tossed off one of his easy-going slippers, stood steadily on one leg without the slightest artificial support, and scrubbed clean the top of the table with the sole of his stocking. But few young men could perform such a feat. Active as I was at that time, being well under thirty, I failed to raise my foot (in the position he stood) to the top of the table. Laughingly he said, "Oh, that's nothing; I'll jump over it." And had I not interposed my person between him and the table, I believe he would have done it with perfect ease. The Misses Edmonstone told me that they had often seen him do such things.

'As the clock struck eight, the Squire rose, held out his hand, and said, "Good-night; I always go to bed at eight, as I rise early. I shall be up to-morrow morning by three. I leave you in good hands with my sisters-in-law. Good-night."

'I was surprised, but merely wished him a good night's rest, and pondered more than ever over this strange being.

'Verily, Walton Hall was a place for surprises, and I had yet to enjoy another before the evening was over. As bed-time approached, I began to wonder what sort of a place my night-chamber would be. The memory of the Squire's wooden pillow haunted me. I am not overfastidious, but, still, I must say that I looked forward with fearful fore-boding. I thought it ominous that, though I had been in the house all day, I had never yet had a peep at my sleeping-chamber. Well, ten o'clock came, and we began to talk of retiring to rest. The bell was rung, and, after wishing the ladies " Good-night," I followed the butler, who conducted me across the hall, where he took up a silver bedroom candlestick, and then, ushering me upstairs, flung open the door of a room, the size of which fairly took away my breath.

' I had often slept in big bedrooms, but certainly this was about the biggest among them. A bright, blazing fire was in the grate. A small table stood on the rug, on which were placed two fine, tall, old-fashioned silver candlesticks, and snuffer-tray to match; a silver inkstand between the candle-sticks, with pens and paper ; a couple of popular books also gladdened my sight ; while, best of all, a comfortable, old-fashioned easy-chair was drawn up close to the hearth. Into the easy-chair I soon flung myself, and took a general survey of this most sumptuous sleeping-chamber ; after which I could not help mentally exclaiming, " Well, well, if my host treats himself badly, he certainly treats his guests regally."

' Tired out, I soon, very soon, went to bed, where I dreamt of animals without interiors, poisoned cocks and feathered arrows, cats of gigantic size and men like pigmies, turpentine and nail-brushes, beds of feathers with pillows of wood. In fact, a complicated muddle reigned in my brain, and when I awoke in the morning, it took me some little time to disentangle the threads of truth from the confused mass of false ideas with which they were mingled in a delicious jumble.

' One of the most beautiful traits in Squire Waterton's character was, to me, his intense love of animal life.* He would never allow a gun to be fired off in his park ; hence Walton Hall became the home of every biped and quad-ruped that could fly over its walls, or obtain access to the place by an opening in them. In winter-time the lake was covered with all sorts of wild waterfowl, some of which were so tame they would sit basking in the sun on the

* Except the Hanoverian rat, which he hated.

narrow piece of lawn in front of the drawing-room windows. To me it was a lovely, mentally lovely, sight to witness their pure and simple faith in man.

'On one occasion Squire Waterton informed me that his great and grand remedy for all the ills that flesh is heir to was the lancet. Go where he would, he never travelled without one. If he felt a fever coming on, he bled himself. If he caught a cold, he bled himself. If he had a colic, he bled himself. Moreover, he assured me that this line of treatment was always successful. On inquiry how often he had tried it, his prompt reply was, "Hundreds of times."

'A smile of incredulity, I fear, flitted across my face, for instantly off went his coat and up went his shirt-sleeve.

'"Look there," he said, "and believe."

'I looked and did believe, for the bend of his arm was literally one mass of lancet scars. More than fifty I counted on his left arm. Then turning up his other sleeve, again my wondering eyes beheld another mass of scars. In all, he said, he had bled himself over one hundred and sixty times.

'"Who, in the name of wonder, was your doctor?" I exclaimed in a tone of amazement.

'"Myself," said he.

'"Well," said I, "I suppose you know that the tenor of the old adage is, that he who treats himself has a fool for a patient."

'"Ah! that may be true," retorted he, with a laugh; "but the advice cost me nothing."

'Not wishing to be outdone, I smilingly replied:

'"Quite true, and yet it may have been dear at the price. Tell me how much blood you usually take away at a time?"

'"My plan is," said the Squire, "to put the wash-hand basin on a table in a good light, stand beside it, dig in my lancet, and let the blood flow till I feel faint."

' "Then you must take about twenty ounces of blood at a time—a large bleeding," said I.

' "Yes," replied my strange friend, " I dare say you think it a large bleeding ; but that is, I should say, about the amount."

' I have already said that the Squire, though but lacking half an inch of six feet, looked a short man, but I ought to have added he was most powerfully built. His calves were big enough for a Scotch Highlander to be proud of, and even at the age of seventy-five were still as hard as iron.

' My dear, kind old friend Mrs. Loudon told me once, when on a visit at Walton Hall, her little daughter Agnes, while walking through the woods by the side of the Squire and herself, expressed a wish to have an egg out of the nest of a bird which had built in one of the high trees, and before she had time to interpose and prevent him, the Squire had off his coat and was up the tree with the agility of a monkey ; in a few seconds more the coveted egg was in the child's hand !

' I had already met many remarkable men in the course of my career, but, as I said to Mrs. Loudon on my return to London, Squire Waterton surpassed them all.

' " What do you think now of his veracity?" she asked.

' My reply was short and to the point :

' " I could never doubt him again ; if he were to tell me he walked from Walton Hall to London on his head, without either using his hands or his feet, I should believe him, for I am sure he would not tell a lie."

' Just when I was about to bid farewell to the ancient mansion, the Squire made his appearance, carrying a long, thin bundle in his hand, and with a smile observed :

' " Here is a treasure for you I don't think I would give to anyone else. You will find in this parcel the bow with which I shot the fish little Agnes Loudon desired "—it was swimming in the lake at Walton Park, and the Squire shot it with a bow and arrow for the child, who had it for dinner—" and a fish arrow. Besides which it contains a broad-bladed arrow and an arrow-gun with its spike in it; so these, with the blow-tube spikes which I gave to you yesterday, make a complete set of Guiana poisoned weapons."

' Most thoroughly did I appreciate the prize, and turned them to scientific account.

' Another present I received from the Squire was on the Christmas Day preceding his death, when he sent me a dozen blow-tube spikes, together with a most characteristic letter.

' In his " Wanderings " the Squire tells the story of how he rode on a living crocodile, a story which many doubted, but which I implicitly believe. He showed me the set-up skin of the animal, with a natural air of triumph. It was not big; so far as I can remember, about eight feet long; and of the thickness of a not very stout man's body.

' He also showed me the famous Nondescript. It was a marvellous production, half nature, half art. The face was beautifully human, the body brutally brute. The face any-one might have admired, but the body could only be loathed; it was all covered with hair, like the true body of a monkey, which in reality it was.

' The face was that of a handsome European, yet not, like the body, the work of God, but the manufacture of man, and that man Charles Waterton, who out of a monkey's face moulded this beautiful image! His modelling talent was truly wonderful—more wonderful than words can express: for how he could transform the face of a monkey into that of a most perfect man is utterly beyond my power of comprehension. Nevertheless, he did it, and I have oftentimes since thought what a splendid mermaid he could have manufactured out of a fish. All attempts at mermaid-making I have ever seen have been more or less failures; but after seeing the Squire's Nondescript, I have never doubted he could have made one that many a scientific man would unhesitatingly have said was a natural creation.

' I ventured to accuse the Squire of having tried to

impose upon the credulity of the public, by asserting that the Nondescript was a production of Nature, when he knew that its merit to distinction was solely due to the cunning of his own hands.

'"I never imposed upon the public," he said, "the public imposed upon themselves; I never asserted that the Nondescript was a Nondescript when alive. They thought I did, but I didn't. Therefore they have only themselves to blame for any deception."

'This seems a little bit of sophistry, for, in spite of my admiration for the Squire, I cannot shut my eyes to the fact that it is not upon what a man says, but upon what he makes others believe he says, that the truth or falsehood of an assertion depends; however, I do not wish to discuss the question, and shall pass on to mention another of his wonderful transfigurations of animal features.

'The Squire, as a good Roman Catholic, hated everything Protestant, and Henry VIII., like the Hanoverian Georges, he held in particular abhorrence. So he amused himself by representing poor John Bull in the skin of a frog, heavily weighed down by the national debt, and Royalty and courtiers, made out of the skin of toads and monkeys, as a motley group of depraved creatures. The design was too complicated for me to describe its details after a lapse of nearly twenty years, from memory, so I shall not further attempt to. do so. Suffice it for me to say that, like all the other works of the Squire, it was a masterpiece of brains and fingers.

'As I am an enthusiastic admirer of physical courage, I must relate a story of the Squire (although I believe it has been recorded already) which interested me greatly. I shall give it as nearly as I can in his own words. I had been telling him how I managed to handle poisonous adders, without ever being bitten by one, when he said:

'"Ah, I can do that, too. When Wombwell's menagerie of wild beasts was on show, the lecturers at the School of Medicine were desirous of making some experiments on

serpent poison, and they invited me to come and see them.
The experiments were performed in a room at the school,
and the serpents were brought there in a box. The last
experiment was to be made by letting a big cobra bite a
large dog; but when all was ready, the keeper could not
manage to get the cobra out from among the other snakes
in the box. After letting him try till he was tired, I said,
' Let me take him out for you.' Casting off my coat and
turning up my shirt-sleeves, I pushed the man quietly on
one side, opened the door of the serpents' box, put in my
arm, and gently moved my hand about among the snakes
till I caught hold of the big cobra by the neck, and out of
the box I safely brought him, when—would you believe it,
sir?—the whole lot of the fellows rushed out of the room,
and left the keeper and me alone with the snakes."

' "Bravo!" I exclaimed; "that beats me, for I never
handle even the adders with a bare arm."

' Now this tale was simply truth unadorned.

' Shortly afterwards I happened to dine at a house in
company with the lecturer on anatomy who was present on
the occasion referred to, who, after hearing me repeat the
story, stated that every word of it was perfectly true, adding
the query :

' "Where could you find another man that will handle
poisonous snakes as you would do eels, with a naked hand
and a bare arm?"

' Ay, well might he ask the question. I know of none.

' The dear old Squire died on May 27, 1865, was rowed
to the end of the lake in the dead of night, and buried by
torchlight (the *Illustrated London News* gave a picture and
full accounts of the pageant) in his own grounds, in a small
mausoleum he had some years before prepared for himself.
His frame is now mingling with the dust. His spirit has
soared to the regions of the blest. His memory is fondly
enshrined in the hearts of many still living, who enjoyed
the happiness of his friendship. Just as the material
world is built of numbers of small atoms which, though

infinitesimal in themselves, are nevertheless essential to the constitution of the whole, so are the intellectual growth and development of the world dependent on the fractional units contributed by each individual man. The vibrations of the tuning-fork extend to no one knows where, and in like manner the ideas of an original mind like Waterton's teach in gradually widening circles.

'Truly the Squire was one of those men who build up natural science!'

CHAPTER XXII.

PEEPS ABROAD.

FROM the year 1870 my father had to refuse all offers of outside active work, such as becoming president of learned societies or joining committees of the same. He did this with many pangs of regret, but he was forced to do so simply because he had to husband his strength for his own work. He had a large and good practice; fees came in abundantly—quite as fast as health would allow him to make them; therefore in the summer of 1874 he determined to accomplish a long-cherished plan and visit Scandinavia, the great cradle of our ancestors. He shall tell the story of his travels himself:

'An international congress of archæologists was to be held at Stockholm, and accordingly I set out for that capital, taking excellent introductions with me—one to the Swedish Minister of Foreign Affairs, another to the wife of the Governor of the Royal Palace, and a third to one of the ladies of the Court. These credentials gave me an immediate entrée into good society—society so good that, on the evening when the King entertained the foreign members of the congress at his country palace of Drotingholm, I had the honour of supping at the same table with His Majesty King Oscar, the Queen, Queen-mother, and other grandees.

'From Stockholm I proceeded to Finland with my friend

and old teacher, Professor Virchow, of Berlin. From
Finland I went to Russia, while there spending ten days
in Moscow and eight at St. Petersburg. Russia proved a
dreadful disappointment. Ignorance and poverty abounded
everywhere, except in the presence of Royalty. Just fancy
in the streets of Helsingfors seeing a soldier of the grand
Russian Empire with great patches on his breeches,
holding up a soleless, or nearly soleless, boot, and asking
alms!*

'At Helsingfors the professor who was escorting Professor
Virchow and myself round the archæological part of the
museum, called my attention to an old brass fiddle, at the
same time saying, "You have nothing of that sort in
England, I suppose?"

'"Pardon me," was my reply; "we have its counterpart in silver."

'I then told him how I had seen one for sale in a
curiosity shop in Wardour Street, London, and added:
"I rarely mention that fact now, however, for on one
occasion, when sitting at the table of a great London
banker, my story of the silver fiddle was turned into
ridicule by a Christianized German Jew, who thought
himself a great authority on musical matters, and coolly
informed the company, with an air of pity for my ignorance,
that the 'Professor,' as he designated me, must have con-
founded a flute with a fiddle, as it would be quite absurd
to make a metallic fiddle, which could bring forth only
harsh sounds."

'I was so completely crushed by this genius, I preferred
chewing the bitter cud of an error of judgment or wilful
misrepresentation rather than give the lie direct to my
accuser, at a dinner-table around which ladies were seated.
Long and deeply, however, did his venomed words make
my *amour propre* smart, and severe was the lesson it taught
me never to tell an improbable tale at a table surrounded

* Things are somewhat better now, *vide* 'Through Finland in
Carts.'

by persons unacquainted with my character for truthfulness.*

'In Moscow the streets are, so far as I know, never swept or watered, the only attempt at the latter I was privileged to see being made by a man who, standing opposite his own door, held a pail in one hand and a big wooden ladle in the other, with which latter he sprinkled the pavement.

'The dust in the streets during the month of August was suffocating, and compelled thorough ablutions and brushings every time I entered the hotel. The inside of this hotel, which was the grandest in Moscow, was on a par with the streets. The dining-rooms were clean, it is true, but the bedchambers filthy. One thing I can state with certainty : mine was never swept out during the ten days I spent in Moscow, for an odd piece of string I saw lying under the table the day I took possession remained there during the whole time I occupied the apartment, and in the same spot I left it, as a legacy to my successor.

'Moscow is most interesting ; but as a description of it would be here out of place, I will only remark that, like Napoleon the Great, I saw it in flames. One day a house took fire, and the conflagration spread so rapidly from one wooden dwelling to another that within twelve hours a large district was totally consumed, a result not to be

---

* '*March* 23, 1877.—To-day, when driving round the corner of Green Street, Leicester Square, I was able to point to the identical fiddle, again hanging up for sale in Davis the pawnbroker's shop-window, concerning which fiddle I find in the *World* this paragraph :

'"Passing through a street hard by Leicester Square the other day, I saw in the window of a bric-à-brac shop a silver violin. It was labelled 'Silver violin from South Kensington Museum ; the only one known.'"

'Silver violins are probably as scarce as tortoiseshell tom-cats or Queen Anne's farthings, but I fancy I could exhibit an even greater curiosity, viz., a tin fiddle ! This bizarre musical instrument belonged to Albert Smith, and figured at many of his entertainments in the Egyptian Hall as an accompaniment to quaint patois songs.

'Here then is evidence of the existence of no less than three varieties of metal fiddles—tin, brass and silver.'

wondered at when it is remembered that appliances for coping with fire were in 1874 of the most primitive description. I opened my eyes in blank astonishment, for the water was transported from the river in barrels on carts !

'From Moscow I returned to St. Petersburg, in order to witness the festivities held in honour of the nuptials of the Grand-Duke Vladimir, who married the Grand-Duchess Marie of Mecklenburg. St. Petersburg was at its gayest. I beheld the whole town, and all the ships on the Neva, including the Emperor's yacht, illuminated ; and, what is more, I saw the great Tzar Alexander II. himself in a rage —a towering rage.

'One Sunday afternoon I and two other Englishmen stopping in the same hotel (Angleterre) hired a droskie to take us to the fortress where all the Russian Emperors lie buried. On the way we were stopped, and told that, as the Emperor was going out for a drive, we could not pass in front of the palace door. Our coachman obediently turned and drove by a short-cut through the royal mews. There I observed an imperial phaeton, to which one horse was already attached, while a groom was leisurely furbishing up the harness on the back of the other close by the door of the stable. They were a pair of handsome young iron grays.

'Arrived at the fortress, we entered the chapel, and began our meditations among the tombs ; but we had been only a short time so engaged ere, while looking at that of Peter the Great, in rushed a warder, who hurriedly turned us all out through a back-door. We moved reluctantly, for the only word we could clearly understand in the excited harangue was " Tzar !"

'Like true Britons, wanting neither in curiosity nor courage, no sooner did we find ourselves hustled out of the back-door than we made our way round the chapel to the front, and arrived just in time to see a commonplace, chocolate-coloured single brougham drive up, out of which stepped the Emperor Alexander and his Empress.

'While we waited, a droskie containing a solitary lady, and drawn by one horse, arrived. After exchanging a few words of animated conversation with the old Major at the door of the chapel, the lady entered. Just as we were wondering who the favoured dame could be—for there seemed no great style about her—the sharp sound of horses' hoofs on the hard, stony avenue fell upon our ears, and, looking in the direction from whence the noise proceeded, we saw a pair of grays tearing along, literally striking fire from the road with their shoes. To our surprise, the phaeton, save for the driver, was empty. What, then, could be the meaning of all this haste? We were left to wonder. The carriage drew up at the door of the chapel, but only for a minute; then the driver walked his horses quietly across the road, and took up his station alongside the brougham, when a lively conversation ensued between the two coachmen, which, although we heard, left us unenlightened, for the sufficient reason that none of us understood Russian. What all the hubbub meant—for there evidently was a hubbub—we could not imagine. First the brougham with Emperor and Empress, next the droskie with the single lady, and finally the furiously-driven empty phaeton. Was it but a storm in a teacup? We were soon to know. Within a quarter of an hour or twenty minutes from his entrance into the chapel with his wife the Emperor reappeared, accompanied only by the old officer. Quickly glancing across the street, he spied the unlucky coachman with the iron grays, and instantly rushed towards him, with flashing eyes, uplifted arm, and passionate words. Shaking his fist in the man's face, he tore open the door of the phaeton, jumped in, and drove off, with the most demoniacal expression I ever beheld on the visage of man.

'A few minutes later out came the Empress and the lady, both of whom were handed into the brougham by the old Major. No sooner had they all departed than the officer beckoned for us to re-enter the chapel. We went, and finding that he spoke French fluently, we soon got into conversation, which he began by apologizing for our having been so hastily turned out of the chapel. His explanation was that on Sundays the Emperor came to pray by the tombs of his ancestors, and no stranger was allowed inside the sacred edifice while he was there.

'After a few minutes I slyly insinuated the Emperor seemed rather put out, and that I should not like to be in the coachman's place.

'"Ah!" he agreed sadly, "pauvre homme, pauvre homme, je ne voudrais pas être lui." And so thought I, for the face of the Tzar had given me strange visions of Siberia.

'What was the cause of the Tzar's passion? His Imperial Majesty had ordered his little private phaeton to be ready at a certain hour. The coachman had mistaken the hour, as was evident by the leisurely way in which we had seen the horses being harnessed in the royal mews. The Tzar waited till his patience was exhausted, then jumped into his wife's brougham, which was ready at the door, leaving the lady who was to have accompanied the Empress to follow by herself in the droskie. The coachman, with the phaeton and the iron grays, finding on his arrival at the palace door that the Tzar had already departed, put speed to his horses and followed at a wild rate. The rest is already told. *Moral :* Even Tzars are liable to little disappointments, and not free from outbursts of human passions.

'On the evening of this same day the Tzar gave a private entertainment at the Opera House in honour of his son's wedding. No one was admitted except by invitation. All St. Petersburg wanted to go. Most were disappointed. Not I, however, for with my usual good luck I had made friends with Professor Bellafont of Paris, and he having received an invitation to dine with Baron L——, one of the imperial household, and occupy a place in his box at the Opera, obtained a similar honour for me. At the dinner-table I met several of the diplomatic corps, as also the

Chamberlain of the Tzar, and after dinner,* which was served in true Russian style, we repaired in a body to the Opera. The scene was splendid. The pit and orchestra stalls were turned into one and occupied by officers in full uniform, representing each shade of colour in the rainbow, regulars and irregulars from every regiment in all the Russias, from the far north of Europe to the very centre of Asia. Stars and medals glittered. The sight was magnificent. The whole diplomatic corps also appeared in full uniform, and sprinkled as they were in the boxes among ladies brilliant in feathers and diamonds, the *coup d'œil* was grand. There in the imperial box sat His Majesty, now all radiant with smiles ; the Empress was not there, on account of the delicacy of her chest, but the Queen of Holland, and some other grandees whose names I have forgotten, also occupied the imperial box.

'Being the guests of the Tzar, we were supplied with refreshments ; the waiters were servants from the imperial household, dressed in imperial livery, the ordinary staff of the theatre having been dispensed with for that evening. The whole experience was a thing worth remembering. On that memorable day I had beheld the Tzar looking like a fiend, and afterwards smiling like a courtier.

'Before leaving Russia I must further remark that the two points in its character which impressed me most were the magnificence of its churches and the poverty of its poor.

'The "Louce Markets," both of Moscow and of St. Petersburg, especially the former, were to me most admirable posts for study.

'From Russia I retraced my steps through Finland viâ

---

* 'The novelties to me were, the anteprandial bear's smoked raw ham and *fresh* caviar, which they ate off glass plates with *spoons*, as if it were Neapolitan ice. Caviar, although a favourite dish of mine for more than twenty years, I had never hitherto tasted in a fresh state. It was excellent, and had just the flavour of a fine native oyster.'

Helsingfors and Abo to Stockholm, and having crossed
Sweden in one direction through the great Gotha Canal, I
recrossed it to the north by the Christiania and Stockholm
Railway. Arrived in Norway, I soon set about making
preparations for a cariole tour through the fine mountain
scenery near the Hallingdal to Bergen.

'Most thoroughly did I enjoy myself, generally accomplishing from seventy to eighty miles a day. The only
drawback was the lateness of the season, for not only did
I find plenty of old snow lying on the uplands, but fresh-
fallen snow often surrounding the log-hut hotel doors.
There were few or no travellers on the road; the time for
them had gone by. One day, however, as I drove along
I passed two gentlemen and a lady walking, and mentally
saying to myself, "English and aristocrats," I thought no
more about them. A mile further on I arrived at one of
the finest of Norway's rural hotels.

'It was drizzling slightly, so while dinner was being
prepared I smoked my cigar sitting in the log porch. I had
not sat long before I observed the trio of English (supposed)
approaching the door. They had gone for a walk, but the
shower drove them back again. The lady passed on with
a slight inclination of the head in recognition of my raised
hat. The gentlemen stopped and chatted. I soon found
that they were intelligent men—both of them above the
average. Unlearned in science, they nevertheless soon
became deeply interested in my account of the Archæological
Congress at Stockholm, and the opening of the Tumulus at
Upsala. Dinner being announced, we parted, and I saw
nothing of them till the following morning, when I found
them breakfasting in the common-room. A separate table
was spread for me; but when they asked if I would not join
them at theirs, I most willingly accepted their invitation,
as it is rather dull work consuming one's meals with no
one to speak to. During breakfast I learned they were going
the same route as myself, and intended to sleep at a little
place immediately preceding that I had selected for my

19

night's quarters. Our meal finished, we parted, they forming a party of five, there being with them an interpreter
and lady's-maid ; but as my cariole was not ordered for an
hour later, it was suggested by one of them that I should
drive quickly and overtake them at luncheon, a plan in
which I readily acquiesced, for their conversation had
greatly attracted me. So we arranged to meet and drive
on later together.

'Off they went, and I was left behind to enjoy the
scenery with a cigar between my lips. I took a stroll; it
was beautiful. I stepped over a long row of planks to an
island on the lake, and there found the biggest ant-hill I
ever saw. It was nearly four feet high, and one would
guess it about ten feet in circumference. Just as I was
starting from the door I asked the hotel-keeper if he knew
the names of the gentlemen who had preceded me.

'"Why !" said he, "don't you know that is your Queen's
cousin, Prince Hohenlohe ?"

'"No," I answered, "I know nothing about them,
except that they seemed nice people. Who is the other
gentleman ?"

'"He is Lord Elphinstone, and the lady is the Prince's
wife."

'"Thanks," said I, and drove away.

'I had not gone far when, with a "Humph !" I said to
myself, "Don't drive so fast; they may imagine you know
who they are, and wish to push yourself upon them."

'For which reason I let them lunch by themselves.
What an extraordinary thing pride is ! Here I, in one way
a mere nobody, was too proud to even deign to be suspected
of trying to push myself on people in a worldly position far
above me. I changed my plans and remained the night
where I was, rather than intrude upon these great folk !

'Next day I proceeded on my journey, always lingering
a stage behind them, as I could tell by reading the names
of Count Gleichen and Lord Elphinstone in the post-books
kept at every station along the postal route.

'In my calculations I was deceived, however, for on driving up to the door of one of the inns, who should step out but Count Gleichen, who, after a kind welcome, said : "Make haste ; we are just sitting down to a hot luncheon, so don't let the fish get cold."

'In I went, and from that moment joined them, first as a fellow-traveller, afterwards as a guest on board their private steamer.

'Their kindness, alas! proved fatal to me. I did not possess their strength. My bodily powers were unequal to the strain of their rapid travelling, and in order to keep myself up to the mark I drank port wine, which, being in Norway unbrandied, I was assured would not induce gout. Vastly, however, had I been deceived, for at V——, partly from exposure to cold, partly from the few glasses of port wine I had latterly been taking, I was stricken for the first time in my life with rheumatic gout. Gout, being hereditary in the family, and I a martyr to it ever since I was nineteen years of age, would not have surprised me; but of rheumatic gout this was my first taste. Not being able to lie up, compelled to travel on when I ought to have been in bed, though two long years have passed between my writing this and its occurrence, I am not free from it yet. Relapse after relapse has laid me up, and left me but a mere wreck of my former self. It has held me in its iron grip; it has haunted me in hours of pleasure, and pursued me at every turn. It seems cruel that fate, which at one time deprived me of sight, has now taken the power from my legs!

'Home I came from Norway, through Denmark (suffering horrible pain while in Copenhagen), through Holstein, by Hamburg to England, and here, nearly two years afterwards, I am sitting, invalided, in Douglas, Isle of Man, on this the twenty-sixth day of July, 1876.'

Just after his return home from Russia and Norway my father received a summons to attend a patient in the country, was put into damp sheets, had another severe attack of

19—2

rheumatic gout, and was compelled to give up work and leave London for two years. Rheumatic gout dogged him to his grave twenty-one years later, and during all that time he was always lame from its effects. But he never gave in. He sat writing stories and reminiscences in the Isle of Man, where he went to seek new health ; he fed birds from his Bath-chair and made friends of robins or herons alike, told stories to children, or plunged deeply into old Manx lore and customs. His busy brain was never idle.

Many men have fought such battles and won, but many more have laid down their arms and died broken-hearted. Those two years in the Isle of Man, although happy enough outwardly—for he always seemed cheery and made friends wherever he went—were in reality a living hell. He had already made two starts in life and, against many odds, succeeded; but he was now an older man, and the battles, though won, had left their mark and enfeebled his constitution. Other men had taken up his line of medicine as specialities ; 'Harley on the Liver' was no longer the sole authority, and yet so determined was he to push himself to the fore again, if only his weakened frame could stand the strain, that he collected a number of his strange cases and strung them together, determined that, as soon as ever he went back to his work, he would write a book on the liver, to be the book of his life.

He did write the book ; it appeared in 1883, and remains the standard book on the subject up to the present day.

The *Lancet* obituary says :

By far the most important work that has appeared from his pen is a large one on ' Diseases of the Liver,' which may be regarded as his *magnum opus*, in which he proved the truth of the motto borne on the title-page, that ' true science is the key to wise practice,' by giving numerous illustrations of the manner in which, when physiological chemistry is discreetly applied at the bedside, it not only elucidates some of the very darkest problems in the etiology and pathology of disease, but furnishes the busy practitioner with a trustworthy guide to successful treatment. Moreover, in it the author strives successfully to prove that Nature, in things medical, as in everything else, invariably acts on one great and uniform plan, and that, notwith-standing the incongruities in the nature and clinical history of the hepatic diseases met with in different quarters of the globe, when the light of modern science is focussed upon them their pathology is found to be everywhere identical, the difference in their degrees of virulency not being entirely due to climatic influences, but partly to the con-stitutional peculiarities of the sufferers, originating in differences in their modes of life.

But his life and work on his return to London after two years' illness must be told in another chapter, for happily rest and pluck succeeded, and the man who for the second time had appeared doomed for life to loss of health and compulsory idleness triumphed.

Mental strength again overcame physical weakness.

CHAPTER XXIII.

SCIENTIFIC HOBBIES.

My father was truly an indefatigable worker. His hobbies were endless—not useless hobbies, but hobbies pursued by a scientific man in pursuit of knowledge. It was more particularly during the latter part of his life that he devoted so much time to curious subjects, and the cause was not far to seek: being lame, and therefore unable to take much physical exercise—during twenty years riding and walking were practically denied him — he found relaxation from his professional work in employing his mind in other directions; for, as we know, ill health had closed the doors of pure science cruelly from the enthusiast. Unfortunately, I cannot do more than give a cursory glance at a few of his hobbies in these pages, but they are so varied and so strange that they are worth mentioning.

As recorded in a former chapter, at one time he collected poisoned arrows; that was in connection with his work on worali poison. Then came a time when coins held their sway, and he became possessed of some marvellous Chinese specimens dating from thousands of years before Christ. Mandarin watches, used long before the days of real watches, fascinated him for a time. All this led him to study Chinese history, and much amusement and pleasure were derived from that pursuit; he unravelled all sorts of theories showing how civilization gradually travelled from the East to the West, and is still steadily advancing in a westerly direction, so that at no distant date China may be expected, after a sleep of upwards of three thousand years, to awake and again take rank as the most advanced country in the world.

Amongst the many hobbies which he was busy working at up to the time of his death were the 'Mummy Eyes of Peru'; the 'History of Drinking Horns'; the 'Origin of Throwing Sticks'; 'Shell Musical Instruments'; 'Talking Sticks,' etc. He was an omnivorous reader, and whatever subject he took up he perused all the volumes connected with it on which he could lay his hand; he verified his facts; many of the theories he had from time to time discussed with different people, and, no matter how trivial the information gleaned, he always managed to turn it to good account, and so connected the links of many a chain.

Unhappily, these facts are many of them in too chaotic a condition to be handled by an outsider like myself, but they all tend to prove that, for centuries before there was supposed to be any connection between the Eastern and Western Hemispheres, there was some kind of communication by which the ideas of one nation were conveyed to the other. This was the point round which his work centred, and it was tracing the similarity of idea of savage men in the East with the later development of the same idea in the West that held for him such fascination, coupled with the similarity of construction in all things great and small. He wrote on many of his hobbies, and those which were 'showable' he lent to scientific societies.

In the Royal Society catalogue of the conversazione on June 13, 1894, with Lord Kelvin as president, I find mentioned the following, shell or bone musical instruments being probably the earliest forms of music known :

'*Exhibited by Dr. George Harley, F.R.S.: Shell Musical Instruments (Trumpets and Flutes).*

1. Shell fog-horn used by fishermen on the banks of Newfoundland (*Strombus gigas*).
2. Welsh shell trumpet used as a dinner summons (small *Strombus gigas*).
3. Miner's blasting signal-horn used in the Guernsey granite quarries (*Strombus gigas*).*
4. Conch trumpet blown at funerals and religious festivals in Southern India (*Turbinella rapa*, peeled and decorated with lotus-flower).
5. Triton shell flute from New Guinea (*Triton tritonis*).†
6. Helmet shell trumpet from New Guinea (*Cassis cornuta*).
7. Figure-ornamented triton trumpet from Japan.
8. Triton shell flute from Solomon Islands.

    The exhibitor is of opinion that shells were the first forms of trumpets and flutes ever employed.'

These shell instruments were collected by my father during many years. People got to know of his strange interest in these matters, and therefore it was that he received a present of one here and one there; among them was a wonderful conch trumpet such as is used to-day by the boatmen of Jaffnapatam and British Honduras. The gentleman who gave it to him explained that the sound

---

* 'I am told they are also used for the same purpose in the Welsh slate quarries.'—Notes of Dr. Harley.

† 'Theodore Bent showed a triton flute shell from Arabia (exactly like my Moresby Island one), with the shell round the opening all worn down by long blowing, showing, moreover, that it had been blown into as a trumpet (in spite of the hole being in its side), instead of as we do into a flute.

'Mr. Preece, the electrician at the Post-Office, told me that when he was a boy they blew a horn to call. the ferrymen at the Menai Bridge across the straits.'—*Ibid.*

could in calm weather be heard at a distance of two or three miles.

The West Indian and Guiana negroes quite commonly use conch shells as trumpets, especially to announce they have fish for sale, and this habit is occasionally copied by the Indians. Indian boys every morning proclaim the beginning of their working-hours by blowing on such shells. Many of these my father collected, showing their gradual growth.

The history of one of the trumpet shells was to be found nearer home. This shell was fairly well known for over a hundred years; for the last fifty years it had been used in a large granite quarry in the Vale Parish, Guernsey, to give warning when a blast or explosion was about to take place. Prior to that it was used on a large farm, now destroyed in part by this very quarry, to call the labourers to their meals.

There are still a few old people in the island who remember distinctly that it was quite a common custom in the large farms to summon the workmen to their meals by blowing a shell. It must be borne in mind that in the early days of the century watches were not common amongst labourers, and they were not all clever enough to judge time by the sun, though possibly a fairly good clock was to be found in the farmer's house. At that period it was also usual for the farmer, his servants and labourers to have their meals together, as they do in Finland to-day.

Another shell of which my father felt very proud was used early in this century at a farm, Rhiwlas in Anglesea, as a horn to call the men in to dinner. This shell, when lying on his library floor, chanced to be seen one day by Major Harman, who explained that exactly the same kind of shells are used by the natives of Upper India to frighten away animals from eating the crops, and also to call the labourers from the fields, and Captain Campbell Tufnell gave him another specimen, which the natives of Southern India blow at their funerals. These are only a few instances of many, to show shells are employed as horns or musical instruments, and are known all over the world.

It would be impossible to describe all the tom-toms made from human skulls, trumpets fashioned out of thigh-bones, and other queer specimens my father collected around him; but, from the notes left behind, he evidently intended to write a book on musical instruments made from shells or human bones.

Next to Professor William Ramsay's ' Spectra of Argon and Helion mixed with Argon,' shown at the Royal Society in 1895, my father again exhibited :

' A sacred bone-trumpet, drum, and flute.

' The trumpet and tom-tom drum are from the temple of a Buddhist monastery in Thibet.   They are made from the bones of priests, and therefore supposed to be more religiously effectual.

' The trumpet when blown emits a rising and falling mournful, wailing sound.

' The drum, when the knobs attached to its strings are rattled against the skins, gives a disagreeable harsh noise which is thought to drive the evil spirits out of the temple.

' The flute is a Carib Indian's, from Guiana, made from the tibia of a deer (*Coassus rufinus*).   From it can be got the notes 1, 2, and 3 in the natural harmonic ratios of 6, 7, and 8, as in the French flageolet.'

In a note on bones as musical instruments, my father says :

' The idea of dead priests' bones being more acceptable as musical instruments sprang from the same line of thought which induced the natives of New Britain to make their war-spear heads from the bones of their slain enemies, in the hope that the power of the dead might be added to their own when hurled against their foes.

'The North American carrying the scalp of his fallen foe has a like origin.

'The ancient King eating the eyes—in which the soul was supposed to reside—of his sacrificed victim, with the idea that it would make His Majesty see more clearly, or tasting the heart with the object of making him wiser, all sprang from the same origin.'

But this subject is endless.

'Peruvian mummy eyes' at one time fascinated my father. In 1868 an earthquake sent a tidal wave over Arica, in Peru, which washed a number of desiccated mummies out of their graves. These mummies had been buried in vaulted chambers, and were generally found in a sitting posture, their knees clasped by their hands and their chins resting on them.

They were rolled up in cotton cloth which glistened like silk, although probably made of the fibres of the aloe, and beautifully dyed with zigzag tartan-like patterns. When the mummies were washed out of their burial place, their eyes were found to be oval with the end flattened, and made of concentric layers deposited round a central point. Many of these eyes came into my father's possession, and he was very proud of them. They were held in the head by a cloth tied under the chin, but when taken out were brittle and shone quaintly. They proved to be the crystalline lenses of the eyes of *Lotigo gigas*, the great cuttle-fish of Peru, which, divided hemispherically, the embalmer substituted for the perishable and lustrous human eye, to give the faces of the dead a more life-like appearance.

In the mummies of the warriors lying on bamboos, suspended in the usual way between four trees at some height from the ground, in the Torres Straits and New Guinea, the eyes were made of mother-of-pearl and the nose of a piece of wood.

This was the same idea as the Egyptian, which probably travelled, according to my father's theory, by the Malay

Archipelago to Peru, in the same way as he thought the North American Indians got their scheme of tree-burial from the Torres Straits.

It is well known certain Buddhist and Mahommedan tribes will not let their portraits be taken, as they think that at the Day of Judgment the picture might claim the soul and the body get none. This is probably the same notion as that of the Chinese, who get their priests to paint the pupil of the eye into pictures. From this we might infer that they think the soul resides in the pupil. After all, the idea is not so extraordinary, for do we not say, 'He has speaking eyes,' as well as, 'His soul is in his eyes'?

Among the Indians of Guiana, they quite believe the spirit, 'the small human figure' called *emmawarri*, departs from out of his eyes when a man dies. This doubtless means, 'the small human figure,' which they imagine to be the departed soul, though only the on-looker's own reflection, which is no longer visible in the dead eye.

All primitive peoples have reverence and dread of the human eye; even to-day in the civilized Highlands of Scotland, there is keen superstition rife anent the evil-eye.

Pearls are all the fashion nowadays; indeed, pearls are far more valuable than diamonds, and may be said to be at the zenith of their social glory. It was not, however, from this fact that my father took up his hobby of collecting pearls. As is well known, the pearl is the result of disease, and therefore as a disease it had its interest for him. His collection showed the formation and origin of their growth and development; but the subject became expensive, because he required large specimens to demonstrate his theories, and big pearls are not to be obtained cheaply.

He called pearls the 'product of disease,' and Professor Ruskin was so distressed by anything so beautiful being spoken of by such a hideous term, he begged my father to speak of them as 'deviations from the normal structure.'

He traced the same chemical growth of pearls in man, beast, vegetable and fish.

Six pearls shown at the Royal Society and elsewhere came from the gall-bladder of an ox, two from a woman, and one from a man, both the latter being patients of his own. In mammals the pearl's composition is an organic white crystalline substance called cholestearin, while in the vegetable kingdom pearls are formed of silica.

The pearls we know and value most come from such shell-fish as oysters, mussels, conch and clam shells. Sometimes the disease is found in the fish itself, and sometimes embedded in the shell surrounded by mother-of-pearl.

Sedimentary pearls are formed in strata, layer upon layer, round a central point known as the nucleus. When cut through, the pearl resembles the rings in an onion, or the age-marks in a tree, or even the rings in a horse's teeth. Then there are crystalline pearls, and others combining both formations.

In speaking of the marvellous works of Nature, my father said ' in the great chemical laboratory of the Almighty He always worked under certain fixed laws; that whether it were a mountain which was in course of formation or only a stone, the system was the same : Nature's laws were fixed laws '; and the formation of a calculus in the human bladder, to which he had paid much attention, was identical with the formation of a pearl, a subject which he thoroughly investigated, and on which he read a couple of papers at the Royal Society in 1888, abstracts of which I quote, as they show the way in which he worked his hobbies into scientific truths.

' One fact,' he would say, ' is worth a whole shipload of suppositions ; whatever we attempt to do, let us try to do it well, for truth, like light, goes quickly and directly to the point, while falsehood wriggles slowly like a snake towards its goal.'

1. As regards oyster pearls. Of these three varieties were examined : British, Australian and Ceylonese.

The qualitative analyses showed they all had an identical composition, and consisted solely of water, organic matter, and calcium carbonate. There was a total absence of magnesia and of all the other mineral ingredients of sea-water—from which the inorganic part of pearls must of course be obtained. Seeing that ordinary sea-water contains close upon ten and a half times more calcium sulphate than calcium carbonate, one might have expected that at least some sulphates would have been found along with the carbonates, more especially if they are the mere fortuitous concretions some persons imagine them to be—a view we cannot endorse, from the fact that, by steeping pearls in a weak aqueous solution of nitric acid, we are able to completely remove from them all their mineral constituents without in any way altering their shape, and but very slightly changing their naked-eye appearances, so long as they are permitted to remain in the solution. When taken out they rapidly dry and shrivel up.

The next point being to ascertain the exact proportions of the substances composing the pearls, and pure white pearls being expensive, from our having ascertained that all the three kinds we were operating upon had exactly the same chemical composition, instead of making separate quantitative analyses of them, we simply selected two pearls from each variety, of as nearly the same size and weight—giving a total of 16 grains—and analyzed them collectively, the result obtained being:

Carbonate of lime* ...	...	...	91·72	per cent.
Organic matter (animal)	...	...	5·94	,,
Water	...	2·23	,,
Loss	...	...	0·11	,,

$$100·00$$

From this it is seen that, notwithstanding that mother-of-pearl consists of precisely the same ingredients, their proportions are quite different from what they are in fine pure white pearls (we say fine pure white, because pearls vary greatly in purity, and those we analyzed were good ones), which are infinitely denser, and consequently harder than the mother-of-pearl constituting the shells in which they are formed. The analysis of mother-of-pearl given in Watts's 'Dictionary of Chemistry' is:

---

* The carbonic acid was estimated by disengaging it with dilute sulphuric acid into a soda-lime tube, and calculating the increase in weight (as described by Lunge and Hurter in 'The Alkali-maker's Pocket-book') ; the amount of the organic matter, by noting the loss by weight after calcining, slightly moistening the mass with a solution of ammonium carbonate.

Carbonate of lime	...	...	...	66·00	per cent.
Water	...	...	...	31·00	,,
Organic matter	...	...	...	2·50	,,

thus showing that while mother-of-pearl contains less than half the quantity of organic matter pearls do, it at the same time possesses close upon fourteen times more water. This fact appears to us all the more surprising as, not alone to the naked eye, but even under the microscope, the structure of the mother-of-pearl of the shell and of pearls is almost identical.

[One can scarcely imagine that the analyst could have possibly employed in his investigation a piece of shell while it was yet in a fresh and consequently moist state.

As regards the hardness of pearls, again, it may perhaps be as well for us to remark that good pearls have a much denser texture than the majority of persons appear to suppose, as may be gleaned from the following facts:

On one occasion, being desirous to crush into powder a split-pea-sized pearl, we folded it between two plies of note-paper, turned up the corner of the carpet, and, placing it on the hard bare floor, stood upon it with all our weight. Yet, notwithstanding that we weigh over 12 stone, we failed to make any impression whatever upon the pearl, and even stamping upon it with the heel of our boot did not suffice so much as to fracture it. It was accordingly given to the servant to break with a hammer, and he informed us that on attempting to break it with the hammer against the pantry-table, all he succeeded in doing was to make the pearl pierce through the paper and sink into the wooden table, just as if it had been the top part of an iron nail, and that it was not until he had given it a hard blow with the hammer against the bottom of a flat-iron that he succeeded in breaking it.

In addition to the foregoing, we may likewise take occasion to mention that shell-fish pearls are not nearly so easily dissolved in strong vinegar as the interesting tale of Cleopatra having taken a large pearl from her ear, and, after having dissolved it in vinegar, drunk it to the health of her lover Antony, would lead one to believe; for during our experiments we have learned that not only does it take many days to dissolve out the mineral constituents of a large pearl in cold vinegar, but that it even requires several hours to extract the mineral matter, by boiling vinegar, from a pearl not bigger than a garden pea. While in neither case, moreover, can the pearl be thus made to disappear, as from the fact of the organic matrix of a pearl being totally insoluble in vinegar, even after every particle of its earthy substance has been removed, it still remains of the same shape, bulk, and almost identical appearance as before. Hence we fear that, if the Cleopatra legend is to be believed at all, it requires considerable modifications ere it can be brought into harmony with scientific truth. There is, indeed, only one way in which a large pearl, such as that Cleopatra is said to have employed, could be dissolved in vinegar at a supper-table, and that is by having it completely pulverized by a hard hammer and a strong arm before applying the vinegar to it. For once the mineral constituents of a pearl have been reduced to the state of an impalpable powder, they not only readily dissolve, but effervesce like a seidlitz powder—though much less strongly—when brought into contact with strong vinegar, and thus on their being diluted with water may be transformed into what might be called a cooling lover's potion, while from the organic matter having at the same time as the mineral constituents been minutely subdivided, its presence would scarcely be recognisable in the solution.]*

2. Composition of cocoanut pearls.

Qualitative analyses of pearls found in cocoanuts have been published by both Dr. J. Bacon and Dr. Kimminis.† But their analyses differ somewhat, for while Bacon found carbonate of lime and an organic substance akin to albumin, Kimminis met with nothing whatever in them except pure carbonate of lime. We subjected a portion of a garden-pea-sized cocoanut pearl, weighing 14 grains (kindly given to us by Messrs. Streeter), to analysis, and found that, like shell-fish pearls, it consisted of carbonate of lime, organic matter (animal), and water.

3. As regards mammalian pearls.

These so-called pearls have been met with in human beings and in oxen. The first person who kindly called our attention to those of the ox was the late Professor Pannum, of Copenhagen, who in 1874 presented us with some specimens he had found in the gall-bladder of a Danish ox.

In so far as naked-eye appearances are concerned, a good specimen of the variety of pearl now spoken of is quite undistinguishable from a fine specimen of Oriental oyster pearl, from its not only being globular in shape, and of a pure white colour, but from its also possessing the iridescent sheen so characteristic of Oriental oyster pearls of fine quality.

In chemical composition, however, mammalian pearls bear no similarity whatever to pearls found in shell-fish, for they are composed of an organic instead of an inorganic material, namely,

---

* Added March 27, 1888.

† See 'Proceedings of the Boston Society of Natural History,' vol. vii., 1861, p. 290 ; vol. viii., 1862, p. 173 ; *The Tropical Agriculturist*, April, 1887 ; and *Nature*, June 16, 1887 (Dr. Hickson and Mr. Thiselton Dyer).

cholesterin. In minute structure again, they bear a marked resemblance to the crystalline variety of shell-fish pearls.

The quantitative analysis of human pearls yielded in 100 parts:

Water	...	...	...	...	2·05
Solids	...	...	...	...	97·95

The solids consisted of:

Cholesterin	...	...	...	98·63
Animal matter	...	...	...	1·37

From this it is seen that human pearls are in reality nothing more nor less than exceedingly pure cholesterin biliary concretions.

George Harley, who was an indefatigable worker himself, always took the deepest interest in young people and their work. Writing to a student, he said:

'Every advance made in theoretical knowledge is sooner or later followed by beneficial scientific results. Hence every advance in scientific theory is followed by a corresponding advance in practice. Try not only to keep on the side of truth, but try also to get truth on your side. Remember Conceit is the handmaiden of Ignorance, in the same way as Self-assurance is the twin sister of Stupidity.

'Don't, however, be easily daunted in your research work, for the same ideas which meet with strong opposition from one may elicit decided approval from another; and all progress, you must remember, is due to those who *think* differently from their fellow-men.

'Work out your own theories with your whole heart; one incontrovertible argument is worth a thousand debatable ones.

'Never lose an opportunity; once passed it will never return.

'Mere reading only crams the brains; thinking alone develops them.'

20

CHAPTER XXIV.

FROM first to last my father's great idea was *simplification*. Whether in science, medicine, or in private life, he always seemed intent to try and make things short and easy. Thus, when invalided in the Isle of Man, he amused himself by suggesting a plan for simplifying the English language, which is so full of incongruities.

Thinking out its origin and many of its difficulties, which had often been pointed out to him by foreigners, interested him deeply, and when the spelling bees were started in the seventies, he was much amused to find that people who spelt most accurately and who won prizes were by no means the cleverest or best-educated. At this time there was a stir among the phonetic advocates, a plan which he never considered feasible, though the idea of suggesting the abolition of duplicated consonants occurred to him, and to this scheme accordingly he devoted much time and thought.

Proving to his own satisfaction the efficacy of absolutely abolishing duplicated consonants from all words (except personal names), he adopted the plan, and for several years wrote everything in that manner, even articles in scientific and medical papers. He made some few converts to his theory, but so few that at last he came to the conclusion—although some similar system is sure eventually to be adopted—society was not at that time ready for such an innovation. Very reluctantly, therefore, he gave it up, and took superfluous consonants into use again, if not into favour.

In a book, 'The Simplification of English Spelling,' he wrote :

A new alphabet and phonetic spelling appears too large a mouthful to be forced upon the nation all at once. It would be better to try and give it in small doses. With this object in view, we beg to propose the following plan, which has the great advantage of causing a minimum of national inconvenience.

Our scheme is this :

Let us begin by following the natural course of linguistic evolution, and omit all duplicated consonants from English words, not one of which is absolutely necessary. Duplicated vowels, on the other hand, must not be interfered with, as they are an essential index to pronunciation. But doubled b's, c's, d's, f's, g's, h's, etc., are totally unnecessary, so we would propose to do entirely away with them, except in personal names.

None but those who have already given special attention to the important part played by consonants in English literature can possibly suppose that the topic of this essay is not only one of national importance, but of personal convenience to every man, woman, and child reading and writing the English language.

The number of doubled consonants which infest English literature is far beyond the power of human calculation. A glance at the *Times* newspaper will suffice to illustrate the truthfulness of this assertion.

Few persons are aware that each full-sized copy of the newspaper which they so gladly welcome to their breakfast-table in the morning contains more than 30,000 doubled b's, c's, d's, f's, g's, etc., and that it daily entails upon their visual organs the necessity of deciphering exactly one half—that is to say, more than 15,000—absolutely unnecessary letters of the alphabet, which not only take up a quantity of valuable space in the journal, but must have consumed much time both in writing and printing. About £10,000 a year would be saved by their abolition.

It was once said by a wiseacre that the majority of men are fools, and if the minor half only got the chance it would lock up the major half of its fellow-men in a madhouse. Be this true or be it false, there is no doubt whatever that many of the actions of perfectly sane men possess in them a strong intermixture of folly. The inveterate force of habit is of itself a proof of this. Our actions are often contrary to our reason, and no more graphic illustration of the innate tendency to folly of the human mind can be given than by citing the case of a poor

idiot lad, who, on being asked by a kind-hearted old gentleman why
he was so very lame, gave the prompt reply, ' A hae a nail in the heel
of ma bute ' (I have a nail in the heel of my boot). ' Why don't you
pull it out, then ?' the gentleman retorted. ' Oh, 'cause a'm yeused
wi'd' (Oh, because I am used to it), was the sage reply. Now,
although this was but the logic of a poor idiot boy, humiliating though
the fact be, it nevertheless illustrates to a nicety the principle upon
which the vast majority of mankind act throughout life ; and the most
formidable obstacle to the removal of the evil of duplicated consonants
from our language will probably be that, like the nail in the heel of the
boy's boot, ' we're yeused wi'd.'

If we glance around us on the fields of agriculture, mechanics, art,
or science, we everywhere encounter the same prominent symptom,
the symptom of ' simplification.' The reaping-machine is employed
because it cuts in the brief space of an hour more corn than a
labourer in a whole day. Steam is applied to purposes of loco-
motion to enable us to travel between dusk and dawn a greater
distance than could formerly be accomplished within a week. The art
of the photographer, again, enables mere manual skill to develop in a
few minutes a more exact likeness than an accomplished miniature-
painter can portray in as many hours. By the simplification of
scientific principles we are enabled to waft ideas across the broad
Atlantic in the twinkling of an eye, which in former years failed to be
transmitted to the same distance within a month.

Let us, indeed, gaze on what side we may, the process of philosophic
simplification ever seems to be in the ascendant. It curtails labour, it
saves time, it engenders speed, and, as time is said to be synonymous
with money, simplification may be regarded as the synonym of profit.

Literature alone hangs fire in the general reform movement.

In Speed's ' Empire of Great Britain ' such monosyllabic words as
son, won, sin, map, lap, stem, and war, are not only spelt with duplicated consonants, but with an additional e at the end of each of them.
Thus they are written—sonne, wonne, sinne, mappe, lappe, and warre ;
and one might, perhaps, be excused asking the question whether it is
the old or the new form of spelling which is founded on the best
philological principles.

In fact, the presence or absence of duplicated consonants has little
or nothing to do with the true etymological understanding of any
language ; therefore their total abolition from the English language
cannot be objected to on purely etymological grounds, except by those
super-acute-minded individuals who are in the habit of ' discovering
subtle intentions in the shallow felicities of chance.'

Many of the present generation will remember that when at school
they were taught to spell wagon with two g's, while it is now spelt

with only one g. Fulfil, skilful, and wilful, each with four l's, and dulness with two. Now, however, each of these words has had its l's diminished to one-half. The diminution, too, came about gradually; first, only one of the l's was quietly dropped out, and we had fulfill, skilfull, and wilfull, and, as is seen, without any regard being paid to the order in which the diminution of the l was made; then, after a short time more had vanished, 'Time,' the executioner, again stepped in with his pruning-hook, and silently cut off the third l, so that the words are now reduced to fulfil, skilful, and wilful.

Life is too short and money too precious to be thrown away un-necessarily; and, as the perfection of an art is to produce a maximum of profit at a minimum cost of time and labour, perfection must be regarded as the goal of human progress, and philosophic simplification —the *ne plus ultra* of the age—the royal road thereto.

Why, then, should we hesitate to apply the process of simplification to the English language, and sweep from it, at once and for ever, many of the inconsistencies which at present hang around it?

It is not improbable that the suggestion of the abolition of duplicated consonants is before its time, and will, therefore, perhaps meet with the approval of but a few of the more advanced philologists, while a storm of invective is raised against it, causing it to appear as if about to be totally overwhelmed in the surf. The raging billows will probably, however, pass over it, and in the quiet water behind it will raise its head triumphantly; for being founded upon the principle of simplifica-tion, the lifebuoy of improvement in this progressive age, and having for its sheet-anchor the saving of time and labour, it is impossible for it, we think, to be permanently swamped, no matter how long or how fiercely the stormy billows of prejudice may rage around it.

All the males of George Harley's family for generations died from gout, yet I believe it has never been on record that a woman of the family suffered from the disease! My father had gout in his teens, and therefore the subject was one that interested him immensely. Almost the last thing he published was an article in the *Contemporary Review* for June, 1896, headed 'Champagne.'

It appeared exactly three months before his death, and created a perfect furore among wine-merchants and re-viewers, for he declared sweet wines did not give gout, but 'sec' or so-called 'sec' wines did.

He began his article as follows:

Champagne—nectar of the gods !—is the favourite wine of the hour. How long its popularity will last none can tell, there being a fashion in wine-drinking as there is a fashion in dressmaking: the admired of to-day becomes the neglected of to-morrow. The life-history of all popular wines, from the time of the ancient Greeks and Romans until now, tells this tale. Even within the last couple of decades or so a notice-able change has taken place in the relative quantities of hock, claret, champagne, port, sherry and madeira, drunk at dinner-tables. The uninitiated think the change is due to mere caprice—to a meaningless revulsion in public taste. It is, however, not so. The appreciative powers of the Briton's gustatory nerves have undergone no change, but the qualities of the wines presented to him have altered. Conse-quently, the fault is not on the side of the consumer, but on that of the consumed.

The reason why one wine after another falls into disrepute is easily explained, on the grounds that, the supply of every vintage being limited, no sooner does a wine become popular than the demand for it exceeds the supply. Wine-merchants, not having sufficient moral courage to confess to their customers that they can no longer obtain a sufficiency of the genuine article, adopt the disingenuous practice of equalizing supply and demand by the addition of more readily obtain-able wines. . . .

Sparkling champagne is nothing more nor less than a still white wine, artificially transformed into an effervescing liquid. Hence there are still champagnes as well as sparkling ones ; still hocks and sparkling hocks ; still moselles and sparkling moselles ; still burgundies and sparkling burgundies ; still astis and sparkling ones.

The effervescence of the wine is due to its being bottled and corked up before fermentation has entirely ceased. And all forms of vinous fermentation are due to the splitting up, by minute living micro-organisms, of the sugar contained in grape-juice, into alcohol and carbonic acid gas. The gas, after the bottle has been corked, finding no means of escape, remains suspended in the wine until the cork is withdrawn, when it instantly rushes in bubbles to the surface, and in escaping from it causes the wine to effervesce and sparkle.

Strange though it may seem, the sugar is the food, and the alcohol and carbonic acid gas the excretions of the minute organisms that cause the fermentation.

There is no such thing as a natural sparkling wine ; consequently, champagne is a manufactured article, in the sense that it is brought into existence by the skill of the viticulturist. The process is a com-plicated one. It consists of three distinct stages, the first being merely the making of a still wine. This step differs in no essential particular from that followed in the making of any other still wine, be it port, sherry or claret; that is to say, it consists in the fermentation of expressed grape-juice in open tubs, at a temperature ranging between 60° and 70° Fahr., and, from the tubs being open, the carbonic acid gas generated escapes into the air as a waste product, the alcohol only being retained in the liquid.

The second stage is the conversion of the still liquid into a sparkling wine. This is accomplished by withdrawing it from the tubs into bottles, and tightly corking them so that none of the gas generated during the subsequent fermentation can escape.

In this stage there is, however, another object held in view. For while up till now it was chiefly alcohol that was wanted, during the secondary fermentation the delectable aromas and flavours upon which the commercial value of the wine mainly depends are sought to be developed. So the fermentation is no longer a rapid one at a high temperature, but a slow one at the low temperature of 43° Fahr. And the fermentation is not, as in the first instance, kept up for merely a few weeks, but for months, or even years, according to the quality of the vintage and the price the wine is ultimately expected to bring.

It ought not to be forgotten that 'bouquet' is a point of paramount importance in apprising the value of any wine, champagne being no exception to the rule.

The bouquet of a wine depends mainly on the following five factors: the species of the grape; the soil of the vineyard; the amount of sunshine; the mode of fermentation adopted; and the temperature at which it is conducted.

As sugar is an essential element in champagne manufacture, it may be stated that its amount in grapes materially depends—other things being equal—on the sunshine and rainfall. The hotter the season, the more saccharine is the grape; the colder the season, the sourer the wine. Moreover, it has recently been noted that the sweetness of a grape is in direct proportion to the size of the vine-leaves; the larger the leaf, the larger being the amount of sugar in the grape, and, as a consequence, the stronger the wine made from it. . . .

Until after its *dégorgement*, the bottled champagne is spoken of as *vin brut*, meaning thereby a harsh, immature article; and brut(e) it might well be called, for in its then state it is acid enough, and acrid enough, to take the skin from the mouth of a crocodile. Consequently, it has to be submitted to a softening process, called *dosage*, to suit the varying tastes of its consumers; for even the grossest palate could not drink the wine in its then condition, notwithstanding what some English wine-merchants, who discourse learnedly upon what they are pleased to call the beauties of ' natural champagne,' tell us to the contrary. The word ' natural ' might, perhaps, with some show of reason, be applied to a still wine; but the word is as inappropriate when applied to champagne as it would be to butter or cheese manufactured out of milk.

The act of *dégorgement* consists in the removal of the cork, which, in consequence of the sudden outrush of the pent-up carbonic acid gas, goes out with a bang, along with all the dirty débris that has become deposited in the neck of the bottle. The operation requires great care, and is performed by men with masks on, as the bottles frequently explode. It likewise requires great skill, in order that the whole of the débris may be got rid of with a minimum loss of wine and gas.

Dosage, the last act in the drama of champagne manufacture, is a most important one in the eyes of the viticulturist, for the reputation of his brand mainly depends upon the skill and care with which he accomplishes it, seeing that, as just said, it is the converting an unpalatable sour liquid into a pleasant beverage.

The *dosage* of inferior kinds of champagne is attended with little difficulty, from the fact that all that unrefined palates care for in sparkling wine is alcoholic strength and effervescing sharpness—two qualities that can be given to the poorest of champagnes with but little trouble or expense. . . .

As Russians', Prussians', Frenchmen's and Englishmen's champagnes all come out of the same vats, the differences in their flavours are solely due to the *dosage* liqueur of the viticulturist. To give some idea of this, it may be mentioned that, while the finest champagnes drunk in France have 8 per cent. of it added to the *vin brut* immediately after *dégorgement*, that for Russia has from 14 to 16; for Prussia, from 11 to 13; for America, from 8 to 10; and for England, from 2 to 4. This extremely low percentage for Britain is a thing of quite recent date, however, for up till about the sixties the best champagnes imported into England received exactly the same amount of *dosage* liqueur as the best consumed in France—namely, 8 per cent. And at that time these were spoken of as dry wines; for dry assuredly they were in comparison with the sweet Prussian and Russian varieties.

The word ' dry,' when applied to wines, is a misnomer, as it simply implies that the wine contains but little saccharine matter.

Not one Englishman in a thousand, unless he be in the champagne trade, can distinguish a sour sparkling wine from one that has become dry by being kept from nine to fifteen years. . . .

A popular erroneous notion is that champagne becomes sweeter by age. So far from this being the case, it does exactly the reverse. The older the wine, whether champagne, port, sherry, burgundy or hock, the more and more its saccharine ingredient disappears, from its being transformed into alcohol and alcoholic ethers.

Does champagne cause gout by reason of the sugar it contains? What is the secret of the immunity from gout among sweet-wine-drinkers of the Continent? The answer is very simple. The widespread notion that sugar causes gout is a mere figment of the imagination. Sugar could never bring on an attack of gout, even in a constitutionally predisposed individual, from the fact that uric acid, which is now conceded by all leading pathologists to be the peccant material of gout, as it enters into the composition of every gout-stone, and is deposited in the form of urate of soda in every gouty joint, contains an element which does not exist in sugar. For uric acid is a compound of oxygen, hydrogen, carbon and nitrogen, while sugar contains no nitrogen whatever. How, then, can uric acid be formed out of sugar, any more than the children of Israel could, during their bondage in Egypt, manufacture bricks from the mud of the Nile without straw? Although this is not a medical paper, it may perhaps be well to add that the idea that sugar produces gout is alike contrary to everyday experience and scientific observation. Because, were it true, children and women, who consume most sweet things, would be more subject to gout than men, which they are decidedly not. And the women in the Eastern harems, who almost live on sweetmeats, would all be afflicted with gout in some form or another.

Besides which the urine of herbivora, whose food is richly sugar-forming, instead of being, as it is, alkaline, would be acid. Moreover, that a fit of gout cannot be induced by eating sugar was shown by Dr. Vaughan Harley's taking, while working at the Sorbonne in Paris, 400 grammes (13 ounces) of sugar daily, until he completely upset his digestion, and totally failed to induce the disease, notwithstanding that he is hereditarily gouty. And while working in Professor Mosso's laboratory at Turin he even took 17½ ounces of sugar in the twenty-four hours without producing a single gouty symptom. . . .

In corroboration of the fallacy of the sugar and gout idea, it may be mentioned that the still more reprehensible dogma in a sanitary point of view that sugar ruins children's teeth is equally false. Indeed, how the idea ever came into existence is a mystery, seeing that the finest, whitest and strongest teeth are found in the mouths of negroes brought up on sugar plantations, who from their earliest years upwards consume more sugar than any other class of people whatever. Those at all sceptical of the value of this fact have only to look round among their personal friends and see whether the sugar-eaters or the sugar-shunners have the finest teeth, and they will find—other things being equal—that the sugar-eaters, as a rule, have the best teeth. The only possible way for accounting for this libel against sugar seems to be by supposing that it originated in the brain of one of our economically disposed great-grandmothers, at a time when sugar was two shillings a pound, in order to prevent her children gratifying their cravings for sweets at the expense of the contents of the sugar-basin.

While all experimental data point to the fact that alcohol and acids are the most potent exciters of uric acid formations, clinical observation has shown that the most alcoholic and acid wines are, as a rule, the chief generators of gout.

There are seven acids in wine—three natural: tartaric, malic and tannic; and four developed by fermentation: carbonic, acetic, formic and succinic.

Acetic acid is so powerful a producer of gout that the vinegar in a salad or a mint sauce will suffice to bring on an attack in some constitutionally predisposed persons in the same way, and for a precisely similar reason, as a glass or two of the acid *très sec* or *brut* champagnes do.

Champagne requires a temperature of 66° Fahr. to bring out in perfection the more delicate of the vinous aromas of sparkling wines. Frozen champagne is wine spoilt.

A few weeks after the champagne article appeared, and within a month of my father's death, he gave a paper at the British Association, September, 1896, in Liverpool, on ' Talking Sticks.'

This article on ' The Stick and Bone Letters of the Aboriginal Australians in Horizontal Straight Lines like Ogams ' was a very profound paper. It was one my father worked at, off and on, for some years, collecting material here, there and everywhere, but it is impossible for me to do more than hint at its purport. He was most anxious for an Imperial Bureau of Ethnology, in order to record, for the benefit of future generations, the now fast vanishing folk-lore of Greater Britain. At the British Association he showed some of the primitive writing on wood and bone of the Australian blacks of the present day, and suggested comparison of this with the picture-writing of other barbaric peoples, in which lies the germ of phonetic signs composing the world's alphabets.

' There are five great systems of picture-writing, which have been independently invented, the Egyptian, Cuneiform, Chinese, Mexican, and Hittite; but as picture-writing is a troublesome and cumbersome mode of communication, it became superseded as tribes advanced in culture by abbreviated signs.

Among the stick letters exhibited by my father was one sent by a West Australian native to a friend. It showed two paragraphs of lines in two parallel columns. There were ten in all, and one of them contained seven parallel columns, the division between them being quite distinct, though without a stem line. At the top of the stick was a knot of human hair, a very ordinary means by which these natives identify from whom their letters come. He also had bits of leg-bone (the fibula) of a kangaroo from King George's Sound, S.W.A., having lines almost identical with some of the ogams on the bone pins found in Irish lake-dwellings, and again he showed two message sticks from Central Queensland, N.E.A., that were sent by Nowwanjung to her husband Carralinga, the strange lines of which represented his name and her name, while the intermediate ones meant ' Come here to-morrow.'

That the past often repeats itself in the present is well known ; particularly is this the incentive to appliances of practical utility, and it was a great pity my father was not able to finish his researches, for he had collected an enormous amount of interesting material. Had he lived to retire from his arduous practice at seventy years of age, as he hoped, he had planned many years of active work outside his profession.

CHAPTER XXV.

MEDICAL SCIENCE was literally groping in the dark when George Harley first came to London. The struggle between Empiricism and Science was then fierce, but when he died, forty years later, Science had, so to speak, conquered.

To sum up in a few words. The use of the microscope early in the fifties was practically unknown. Microscopic Anatomy, both of healthy and diseased structures, is at the present day one of the most important factors in medical teaching. No scientist and no medical man can do much without a microscope, yet half a century ago only a handful of men knew how to use one.

My father, through the knowledge gained during many years' study at foreign Universities, was able to introduce new methods of teaching into London, and to show how the microscope could be employed in Medical Science.

The very first Chair formed for the teaching of scientific methods as applied to Histology was at University College, and George Harley was the first Professor in England of Practical Physiology, a Chair afterwards held by Michael Foster and Burdon Sanderson.

The teaching in the hospitals, as we have already said, was most rudimentary, and, one might almost venture to say, at the Universities equally so.

Although this is not a scientific work, it may not seem out of place to give a brief sketch of some of the advances that have taken place in the science of Medicine, and through them in medical practice, during the time George Harley lived : for it was with interest and enthusiasm that he advanced step by step with each fresh discovery, and, one may well say, at the time of his death took as keen an interest in the scientific discoveries of Bacteriology as he did in his youth in his early microscopical experiments. It seems hard for us at the present day to conceive the condition of affairs that existed half a century ago, when Darwin's doctrine of Evolution was unknown. Through the teaching of Darwin and his followers, we are now one and all able to see a mental picture of how the different forms of life around us can not only be modified by artificial selection, but also by natural selection or by the surroundings in which they are placed. This biological fact has the greatest importance on the medical teaching of the day, for it opens up in the young man's intellect a pathway of reasoning and understanding, showing how one thing in Nature can be connected with the other in consecutive order, and not, as in the early sixties, by jumping from one form to another without any sequence.

Still further, the modifications produced in the animal and vegetable kingdom by the surroundings, explain how the same thing applies to tissues under diseased conditions.

When we turn from this preliminary of Biology, we come to the other step which so greatly helped the advance of medicine, namely, Physiology. ' The precise recording apparatus ' have all been introduced in this space of time, and owe their origin to men like Ludwig and Du Bois Raymond. By means of such apparatus as the kymograph, accurate records of the movements of the heart and circulation can now be obtained, and careful comparisons made. How this has modified our present view of circulatory disease it is needless to remark, for now medical men no longer grope darkly after the movements of the heart, but know definitely how they act and under what circumstances they may be deranged.

In Physiology even greater advances have been made in

the knowledge of the nervous system. The experiments of
Ferrier, Horsley, Schäfer, and others in this country, as
well as of numerous foreigners, have led to the mapping
out of certain areas in the brain for each definite movement.
Still further, from these motor-sensory areas the course of
fibres can be traced down the spinal cord, and hence into
the various nerves to the regions supplied, and thus we are
able to follow how a nerve impulse flows from the centre in
the brain to any muscle or gland, and by seeing how the
distant end is deranged are able to localize a lesion somewhere in that course.

It is now not sufficient to say that a patient is suffering
from paralysis, for even the student in the hospital tries
to localize the seat of nerve lesion, and the successful
results thus obtained are so palpable that no tyro can help
admiring the advances made.

When we turn to the Chemistry of Physiology, we must
bear in mind that really it is within the last forty years
the whole of Physiological Chemistry has been developed.
Liebig was practically the founder of Physiological
Chemistry, but how amazed he would be to-day to see
the results of his work !

In France, Claude Bernard proved by Experimental
Physiology how the various secretions—gastric, pancreatic,
and biliary—acted, and Physiological Chemistry was still
further expanded by Hoppe Seyler and Voit in Germany ;
so that now we are able to follow the chemical changes
which take place in the body when food is introduced, in
the progress of digestion, and still further during assimilation, while up to a certain extent we can see how the
chemical constituents of the food have yielded their energy
to allow the movements, etc., we call life. The food
required can be calculated out in calories, and up to a
certain point accurately measured to each individual's
requirements, in the same way as a fire can be stoked with
a given amount of coal to yield a certain amount of heat.

It was in the fifties that Helmholtz introduced the

ophthalmoscope, and, although greatly modified in form, the modern instrument allows us to see inside an eye, and has yielded wonderful results to the oculist, as well as in the diagnosis of brain disease.

In the days when my father came to London, Anatomy and Physiology were taught together; now not only these have been separated, but a new subject has developed, that of Pathology, and in each of these subjects it is no longer possible for a medical man, however great his ability, to keep continually up to date, therefore he must 'specialize.' The Anatomist, Physiologist, and Pathologist, although working much on the same line, each diverges on his special course; while Pathology has now developed an off-shoot, so that a fourth specialism has come into existence, viz., Bacteriology.

Pasteur's study in fermentation first introduced Bacteriology, a science that has done more to revolutionize medicine than any other, while the more plodding work of Koch led to the definite establishment of consumption and various other tubercular diseases, showing they were due to the action of one and the same bacillus, namely, the 'tubercle bacillus.' In consequence of these successful experiments, it has been found that various other infectious diseases are caused by special bacilli.

The discovery of the special bacilli for various infectious diseases led to the development of serum therapeutics. As an example of this we may take the diphtheria antitoxine. It was first found that a special bacillus formed the diphtheritic membrane, and the products of this bacillus passed into the body and produced the various symptoms we know as diphtheria. It was still further found that animals could be inoculated with diphtheria in so modified a form that they had no severe, indeed almost imperceptible, diphtheritic symptoms; at the same time they became under treatment incapable of taking diphtheria, for which reason these animals might be considered 'immune.' It was found the serum collected from 'immune' animals was capable of preventing further development of diphtheria in patients already suffering from that disease, and by this means already many lives have been saved, and the value of such methods of research has been demonstrated to the general public.

Since the discovery of the diphtheria antitoxine various others have also been found, such as that against tetanus, erysipelas, etc., so that we are now in a new field for the treatment of disease. The prevention by inoculation of hydrophobia is on the same lines, though, strange to say, while the preventive has been found and proved successful in thousands of cases, up to the present moment the actual bacillus which causes rabies still remains unknown.

In tracing the study of Bacteriology, one naturally turns to antiseptics, for it is true the proof that spontaneous generation did not exist led my father's old friend Lord Lister to his great discovery of antiseptics, so that now one can treat wounds without danger of contamination, while the healing of such wounds is practically painless.

The discovery of anæsthesia also came prominently before the public in George Harley's lifetime. He worked for years at the subject of anæsthetics himself. The experiments made for the committee of the Royal Medical and Chirurgical Society on chloroform, drowning, and hanging, were carried out by my father in his own laboratory at University College. The perfection of anæsthetics has not only led to a great diminution of human suffering, but has freed the surgeon from the horrors attendant upon carrying out an operation on an individual suffering pain. Now the surgeon can operate at his leisure, consequently operations are performed which would not formerly have been conceived possible. No longer is Surgery limited to the lopping off of limbs, but every region in the body has been attacked by the knife with the most marvellously successful results. Thus the use of antiseptics and anæsthetics has revolutionized Surgery.

In a non-scientific book like this it would be out of place

to enter into descriptions of purely medical and surgical work; but we may remark that abdominal Surgery has proved effectual in the saving of life and suffering, that the thorax has been attacked with successful results, and the surgeon has explored the inside of the skull, so that abscesses and growths have been taken from the brain itself, their exact position having been previously diagnosed by means of the advances taught by Physiology.

We now come to consider Medicine proper, and we can boldly state that there has hardly been less done in that direction than in Surgery, although the advances in Surgery have been great, and allow the eye of the uninitiated, perhaps, more easily to grasp their significance. At the same time, the strides made in Medicine have been immense, and owe their origin to the more accurate and careful methods of observation which have been introduced during late years by Physiology and Pathology.

We now know the proper treatment of consumption, and openly attack the tubercle bacillus. The open-air treatment of phthisis has come into vogue, and we are aware that phthisical individuals, in whose bodies the bacilli are already present, require to be fed up, so as to make their tissues so resistant that they will conquer the disease known popularly as consumption.

Further, we have learnt the hereditary tendency to consumption, which used to be so feared, is due, not to the patient absolutely inheriting consumption, but that he inherits a weakness in his tissues, so that the tubercular bacillus can and does more easily grow in such a soil. Consequently, children of consumptive parents ought to be guarded in every possible way against the possibility of the tubercular bacilli obtaining access to their bodies, and lately this has been attempted by a more careful sterilization of milk, etc.

In diseases such as gout and rheumatism our knowledge has grown enormously. Doctors now know the chemistry of gout, and can view it in a rational manner, being thus

21

successful in its treatment. In the cure of rheumatic fever the discovery of the use of salicylate of soda has been made. Instead of the patient suffering weeks of agony, a doctor is able, with a few doses of salicylate of soda, administered at the proper time, to charm away the pain as if by magic.

In diseases of the circulation the 'accurate recording apparatus' of Ludwig, etc., have led medical men to modify their methods of treatment and diagnosis, while the proper action of cardiac tonics, such as digitalis, has been carefully demonstrated, and the value of substances like nitrites in angina pectoris, no less marvellous.

As an example how wonderfully Medicine has advanced let us take one piece of work, and that is the result of research on the thyroid gland. Schiff long ago showed that in animals the removal of the thyroid gland led to disastrous results ; Gull, in 1873, described a condition of cretinism which occurred in old age, and Ord gave to this condition the name of myxœdema. Later, Kocher showed that very much the same condition—if not absolutely the same condition—as described under the disease myxœdema was seen in patients after the removal of goitre.

In 1885 Horsley removed the thyroids of monkeys, and showed that a cretinoid condition was thus produced, and proved, moreover, that if grafting of the thyroid gland was performed this cretinoid condition could be averted. In consequence of this George Murray suggested the administration of the thyroid extract to patients suffering from myxœdema—that terrible sort of imbecility which has caused misery in so many homes—and by this treatment the myxœdemic condition disappears. It appears almost impossible to realize within how short a time such an amount of knowledge has been gained.

Truly, the careful way in which fresh discoveries have been made and followed step by step, both by clinical observation and experiments, to their legitimate end is a good example of modern methods in Medicine.

At the end of the nineteenth century this progressive mode of reasoning has been brought into general hospital work, and no longer do doctors or students jump from one conclusion to another, for nothing is accepted as proved till it has been absolutely followed to its sequence.

The last advance which has been made is the discovery in the blood of patients suffering from malaria of a special plasmodium which is now proved to be the cause of malaria, and the painstaking researches of Dr. Ross have still further shown that the plasmodium reaches the human blood by means of mosquitoes !

One of the foremost results of the better knowledge of the etiology of disease which has been obtained in the last half-century has led to the introduction of Preventive Medicine, or Public Health. The advances in Preventive Medicine have prolonged the average life some three or four years, and this alone is a wonderful step, when one considers what it means. Public Health is no longer merely looking after drains and smells, but has developed into a science of its own, and now every town has its special health officer. In consequence of this, when an infectious disease springs up it is at once attacked in a scientific manner. This was lately demonstrated at Maidstone, when typhoid fever made its appearance so suddenly. The public health officer stepped in and discovered the cause of disease, and prevented its spreading. The same thing holds good throughout the kingdom, and now our public health and sanitary arrangements become more perfect day by day. A step is now being taken to insure that animals shall only be killed in certain places and under the direct supervision of the health officer, and, still further, that the collection and distribution of milk is to be under supervision.

I cannot leave the subject of the advance of Medicine in the present day without referring to the changes produced in the treatment of the sick poor by the introduction of nursing by skilled hands. My father often told stories of

21—2

the want of experience of nurses when he first came to London; such a state of things as he described can hardly be said to exist now, when nursing has become, so to speak, a science.

Viewing the perfection of nursing to-day, it seems impossible to realize that it was only in the middle of this century that real nursing came into existence at all. The pioneer in this country was the Quakeress, Mrs. Elizabeth Fry, who inaugurated the Institution of Nursing Sisters in 1840.

She did her best to have her nurses taught at a general hospital, and ten years later King's College Hospital and St. Thomas's organized classes for regular training.

Then came the terrible troubles in the Crimea; heart-rending accounts of the sufferings of the soldiers were sent home to England. At once great public interest was aroused, and Miss Florence Nightingale came forward and volunteered her services. Hospital nursing was organized at the seat of war, and so began the wonderful reformation which has achieved such universal success, both in military and other hospitals; and I think every physician and surgeon will own that he owes much of his success to the good nursing of the present day.

Although the short résumé which I have given is but cursory, I have endeavoured to show how the training of the medical man is now carried out, and how a diagnosis is rightly made and treated in a scientific spirit, in a very different manner from what it was when my father first started practice.

CHAPTER XXVI.

LAST YEARS.

Many people doubtless remember the enormous excitement caused by the opening of the Imperial Institute in 1893 by the Queen, who had not taken part in any public ceremony for some time.

It chanced one beautiful morning that I drove to Harley Street, intending to go on from there and do some shopping, when I was, to my surprise, met in the hall by my father arrayed in his scarlet gown and black velvet cap. Before I quite realized the situation, I found myself whirling away with him in his brougham to the Imperial Institute. The matter came about in this wise : Sir Andrew Clark, as President of the Royal College of Physicians, had received a ticket for himself and a lady, and at the last minute, finding it impossible to go, sent the ticket—as was his wont on such occasions—round to my father, begging him to represent him and the College at this function. Thus it happened that, arriving at the exact moment, I chanced to be the favoured one.

By the time we reached the Serpentine the crowd was tremendous ; however, policemen peeping in the carriage window, and seeing my father's gorgeous attire, called from one to the other, 'Let the Ambassador's carriage pass !' And so in great state we finally drove up to the door of the Imperial Institute just behind the Duke of Cambridge and immediately in front of the Queen. I remember it as one of the most awful ordeals in my life, for I had not on my best frock—merely a plain morning-gown; and when we arrived, it was to find everyone else dressed in their very best, and bedecked with diamonds and lace. Almost all present were in their seats as we entered the vast hall containing the presidents of the learned societies, Ambassadors representing various countries, Ministers past and present, Bishops and Judges of England. It was a wonderful spectacle, but for me a terrible one. My father took my arm, and with the aid of his stick in his other hand we walked slowly up that vast hall; for our seats were at the very top, and we found ourselves placed immediately to the right of the royal daïs. In passing to my place I crushed the beautiful lawn sleeves of the Archbishop of Canterbury, who was waiting to open the service!

Really, the great hall was a magnificent sight. Gaily-attired ladies, men in Court dress, Ambassadors in robes, military and naval uniforms, Judges in their red and ermine gowns and wigs, and the splendid dresses of the Indian Princes. A blaze of colour, a wonderful scene, the dancing sunlight adding brilliancy to the effect.

Immediately opposite to us sat Lord Salisbury, Mr. Balfour, and all the then Ministers, while the front row below us contained those of the last Administration; then a row of Ambassadors and their wives, the Chinese, Japanese and Turkish being magnificent. In the third row we sat with Lord Kelvin on one side, who represented the Royal Society, on the other Sir Frederick Leighton, representing the Academy, while next, again, was Sir William Flower, of the Natural History Museum.

This was the first appearance of the Duke and Duchess of York as an engaged couple, and they received a perfect ovation. Her Majesty appeared thoroughly to enjoy herself, and when not actually engaged with the ceremony, held up glasses with long handles, and looked around at everyone and everything, making remarks ever and anon in her clear, bell-like voice to the Prince of Wales and the Duke of Edinburgh, which we could hear distinctly.

The Prince of Wales read his address in that loud, rich tone and slight foreign intonation of the letter *r* we know so well; and every time he referred to 'Your Gracious Majesty,' he made his mother a slight bow, which she pleasantly acknowledged. The Queen read her reply sitting, and without wearing glasses. Her voice was perfectly clear and strong, much more like that of a young woman than a lady over seventy years of age. She only referred to the Prince of Wales once, and then as 'my dear son.' Her rendering of the little speech was so expressive, it was quite dramatic. After she had finished, the Prince of Wales declared the building open on her behalf, and touched an electric button in the silver model of the Imperial Institute on the table before the Queen. Instantly the bells began to peal, and very musical they sounded as they rang forth for the first time. Albani sang ' God save the Queen ' so beautifully that the ruler of a quarter of the world shed a silent tear! There were not many dry eyes.

My father quite enjoyed the ceremony, as he always did anything of a like nature, such as his friend Mrs. Keeley's ninetieth birthday celebration at the Lyceum Theatre a few months before his death. He retained to the last the keenest interest in everything and anything; indeed, a friend persuaded him to go to Ascot on his drag, sit in his box on the grand-stand, and lunch in his private dining-room! My father had not been to a race-meeting for many years; but when everything promised so delight- fully he accepted, and went off with the enthusiasm of a schoolboy, although climbing to the box-seat by the little ladder was a very serious matter to his lame leg; but he did it, and enjoyed himself thoroughly.

Surgeon-General Sir William Moore and my father were great friends. Sir William was a well-known man, the inventor of ' Moore's test,' and author of many medical books which still circulate widely in India, where he resided for thirty-five years. In England, however, he is chiefly remembered in connection with ' the Opium Inquiry.'

While in India he studied exhaustively the whole question of opium-smoking, with the result that he became an ardent advocate for its non-abolition, stoutly maintaining the denounced custom was of real service to a people addicted to its practice from time immemorial. He said though a few might indulge in the habit to excess, a large majority smoked in moderation, and added that, even to those destitute of self-control, opium was much less deleterious than alcohol, since the latter fires the brain and incites to quarrelling, while the former only soothes to sleep. An opium smoker never fights; after inhaling a few pipes he drops into a sweet slumber, and enjoys dreams of heavenly bliss.

One day in March, 1895, just before Sir William delivered his remarkable address in favour of opium at the Imperial Institute, he and Lady Moore lunched with us in Harley Street. After coffee had been handed round, a wooden box was brought into the room, which contained half a dozen opium-pipes. The ordinary pipe used by the poor people of India is made of bamboo, the handle or stem of which is about eighteen inches long and some two inches in circumference; it has an open hole at one end, which is put in the mouth. At the other end is a little blue-and-white china pot, something like an ordinary ink-pot, into which the bamboo stick is thrust, like a cork in a bottle, a little bit of thread being tied round the bamboo in such a way that no air can enter or smoke escape. At the side of the little china inkpot is a small hole the size of a pin's head. At the side of this hole, and not in the pot itself, some opium mixture, about the size of a pea, according to custom, was carefully placed by means of one of the long thin opium spoons. A spirit lamp was next lighted, and then, holding the pipe to his mouth and the opium pea so near to the flame that it almost caught fire, Sir William began to smoke. In a moment the queer smell of the opium became noticeable. Half a dozen whiffs only; the stuff was burnt to a little brown cinder, and that pipe was done. No wonder opium-smokers take from six to twelve pipes of such a transient joy. This rapid ending to the pipe solved our amazement on learning four or five were necessary to produce any effect at all, for, naturally, an English person had in his mind ordinary tobacco-pipes, whereas the opium-pipe contains little more than a whiff.

My father and my brother Vaughan quickly followed Sir William's example, and soon the atmosphere grew heavy and thick with the fumes of opium. As I always like to try everything—novel experiences are so delightful—I carefully picked out the largest and most elaborate-looking pipe from the wooden box lying on the table. While the small Indian pipes had only cost sixpence apiece, this Chinese specimen was worth four or five shillings. Instead of having a pot at the end, it was tightly fastened by means of a piece of ivory or bone, while about six inches from the top was a projecting kind of copper cup, on the outer edge of which appeared the same little hole observable in the other pipes. Over this hole some of the black mixture was smeared, it being thicker than treacle and like the dubbin used for boots. It was prepared by a simple process of treating the opium with hot water and filtering, the filtrate being evaporated down to a semi-solid consistence, and kept in pots ready for use. Opium, as most people know, is really the juice of poppies, the growth of which in India returns a large revenue. The poppy-seed is not prepared for smoking, but is eaten with sweetmeats, made into a cake for cattle, and also affords an oil which is extensively used. Besides the revenue it yields, the opium industry gives employment to thousands of persons, so that its abandonment would be very much more serious to India than at a casual glance one might suppose.

With great excitement and a sort of dread, I placed my opium pea in the flame of the lamp and began to inhale. How shall I describe the effect? There was a curious burnt taste, as if I had toasted a little bit of bread to a cinder and was eating it; beyond that there was at first no sensation, pleasant or otherwise. Puff, puff, puff, and the pipe came to an end, so I decided to follow the men's example and try another, each lasting but half a minute. With the second one I succeeded in inhaling more satisfactorily, and gradually felt the effect of the smoke in my lungs. It was like having a cold on the chest, and breathing through cotton-wool. But where were the pleasant feelings one had heard about, the delightful contentment, the dreamy, sleepy beatitude? My experience of the drug was a choking, struggling effort to breathe through a bad chest cold, with a little cough thrown in—very different indeed from a peep into Elysium.

Not caring to be beaten, however, and having three members of the medical profession close at hand, ready to come to my rescue if results proved dangerous, I insisted on trying another pipe. But, alas! that also proved ineffectual. Only more choking, more discomfort, more the sort of feeling one might experience from imbibing the fumes of chopped hay or brown paper. Like other forms of smoking, opium probably requires practice to produce great happiness. Nevertheless, as I hate failing in any endeavour, I wanted to try another pipe, to smoke, in fact, until I felt the delicious drowsiness so loved by Easterns; but I was not allowed to have my bad way, therefore can give no personal experience of its charms.

Those three good doctors smoked on, however, compared notes, and generally enjoyed their little experiment, the results of which Sir William Moore gave a few days later in his address at the Imperial Institute.

No sketch of the life of George Harley of Harley Street would be complete without a few lines concerning the Savile Club, where he spent some of his happiest hours. One of the original members, he belonged to the old club in Savile Row for many years without making much use of his privileges, but after he became lame and the club moved into Piccadilly, he generally managed to finish up his afternoon consultations by looking in 'for tea and gossip' at this temple of literature and fame.

In summer my father was wont to sit in one of the big windows of the smoking-room overlooking Piccadilly, his blotting-pad upon his knee, an attitude essentially his own, writing the thoughts that were ever floating through his busy brain, ever and anon laying his work aside for half an hour's chat with some congenial spirit. In the winter the arm-chair, which by the kind courtesy of the members was considered sacred to him, was wheeled close to the blazing fire, while a little crowd gathered round to listen to experiences graphically told, or enter into some discussion which the lame doctor was carrying on with an animated adversary.

He never came home without having met people of interest who had come up to have a talk with him, for his lameness made him dependent on the members seeking him out.

Many of his club friends were quite unknown to us except by name. As the following note to my mother is from a total stranger, it may possess some interest, and I hope, therefore, I shall be forgiven for inserting it :

'DEAR MRS. HARLEY,

'You may possibly not remember my name, but as one who long knew and greatly respected Dr. Harley I venture to write. It would, I am sure, be a solace to you in your great sorrow to know how much his loss is felt at the Savile Club, and with what affection many members who were in the habit of meeting him speak of the friend who has passed away. It was not only that his wonderful knowledge of men and manners made his conversation a delight; there was a sincerity and kindness of nature that made the man beloved. Only a few days before I last saw him, Sir Charles Cookson spoke to me with great enthusiasm of the pleasure he felt, on his annual visit to England, at renewing his acquaintance with that " dear soul."

'It is a relief to me to tell you this, for it seems to me a sad thing that a familiar and ever-welcome face should disappear from our circle, and that those whom he loved should never know their grief found a deep reflection in the regrets of those who knew him outside his home.'

At a big literary dinner in June, 1898, I met the Rev. Edward Hawkins, whose brilliant son 'Anthony Hope' was in the chair. The former began asking me if I had nearly finished my father's Life. 'I never now enter the Savile Club,' he went on, 'without missing the cheery smile of George Harley and his brilliant conversation. The place has never been the same since. He was one of the centres of talk there during the last twenty-five years.'

Edward Clodd was another of George Harley's close friends. They had much in common, and discussed the ' Childhood of Religions,' the ' Childhood of the World,' and the ' Story of Creation,' before the days when those well-known works saw the light. Writing to me recently Mr. Clodd says :

' Your dear father's brilliant and informing talks were always enlivened by some bit of personal reminiscence, when the members gathered together in the smoking-room, where his chair was always reserved. I must apply to him that immortal tribute which Callimachus pays to his dead friend Heraclitus. Let me quote it for the beauty and pathos that inspired words thus Englished by William Cory :

' They told me, Heraclitus, they told me you were dead ;
They brought me bitter news to hear, and bitter tears to shed ;
I wept when I remembered how often you and I
Had tired the sun with talking, and sent him down the sky.

' And now that thou art lying, my dear old Carian guest,
A handful of gray ashes, laid long ago at rest,
Still are thy pleasant voices, thy nightingales, awake :
For Death, he taketh all away, but these he cannot take.'

This is enough to show that my father was one of a little circle of friends. He always spoke with the greatest affection and esteem of those who clustered round him over his cup of tea.

One of the younger men who never entered the club without seeking my father's particular corner was Charles J. Cornish, the well-known writer on natural history subjects. Mr. Cornish often quoted the doctor in his books, and is good enough to say : ' Many young men like myself owe much to the interest and sympathy of George Harley. He was ever ready to give the benefit of his advice and experience.'

Everyone knows by reputation the Royal Society, which allows its Fellows to use the magic letters F.R.S. after their name, but everyone does not know that there is a small and distinguished Royal Society Club, a little dining coterie belonging to the parent stem. It has nothing whatever to do with the Royal Societies' Club, which has very closely encroached upon its name, but is a different affair altogether, being an ordinary club, presumably for members of different Royal Societies, but comprising outside members. The real Royal Society Club is very small and select; I believe, all told, it comprises only about fifty members, and these, forming themselves into a body, elect a new member from among their *confrères* at Burlington House when a vacancy occurs. No one is actually ' put up,' therefore no one knows anything about his probable election until he receives a letter such as the following :

' *To Dr. George Harley, F.R.S., 25, Harley Street,*
London.
' 56, Lexham Gardens, W.,
' *June* 24, 1887.

' MY DEAR SIR,
' I have the pleasure to inform you that you were yesterday elected a member of the Royal Society Club. I enclose you a copy of the rules of the club.

' The admission fee named in Rule X., together with the annual subscription, viz., £1, are payable to R. H. Scott, Esq., F.R.S., 6, Elm Park Gardens, S.W.

' A card containing the members' names, with the days

of meeting, will be sent you in due course. The first club meeting is on November 17.

'I am, my dear sir, yours faithfully,

'GEORGE HENRY RICHARDS

'(Treasurer).'

This little coterie dined once a month during the winter at Limmer's Hotel, and it had to be something extremely important which ever kept my father away from these exclusive gatherings. A few distinguished guests only were allowed to be present, when all that was best in science was discussed. Anyone who had a new invention to show or a new theory to expound always tried to show or expound his novelty to the select few at the Royal Society Club dinner. The following may prove interesting:

ROYAL SOCIETY CLUB.

Members of the club are reminded that it has been decided to commemorate the one hundred and fiftieth anniversary of its foundation, October 27, 1743, at the opening meeting of the present session, November 16, 1893.

The bill of fare and the price of the dinner (one shilling and sixpence) will be the same as were usual for the club at the date of its foundation.

The earliest dinner of which the bill of fare has been preserved is that of March 24, 1748, and is as follows:

Old Menu, 1748.	*New Menu*, 1893.
	DINNER TO COMMEMORATE THE ONE HUNDRED AND FIFTIETH ANNIVERSARY OF THE ROYAL SOCIETY CLUB.
2 dishes Fresh Salmon, Lobster Sauce.	Cod's Head.
Cod's Head.	Smelts.
Pidgeon Pye.	Calves Head.
Calves Head.	Pidgeon Pye.
Bacon and Greens.	Bacon and Greens.
Fillett of Veal.	Fillett of Veal.
Chine of Pork.	Chine of Pork.
Plumb Pudding.	Haunch of Venison.
Apple Custard.	Plumb Pudding.
Butter and Cheese.	Apple Custard.
	Butter and Cheese.
	Limmer's. 16 *November*, 1893.

As the attendance may probably be large, it would be convenient if any member proposing to dine would on this occasion send in his name beforehand, and also say if he intends to bring a guest.

The usual cards will also be issued as the date of the dinner approaches.

ROBERT H. SCOTT }
JOHN W. HULKE } *Treasurers.*

Always having been a great diner-out, as well as giver of dinners, my father was much interested not only, as we have seen, in queer foods, but in strange menus, and among a number of the latter the following seems so funny I insert it. Two legs of mutton for 2½d. must send a thrill of envy through the bosom of every housewife !

Bill of fare for Barber-Surgeons, Wax and Tallow Chandlers' Company, on October 28, 1478, in the reign of Edward IV. :

	s.	d.
2 loins of veal - - - - -		8
2 „ mutton - - - -		8
1 „ beef - - - - -		4
2 legs of mutton - - - -		2½
1 pig - - - - - -		6
1 capon - - - - - -		6
1 rabbit - - - - - -		2
1 dozen pigeons - - - -		7
1 goose - - - - - -		4
1 gross eggs - - - - -		8½
2 gallons wine - - - - -	1	4
18 „ ale - - - - -	1	6
	7	6

One hundred and twenty-four men dined off the above.

By chance and through a foreign source my brother became assistant to the famous Victor Horsley, in 1892, a piece of good fortune which was soon followed by another, namely, that of being appointed assistant professor at University College, London. The last months of my father's life were very happy ones. Professor Horsley determined to retire from his arduous labours at the college, and then the vastly accumulated work was divided into two parts, Dr. Sydney Martin, F.R.S., taking the Pathological Chair, and Vaughan Harley the Chemical Pathological Professorship. Thus the son became the first Professor of Chemical Pathology in England, as the father had become the first Professor of Practical Physiology in this country thirty-six years before !

My father took immense interest in Vaughan's work, and all his scientific enthusiasm lived again in his son, whom he educated to follow in his footsteps with all the care and knowledge he had to bestow.

CHAPTER XXVII

My father spent his holidays in 1896 with me at Gillie-
brands, Chalfont St. Peters. He loved the little red house
belonging to Sydney Roscoe, the Registrar and well-known
writer, who did much to make our stay in his neighbourhood pleasant. That house, which was built nearly 300
years ago, and is similar to Milton's famous cottage,
situated at Chalfont St. Giles, a couple of miles away,
stands nearly 500 feet above the sea, and in front commands a beautiful view over the Denham and Rickmans-
worth Valleys to the Downs and St. Albans. Behind are
the Chalfonts, famous as the homes of Milton, Waller,
Penn, and Thomas Elwood, while away in the distance lie
the Missendens, Wendover, and Aylesbury.

My father and I drove from town one beautiful day
towards the end of August. It is twenty-four miles from
the Harley Street door to Chalfont, but the pair of fine
black horses, in which he took much pride, trotted the
distance in less than three hours without drawing rein.
He had several times driven the road before, and chatted
all the way about the histories of Shepherd's Bush, Acton,
Ealing, and Uxbridge.

It proved a sadly wet September, and I was busy at the
time writing ' Through Finland in Carts,' having just returned from that country ; but in spite of the weather and
my lack of leisure, he was perfectly happy and contented,
for he had a marvellous power of amusing himself, reading

22

or writing, and was ever ready to tell stories to my two
small boys, who sat spellbound while listening to his
natural history tales.

When he could not sit out under the coloured awning,
he prepared his notes on ' Talking Sticks ' for the British
Association, to be held in Liverpool at the end of the
month.

All through that wet September he worked at his paper,
drawing comparisons from Runic, Ogam, Chaldean,
Phœnician, Samoyed, Esquimo, North American Indian,
and Australian writings; for his knowledge was wide and
his industry and memory amazing. I made sketches of
the ' talking sticks ' for him, but if I put 399 lines or curves
when there were only 398, my fault and inaccuracy met
with dire disapproval. He was intensely thorough.

When the weather was favourable we drove to Stoke
Pogis, where Gray wrote his famous ' Elegy,' to Burnham
Beeches, or to Hampden, where the famous Cromwellian
who refused to pay the Ship Tax once lived. At Wendover
we lunched at the Red Lion Inn, the host in truly ancient
style taking his place at the head of the table and carving.
This inn still boasts of its ' ordinary,' and in good old
English fashion the beer is home-brewed, the mutton
home-fed, the bacon home-cured, and the bread home-
baked.

Then news came of the meeting of two of our friends—
Nansen and Jackson—an event I had prophesied a couple
of years before, in the third edition of ' A Girl's Ride in
Iceland.'

Frederick Jackson, on his return to England a year
later, named an island after my father on his map of Franz
Josef Land. George Harley Island lies a few miles north
of the place where Dr. Nansen passed that famous winter,
1895-96; while Alec Tweedie Bay is a little to the south-east.

The days passed pleasantly enough in our tiny cottage,
and the life and soul of the party was George Harley.

One sad day, however, a telegram arrived which upset

my father greatly, for it told us of the death of his valued
friend and colleague, Sir John Erichsen, with whom a close
friendship had existed for nearly forty years, 'Uncle John,'
as we called him, seeming to us like a second father. Both
had been at University College, as had also their old
colleague, Sir Russell Reynolds, who died only a few weeks
previous to Sir John.

Every medical student has heard of Erichsen's 'Surgery,'
which is a standard work, but to know its author was a
privilege. Blessed with the sweetest nature, well-read,
travelled, and of courtly bearing, Sir John was a delightful
companion and an enthusiastic friend. He retired from
practice some years before his death, after which he would
laughingly say, ' I am more proud of making an odd guinea
now than I was of a hundred times that sum a few years ago.'

Science and religion are proverbially antagonistic ; what,
then, were my father's religious views ?

Well, he was brought up in a strictly orthodox Puritanical
school, such as dominated Scotland in the middle of the
century, and its doctrines hung around him to the last ;
a sort of strange idea that the Sabbath should be kept
rigorously clung to him, though reading and thinking had
made him in other respects very broad-minded.

Taken twice to kirk on the Sabbath as a child, taught
long chapters of the Bible, he was yet allowed to walk out on
Sunday with his mother for pleasure, even to read instructive books, although the piano was forbidden and no letters
were opened or written.

As he grew up, he gradually threw off many strict
Sabbatical observances, but he remained deeply religious.

Religion and its origin fascinated him, so much so that
for years he read deeply on all the beliefs of the world ;
and some time in the seventies, having collected a vast
amount of information and formed many theories, he wrote
a book on ' The Science and Origin of Religion.' This he
showed to Nicholas Trübner, then one of the leading

publishers in London, who was so fascinated with its originality that he offered him an extravagantly large sum for the work, which he thought would create as great a sensation as the ' Vestiges of Creation ' had done, although he declared it was *very* advanced, and in some respects startling.

Home my father came delighted. All glee, he rushed upstairs to my mother to tell her at last his ideas were to see the light—at last he would convince people ; for the money part did not appeal to him so much as Trübner's appreciation and the prospect of the appearance in print of his dearly-cherished theories.

His enthusiasm met with scant sympathy. My mother did not approve of the book appearing, for, as she said, ' If it comes out and is a failure, it will do you harm in your profession ; if it comes out and is a success, it will do you still more injury, for everyone will say you took no interest in practice, so wrote about theology to occupy your idle time. You are a doctor and a man of science, not a theologian or philosopher.'

Thus wisely she argued, and he—well, he always gave in to her sound, practical common-sense : Trübner's offer was refused, and the book never saw the light.

The study of theological problems stepped in and out of his life and excited his earnest attention, as many other subjects had done ; still, although devoted to science, a reformer in his own branch of medical science, he warmly maintained science need not destroy religion, although it shook many of its superstitions and crumbled them to the dust.

Although a deeply religious man in his life and actions, he declared ' dogma killed all true religion.' On a scrap of note-paper I find his ideas summed up in these lines :

' RELIGION.

' There are no sects in the sight of God. When standing before the Judgment-seat, one will not be asked if he be a

Papist or a Baptist, an Episcopalian or a Nonconformist, a Buddhist or a Mohammedan, for it is not according to his accepted or rejected doctrines that he will be judged, but by his thoughts and deeds alone.'

My father's interest in so many things may, of course, have been an acquired art, for lameness during long years prevented much physical exercise, and threw him on his mental resources. When he could no longer walk over to Tattersall's on Sunday afternoon, or peep into Christie's on his way to the club, pay visits to queer old shops and gaze into the wonders of Wardour Street, he took to collecting facts and fancies—teapots, cups, silver drinking-mugs of all countries and ages, horn shells for blowing, talking sticks, watches, rings, etc.

Had he possessed the means, he would have stopped at nothing. He was a widely-read, well-informed man, interested well-nigh in all subjects, and every hobby he took up he sifted to the bottom in a most marvellous way.

During the last years of his life, my father delighted at the stride made in this country scientifically. He knew about and was interested in all the latest engineering improvements, chemical discoveries, electric apparatus, etc.; indeed, he would often rub his hands and say, 'Now England is beginning to assert her own, and in pure science takes the foremost place.' He ever admired the advance of surgery, in which he was himself very skilful, though, funnily enough, he never cared to operate even in his student days, and used to laughingly say, ' Why, soon, if they go on at this rate, they will take us all to bits, look at us, wash us, tidy us up, and put us all together again !'

He keenly appreciated every new discovery in medical science, and took care to make himself acquainted with the details, even while with a sigh he would say, ' Alas ! I am no longer one of the pioneers.'

To the day of his death he felt very keenly his enforced retirement from scientific research, although he managed to get through a vast amount of scientific work up to the very last. What changes he saw!

From the Buckinghamshire cottage he went, as has been said, to Liverpool for the British Association, where he stayed with his brother-in-law, E. K. Muspratt, one of the vice-presidents; Professor William Ramsay, of Argon and Helium fame, and Sir Frederick Abel being of the party.

The paper on talking sticks was read. My father, apparently in the best of health and spirits, attended meetings, garden-parties, dinners and receptions, and thoroughly enjoyed seeing so many old friends. About the beginning of October he returned home to his work in London, refreshed mentally and bodily by his holiday.

Later on he caught a slight bronchial cold, but feeling much better on Tuesday, October 27, he got up for breakfast, a thing he had not done for the two previous mornings. He was in splendid spirits, dressed, came downstairs about nine o'clock, read his letters, including one from me asking what he knew about Baal fires—he was always my encyclopædia, and I wanted some information on the subject for my Finland book. He jotted on the border of the manuscript two or three notes in pencil, and about ten o'clock went to his room.

The butler saw him then, and some ten minutes later, having occasion to ask him some question, knocked at the door. No answer being returned, he knocked again, and knowing that when writing my father had the most marvellous power of concentrating his thoughts, not even noticing pianos or hurdy-gurdies, turned the handle. Meeting with some resistance, a very unusual thing, he put his head in, and, seeing to his horror my father lying on the floor with his head against the panel, called for help. In a moment my brother Vaughan reached the room. It was only about a quarter past ten a.m., and yet at five houses in Harley Street the page-boy called before he could get a doctor! Meantime my brother and the butler had laid the stricken man flat on his back; Vaughan, having only just returned from seeing a patient, had his stethoscope in his pocket, which he used, but found no heart-sounds and could feel no pulse.

Minutes went by—or hours, as those two watchers felt them to be—ere a doctor arrived, but at last one came.

Vaughan met him in the hall.

'I can hear no heart-beats,' he said, ' but it may be only nervousness on my part—listen.'

The doctor listened, felt for a pulse-throb, then answered:

'Alas! it is not nervousness. He is dead!'

Yes, he had passed away without one moment's pain, without a struggle. He was dead, the ink still wet on the paper of an article he was writing for the *Lancet*.

It was as he had wished to die. He who had suffered much pain in life, and knew its horrors, always hoped for a sudden death, and when my husband passed away in his sleep a few months before, he repeatedly said, 'A beautiful death—may mine be as peaceful !'

And so the father-in-law followed the son-in-law within a short five months.

Even in contemplating death his love of science, his love of knowledge, haunted him. He always said it was 'the duty of the dead to give up their secrets to the living.' Years before, when his son Vaughan first took up medicine, he had expressed the wish :

'When I die it is my desire for a post-mortem to be made, and, if possible, I should like you to see to it yourself. My case is ambiguous, and, for the benefit of others, I wish what is wrong to be clearly ascertained.'

Thus he talked, discussing his own body, and in the interests of science insisting that his son should prove or disprove his theories.

More than that, in his cash-box was a letter, stating he wished after the autopsy that his remains should be cremated, the ashes weighed, and the facts noted and compared with what he had calculated they ought to be.

My father, be it mentioned, was one of the first to advocate cremation in this country. As far back as 1865 he worked at the subject, and never let an opportunity pass of advocating its claims.

Death had for him no horrors; this desire for a post-mortem arose from no morbid feeling—it was the true longing for information, the belief that the living really ought to benefit by the dead. Further, he had repeatedly during his lifetime experimented upon himself when in search of some scientific truth.

His wishes were carried out; there was a post-mortem, which proved he died from rupture of one of the arteries of the heart-wall, and also that his lameness was not due to locomotor ataxia, as some had supposed—he always thought erroneously—but was caused by an injury to the spine, as he had himself diagnosed.

Verily, all the theories he had written down proved on investigation to be correct, even to the weight of the ashes!

Often when invitations came to funerals, official and otherwise, he said:

'Remember, when I die I wish to be cremated and buried quietly. I want no one to be invited, no one to make martyrs of themselves or risk cold and death for me; neither must they spend their money on flowers. I wish no flowers; they can do me no good. I wish no mourning—certainly not crape. In fact, I desire to be got rid of as quickly and simply as possible, and not to run the risk of injuring any living thing.'

Simply as he had lived was he buried.

Thus ended at the age of sixty-seven the life-history of one who evinced ceaseless and varied activity, a pioneer of scientific medicine, whose bravery during his own ill-health often worked against serious odds.

George Harley of Harley Street, as we have seen, was an indefatigable worker and a thinker whose personal influence accomplished much. He struggled against well-nigh overwhelming difficulties; well born and highly strung by temperament, his brain aimed at more than his body was capable of enduring. Overwork and untoward accidents twice in twenty years forced him to retire from his career apparently a doomed man. Sheer pluck and strength of will conquered, and he three times began his professional life, so to speak, and always with success.

Then George Harley lived before his time. He was a pioneer of medical science, which in the days when he came to London was practically nil, and consequently all his professional life was spent in battling against old traditions, fighting laws, the outcome of custom, by which most of the medical profession were then fettered. The wonder is that he did not make more enemies, considering he was always uprooting men's dearly-cherished ideals; for, as we know, no hatred equals that engendered by jealousy.

Does his life not teach a lesson? Does it not show how in the darkest hours we need not despair? how courage and time will triumph over adversity? and how, when well-nigh defeated, success is oftentimes possible?

He worked bravely. It was through his medium many discoveries were arrived at in the use of chloroform, that wonderful drug which nearly cost him his life, and which so interested him that for years he experimented towards its perfection.

He lost his sight nigh unto blindness through his experiments with the microscope, one of which bears his name, or rather, I should say, bore; for science now moves so rapidly that what is startlingly new to-day is ancient history five years hence. He discovered many wonderful methods of treatment for diseases of the liver—which are too medical to deal with here—and died in harness at the age of sixty-seven, with all the enthusiasm of youth still unabated, although greatly impaired in health.

'True science is the key to wise practice' was a little self-made motto he was never tired of repeating.

As children, he often used to explain to us how Force was

never-ending; how we could set the waves of air moving, maybe only with a bend of the hand, but the movement went on to all eternity, through all space — a fact that to our childish brain seemed too vast for comprehension. But now I feel and understand the many waves of thought, of love and goodness, which my father ' set going' during his span of life are still moving, and though the home knows him no more and the chair is vacant, yet his influence and his individuality are amongst us still.

The influence of a good or a bad life exists for all time!

DR. GEORGE HARLEY AS I KNEW HIM.

BY MRS. J. H. RIDDELL.

'A GOOD beginning is half-way towards a good ending,' says an old proverb, which may be true, but certainly its converse cannot be right, since, if it were, I should never have been asked to write any word of sad recollection concerning my kind dead friend Dr. George Harley.

For ours was not merely an unpromising, but a bad beginning. We met for the first time at a large and very successful party, in rooms so crowded it was impossible, in the language of that time, 'to see whether the carpet had a pattern,' and where no one voluntarily sat down—there were, indeed, but few chairs on which to sit—lest he or she should be doomed for hours to utter solitude or boredom.

I was standing among a number of, to me, utterly unknown people—myself unknown to almost everyone present—when a voice at my elbow said : 'You should not eat strawberries with your gloves on ;' and, turning my head, I saw a black-haired, dark-eyed, handsome, well-dressed, youngish man, with a not unpleasant air of dandyism pervading his whole appearance, looking at me with an exasperating expression of good-humoured amusement.

I was so amazed at receiving this piece of 'general information' from a total stranger that I did not take the gift in a right spirit ; consequently our conversation for a short time was on my side more crisp than courteous, till at last, growing restive under the influence of his cool, nonchalant manner, I said :

' May I ask if you *never* talk sense ?'

At once there came an indefinable but marked change, and he answered :

' *Never*, unless I am paid for it.'

' And your charge ?' I inquired.

' One guinea '—which told me he was a doctor, a fact no one would have suspected.

' Then, if I am ever likely to meet you again, I will bring a guinea and consult you,' was my snappish answer, shortly after receiving which he left me—as I subsequently learned from our hostess, to ascertain my name.

He returned ere long, but my impression is we did not get on much better later in the evening, which proved a disastrous one, for our mare — Irish, of course — while waiting, employed her elegant leisure in eating the varnish off the back of his carriage, fresh from the coachbuilder's renovating touch.

Most men would have been annoyed, but he was not. He refused to receive compensation for the damage 'Tottie' had done, and soon after rode seven miles in order to call, when truth compels me to say we squabbled dreadfully, the reason for which may have been that all his life Dr. George Harley was much interested in noting the difference, moral and mental, between men and women, a subject that when young held no more attraction for me than it does now.

Some people are content to take things as they find them, but Dr. George Harley never could do this. He always wanted to know the why and the wherefore even of matters that can never be understood on this side the ' Great for Evermore.'

Many years after we became acquainted, while staying at Scarborough, where, no doubt, he had fine opportunities of studying the great feminine question, he wrote the following lines, which show the problem I always declined to grapple with was still perplexing him :

'Men and women are not one, you know;
Their thoughts are different as is rain from snow;
Although the element of both's the same,
Yet widely different is fair snow from rain.'

My opinion is that, spite the glorious samples of woman-kind Dr. George Harley was happy enough to know, in the persons of his mother, whose memory he worshipped, and his wife, loving, devoted, his very right-hand, he did not, for some reason, believe 'fair snow' was the weaker sex characteristic. But all that is not of much consequence.

Though personally disinclined to enlist under either banner, preferring to think and speak of the merits appertaining both to rain and snow, I cannot forget Adam failed to come out of that little apple business with flying colours, perhaps because he was wiser—after the event—than poor foolish Eve!

Possibly it was the divergence of opinion between Dr. George Harley and myself—or, rather, indifference on my part—which hindered the rapid growth of acquaintance, for it was not till I knew Mrs. Harley, that the friendship began which ended only with life.

There may be other homes in London—I hope there are many—where, within sound of the hurry and bustle of a great city, peace reigns supreme; but it can be only in a few the uniform calm obtains which made 25, Harley Street so welcome a haven for any storm-tossed human barque to turn into and—rest.

How many sought that haven will never be known on earth. Sure am I neither husband nor wife kept a record. For myself I have always thought of the house as Home, since Death wrecked mine.

The kindly smile never changed; the cordial welcome was warmer, if possible, through long years of trouble than in my brief hour of prosperity. I could not say, I could never tell, what that acquaintance, which opened so in-auspiciously, has been to me!

I was made free of that delightful household, where

everything went calmly, without fuss, friction, fret, or hurry. Were I asked the reason for the peace which reigned within those walls, I should answer Self-Control, a virtue fast departing from this world, if one may judge by what meets eyes and ears daily.

Trouble often knocked at the door, and did not stay outside. Quite unequal battles were fought and won in the quiet rooms; mind grappled with bodily anguish, disappointment, loss of income, and conquered; but nothing was said about the pain, the struggle, the gallant and successful effort to make up leeway. All were met with the dignified spirit that would not have triumphed excitedly had Fortune emptied her cornucopia into the old house.

Save a half-laughing exclamation when toiling upstairs, one hand on the balusters, the other holding my arm, I never heard one syllable of complaint pass Dr. George Harley's lips.

He must have suffered horribly; but he suffered in silence, and maintained a cheerful spirit simply because he did not aggravate his pain by dwelling on it. How he got through the amount of work he did I cannot imagine. He must have utilized every spare moment, and yet he was always ready to talk or to hear.

Unless I chanced to be staying in Harley Street, it was generally at luncheon we met. He would come and join us at that meal looking a little tired, perhaps, after seeing a number of patients; but next moment his kindly face would light up with pleasure, and he would grasp my hand or that of any other friend with a cordiality not to be forgotten (it was wonderful how so small a hand* could clasp another hand with so strong a grip!), the while he asked earnestly how things were going or had gone; what was the news, etc.

---

* Dr. George Harley's hands and feet were exceptionally, marvellously small.

In my own case, possibly a new book had been arranged for or just brought out ; and, busy though he always was, when a serial novel chanced to be in progress, he never failed to write a cheery word of praise and encouragement, simply, kindly, or he would speak that word if I chanced to call. It was all just as it might have happened in a brother's house. Can the reader wonder 25, Harley Street will ever remain stamped on my memory, and that I linger a little over the days that can come back no more ?

After luncheon dear Mrs. Harley was wont to say, ' Now, you two want a talk, I know, so I am going to leave you for an hour,' which in latter years, when he was not so busy, ran generally to two. Then, as a rule, he talked while I listened ; people can sometimes contribute as much to a conversation by listening as by talking.

I told him all I had learned about reptiles, all I had gathered in the way of folklore, anything new I had heard concerning vegetable poisons—all I knew, in fact, about anything, which was not much, but still interested him. He liked to hear what I, living in the country, had to say regarding animals, the gossip I was able to collect anent rural matters, quaint sayings, and so forth ; but my little budget was soon exhausted, and then he took up whatever subject chanced to be uppermost in his mind or had been suggested by some casual remark.

His apparently inexhaustible stock of knowledge was amazing. Let the topic selected be what it would, he seemed not merely well-informed concerning all its details, but able also to add some fresh idea which lightened up the whole. Occasionally this light was so unexpected as to prove startling.

We were speaking, for instance, one afternoon about a country ' cut off,' so to say, from the rest of the world, where, nevertheless, the remains of magnificent buildings are to be met with—ruins which would seem to indicate a settlement of, or close intimacy with, cultured races at some extremely remote period—when I expressed wonder as to how civilization found its way to such an out-of-the-way part of creation.

For the moment his answer produced a sensation of giddiness. 'There is no difficulty in the matter,' he said. 'What is now sea was once dry land, and communication therefore easy. Like changes are going on all over the world, only the majority of people do not notice them.'

A few thousand years—indeed, a few million—were nothing to him, and eventually became nothing to me.

I grew quite accustomed to walking with him over countless ages to a point whence I could see oceans forming where firm land had been, lakes drying up, channels opening—our own 'silver streak,' for example—the 'everlasting' hills changing the place of their abode, and could even imagine hard granite leaving its birthplace and taking a long lease of premises remote from boyhood's haunts.

And why not? I have seen with my bodily, matter-of-fact eyes the inroads made in fair Erin by water, which pays no heed to the command of men. Even in England what was formerly a town now lies fathoms deep under the salt sea—graveyard, houses, once pleasant gardens, where less than a hundred and fifty years ago the mother of a lady I once met was married in the church of which not one stone remains on another; while on the Kentish coast the boatmen, when well away from land, rest on their oars, and say, pointing below the rippling waves: 'That was once the main street of Whitstable.'

It all seems quite natural when a person gets accustomed to the idea—my difficulty was in getting accustomed. Now millions, billions, of years seem as natural to contemplate as thousands did once, for have I not in imagination explored with Dr. George Harley the England of old, when there was no 'silver streak,' and animal Goliaths with unpronounceable names roamed through forests since cleared for the site of London?

Did not one of those, to our thinking, unwieldy creatures select what is now Euston Square as a desirable place of sepulchre? and when we learn to regard such wonderful changes as mere matter of fact instead of legend, why should millions of the continually dropping sands we call time affright or appal us, *if* only we go back far enough—firm in faith?

The idea appalled me at first, but now I can see no just cause or impediment why even the New and the Old World should not have been in some way originally one—why the legendary path between Scotland and Ireland might not really have existed—why the many theories and fancies with which Dr. George Harley beguiled years of pain and compulsory idleness may not have had a solid foundation in truth.

What a variety of subjects he ranged over, what infinite thought he must have given to many an apparently trivial matter! And the curious thing is, he did not take up an idea, work it out, lay it down and forget. No; if it were spoken of years afterwards, he would discourse as eloquently on the theme as in the days when it seemed the one topic of interest.

He was a wonderful man, and if I could not always follow or agree with what he said, at least he taught me never to reject any new idea because it appears strange and impossible.

I cannot recall the exact time when it first occurred to me Dr. George Harley was a disappointed man. Success and failure lie not in what a person has done, but in what he hoped to do; and I can see now his genius was never fully recognised, and that he felt what all in advance of their time must feel—viz., that Ignorance and Prejudice still keep solemn guard over honours and treasures few who see too soon may hope to win.

Lately, when reading the very clever life of William Harvey,* I could not help being struck with the opposition

* 'William Harvey,' by D'Arcy Power, F.S.A., F.R.C.S.

that great physician met with when at last he ventured to give his discovery to an ungrateful public. 'The Circulation of the Blood' caused a perfect storm of opprobrium amongst those who believed 'they were the people, and wisdom should die with them.' And in like manner Dr. George Harley's new ideas were, as a rule, received coldly, if not with disapprobation. Each original thinker has to pass through the same experience, but it must be hard to bear, more especially when, as in Dr. George Harley's case, ill-health aggravates the evil.

Never had man, however, a sunnier temper. There never existed anyone less given to take sorrows home to nurse. He loved a good story ; he delighted even in simple talk. It was charming to hear him accommodating his words to the immature understanding of his grand-children, and more charming still to see his trust in, and dependence on the best wife that ever lived—a helpmeet indeed, his very right hand ! He was sympathetic to a degree. When we have been at the theatre, I have known him weep over some pathetic scene, making no effort to hide his tears. And he could laugh as heartily. Ah me !

He had but small belief in the uses of affliction. It was the joys of life which appealed to his temperament rather than the trials that seemed to him terrible, wherein he was wrong, for there were depths in his nature the full virtue of which could never have been stirred had not the angel Sorrow descended into the waters and troubled them.

Well, he has gone, and left many a grieving friend to mourn his loss. I remember hearing him laughingly say how he should like to die—'after a quiet evening spent with friends to go to sleep and *wake dead.*'

He did nearly so die, waking not to death, but, as we humbly hope and believe, to the fulness of Eternal Life.

If one of the delights of heaven be, as some suppose, climbing peak after peak of knowledge, and seeing from thence the vast plains of science humanity longed in vain to explore below, then in the Far-away Land George Harley is happy retrieving the hours stolen by illness from research here, and adding to the facts wrested from Nature on earth more wisdom vouchsafed by the Most High.

INDEX.

A

ADDISON, Colonel, 219
Aitken :
    John, Mr., 21–23
    William, Dr., 20, 21, 23
Alexander II. and his Empress,
    285–288
Alison, Professor, 23
Anderson, Mrs. Garrett, 166
Arnold, Matthew, 135, 177, 179
Arran, 37–39
Austin, L. F., 257, 258

B

Bacon :
    Charlotte, Lady, 229, 230
    J., Dr., 304
Bastian, Dr. Carlton, 172
Baumann, Dr. John, 41
Bell, Robert, 128, 135, 218
Bennett, Professor, 114
Benoni, curator of Sir John Soane's
    Museum, 218
Bernard, Claude, 40, 50, 318
Blanc, Louis, 57, 128, 135, 218
Blessington, Lady, 128
Bond, Sir Edward, 218
Brantwood, 234, 235
Brewer, Rev. Dr. Cobham, 172
Brewster, Sir David, 135, 167,
    236
Brookes, Mrs., 185, 186
Browning, Robert, 232
Buckland, Frank, 135, 164, 218
Bunsen, Professor, 114

Burke, 31, 32
Byron, Lord, 229–232

C

Catlin, George, 218, 242–245, 249
Chaillu, Paul du, 218
Chevallier, Nicholas, 217
Clark :
    Andrew, Sir, 212, 255, 325
    James, Sir, 133, 135
Clodd, Edward, 332
Cole, Sir Henry, 236, 237
Colney Hatch, 202, 203
Coniston, 233–235
Conneau, Dr., 83
Cornish, Charles J., 186, 333
Cox, Mr. Sands, 111, 112
Cruikshank, George, 135, 170, 218
Cubitt, Mr. Thomas, 237
Cushman :
    Charlotte, 134, 142–146
    Susan, 142, 144, 145

D

Davy, Sir Humphrey, 165
Delepierre, Octave, 169, 219
Denham, Captain, 141
Dickens, Charles, 135, 218
Dow, Mr., 256
Dunbar, 20–22

E

Eastlake, Sir Charles, 135
Edmonstone, Miss, 273, 274
Eliot, George, 135

Elizabeth, Queen, 4, 6
Ellis, Professor, 116
Elphinstone, Lord, 290
Elwood, Thomas, 337
Erichsen, Sir John, 173, 218, 339

F

Faraday, Michael, 135, 169
Farquhar, Maurice, 255
Faucet, Helen, 135
Fergusson, Sir William, 133, 135,
    202, 203
Ferrier, 318
Finland, 282, 283, 288, 297, 337, 342
Flourens, 47
Flower, Sir William, 326
Foster, Professor Michael, 121, 316
Froude, Mr., 44, 251
Fry, Mrs. Elizabeth, 324
Fuller, Francis, 236-239

G

Garrod, Sir Alfred, 133, 173
Gay-Lussac, 249, 250
Geibel, 162
Giessen, 84, 100, 102, 114, 141, 163
Ginsburg, Dr., 254
Gladstone, W. E., 207, 241, 242
Gleichen, Count, 290, 291
Glyn, Mrs. Dallas, 135
Graham, Professor, 135, 169
Gray, John, 21
Grossmith :
    George, 146, 255
    Weedon, 255-257
Gull, Sir William, 218, 322
Gunn, Dr., 24

H

Haddington, 1-3, 5-7, 9-16, 22-25,
    37, 131, 136, 155
Hall, Dr. Marshall, 123, 125
Hare, 31, 32
Harley :
    Adam, Friar, 2, 9, 10
    Brilliana, Lady, 168
    Charlotte, Lady ; Bacon, Lady
        Charlotte. *See* that title
    George, Mrs., 102, 103, 135,
        148-150, 156, 160, 162, 163,
        168, 176, 181, 185, 187, 190,

Harley, *continued :*
    195, 234, 235, 240, 250, 331,
        340, 349, 351
    George Barclay, 5, 14
    James, 4
    John :
        Friar, 3
        Rev. Dr., 3
    Patrick, 16
    Robert :
        Earl of Oxford, 133
        Sir, 168
    Vaughan, 54, 240, 313, 329, 335,
        336, 342, 343
    William, Sir, 4, 6
Harman, Major, 297
Harvey, Sir George, 142
Hawkins, Rev. Edward, 332
Hayes, Miss Catherine, 129, 135
Heidelberg, 88, 114, 135
Helsingfors, 283, 289
Hewitt, Grailey, 127
Hill, Sir Rowland, 154, 169, 218
Holland, Sir Henry, 135
Home, 128, 129
Hook, Theodore, 135, 239
Horsley, Professor, 318, 322, 335
Hullah, John, 228

I

Isle of Man, 226, 227, 291, 292, 306

J

Jackson, General, 247
Jenner, Sir William, 133, 173
Jones, Dr. Bence, 117, 121, 133, 135

K

Kean, Mrs. Charles, 135
Keeley, Mrs., 327
Kelvin, Lord, 295, 326
Kemble, Fanny, 57, 135
Kingsley, Charles, 146, 228
Knowles, James Sheridan, 140, 147
Knox, Dr., 30-32
Koch, Dr., 319
Kölliker, Professor, 113, 116

L

Landseer :
    Charles, 135, 169, 170. 218
    Edwin, Sir, 135, 170, 218

Lawrence, Sir William, 36, 247, 248
Leech, John, 135, 218
Lemon, Mark, 135
Liebig:
    Baron Justus von, 103, 141,
        160–165, 168, 169, 249–251,
        318
    Herman von, 102
    Nannie, 102, 103, 160, 162, 251
Lieshman, Mr., 25, 26, 29
Linton, Mrs. Lynn, 239, 240
Lister, Lord, 320
Loudon, Mrs., 128, 261, 277
Lover, Samuel, 135, 146
Ludwig, 317, 322

M

Macbeath, Mrs., 24–29
Marcet, Dr. William, 39, 64, 65,
    228, 229
Martin, Dr. Sydney, 336
Maurice, Frederick Denison, 228
Mazzini, 135
Milligan, Professor William, 218,
    253–255
Milner-Gibson, Mrs., 129
Mons Meg, 17–19
Moore, Surgeon - General Sir
    William, 327–330
Moscow, 283–285, 288
Munday, Mr. George, 238
Munich, 102, 103, 141, 160–164, 169
Murray, George, 322
Muspratt:
    Edmund Knowles, 140, 146,
        342
    Emma. Harley, Mrs. George.
        See that title
    James, 135–142, 147, 148
    Sheridan, Dr., 136, 140, 144

N

Nansen, Dr., 338
Napoleon III., 64, 69, 72–83
Nightingale, Miss Florence, 324

O

O'Neill, Miss Eliza, 139
Omar Pasha, 91, 92, 95, 97
Ord, 322
Orfila, Mathieu, 56, 57, 128

P

Palmer, 122, 123
Pannum, Professor, 304
Parry, John, 146
Pasteur, 54, 319
Peel, Sir Robert, 237
Pfeuffer, Dr., 160, 161
Powell, Sir Douglas, 172
Priestley, Sir William, 56
Prince Consort, 237–239
Prince of Wales, 326, 327

Q

Quain, Sir Richard, 133, 173, 218
Queen Victoria, 325–327

R

Ramsay, Professor William, 298, 342
Reynolds, Sir Russell, 173, 339
Riddell, Mrs. J. H., 37, 347
Ringer, Dr. Sydney, 172
Roberts, Dr. Frederick, 172
Ross, Dr., 323
Ruskin, John, 233–236, 249, 300
Russell, Mr. Scott, 236–238

S

St. Petersburg, 283, 285, 287, 288
Sanderson, Professor Burdon, 56,
    121, 316
Savile Club, 330–332
Savory, Sir William, 218
Scherer, Professor, 113, 117
Schiff, 322
Scott, R. H., 333, 335
Seaforth Hall, 135, 136, 141, 142,
    146–148
Seyler, Hoppe, 318
Sharpey, Professor, 116–118, 124,
    125, 127, 130, 135, 169, 218, 249,
    251–253
Shelley, 231, 232
Simpson, Sir James, 109–114, 117,
    118, 132, 164, 165, 218
Spain, 149–158, 229
Stanley, Dean, 167, 242, 254
Stebbins, Miss, 142
Stein, Baron von, 103, 106–108
Sterling, Madame Antoinette, 135,
    255

Stockholm, 282, 289
Syme, Professor, 35, 36

T

Tennant :
  Charles, Sir, 140
  Emerson, Sir, 151
  John, 140
Tennyson, Alfred, 228
Thackeray, 135, 242
Thiersch :
  Carl, Professor, 162, 251
  Ludwig, 162
Todd :
  Charles, Sir, 224
  Professor, 196
Tree, Mrs. Beerbohm, 256, 257
Trelawny, 230–232
Trieste, 92–94, 97
Trübner, Nicholas, 339, 340
Tweedie :
  Alec, 246, 247, 249, 344
  Alexander, Dr., 246–248
  Alexander, George, 247–249
Tyndall, John, 135, 218

U

University College, 115, 117, 119–121, 125, 133, 164, 167, 172–174, 192–194, 196, 212, 229, 252, 316, 320, 335, 339

V

Virchow, Professor, 113, 282, 283

W

Wakley, Dr., 123, 125
Waller, Dr. Augustus, 121
Walsh, Mr., 173
Walton Hall, 260–263, 273–275, 277
Waterton, Charles, 249, 260–281
Watson, Sir Thomas, 126, 133, 187–189
Williams, Sir John, 133, 172
Wurtz, 39, 228
Würzburg, 89, 100, 101, 113, 114, 264

THE END.

BILLING AND SONS, PRINTERS, GUILDFORD.

Lightning Source UK Ltd.
Milton Keynes UK
UKHW010757060223
416537UK00008B/1890

9 783337 849580